Praise for *Hawker*

'A brutal, brilliant tale, told with terrific creation'

Bernard Cornwell, author of the Last Kingdom series

'A highly enjoyable ride through a story rich in detail. Bale takes the reader from the terror of battle where a crown is lost and won to the sparkling jewel that is Venice, teeming with intrigue and treachery. Loyalty tested, love for a woman reclaimed, a quest beckons to reclaim the English crown. Great storytelling'

David Gilman, author of the Master of War series

'An absolute gem of a novel. I was taken aback by Bale's skill and talent. Meticulously researched, with a totally authentic medieval feel, the novel fizzes with action, romance and intrigue. A gripping yarn'

Angus Donald, author of the Fire Born series

'This character-driven plot holds the interest to the end. Hawker is an ageing, flawed character and it is in his description of the man's inner turmoil, his bursts of energy and, above all, loyalty that the author has created a living soul. Compelling, authentic characters, a tight narrative which drives the story with verve; dialogue which is neither mock Gothic nor anachronistic, all allow the reader to feel part of the sounds and sights of the late fifteenth century. The novel deserves high praise'

The Richard III Society

Praise for *The Lost Prince*

'*The Lost Prince* is certainly a page-turner. It is exciting, tense and action-packed as the protagonists grapple with multiple enemies and detractors, never quite sure if they can trust all of their friends... The author keeps us guessing about the outcomes until the final pages... Tremendous fun and a great read'

The Richard III Society

The Knight's Redemption

ETHAN BALE

CANELO

First published in the United Kingdom in 2024 by

Canelo
Unit 9, 5th Floor
Cargo Works, 1–2 Hatfields
London SE1 9PG
United Kingdom

A CIP catalogue record for this book is available from the British Library.

Print ISBN 978 1 80032 972 0
Ebook ISBN 978 1 80032 971 3

This book is a work of fiction. Names, characters, businesses, organizations, places and events are either the product of the author's imagination or are used fictitiously. Any resemblance to actual persons, living or dead, events or locales is entirely coincidental.

Cover design by Blacksheep

Cover images © Depositphotos

Look for more great books at www.canelo.co

Printed and bound in Great Britain by Clays Ltd, Elcograf S.p.A.

I

For Lady Kay

Deliver me from mine enemies, O my God: defend me from them that rise up against me.
Deliver me from the workers of iniquity and save me from bloody men.

Psalms 59

Prologue

'It's sanctuary. *Holy* sanctuary.'

The young soldier pushed the brim of his helm up on his forehead, licked the sweat from his top lip, and wiped his mouth with the back of his hand. His eyes remained upon his comrade-in-arms, John Hawker. 'Is this what the duke wants? What the king wants?'

Hawker fixed him squarely. 'It is what the king has *ordered*. Gloucester obeys his king. We obey them both.' He then looked at the other three soldiers in turn and the ten beyond them, a mix of well-seasoned men bearing hafted weapons: bills, glaives and pole-axes. 'Is that understood?'

Reluctant nods followed, all around. John Hawker, man-at-arms to King Edward and doer of whatever needed doing, nodded back at them. 'Good.' His own harness, fine bright Milanese and fitted, now bloomed orange with rust after days of marching across the countryside. Two days earlier, he had taken part in a great battle a stone's throw away, and witnessed the victory of York and the utter defeat of the Lancastrian cause.

He looked over to the great hulking abbey nearby, frowned, and then turned to glance behind him, a hundred feet away, to where Richard, Duke of Gloucester sat on horseback alongside his companions. He had helped train the youth since he was fourteen – at his brother's request – had given him a few bruises and lumps, taught him decisiveness in battle, and moulded him into the knight he had become. Moments ago, standing at Richard's stirrup, Hawker had been given his latest orders.

'John Hawker,' Richard had said, 'today you must be chief rat-catcher in the abbey.'

'We will bring them out, my lord. Willingly or otherwise.'

The still boyish face of the duke had smiled down at him. 'John... don't make a slaughter of it. You understand? Unless they resist. Then it will be upon their heads. And theirs alone.'

Hawker turned back to his men, the conversation echoing in his mind. He gave a deep sigh. 'We're going in. We enter at the front.'

The men-at-arms walked forward, armour clanking and jangling.

'Will they fight?' asked the man next to Hawker. 'Inside the abbey?'

'They'd be unwise to try it.'

The man on Hawker's left spoke up. 'If we spill blood in there... we will be damned. Our souls will burn for eternity, they will.'

'Traitors don't deserve sanctuary,' growled Hawker. 'And if you thought your soul wasn't damned already, William Blaye, then you're a bigger fool than I thought.'

The word had already spread that the Duke of Somerset, Sir John Langstrother, and a dozen or so other Lancastrian nobles and gentles were to be removed from the abbey where they had taken refuge after the battle. Many townsfolk stood at a safe distance from the troops that milled about the abbey grounds. Hawker reached the western tympanum and entrance to the nave and signalled for two men to open the doors. Both doors were unlocked. Hawker looked down the aisle. Ten feet inside stood more than a dozen black-cowled monks. One, holding a large golden cross, stepped forward and spoke, holding out his hand.

'Do not do this thing! You are violating the sanctuary of this holy place. These men are under the protection of the Church.'

Hawker looked down at the little cleric. 'Father, step aside.' His voice was without emotion. 'Your charter enshrines no such right to confer.'

The abbot glared at him. 'You do not strike me as an expert in ecclesiastical affairs. Turn around and leave this place.'

Hawker stepped into the nave and his men followed, spreading out around him. One monk sprang forward to place himself in the way, but a soldier punched him with a gauntleted fist, dropping him into a heap on the stone floor. The abbot raised his hand and the other monks then parted like a black sea, a silent rippling wave, allowing the soldiers to enter. Hawker moved ahead, walking slowly down the length of the nave.

The abbot was on Hawker's heels. 'Sir Knight, if you spill blood this day your soul will be blackened for ever. Desist this action now, I implore you.'

Hawker kept walking, his eyes darting, searching for armed men. 'I am no knight, Father. Nor am I likely to be.'

He reached the point where the north and south transepts began before the entrance to the choir. Overhead was a riot of reds, blues and gold upon the glorious vaulted ceiling high above. He heard a metallic rasp to his right, and he changed his path, veering into the south aisle. At the entrance to the south transept stood ten men in armour, arrayed shoulder to shoulder. They were squires and knights all. Their weapons were drawn and held in front of them. In the bright sunlight that streamed through the stained glass above, Hawker could see several had dried blood on their harness along with splattered mud and filth. Most were bareheaded. Hawker scanned their faces and saw a mix of fear, fatigue and determination.

Hawker put his hand to the hilt of his arming sword, still in its scabbard. 'Good gentles, your rightful king demands that you yield to me. The field was fairly won. Surrender now.' Hawker's men fanned out, blocking any escape past them. Behind the Lancastrians lay a door, which Hawker knew led to the Chapter House and dormitory, no doubt where Somerset was hiding. No one said a word.

'This will end only one way for you,' said Hawker, edging his voice towards conciliation. 'I beg you to yield, gentlemen.'

A soldier not much more than a boy – squire to a knight no doubt – shouted out, voice wavering, 'Not to a knave like you!'

Hawker smiled. At his back he could hear the plaintive, chanting prayers of the monks.

Sir John Langstrother, prior of the Knights of Saint John, stood halfway down the line of steel. He spoke, his voice soft and composed. Hawker recognised him from happier days, even without the help of the Maltese cross embroidered upon his tabard. 'The lad speaks the truth, John Hawker. Henchman and churl to a house without honour.'

The voice of the abbot rang out, echoing. 'There will be no blood drawn here! Whoever throws the first blow is *excommunicado!*'

Hawker lifted his left hand and pulled down the visor of his sallet helm. 'If that be your choice then, Sir John… lay on!' Hawker drew out his sword in one swift motion, bringing it up into a hanging guard.

A part of Hawker wanted it to end differently, and it might have, if the monks had had more time to convince. But boys are impetuous and drawn to glory like a moth to the flame. The young squire dashed forward, a cry upon his lips. 'For King Henry!'

And the long blades of Hawker's men rained down upon them like the threshers of corn in the yard.

–

Five hours later, Hawker stood in the town market square, watching the grim spectacle before him. The low, makeshift scaffold creaked with the movement of the condemned and the executioner. And the ritual repeated itself once again. A quick prayer, the condemned on his knees, neck upon a blacksmith's borrowed oak block, the rise and fall of the axe. The crowd's silence replaced with a collective groan as the head was held aloft. Thirteen went that way. The Earl of Somerset, Langstrother, half a dozen other knights and their squires. They'd dispatched four inside the abbey before the rest had surrendered and were dragged out. Maybe that was the better way to go, mused Hawker, watching the gory head of the prior of Saint John's being tossed into a wicker basket. *Sweet Christ!* The man had spent his youth defending Rhodes from the Turk. Hawker's emptiness deepened, a gnawing pit inside him. A man-at-arms threw another armful of straw onto the slick platform.

The king had not watched. Richard, as lord constable of the kingdom, had judged them all in the company of the Earl Marshal, Duke of Norfolk. Richard stayed long enough to see Somerset executed and then left. The war was won – again. Hawker turned and prepared to gather his men. But a messenger found him and handed him a sealed note.

You are commanded to come to me without delay.

Hawker scowled to himself, folded the paper, and set off for the Ox, a few streets away. The inn was well guarded, but the men recognised him and he went inside. Officials gathered and argued downstairs, courtiers laughed and drank, and bored sentries slouched in the corners while leaning on their halberds. He doffed his helm, went to the stairs, showed his note to the captain of the guard stationed there, and ascended the wide staircase.

Upstairs, the two large chambers had been requisitioned by the royal household. The first room, where Hawker entered, was the antechamber. A large, carved door at the other end led to the main solar, which was serving as King Edward's reception chamber. Hawker looked at the faces around him: newfound hangers-on, loyalists from years gone by, two Burgundian gentlemen (from their ridiculous hats and shoes), and four of the queen's ladies-in-waiting, conspiring and giggling in one corner.

And there was the Duke of Gloucester. The young noble stood in the centre of the chamber in quiet conversation with his companion – someone Hawker knew also – the

Baron Lovell, a fifteen-year-old boy destined for high office at the Yorkist court. He had been a ward at Middleham where Hawker had instructed them both in sword and buckler. Richard saw Hawker and beckoned him.

The man-at-arms approached and gave a bow.

'Hawker, you are always so glum these days! Be of good cheer!' He quickly turned to Lovell. 'Francis, you remember your sword master, don't you? He gave you a fair few bruises, I seem to remember.'

The fine-featured boy nodded to Hawker. 'I do remember. Perhaps one day I will be skilled enough to repay the favour.'

Richard chuckled. 'You will have to train a bit more to best Hawker, I would wager!'

Hawker grimaced a little, unable to offer up a smile.

'You do know why you're here, don't you?' asked Richard. 'The message.'

'I wait upon His Majesty's pleasure,' said Hawker quietly. 'The note said nothing else.'

Richard of Gloucester grinned widely, his strong jaw jutting. 'My brother is this day making you a knight bachelor!'

Hawker's brow creased up in confusion. And then, as if planned, the herald at the door called out his name.

Richard leaned closer and whispered. 'Go on. Receive your reward.'

Part I

SALT AND SALVATION

1

The Lagoon of Venice, March 1486

Sir John Hawker, knight without a lord, stared out across the grey waters towards the spires of Venice, one league distant. His nostrils were filled with the harsh, acrid smell of salt and sulphur, a stench he had been imbibing for some ten days. The island of Torcello was a forgotten place now, squatting in the middle of the *laguna Venesia*, the shallow bay that also sheltered those islands not forgotten in the past: Venice and Murano. Torcello, however, was in its death throes. A place of pestilence, its canals were silted, its *palazzos* demolished and abandoned, pigs rooting in their ruins. In its reed marshes a few fishermen eked out a living and the noxious salt flats provided some poor folk – their hands burned raw – with work drying and then bagging the stuff ready to be ferried across to the Serene Republic.

If stone and brick could shed tears, mused Hawker, then the Cathedral of San Maria Assunta (which loomed at his back) would have cried copiously to the heavens, a flooding river of lamentation for its loss. The once great Byzantine church now had few who worshipped, its dwindling flock catered for by a single priest who had likely offended some *monsignor* in Venice to be sentenced to such a parish of hardship. The resident bishop had long departed the island, leaving it to the salt gatherers and the raucous cormorants. Yet it was Torcello's misfortunes that had led Hawker to choose to land there. For those who did not wish to be seen by the many eyes of the Republic, it was the safer choice to hide.

Hawker's last remaining man-at-arms, Jacob de Grood, approached, the salt-crusted, dead vegetation of the shoreline crunching under his boots.

'Sir John... they're here. Your spies from the Terra Ferma. They say they have intelligence of San Polo... and the lady.'

Hawker turned, pinching his proud nose to clear away the strong smell that lingered, carried upon the breeze blowing across the tidal flats. He regarded Jacob, the Fleming's deep, sweeping cheek scar giving him a permanent grimace. 'Good. We've waited long enough for their return.' He yanked his belted jerkin down with both hands, straightening the leather, and rested his left palm on the pommel of his *cinquedea* dagger. 'Take me to them.'

The little stone house lay at the edge of the remaining settlement, a short distance from the square of the basilica. It had been fashioned from larger marble and sandstone blocks scavenged from the ruins of some *palazzo* by the hardier denizens of Torcello. Its masonry looked sadly out of proportion with its small size. Outside, waiting, stood three men, well-fed soldiers, by the look of them. Short and broad-chested, all three bore long daggers showing beneath their homespun wool cloaks. One stepped forward, giving a nod of recognition towards Hawker, and then, grasping both of the knight's forearms in greeting, shook them.

'Don Falco!' he said heartily in sibilant Venetian. 'I greet you well. And we bring news of whom you seek.'

Hawker smiled and gripped the man's elbow. 'Marco, I am eager to hear what you have learned. Come inside.'

He beckoned them to enter, along with de Grood, and, glancing around to see if any observed in the street, followed them in last. The sunken floor was earthen, the front room, which served as the hall, held a large trestle table and some benches but little else. Seated there were three others: an elegant and tall blond youth, fair of features, a thin handsome, dark-haired man with a pointed chin, not yet in his middle years, and a boy on the cusp of manhood, his upper lip covered in wispy ginger whiskers so sparse they might be counted. All three rose up when the newcomers came in.

Hawker guided Marco Rosso and his men into the candle-lit room, shutters fixed tightly to discourage eavesdroppers. He gestured for the scouts to sit. 'Jack, fetch these men some wine!'

The lad, Jack Perry, a very long way from his home in Lincolnshire, nodded vigorously and jumped to the task.

Hawker's eyes glistened, opened wide by necessity of the dimness of the chamber. He seated himself across from Rosso. 'Tell me what you've found, my friend.' Rosso had served him well, years before in the Terra Ferma, the mainland possessions of the Republic, which spread out as far as fair Verona and challenged the Duchy of Lombardy. He had sought Rosso out, lucky to find the old soldier was still alive and living in Treviso where Hawker had last seen him a decade earlier. The company had ventured near to there, overland from Trieste, after many weeks of dangerous travel across the Hungarian lands, the taste of their forlorn quest in the east still bitter in their mouths. Hawker knew it would be unwise to venture into Venice himself to find whom he sought. Better to leave that to those who would be unlikely to draw attention. The price upon his head, and that of the young nobleman who travelled with him, meant he would have but one chance to enter the city: when the deed itself was to be done and not before.

Rosso reached out to retrieve the wooden beaker set before him. He drained more than half of it and set it down, wiping his chin. 'You may not like all we have to tell you, Don Falco.'

The blond youth – Sir Giles Ellingham – bastard son of Richard Plantagenet, stood in the background, arms folded, head leaning in and a scowl on his face, the Venetian dialect clearly a challenge for him. Equally, his companion, Gaston Dieudonné, another survivor of the debacle of Bosworth Field, stood at his side watching the proceedings with narrowed eyes. Hawker would explain all later but was more interested in hearing from Rosso – without interruption – just how difficult things were going to get.

Rosso rubbed his bear paw of a hand over his shaved pate and glanced over at Hawker's companions. 'This is your army, Don Falco?'

'Sometimes fewer are better.'

Rosso snickered. 'Indeed, that is sometimes true. I pray that it will be your fortune this time.'

With a flick of his forefinger Hawker signalled for Jack to pour the wine again. 'Marco, where is she? Who has her?'

Rosso rapped his fingertips against the wooden cup, his eyebrows raised. 'Aye, well, it wasn't difficult to find her where-abouts. It is still the talk of San Polo. The woman is held in the household of her father-in-law – an old merchant. Benedetto Contanto.' Rosso raised his left hand, pressing thumb and fore-finger together. 'He is like *this* with the guilds. Much influence.'

Hawker leaned in. 'Did you see her? Even glimpse her? How does she fare?'

Rosso shook his head, stuck out his lips, and tugged at the gold earring in his right ear. 'We watched for two days straight. No one sees her. The word in the calle is that she is under house arrest. The Council of Ten seems to be divided on her fate. Nobody knows why. Some say she is a murderess... or at the very least a faithless adulteress. Others say that Don Falco murdered her husband.' Rosso gave a sheepish smile. 'But, I suppose... only you would know that.'

Hawker ignored the implication. 'So, Chiara may face trial... at the very least for adultery.'

Rosso nodded slowly. 'And, more likely, for murder. Her father-in-law will want his son to be avenged. The man has much power with the Council. And if he can't find the one who wielded the blade, then she will do.'

'How much time do we have?'

Rosso blew out his cheeks and sat back. 'Don Falco, you ask what I could not know – nor discover. She is lucky she's not wading knee-deep in the stinking wells at the bottom of the Doge's Palace. If you force me to guess... they will take her away in days – not weeks. The whole affair is making the Council look weak. Weak on those who go against the natural order of things.'

Hawker, too, sat back and then rubbed his eyes with both palms in frustration and anger. He had left her there when they had fled Venice. Too much the gallant, he had obeyed her wish to be a martyr when he should have thrown her over his shoulder and carried her off. He looked over to Jack Perry – ignorant of the words that had just passed over the table. It was the boy Jack who had killed Luca Contanto. Killing him as the enraged husband tried to strangle Chiara. Jack had saved her only for him to lose her hours later.

The ageing knight leaned forward again. 'The palazzo. Describe.'

'Front's a small waterway off the great canal from the north. At the border with Cannaregio. But there is a servants' entrance off to the side. Can be reached along a narrow street that runs along the back of the row of palazzi. Where the walled gardens are laid out. You can escape by that way to reach the great canal again. You still intend to gain entrance as you told me?'

Hawker nodded, face grim. 'I do, Marco.'

'Then have a care. Contanto has many retainers. Young grooms of sturdy limb.' He looked at the four of Hawker's company. 'These fellows are stout, no doubt. But you will have a devil of a time getting in and out in one piece.'

Hawker, in spite of the worry that tugged at his chest, broke into a smile. 'We have a saying in England. Old crows are hard to catch.'

–

Rosso and his companions had taken their leave. They would return on the morrow, late afternoon, with two small boats this time instead of one. Ellingham and Dieudonné had listened in

13

silence as Hawker told of Rosso's intelligence. When he had finished, adding the details of his own plan for the intended rescue, Sir Giles Ellingham, still gaunt from the hard travels of several weeks across Europe, gave a wide smile and shrugged.

'I expected no less, Sir John. There will be no better time and no better way. God grant us fortune.'

Gaston Dieudonné inclined his head in a mark of respect. 'We are with you, Sir John. But have you thought well upon who will go into the palazzo and who will remain with the boats? There is a price upon the head of this prince we have in our midst. Perhaps entering Venice is best left to you and me.'

Before Hawker could get the words of reproach from his throat, Ellingham had pulled back, turning to face the Burgundian directly. 'Gaston, do you impugn my courage? I am no prince. I am a bastard. And I have given my word we will save this innocent woman if the Lord grants us His protection. Do not seek to rob me of honour.'

Dieudonné gave a court bow, ridiculous in the setting of the lowly, decrepit hovel. 'My lord, I seek only to preserve you for the greater fight. That of the cause of the White Rose.'

'You will *both* be in the boat with me,' growled Hawker. 'Jacob and Jack will make sure that Marco holds his nerve and waits for us while we will take the House of Contanto together. It is no coincidence we do this thing on the morrow. It is the eve of the Feast of the Annunciation. The Lenten fast is lifted for a day and a night.'

Ellingham grinned. 'Very good, Sir John, very good indeed. They will all be eating and drinking to their hearts' content. And we shall have them.'

Hawker gave him a smile. 'We must make the odds the better… and hope that Bacchus aids us.'

Dieudonné inclined his head in a little bow once again. 'Clever, Sir John. *This* is why we follow you.' But Hawker saw that the Burgundian's eyes didn't sparkle with the enthusiasm of Giles's. They were almost dead, expressionless, and Hawker could not see what truth lay behind them.

14

'Rest, gentlemen, for the remainder of the day. Tomorrow will test all of us.' He left them and went outside in the chill March wind that blew across the salt flats and into what remained of the town. His bravado was hollow. There were a thousand things that could go awry, not least of which was Chiara's present condition. If she was bed-ridden or had been beaten. Immovable in body or even in mind. And three of them, even if they were fighting men, what could they do if an entire household rose up to defend? Getting in might be the easiest part, getting out and escaping from Venice once the alarm was raised across the neighbourhood... *that* would be the true challenge. He had to hope the celebration of the archangel's news of the Saviour's coming to the Virgin Mary would keep them all well occupied.

He found Jacob sitting on a half-rotted willow bench, oiling his sword with a dirty rag. 'Where is Jack gone now?' he asked the Fleming.

Jacob paused. 'The lad said he was going to the basilica.' He then looked up at Hawker, eyebrows raised. 'To pray for the salvation of his soul.'

Entering into the great Byzantine cathedral from a side door, Hawker, at first, did not spy him. An iron brazier and few torches had already been lit in the fading light of late afternoon. The sole priest of San Maria Assunta bustled about the nave, preparing for Evensong. Jack, however, was not watching. Nor was he in the pews. Hawker found him standing at the western end of the ancient place, staring at an immense fresco that rose from floor to ceiling. Hawker stood a few paces behind the boy, who was still unaware of his presence, and regarded the work before him. Painted a few hundred years before, it depicted Doomsday and the Final Judgement.

From the angle of Jack's craned neck, Hawker could see the lad was not fixated on the triumph of Christ and the host of angels high above, but rather, further down upon the army of demons who were tormenting the naked souls of the dead.

They writhed in the vermillion-red flames of the Pit, while below them a sea of skulls floated, mocking the beholder.

Hawker gently reached out and placed a hand on Jack's shoulder. The boy flinched and wheeled, recovering when he saw his knight before him.

'Sir John, begging your pardon! Forgive me… I only wanted to do penance before, we…' His words trailed off.

Hawker stepped forward and wrapped an arm about his shoulders. 'You have no need for my forgiveness. Stay. Make your prayers and your peace. Then we must speak about tomorrow. What we must do and how we are to do it. I will leave you now.'

He pulled away, eyes glancing up to the riot of colour still vibrant after so many years. Christ's eyes seemed to be watching him.

'Sir John,' said Jack, voice quiet but still echoing slightly in the cavernous space. 'Am I damned?'

Hawker swallowed. 'What does your catechism teach you, boy?'

Jack winced a little in uncertainty. 'Salvation and the forgiveness of sins?'

Hawker smiled reassuringly. 'That is what we are taught, no? You must believe it. Christ's blood was spilled for all of us. Say a prayer for me, eh?'

Jack nodded and Hawker nodded too, then turned and walked back the way he had come. The priest had robed and a few of Torcello's last remaining townsfolk had wandered in, filing into the pews and kneeling in penance.

Hawker's face dropped as he walked out, the reassuring smile melting away. *We are all damned*, he thought.

2

Jacob grunted, hefting the hempen sack of dried salt then placing it into the bottom of the small, narrow *caique*, its lateen sail furled around its single mast. He tripped over the stowed oars and cursed. Hawker threw him a second sack and the Fleming centred it along with the first. They were, like Ellingham and Dieudonné both, dressed in greasy jerkins and old woollen cloaks, stained linen coifs covering their heads. A keen eye might question the fine green hose of Ellingham and the Burgundian, but most would take them for tradesmen and labourers. At least that was Hawker's hope. The long daggers they wore might be more difficult to conceal.

Jacob nodded to Hawker and then took his place in the other *caique* along with Jack and one of Rosso's men. Both *caiques* were old, probably thieved, their peeling green and red paint looking like the scales of a dead fish.

Rosso looked at Hawker and smiled, eyes twinkling with the love of the risk. 'Shall we, Don Falco?' He gestured towards the boat. Ellingham had already climbed aboard, making his way to the bow. Dieudonné seemed to sniff the air around him a moment and then climbed in and seated himself on a bench, the boat rocking again as he did so. Rosso steadied the boat at the gunwale and nodded to Hawker.

The knight cinched up belt and *cinquedea* in one hand and splashed knee deep into the sea, stepping over the side and into the vessel. Rosso gave a shove and with a rasping sound the *caique* edged out into the lagoon, the Treviso mercenary hopping aboard with a jump. Oars out, he rowed until he could get the sail raised. No one said a word and Hawker watched Ellingham in the bow, the youth's gaze fixed on the soaring campaniles and chimneys of Venice. Hawker was still deeply beholden to the young man's offer of aid on what was a private matter of honour. It was being done out of loyalty and friendship – not for reward – and at great risk of death for this Plantagenet castaway. He would not have expected anything so courageous from one of his age and inexperience. But Ellingham had, by necessity, learned much in the last several months.

Despite the shallowness of the lagoon, little whitecaps danced across the face of the sea, the cold breeze stiffening as they pushed further out. Hawker reckoned once under sail they would be at the northern entrance to the great canal before even half an hour had passed.

They all remained silent for the first several minutes while the boat drew further away from Torcello. Rosso deftly guided them out, one hand gripping the steering board on the side, the other keeping the line taut on the lateen sail. Hawker watched the other boat, which bore on a parallel course a little ways off. Jack seemed to be wearing out Jacob's ears, but the Fleming appeared tolerant of the lad's overexcitement. He smiled a little despite his fears for the boy. Jack had come too far now to go back to any other life. One learned by staying alive.

Hawker looked down into the sloshing bilge of the little craft. His thoughts went to Chiara. Rosso could give him no clue as to whether she was ill or in health, beaten or pampered. And part of him worried about something else. Not whether he could free her but whether instead of being hailed a saviour she would denounce him as an abductor. Hawker knew full well she blamed herself – and maybe him, too – for their adultery and her husband's death. Despite it all, he decided he would bear the risk. He never should have left her when he fled Venice, even though she had begged him to do so. He would not make the same mistake this time.

Dieudonné caught him looking lost in thought and addressed him in French.

'You are thinking about how many will die, no? It is inevitable that the household will defend.'

Hawker looked up and locked his gaze on the Burgundian. 'I told you. No bloodshed if it is to be avoided. Pommel them if they resist. Disarm them. But kill only if needs must.'

Dieudonné gave a shrug. 'Easier said than done, my lord. A double shame as it's the eve of the Virgin's day and the archangel's good news.' He grinned at his own jest.

'Listen well,' Hawker growled. 'No needless deaths. Understood?'

The Burgundian nodded once, slowly. 'Of course, Sir John. Your word is my command.'

His eyes, however, remained stubbornly defiant. Hawker had watched the Burgundian's little challenges grow since they had left the Hungarian kingdom. Half in jest, half goading, Dieudonné's quips were a pebble in the boot. One he would probably have to rid himself of before long. But for the moment, he needed every sword he had.

Rosso called out to him from the stern. 'Don Falco! If we are challenged on the way into the canal, who does the talking?'

'Your accent is the more convincing. We are delivering salt to our customers – and looking to have a little fun on the feast day. Make a joke of it.'

Rosso laughed, all his large, white teeth showing save for one wide gap. 'A joke? A joke upon which much depends! Aye, well, we will brazen it out if it comes to it.' He leaned against the steering board and the boat heeled, turning its course away from a large barge that was approaching from the south. They continued on, drawing ever closer to Venice. Hawker could see the forest of masts from the Republic's many galleys anchored in the basin of the Arsenal. Further along, church spires and domes of red tiles, soaring campaniles, and funnel-topped chimneys of the *palazzos* all dotted the shoreline. It was a sight he had not expected to ever see again.

Five months earlier they had barely escaped the Republic with their lives; and not all of his company had made it out. Hawker owed their survival to the timely intervention of a third party, one who dictated the terms of his salvation. She was Maria Hunyadi, an adventuress of skill and daring who sought something that he had: a precious stone she claimed was of her family. That was the price of their escape and that is how they had journeyed eastwards to her Hungarian lands and joined her in a doomed quest to find her lost father, a prince of Wallachia. The result had been more death and deceit, and little to show for it. Yet they had survived and clawed their way west again. Now Hawker knew he had one wrong that he still could right if God favoured him: rescuing the woman he had left behind.

Rosso edged the little boat harder to larboard. The Cannaregio canal loomed, and Hawker could see other vessels coming and going into the great artery that led to the heart of Venice. Their other boat followed into line behind them and they pushed on. The stockade lookout post at the mouth was manned, but none of the men there bothered to even give them a glance. Moments later they were gliding deeper into the city, and Rosso hurriedly dropped sail and took to the oars. They snaked their way south, passing other vessels loaded with goods or ferrying wealthy merchants in their finery to the vigil Masses held on the eve of the Virgin's day. Hawker and his masquerading labourers were ignored.

Rosso grunted with effort, turning the boat into a smaller canal. Up ahead, the canal turned into a boat slip, green with algae. He pointed ahead to the little square that could be seen above. 'Follow my hand. See the fourth palazzo – the one nearest the fountain? That is Contanto's.'

Hawker saw it, his eyes then scanning for any nearby militiamen. The secret spies in this part of San Polo – the feared *sbirri* – would be harder to spot. 'I see it. The great red door.'

Rosso nodded. 'Yes. That is the one.' He moved his hairy hand again, pointing. 'To the right, past the fountain, the square continues. You will clearly see another canal at the end. That is where we will be waiting for you. From there we can cut through another and join the Grand Canal. We run for it out the western end.'

Hawker turned and told Ellingham and Dieudonné, in French. They both raised their heads to view the *palazzo* and the square. The Burgundian pulled a sour face.

'So… we make our escape by *rowing* – as fast as snails – until we're out? Is that it?'

Hawker narrowed his eyes. 'That is it.'

Dieudonné met his glare. 'Then no one must be permitted to raise the alarm,' he said, almost reverently.

Ellingham's eyes looked over to Hawker. The youth's concern was painted upon his face. Hawker reached down into the boat and lifted a satchel lying on a salt bag. 'Here is rope. We tie them up. Stuff a rag in their mouth. In and out. No more blood!'

Dieudonné grinned. 'My lord, you are a true Christian.'

Rosso cursed. 'Don Falco! Do this thing or do not! We cannot linger here.'

Hawker muttered his own curse and nodded. 'Take us in!' As Rosso took to the oars again, Hawker looked past the mercenary's straining back and over to where Jacob and Jack sat in their boat watching. He gave a wave to them and nodded, signalling all was well. He then touched Ellingham lightly on the shoulder. 'All will be well. We *will* save her.'

–

The cook, a portly woman of middle years, head tied with a kerchief, narrowed her eyes. 'I have bought no salt of late! You are at the wrong place.'

Hawker hefted the sack on his shoulder and grunted. 'Good lady, this *is* for Don Contanto's house! We are not taking it back now! Go, ask the others in the kitchen. They will tell you.' He was glad of the side entrance to the *palazzo*, which directly led into the house. An argument at the main door would have been far too visible to observers.

Dieudonné shifted his sack from one shoulder to the other, grunting as he did so. The cook muttered and waved them inside. It was a large cold room, dimly lit with a long refectory table of oak at its centre. A fire crackled away in the stone hearth over which two large pots were set.

'Where is the mistress of the house?' asked Hawker. 'We are still owed.'

The cook crossed her bare arms, scalds visible from years of kitchen toil. 'The mistress is dead. I handle the household now.'

Her words took Hawker as if by the throat. His mouth opened as he fought for his next utterance.

'Don't worry,' she continued, chuckling, 'Don Contanto does not mourn her any more after two years. He already has his eye on another.'

Hawker smiled at her, relief swelling in his chest. 'But where is the mistress Chiara then? Surely she would serve to manage the household.'

The cook swept her kerchief off her head, her eyes drilling into Hawker. There was a pause longer than Hawker liked. 'Leave the salt there and wait outside while I fetch your coin.'

Dieudonné tilted his head to the side and raised his dark eyebrows nearly to his hairline. He turned and shut the heavy, studded door. The cook took a few steps back and wheeled around to make for the next chamber, but Hawker grabbed her from behind, wrapped his palm over her mouth and dragged her back into the kitchen. She fought hard and Hawker found himself revolted by what he was now doing. He signalled for Ellingham and the youth brought forth a length of hemp cord to tie her hands and feet. Hawker admonished her, the whites of her eyes fully visible in terror. He released his hand long enough for her to let out a short scream in which time he had shoved her balled kerchief into her mouth. They rolled her under the table, moaning.

Hawker led the way up onto the first floor, the staircase becoming more intricately carved and ornate the higher they climbed. He could hear male voices – servants by the sound of their conversation – and he whispered for Ellingham to be ready to take them down. 'They must not run,' he hissed. Coming out onto the next floor, they saw them. Two liveried footmen in red-and-yellow doublets. They were barely more than Ellingham's age, by the look of them, and both froze in confusion upon seeing the rough tradesmen appear at the top of the stairs. Before Hawker could move, Dieudonné had launched himself at the two, dropping one instantly with a punch before leaping upon his startled companion. Their cries required drastic action and Hawker saw his hope of a bloodless rescue evaporate. Even as Ellingham tied one of the footmen while Hawker restrained him on the floor with an elbow across the throat, the Burgundian had punched the other into unconsciousness, red oozing across the glazed tiles of the floor.

Ellingham managed to gag the other footman, who now remained stock still. Hawker suddenly smelled the strong stench of piss. The fellow had soiled himself. Hawker staggered to his feet, breathing heavily and looked around. The bed chambers were probably a floor further up. He hissed again to Dieudonné who was wiping his hands on his dark hose and indicated they had to move higher.

Hawker led the way, hand on the hilt of his dagger, ready to draw. Tall, narrow cathedral windows at the front of the *palazzo* let the early spring light filter into the hall, though it was fast fading. They emerged onto a landing more like a gallery from which other chambers branched off. A young woman – another servant – emerged from one of the rooms bearing a ceramic pitcher. She froze upon seeing the intruders, her mouth gaping. Hawker slowly placed a finger to his lips. She blinked several times.

'Giles,' said Hawker softly, 'see to her.'

Ellingham approached her, his palms spread. He then pulled a length of cord from his belt and went behind her. He took her pitcher away, drew her hands together and began to tie them. Hawker heard the girl begin to whimper but she did not cry out. Dieudonné crept like a cat back to the stairwell to keep watch. His eyes said he was revelling in the raid. Hawker felt his stomach begin to turn, a sour belch coming up from inside him.

'Where is Chiara?' he asked the terrified girl, sitting her down so that Ellingham could tie up her ankles. She burst into tears. Ellingham shot Hawker a look of helplessness or guilt, the old knight wasn't sure which.

'We are here to help her,' continued Hawker in soft Venetian. 'I beg you, tell me where she is.' The girl blinked her tears and indicated with her head the room she had just emerged from. Hawker arose and moved quickly to the door. He exhaled, trying to calm himself, turned the brass lever, and walked inside.

Chiara Contanto stood there, one arm clutching the barley-twist poster of the canopied bedstead. He stopped just over the threshold. She saw him and he could tell she was not believing what her eyes were telling her. It was the look not of surprise, but rather, of someone who was having a vision. Her lips parted slightly.

Hawker's voice was raspy and choked. 'Chiara.'

He saw that her eye was blackened, cheekbone swollen and yellowed with bruising. Chiara's hand fell from the bedpost, and in so doing, the folds of her blue gown moved away, revealing her white chemise and form underneath.

And Hawker saw then, and only then, that she was heavy with child.

3

Hawker took a few tentative steps forward into the bedchamber. Chiara's eyes welled up but she stood motionless next to the bed. She shook her head in disbelief, eyes scrunching, but no words came from her.

'Chiara,' repeated Hawker, trying to assemble his tumbling thoughts into words he could utter. 'I could not leave you. The pain in my soul… unbearable.'

She fell towards him, sobs breaking from her, and he enveloped her in his arms. Her round belly pressed into him. The child that had been taken from him years ago through the death of his first wife might now be restored. A quiet joy ran through him but then instantly was replaced by the thought that it might be Luca Contanto's child, or worse, the result of her being ravished after he had fled the city and left her to her fate. He touched her face and she regarded him with her eyes of sea grey, sparkling with the wetness of tears.

'Giovanni, you should not have come back,' she whispered, still holding him tightly. 'They will kill you now.'

'Who has beaten you?'

She loosened her hold upon him, pulling away slightly. 'My father-in-law. He would see me hang… If it weren't for…' And she framed her belly with both hands. She looked up again at Hawker, her face suddenly becoming defiant and brave. 'It is *yours*, my love. Yours. And I have told him so. He tried to make me drink tansy root – to end it – but I fought him. He has beat me ever since. Hoping…'

His sudden elation over her child – *his* child – was sullied and dulled by his rising hatred of her tormentor. Hawker kissed her forehead. 'We are taking you away from here. Now.' He turned and cast his eyes across her chamber. 'Gather a few things while you can! We must be quick!'

She frowned, confused. 'And go where? How? How can I flee… like *this*?'

Hawker bit his lip. 'We have a boat. We shall make it to Terra Ferma. Trust me! But we must move now, Chiara.'

Her voice grew small. 'I cannot make such a journey. Not now. With you… and your soldiers?'

Hawker moved to her again and gently held her by her shoulders. 'I have planned everything. Do not fear. I won't let you remain to face trial for something you did not do. I should never have left you here, alone.'

'Hawker!' It was Dieudonné calling from the hall. Hawker went out and saw a tall grey-haired patrician slowly descending the staircase from the higher floor of the *palazzo*. He was dressed in a red worsted doublet and black hose, his forest green silk brocade *cioppa* framing his broad shoulders and cascading down to his ankles and fine shoes. The man stopped halfway down to the hall landing, one hand resting on the hilt of the dagger that hung from his waist. His eyes took in the sight of his servant tied up on the floor, and the three roughly dressed brigands who had invaded his house.

'Who are you? You will all hang for his outrage.' Benedetto Contanto's voice held no fear but dripped with scorn. He leaned over the dark oak railing and called down the stairwell. 'Toderino! Nicolo!'

'They are not coming,' said Hawker, darkly.

Contanto swivelled around again, eyes narrowing. 'Murdering bastards. *Foreign* bastards.'

He yanked a set of keys from this belt and tossed them down to the landing. 'There is a strongbox upstairs. Take what you like. But you will have to pass me first.'

Hawker's *cinquedea* rasped from its scabbard.

Contanto laughed. 'A gentleman's weapon? Truly? Something else you thieved?'

Hawker felt his face flushing with rage. 'Giles, see to the mistress Chiara. We are leaving now.'

'Frenchmen? Where is the rest of your army? Get out of my house!'

Chiara emerged, led on the arm of Ellingham. Hawker saw the hateful look she gave her father-in-law.

'Ah,' said Contanto, 'you would steal the whore as well. You are welcome to her. Murdering adulteress. Traitor to her blood!'

Hawker balanced the dagger in his hand, knuckles whitening. 'You would beat a woman with child? There is no honour in you. She's innocent of what she is accused. Blameless.'

Contanto raised himself up and focused on the man before him. He then let out a harsh laugh. 'Don Falco! The Englishman. The randy old dog, come back for his whore. What a fool to return for so little!'

Hawker sprang forward and leapt up the four steps, seizing Contanto by the doublet with his left hand. His right sent the wide *cinquedea* blade thrusting full into the man's stomach. Hawker drew out the dagger and Contanto tumbled down onto the landing. The bound servant girl screamed through her gag and Hawker turned to see Chiara's face contorted in horror. Ellingham stood motionless, eyes wide in near disbelief. Hawker steadied himself on the railing, revulsion flooding his gut.

A slow, steady clap of hands sounded from below. Gaston Dieudonné.

Contanto coughed a fountain of blood from where he lay on his back. He tried to raise an arm but failed, his eyes rolling upwards into his head. And then he was dead.

Hawker didn't move, the dripping dagger still at his side.

'Sir John,' said Ellingham, 'we must leave.'

Hawker nodded and swallowed.

They made their way down the stairs and out back to the kitchen. The cook was still lying there, trussed like a pig, eyes wide in terror that this time she would be dispatched. Hawker threw a blue woollen cloak around Chiara's shoulders and guided her outside. Dieudonné, the last to leave, turned and blew a kiss to the cook before shutting the heavy door.

'Giles, in front. My lord Gaston, you too. Head straight across the piazza. Do not hurry!' He leaned into Chiara's hood, pulled up fully, obscuring her face. 'I am just one pace behind you. Do not fear.' Hawker's hope was that folk would see a lady out with her servants and nothing more. But he knew the lack of a maidservant would raise eyebrows. Chiara walked unsteadily, clutching at the embroidered, claret-coloured sack, into which she had managed to put a few things.

A few merchants were in the square, conversing. And though Hawker gave them a wide berth he saw that they were watching, their conversation now stopped. They passed the gentlemen and continued to the far end, the other canal revealed. Hawker risked a backwards glance. He saw one of the merchants walking briskly towards Contanto's house.

Once the alarm was raised, they would probably be overwhelmed, the outcome bloody but not in question. Hawker felt his back tingling with an onrush of sweating. The canal was at a right angle to them, a short wooden walkway running along its length. A narrow costermonger's gondola was tied alongside. But Rosso's boats were nowhere to be seen.

Ellingham turned. 'Sweet Jesus! Where are they?'

Hawker saw that the merchant had disappeared – probably inside Contanto's house to investigate. It was now a matter of moments until the footmen would be coming for them along with anyone else at hand.

'Get her into this boat!' ordered Hawker. 'You pole it out from here. I will stay and fight them off.'

Ellingham nodded solemnly. 'I will safeguard her, Sir John.'

Dieudonné whistled softly. 'Don't be rash, my lords. Here they are.'

Rosso and his companions were now in view, moving their two boats up through a knot of other vessels further along. The mercenary had somehow obtained long poles and shipped the oars, the better to navigate the cramped side canals.

They were making good progress but at any moment Hawker expected to see half a dozen burly Venetians sprinting across the piazza. Sure enough, just as Rosso pulled alongside, his companion's craft also butting up alongside the jetty, Hawker saw figures exit Contanto's house, stop, take their bearings, and then move into the piazza. He could see that two bore glaives.

'*Allora*! Don Falco!' exclaimed Rosso. 'We were held up at the other end.' He reached up, offering his hand to Chiara while Ellingham helped ease her down into the boat.

'For the love of Christ, get us out of here!'

Dieudonné leapt into the boat with Jacob and Jack, not waiting for further orders while Ellingham helped push the nose of Rosso's boat out.

'Sir John, climb in, I beg you!'

The group of Venetians were now rushing closer, guttural shouts already reaching the canal.

'I shall be the last to leave a boot print in this city,' said Hawker, pushing Ellingham before him and into the vessel. He then put one leg in and pushed off from the jetty with the other, falling into the boat. Rosso, standing, pushed hard and poled the craft down the canal. The other boat was already under way. They passed the edge of the piazza where buildings rose up either side of the canal and Hawker saw the first of the footmen arrive. The man gesticulated and shouted at them, waving his glaive. He was soon joined by others and then all disappeared from view.

'They will try and cut us off,' shouted Rosso, pushing and pulling his pole as fast as he could. 'We must get out to the Grand Canal! I can't raise canvas here!'

Hawker saw Contanto's henchmen and others pounding over a narrow wooden footbridge further down, racing parallel to their own course. They were now on the same side of the island. Rosso followed the companion boat's course into yet another side canal. It was straight and narrow and some three hundred yards ahead, Hawker could see it opened again. The wide Grand Canal lay in front of them.

Rosso grunted with his efforts, the boat seeming to just inch its way along. Hawker placed a hand on Chiara's back, leaned in, and whispered to her.

'God is with us. We will make it out.'

Hawker heard yelling and saw the armed party crossing another footbridge across a side canal parallel to them. Then the view was shut off as they glided past houses. When they reached another side canal Hawker heard Ellingham – who crouched in the bow – shout '*Handgonne!*' and turned to see men standing on a bridge twenty-five yards away, one aiming the weapon balanced over the railing. Hawker could see the burning taper being put to the breech and then a flash. He leaned over Chiara, shielding her, as the explosion echoed off the buildings around them. Stucco blasted from off the house opposite them sending shards of brick splashing into the water.

Rosso swore aloud, crossed himself, and resumed his frantic poling of the boat. Hawker could hear the shouts of their pursuers a few alleys away, but they emerged into the swiftly swirling waters of the Grand Canal before they could be cornered. Rosso tossed away his long pole and began to hoist sail. They were already nearly at the end of the great waterway at the point they entered it. The little boat picked up speed and Hawker took a great gulp of salty air, a cold wind cutting across them.

Ellingham turned and gave Hawker a wide grin of boyish relief. Hawker nodded and leaned down again to speak to Chiara. She was shaking visibly in her cloak and he wrapped his arms around her.

'We don't sail for long, my love. Torcello is close by. From there… Terra Ferma. Be brave!'

Her reply came in little bursts of speech, weighted down by shock and anxiety. 'We'll never… be safe… they will hunt us.' She turned in his arms, glancing backwards as they rounded the tip of the island, passing by the great red campanile of the church that bore her name: Santa Chiara. Leaving the shelter of the canal and entering the lagoon, another blast of wind buffeted them, tossing their boat. 'I will never go back. Ever.'

–

Ellingham leapt from the boat once it had run into the sand. Sloshing in the shallows, he pulled the prow further up onto the shoreline with Hawker wading in as well to push from the stern. In the fading light of the day, it appeared they had not been pursued – as of yet. Hawker knew they would come. His rash action had guaranteed it.

Carefully and with trepidation, the two knights lifted Chiara out and guided her up the beach. Hawker yelled over for Jack Perry and the squire was quickly there.

'Jack, take the mistress's arm, there's a lad. Get her up to the house and take it slowly.'

Rosso and his men now brought the boats up further beyond the tide mark and then joined the rest of the company. Hawker felt sick. It had not gone as he had expected or wanted. The joy of finding Chiara had been spoilt and dirtied by the lowness of the enterprise, a squalid business in which they had played brigands while he had arguably committed murder. Hawker watched as Chiara made her way past the scrub and into the trees, guided by Jack.

Rosso stepped forward and gave a little bow of his head to Hawker. 'We have done as you asked, Don Falco. I would counsel against remaining here much longer though.'

Dieudonné crossed his arms and looked out towards Venice. 'We have left them a trail of salt to find us, Sir John. We might just as well have told them we came from this island. There's no disguising the fact.'

Hawker didn't like having his nose rubbed into a turd of his own making. He felt his face grow hot.

'That was to be expected, my lord,' said Ellingham, in defence. 'The deception gained us entry though. We have made it back.'

'Yes, indeed,' agreed the Burgundian, 'with *two* rescued instead of one, it would seem.'

'And what would you have done, my lord,' said Hawker, parrying weakly.

Dieudonné shrugged. 'I would not have left *any* witnesses. That would have solved the problem. Rather neatly, too.'

Hawker muttered a curse, aimed more at himself than the rash Burgundian. He turned to Rosso and spoke in Venetian. 'Can we make a run to the mainland tonight? Under darkness?'

Rosso frowned. 'By lantern light? Too treacherous, Don Falco. And your passenger is in a delicate condition, I think. Better to hope the sbirri and militia don't like night sailing either.'

Hawker nodded. 'Then we leave at first light.' He turned to the others again and told them his decision. He could see the look of disapproval on Jacob's face. His long-serving man-at-arms knew full well the risks they were running.

'I shall stand watch,' the Fleming said, voice hollow with resignation.

'And I too, after you,' said Ellingham, with the enthusiasm of youth and the fire of adventure still burning.

Hawker turned back to Rosso. 'You've served loyally and with honour. I will pay you ten ducats more than agreed… In the morning,' he added.

Rosso laughed. 'You have not changed your way of conducting business, Don Falco. Very well, we stay with you tonight. God grant us a peaceful slumber with no surprises!'

When they reached the small house, Hawker found Jack had made every effort to make Chiara comfortable. He had wrapped her shoulders in a dry cloak, kindled a fire, and was fussing about her like a mother hen. Hawker approached her, knelt at her side, and grasped her hand. The original fear that he had carried for days – that she would resent his return – had crept back into his heart. Now that he had subjected her to witnessing him killing her father-in-law, that fear was magnified hundredfold.

'Forgive me, Chiara. I beg of you. I had to come back… to find you.'

She beheld him with tenderness, not anger. She had stopped shaking and a calmness had descended upon her now that she was out of the elements. Yet he could see how much the wild flight from the city had taken out of her. Fatigue showed through, pulling at the corners of her eyes. 'I told you not to take me with you all those months ago. You know that is because I wanted to pay for our sins, Giovanni. But that was before I knew I was with child. Now, I am the vessel for another. And I must live.' She pressed his hand to her cheek. Hawker saw Jack turn his back and bow his head, to try and afford them privacy where there was none. 'I thank the Virgin that this day – of all days – you *did* come back for me.'

Hawker folded her hand in both of his. 'Are you strong enough for the journey? It will be long and arduous even if you are in a cart. I fear for you and for the child.'

She smiled at him and Hawker saw the determination in her eyes. 'I am stronger now than ever have I been. Contanto did not break me. Now he joins his foul son in hell. I will follow where you lead me, Giovanni. Of mine own free will.' She called to Jack and motioned for him to bring over her bag. She reached in and pulled out a small, tired-looking sack of dark red leather, tied with a rawhide lace. She placed it into Hawker's palm, the weight of it alone revealing its contents.

'I will not give them the satisfaction of the last of my dowry. I have taken back what is mine. And what is mine is now ours, my love.'

4

If they thought they could be inconspicuous, they were only fooling themselves. At best, thought Ellingham, curious onlookers might think them a company of household men from some Venetian *palazzo*, escorting a noble woman of questionable worth who had fallen on hard times. Who else would ride in a two-wheeled farmer's cart pulled by a bony nag and driven by a fuzzy-chinned boy? No, he mused to himself, riding at the rear of the parade, here was a company surely running from something.

Although they had piled most of their armour in the cart, stacked neatly by Jack Perry behind the semi-reclined Chiara, they wore their breastplates over their gambesons, cloaks thrown over these, as some insurance in case of surprise. As the morning wore on, filled as it was with bright sun and the promise of an early spring, Ellingham dared to consider that perhaps they were not being pursued after all. The flight from Torcello at the first hint of day had gone smoothly. Rosso's loyalty to Hawker appeared unshakeable: horses and cart were already waiting at a small vineyard farm on the mainland shore, a wizened old man there embracing the Treviso mercenary with a warmth that betokened a tie of blood. And now Rosso and his two companions were guiding them all the way to Treviso. What had Hawker done so many years earlier to earn such devotion? Part of him yearned to know more of the old knight's adventures as it struck him that, even after nearly a year, he still knew very little about Sir John.

Now, it seemed, Sir John had gotten more than he bargained for. Hawker had freed Chiara but had gained two charges, not one. And it was Ellingham's own words which had launched the adventure some two months earlier. He did not regret his decision to help Hawker free the woman. He had seen the guilt eating away at the knight and the deep pain of loss. Had his own loss of Maria Hunyadi played a part in his enthusiasm to aid Hawker, even unconsciously? Probably. But Maria was God knew where now, playing her lethal games of chance in the Hungarian lands... or Poland... or—

'Your horse cannot carry such a heavy burden of ill thoughts for much longer. It can barely carry you.'

Dieudonné had come up alongside him, reins held high near his chest, slowing his mount to match Ellingham's pace.

Ellingham smiled and shook his head. 'I was thinking about what lies ahead.'

'Hopefully not an armed party waiting for us,' laughed the Burgundian. 'We've been more than lucky thus far. It would be unnatural for such good fortune to continue much longer, don't you agree? What are the odds that dear Marco has set up a welcome for us with the authorities?'

Ellingham kept his eyes ahead, watching Hawker, Jacob, and the men of Treviso riding out in front. 'This Venetian has had ample opportunity to betray before now. You should have more faith, Gaston.'

'Well, we shall find out soon enough. I can see a church spire ahead. We are nearly there.'

They were on the outskirts, the town similar in ways to Venice itself, little canals snaking their way through the tall houses. Humpback bridges of brick and stone could be glimpsed in between and tall willows gave proof of water in abundance. Two dogs, unseen but nearby, engaged in an excited exchange of barking. On the side of the road, a small group of townsmen were in deep conversation, but stopped and turned to watch the company as it made its progress. They passed a mill and its high wooden wheel turning slowly. The garden beyond had what looked like beige cloth drying on lines but which, Dieudonné corrected him, was actually newly made paper. 'Growing demand for death warrants, you see. More paper needed. Vellum too dear.'

Ellingham pretended to ignore him.

Dieudonné changed his tack. 'I know what bothers you, Giles. It's what lies ahead for *you*. In Flanders. There are choices to be made there. Return to seek the favour of your aunt the dowager duchess… or take one's chances in England again? A journey incognito, perhaps?'

Ellingham turned to regard Dieudonné but still did not deign to give a reply. He found it disturbing how the Burgundian seemed to know his every thought. Was his heart so transparent to all?

Dieudonné's right hand shifted the pommel of his arming sword and he leaned over his saddlebow, closer to Ellingham. 'I tell you honestly, I do not know what lies ahead. Not with Sir John's mistress in our midst and her with child. That complicates decisions for him. And *that* complicates decision for you, my dear Giles.'

Ellingham narrowed his eyes. 'Explain.'

'I do not think that Sir John will have much stomach for fighting any more. Not with a wife and an infant to think about. She would be a fool to let him go off again. Besides, even he knows he is growing old. But I will stand by you. My only tie of loyalty is to you… and your house. You may rest assured of that.'

Again, no words came to him. He did not know what to say. He gave a nod of acknowledgement instead.

Up ahead, Rosso raised an arm high, signalling them, and then pointing left to a cobbled road between two houses.

'Seems we've arrived. Suppose it will be another mean little hostelry,' said Dieudonné, the doubting tone of his voice almost sarcastic.

'If it has a bedstead and a mattress, I will be satisfied,' said Ellingham, annoyed by Gaston's continued vinegar-laced darts but disconcerted by the Burgundian's underlying plain truths.

They passed under a wide stone archway and into the yard of some ramshackle estate, the older fashioned of stone, the newer portions of wooden frame. A barn had been tacked onto the end of the house, its sloping, red-tiled roof dipping ominously inwards. Casks were stacked one upon another across the yard and Ellingham guessed it was the house of some wine merchant. The smell of spilled, stale wine on the cobbles was strong in the air.

Jack brought the cart to a halt and Hawker and Jacob dismounted. Instinctively, Ellingham turned and guided his horse back to the gateway, just to make sure they were not being followed. All was quiet. The dogs had even stopped their protests. Hawker and Jack gently helped Chiara down from the cart. She was enveloped in a great cloak and a coarse blanket on top of that. Ellingham was impressed with her fortitude for one bearing such a precious burden. Satisfied that *ambuscado* was not likely – at least not yet – he dismounted too.

When he joined Hawker and Rosso, the latter was explaining something to the old knight, his voice subdued. He paused at Ellingham's approach and gave a slight bow of his head. 'Signore.'

'This is the house of an uncle,' translated Hawker. 'He has agreed to put us up for the night until we move west in the morning. The man knows only that I was a condottiere and that we are paid to escort a noblewoman to France. He will ask no questions of us.'

Ellingham nodded. 'Does he think we have been pursued to this place? I for one won't rest easy this night.'

Hawker pursed his lips. 'We have no way of knowing, I grant you that. But even if they track us to Torcello, they would have no idea exactly where we might be headed on the Terra Ferma. That is much ground to cover... even for the doge's henchmen.'

Dieudonné had eased his way into the little group, taking his place at Ellingham's right shoulder. 'But they probably know it was you, Sir John. Not some housebreaking brigand.'

Hawker raised his chin slightly, looking down his aquiline nose at the Burgundian.

'You see,' continued Dieudonné, 'Contanto guessed who you were. And he called you out by name. He may be dead but that servant girl... trussed upon the floor... I'd wager she had ears like an oliphant. The footmen below might have heard your name too. The sbirri will put the word out far and wide for Don Falco.'

Hawker smiled at the Burgundian. Ellingham saw that it barely masked contempt.

'That is a risk we must accept. You have always been free to seek your own way, my lord. It would be unfortunate to lose a good sword arm... but you must decide which path to follow. After all, you joined us by chance. Chance might decide when you leave us.'

Dieudonné laughed lightly. 'Good my lord, who is speaking of taking leave? I was only pointing out that we must be on our guard until we are well out of these lands.'

'Then we shall speak no more it. And you can take the first watch.'

Hawker and Ellingham went inside and were met by an old man who, bowing and scraping, then wordlessly showed them to chambers in the sprawling run-down place, which smelled musty and dank. Hawker escorted Chiara by her arm, Jack close on their heels.

Ellingham didn't follow. He went back outside and joined Dieudonné, who was licking his wounds from the short encounter with Hawker. The Burgundian was leaning against the cart and staring out past the stone gate. Dieudonné looked over to him and smiled. 'I tire of this land, dear Giles. And we have each been far too long upon Fortuna's wheel. It will turn again soon, I fear. I feel it in my bones.'

Ellingham had grown tired as well. He had kept his word to Sir John and aided in Chiara's escape. It had been the right and loyal thing to do. But it was time to go north again, to the court at Malines. He knew not whether his lofty aunt would acknowledge him or imprison him should he reveal himself. But the desire to do so was building within him. That and the desire to begin a quest of his own. Just weeks earlier, Hawker had revealed to him that he was not the only bastard of the late king. A sister, Katherine, newly wed to the Earl of Huntingdon, might be far out of reach in England but his brother – this John of Gloucester – might yet be still in Calais. That was a journey he knew he could make even though it might be one of uncertain outcome.

And crowning it all, the threat which hovered over his head still. Whether Henry Tudor – determined to snuff out the last males of the Yorkist line, legitimate or not – would still seek him out.

'I will keep you company a while, dear Gaston. I tire of this place as well. But pray you, speak no more of fortune. Good or ill.'

—

It was a small room, but from the finely woven wall hangings, tiles and carved sideboard, Hawker thought it probably the finest room in the house. The old wine-seller had seen fit to offer it to his unknown guest whether he noticed she was with child or not.

Hawker sat Chiara down on the bed, knelt down, and grasped both her hands, cold to the touch. He looked into her grey eyes and she smiled down at him.

Hawker gave her a slow nod, acknowledging what he saw in her face. 'Chiara, God has seen fit to bring us together again, but I cannot tell you how long we may have. That is for the Lord to decide. But I pledge my troth to you, my love. I cannot be parted from you again except by death. If you will have me as your husband, I will honour you and protect you. And our child.'

She squeezed his hands hard. 'Giovanni, I have been married to you in my heart all these long months. You *are* my husband. I swear by the Virgin on this day – her day – that I will follow where you will lead me. I am not afraid any more.'

'It will be arduous, my love. I cannot tell you otherwise. You must be strong.'

She nodded. 'You give me strength. It flows from you into me. I am ready.'

Hawker smiled at her, feeling a surge of joy where he thought there could be none. He pulled forth a small plaited ring of yellow gold from his doublet and set it upon her hand. 'There then, it is done. You are my wife under God's all-seeing eye and to all in the world.'

He embraced her gently, pulled back a bit and kissed her fully, a kiss she returned eagerly. Their lips parted and she cupped his left cheek, stroking it tenderly once.

'Tell me the place we shall go. That I may dream of it.'

He swallowed. 'We go to Mechelen… *Malines*, my love. We have friends there. Good friends. Those who will keep you and the babe safe. The Burgundian lands are far from the doge's reach. And I will tell you of it, a little each day, so that you will see it clearly in your mind's eye.'

But he did not know if they would ever see it.

5

Hawker sat in a carved wooden chair near to a fire which blazed in a great stone hearth. He sipped at the goblet of strong dark wine he had been handed, savouring the burn on his tongue. The afternoon had passed slowly and uneventfully. Ellingham sat near to him on another chair while Gaston Dieudonné was on a bench on the opposite side of the hall, back to the wall and silently observing all. Chiara yet rested in the bedchamber where Hawker had left her to recover from the bone-shaking journey. Jacob and Jack he had put to keeping a watch outside, while Rosso – whom he had no true hold over – had left, promising a return in the evening. He had already paid him for his good and loyal service, and the Trevisan had been away from his home for several days now.

Sitting opposite from Hawker was the wine-seller. He had introduced himself as Ser Francesco Querini and despite his rather drab and hole-shot garb of brown and black, had explained that he had once too been a captain of men – like Hawker. He had come to the wine trade later in life, tiring of the endless campaigns across bickering republics and dukedoms. *In vino veritas*, he had reminded Hawker with a grin. What was left of his hair was wispy and white, a glistening pate crowning the top of his skull. But his shoulders were broad still, his frame upright, bespeaking a former vigour and strength. His dark brown eyes held intelligence and despite the easy-speaking manner of a wealthy and comfortable merchant, Francesco Querini failed to conceal a probing curiosity concerning his guests. That was something which rankled, for Hawker had been assured no questions would be asked of him.

His host took a sip from his goblet and hefted it towards Hawker. 'Your good lady travels lightly, I have noticed. If only my own had been as frugal, rest her soul. So many maidservants around her. Like a flock of excitable, fussing hens – and costing me a small fortune besides.'

Hawker met his gaze and slowly took another sip of wine. 'Tell me, what kin is Marco to you? He did not tell me much.'

'Marco. Yes, he is a son of my sister. I suppose it was me who fed his imagination with tales of fighting the Milanese. He was a good man-at-arms, I have been reliably told. Good enough to have survived the wars, at any rate. He was under your command, then?'

Hawker inwardly cursed himself that he could not recall any captain called Francesco Querini though the man had to have been in the service of the Republic. Venice held all the towns and cities of the Terra Ferma tightly in its grasp all the way to Brescia. If he owned any land, a man from Treviso would be in the service of the doge and no one else. 'Marco was with me. In the Friuli… against the Turks.'

Querini nodded. 'Yes, that makes sense, Ser Giovanni.'

Hawker had not revealed his name to the man. Marco must have done so. He was beginning to feel uncomfortable and the small amount of trust he had for his host was dissolving like a sugar drop on the tongue, leaving nothing.

There was a sound of footsteps on the flagstones beyond and Chiara entered, with a heavy cloak wrapped over her dress. Her long hair was tucked and covered in a veil and she looked slightly confused in her surroundings. Ellingham leapt up and gave her his arm, seating her in the chair he had been in. Hawker arose too, and folded her hands around his wine goblet, proffering it to her.

'I grew cold,' she said apologetically. 'I did not wish to disturb you, my lords.'

Querini bowed his head to her. 'My lady, you are welcome to sit here by my fire. We will take some food shortly. You must be hungry from your travels.'

Hawker noticed that Ellingham looked uneasy, probably for his lack of understanding the Venetian tongue. Dieudonné seemed to have disappeared entirely, most likely bored for the same reason. And Hawker was now uneasy, too. Querini either knew or had guessed that Chiara was with child. It was more than passing strange for a woman expecting to be out of her confinement, never mind embarking upon a journey across Christendom. Even young Ellingham had already expressed concern about whether Chiara could safely make the trip in her condition. But there was no going back, not for any of them.

'I must offer my apologies,' continued Querini, 'that I have only two servants remaining. I will, of course, make sure the girl waits upon your pleasure, my lady.'

Chiara offered up an awkward smile.

'We will be on our way at dawn,' reminded Hawker. 'There is no need to do more than you already have.'

Francesco Querini nodded. 'As you wish. I must tell you that I am expecting another guest. Their arrival is imminent.'

Hawker softly translated the Trevisan's words for Ellingham.

Ellingham stood up. 'Are we betrayed, Sir John?' he said quietly in English.

Hawker stood too, pulling his *cioppa* away and setting his hand upon the grip of his *cinquedea*. 'What game are you playing, my lord?'

Querini remained in his chair and raised up his hand. 'Do not be alarmed. It will be in your interest to meet them... Don Falco.'

'Giles, go to the door. Fetch the others in here.'

Ellingham opened the door to find a soldier barring his way. The man wore a red leather brigantine with shining brass rivets, a barbute-style helm seated on his head. He took a step back and balanced his glaive in his hands, ready to swing.

43

Hawker looked past the soldier and saw that Jacob, Jack and Dieudonné had been surrounded by an armed party, crossbows at the ready. He beckoned to Ellingham to return to the fire, took up station in front of Chiara, and then drew his dagger.

'So, Marco has sold us. To you.'

Querini was unconcerned, still holding his goblet. He shook his head. 'Marco does not know who is coming. Do not blame him or question his loyalty.'

'His loyalty to you, or to me?' snarled Hawker.

'Giovanni?' Chiara raised herself up and Ellingham leaned down to restrain her.

'Do not be alarmed, my lady,' said Querini.

Hawker stepped forward, knocked the goblet from the man's hand and placed the point of his dagger at his throat. 'You will not live to see the benefit of your treachery.'

Querini was unafraid. 'Think of your lady, Don Falco. None of you will leave here alive if you kill me. I only ask you hear out my other guest.'

Hawker swallowed hard and took a step back. He turned to Ellingham. 'It seems we must bargain for our lives.'

Ellingham's jaw went slack. 'Do we fight?' His voice had shifted in pitch.

Hawker shook his head. 'We talk.'

There was a knock on the door, a moment's pause, and it opened. A middle-aged man entered wearing a gold-and-green brocaded doublet, black hose and boots, and a heavy riding cloak over all. On his head he wore a wine-coloured velvet bonnet, a large silver brooch at his brow. He was followed in by the brigantine-armoured soldier who now barred the way out.

The newcomer moved closer to the hearth and then turned to the company, blocking the warming fire. He nodded towards the old Trevisan captain. 'Querini.' He then pivoted and faced Hawker, a smile on his thick lips. His large, protruding eyes moved to Ellingham and then his double chin dropped so he could better look upon the woman seated in the chair. His gaze lingered for more than a moment before Hawker sidestepped, blocking his view.

'This is the Barone Celsi,' said Querini. 'He wishes to speak with you.'

Ellingham growled a curse and stepped forward, but Hawker raised his hand and threw him a harsh glare to halt his move. He then turned back to the baron.

Celsi tilted his head with a grin and a look of mock mischief. 'Don Falco? Returned? May we parley?'

'To what end? We are your prisoners. It is less than a day's ride to Venice.'

'Even so. Will you hear me out?'

Hawker gestured with an annoyed wave of his hand.

The baron leaned against the stone fireplace lintel. 'It was the captain here who passed word that you were staying. He knows his duty. Old soldier that he is.'

Hawker did not know the nobleman. Some plodding merchant raised up as reward for his largesse to the oligarchs of the Republic, no doubt. 'He should learn better manners as a host. Especially when he has given a promise to his kin.'

Celsi grinned again. 'But you had some good wine here at least, I trust. I'm not here to discuss your conditions as a guest, Don Falco. That was very bloody business yesterday in San Polo. And I must say, I think you were beyond brave to return to the La Serenissima. Or just very foolish. And you came away with only... a woman. A very honoured woman for you to risk your life and those of your company for. *But*, Don Falco, a condottiere of the Republic... hero of Dalmatia! He is alas now a common thief, a kidnapper. A murderer.'

Hawker stood stiffly, feet evenly braced, the words sinking into him. He had led Ellingham into a trap, had now lost Chiara forever, and he would be lucky if he died quickly in the bowels of the doge's palace. Which was unlikely. 'I have heard no words of parley from you yet. Speak, sir, or take us away.'

The baron smiled with amusement. 'Benedetto Contanto had many friends. But he had even more enemies. He will

45

not be mourned or missed. And I think your reputation has probably not suffered by your overzealousness. Speaking for myself –' he placed his open palm over his chest '– the rescue of a lady, even if an adulterous one, is a noble cause. The cause of love.'

'What do you want?'

'We come to the heart of the matter then. The Tears of Byzantium have come into your possession. Give them up and I will give you safe passage north out of the Terra Ferma. To the border of the Austrians.'

Hawker's expression remained set in stone. He did not reply.

'You're thinking I could just take them anyway if they are on your person. True. Or you could hand them over from wherever you've secreted them, and I would send you to the doge just the same. True, also. But I will not. I swear to you.'

'I have no reason to believe you,' growled Hawker.

'And I have no reason to hand the rubies back to the doge. If you take my meaning. You can consider the stones a departure tax.'

Hawker bit down on the inside of his lip. He looked over to Ellingham, the youth still frozen in place, his eyes searching out Hawker's. He looked down to Chiara. She looked up at him, eyes filled with unquestioning love, devotion, and the glimmer of fresh tears. She gave the merest hint of a nod. The decision was his.

Hawker popped the top button of his doublet, reached into the neckline and pulled forth a small leather pouch. He yanked the thong from his neck, breaking it, and looked again to Ellingham. The youth's lips pressed tightly and thinned. He understood what was happening without needing translation. Ellingham nodded to the knight, once.

Hawker held out the pouch to Celsi.

The baron gingerly accepted it and emptied its contents into his palm. 'Only two stones? Well… one cannot be greedy about such things as rare as these.' He let out a sigh. 'Very well, Don

Falco. I will take your word as a gentleman that there are no more to be had.'

He observed the look of cold menace on the old *condottiere*'s haggard face. 'Ah, Don Falco! Be of good cheer. Sleep well tonight and tomorrow you will have an armed escort to the Alps. Gratis!'

Part II

PAX BURGUNDIA

6

Malines (Mechelen), in Flanders, February 1487

Hawker looked down at the cot at his feet and into the wide blue eyes of the babe lying there. The sight gave him a strange comfort he was still unaccustomed to, even after seven months. A warmth flowed up from his chest, a sense of well-being and not a little pride as well. God had seen fit to deliver him a son. A healthy, lusty son arriving after the loss of his firstborn all those years ago, wife and babe taken away from him by an angry God. He had believed then that he was being punished for his own sins, sins in the service of King Edward. The Lord had perhaps forgiven him now, his prayers and repentance divinely answered.

Chiara Contanto, now Dame Hawker, stood nearby, watching him adore his son. Hawker looked up again and smiled at her. 'He is so quiet sometimes. And for so long. I wonder what he is thinking about.'

'He has been fed, and burped, and wrapped up again. He needs nothing more for now. Would we were all so easily satisfied.'

They had named him Nicholas. Chiara said it was that saint who had seen her through the journey safely – over the Alps, into the Austrian Tyrol, the Helvetian lands, the vast territories of the Holy Roman Empire and then into the Duchy of Burgundy. Saint Nicholas, protector of children and a comfort to those who travelled by sea or by road. Hawker agreed that it was fitting and right. In the mountains, he had convinced himself that Chiara would not make it, that she would lose the child upon the road, maybe dying herself as well. But she had shown a force of will that still amazed him and, against all odds, her spirit had never flagged over all the many leagues they had travelled. And his love for her had grown more ardent with each passing week and each milestone reached, bringing them all closer to relative safety and peace in Flanders.

Chiara approached and embraced him, pulling herself into the voluminous black mantle that covered his mulberry-red doublet and squeezing tight. He wrapped his arm around her waist, tugged away her pale linen headscarf, and then tenderly stroked her cheek with his rough, scarred hand. She had grown closer to him over the past months, but he had also noticed her neediness. She was lonely. The Flemish tongue came to her with difficulty, and she struggled. The tall, narrow house was probably growing smaller to her with each passing week, shared as it was with Jack Perry, a nursemaid, and with nearly daily visits from Jacob de Grood.

Hawker tilted her chin up. 'It will be spring soon. The coming of the green will raise both our spirits. We have a little garden here, don't we? Not to rival the duchess's gardens but enough for us and Nicholas when he begins to crawl. It will be a joy to us just as the boy is.' He tried to believe it himself in the sinking, cold gloom of a late-winter afternoon.

She looked into his eyes. 'Where will you go next?'

'Go? Why should we have want to leave this place? I am in service to a noble house again, am I not?'

She nodded unconvincingly. A log in the hearth snapped loudly, cracking and falling in on itself as if a sign. 'My love, I still don't fully understand what it is you do at the palace. I sometimes think that I have winkled it out of you, but you never confide in me. Not truly. Or fully.'

'Chiara, I cannot tell you all. Know that we are safe here. With a roof over us and with coin to buy us food and drink. What more do we need?'

Her eyes grew questioning. 'I think you do need something more. What it is I do not yet know. But I think you'll need more than a chain of office around your neck. Neither of us are from this place, this land. Nor is Sir Giles. And the *other* boy you've adopted – Jack – what will become of him here? He is grown big – and restless. This house is too small for us all. And I think you may grow restless when summer comes and men go to war again.'

He laughed lightly. 'Then you have not read my heart. I swear I am content to stay here with you and the babe. I have had enough of the field. Of swinging a sword. I'm too old besides.' He was not lying. The adventure of Wallachia seemed to have sapped him of the last of his strength and desire to make war. He had tempted the Fates for far too long. But he knew the real meaning of her words. His promise to Sir Giles. A promise that he had not fulfilled, despite the young landless knight's own promise to him to free Chiara. A promise Giles had kept.

It was as if she had read his thoughts there and then.

'You have put off Sir Giles for months. I know he must be growing impatient. It is only his great loyalty to you that has stopped him from going off on his own. And with that Burgundian who follows him like a stray dog. The longer I know that man the less I like his countenance.'

He could not keep it from her any longer. 'You are right. I have promised him we will go in search of his half-brother. But only as far as Calais.'

'When?'

'Soon, I hope… when the weather clears.'

He felt her stiffen a little against him, then pull away slightly.

'My love, it is no distance at all. And there is little danger. We will be back in two or three days.'

Nicholas began a soft mewling, which quickly grew louder. His pout then turned into a cry, as if angered by their talk.

Chiara bent down and retrieved him, hugging him to her breast and then rocking him gently. 'Giovanni, you have told me before that Calais is held by the enemy. And you think you may ride in and find who you are looking for?'

'They... are not the enemy... not all of them,' Hawker growled. 'They are English.'

'They are Henry's men now. Do not think they have forgotten who *you* are. Or Sir Giles.'

Hawker reached over and touched the head of his son. 'We will be as shadows. In and out.' He could see her jaw tense, a slight twitch of her cheek. 'I owe Giles a great debt for he helped me to save you. And our child. You owe him this as well.'

He watched her sink down a little, folding the baby deeper into her embrace. 'Yes, you must do this thing.' Her voice was resigned, recognising both his duty to his honour and to a friend. 'But then... when you return... we must speak of what is best for this child. What is best for all of us.'

He leaned in and kissed her forehead. 'I swear to you, all will be well.'

There were three loud fist raps upon the outer door, rattling the iron hinges and lock.

Hawker raised himself up, recognising the insistent style of the knock. Chiara shook her head slowly. 'Your great duchess calls you, Giovanni. Do not leave her summons waiting.'

Hawker opened the black oak door and there stood two German halberdiers, red cloaks over puffed doublets, their multi-coloured hose and codpieces garishly on display. Large bonnets made of alternating panels of red and white fabric sat at jaunty angles upon their heads, ostrich plumes wilting under the scattered raindrops that were falling. One tucked his halberd up into his right armpit, nodded to Hawker, and handed him a small, sealed envelope of rough brown parchment.

Hawker accepted it, broke the seal and read the elegant rolling French script. It was a curt if courteous missive.

Sir John, I commend me to you, trusting you are in good health. By the command of Her Grace, Margaret, you are to repair to the palace upon receipt of this. – O. de la Marche

Hawker sighed quietly and refolded the parchment. Sir Olivier, *châtelain* to the duchess dowager Margaret of Burgundy, could not be refused. Ever. The two guardsmen stood rooted in the doorway. They were waiting for him to accompany them.

'Take two steps back!' barked Hawker in German. 'And give me time to fetch my hat and sword!'

–

Sir Olivier de la Marche, knight of the Golden Fleece and tutor to nine-year-old Philip, Duke of Burgundy, was waiting in a room between the Great Hall of the palace and the maze of apartments under construction at the rear. It was a room Hawker had not seen before and it appeared to be an ante-chamber of sorts: neither here nor there. A fire crackled away in the huge stone hearth whose chimney breast soared up to the ornately decorated plastered ceiling. Hawker was escorted in by the halberdiers who promptly turned and left him with his host. The man was standing near a great sideboard where porcelain vessels balanced precariously on every shelf. He had in his hand a wine goblet and another rested on the sideboard.

'Sir John, welcome. I thank you for answering my summons so quickly.'

'Did I have a choice?'

De la Marche smiled, lifted the other goblet and proffered it to Hawker. 'To lift the damp from your spirits. A good strong wine from the south. Spicy upon the tongue.'

Hawker took the cup and drank with the ageing knight of Burgundy, a man who had loyally served Charles the Bold and the House of Valois until tragedy brought it to an abrupt end, paving the way for the Habsburgs to take the reins. It was a noble house which he had quickly embraced, seeing in it the salvation of the duchy in a time of great danger and uncertainty.

'Was it the duchess who demanded my presence?' asked Hawker. 'Or was it just you?'

'She is indisposed. Other affairs of state. But I am fully versed in her instructions and wishes. As I am for her son-in-law, the king. And it is upon the latter's wishes that I have brought you here.'

Hawker nodded. He had not met Maximilian, but as the widower of the daughter of Charles the Bold, Maximilian now held what was left of Burgundy in the name of his young son, Philip. In time, both father and son would be crowned Holy Roman Emperor. Hawker, having taken a shadowy commission from the duchess the previous summer, now had several masters, it seemed, and not just Margaret of York.

The nobleman gestured to a pair of chairs near the leaded windows, carefully pre-positioned to facilitate discreet conversation. Hawker waited until de la Marche took one and then seated himself. De la Marche leaned in, elbow on his knees, his wide-set, frog-like eyes searching the Englishman's face. 'You are a strange one, Sir John. I thought that when first we met a year ago, and later, after your mysterious return here, I was not disabused of that notion. I do not doubt your wish to be of service, but I am not always certain of whom you wish to serve.'

Hawker took a tentative sip of the wine and leaned closer still towards the gatekeeper of the royal house. 'My lord, I took employment in the service of her Grace, the Lady Margaret. I am sure your other spies would tell you if it was now otherwise.'

'Indeed they would. And on that score, there is nothing to say. Yet. But I have called you in as to the matter of your request a few weeks ago for a letter of safe conduct into your English enclave of Calais. You mentioned it was to gain intelligence of loyalties within the garrison. Whether Yorkist sympathies might be tapped. And you knew that would appeal to her Grace.'

Hawker nodded. 'That is the truth. I have made no bones of it. You know full well that, as Richard's liege man, I would help the cause of the House of York if it be in my power. Any intelligence gained would be relayed to you – and to supporters in England.'

De la Marche smiled with amusement, a good-natured grin that bore no derision. 'Loyalty I value above almost all other knightly virtues. It suits you well, Sir John. But you are a landless gentleman, no property. No armed retinue. I would not dare hazard a guess as to what gold you possess, knowing your service in the Italian lands. But if there is any there's little evidence you are showering it upon our city. And yet, still… you would fight the cause of a shattered noble house.'

'I am a poor knight. I have lost most of my wealth. But I still have a sword… and a true heart.'

De la Marche leaned back. 'And secrets.'

Hawker said nothing.

'You somehow avoided getting involved in the little rebellion against Henry Tudor last summer. Lord Lovell's gamble failed and he is lucky to have escaped. Perhaps you knew better than most that the chances of success were always poor. You do know he is here now at the court?'

Hawker knew Viscount Lovell had arrived in Mechelen. A man with nine lives: he had survived Bosworth, led an uprising in the north that failed, gone on the run, escaped, and then, finally, made it across the sea to safety. And though he was someone whose path had crossed his own before the disaster of Bosworth, Hawker had not sought to meet Francis Lovell since that noble knight's arrival. For Hawker knew his circumstances were now much changed. New responsibilities to add to old promises. He had no desire to be drawn into a new conspiracy. Not yet, at least.

Hawker leaned forward, his creaking chair, echoing across the chamber. 'I was in no fit position to leave for England when I returned here. My wife heavily pregnant. Robbed along the way. And I knew nothing of the rebellion being planned. It was all I could manage to get my company back from Hungary. My captaincy there did not go as planned. That, you know. Always the risk of a condottiere.'

De la Marche listened, sipping his wine. 'Yes. The Serene Republic. That is a tale we have yet to hear from you, one I still eagerly await. And, of course, Sir John, I can understand your duty to your new wife and child prevented you from more active affairs here in the west. As well as the duty to your friends... Sir Giles Ellingham, for one.'

Hawker tried not to show any outward concern, but he felt his face grow hot. He did not know how much the Burgundian knew about Ellingham. But de la Marche was a wily diplomat with many sources of intelligence. And he had the money to pay for wagging tongues. 'Sir Giles is a loyal knight of the White Rose. And a good friend. He has shared my poverty since Bosworth Field and that in itself is something. I think you spoke of loyalty.'

The nobleman smiled again. 'I have decided to grant your request for your letter of safe conduct. I won't ask you your true motives for this journey. Not now, at any rate. But remember well who your landlord is and who it is that pays you good coin each month. I want you to gather any word on Henry's intentions towards the cities in Flanders. He owes his throne to the French and I would see Calais remain English. I wish to learn whether he will support the uprisings against our king and emperor in Ghent and Bruges, something the French greatly desire. Calais could become a major conduit of arms to the Flemish guilds and their militias. We will not stand for it. Understood? Find out who has the upper hand. Henry's garrison or the leaders of the town's wool merchants. They, at least, have been on *our* side.'

Hawker, still on tenterhooks, nodded thoughtfully. 'The Welsh bastard will do what he can to tip the scales – if he thinks Burgundy intends to support his enemies. But he needs to sell his wool here, too. He would do well to think long upon acting rashly.'

'As would we all,' agreed de la Marche, somewhat archly. 'Your stated business will be noted as an agent of the weavers' guild here in Malines. If you are recognised as Sir John Hawker – outlaw – I will not lift a hand. You will be on your own.'

'I accept the conditions.'

De la Marche took a long swig of his wine and then studied the goblet. 'And do not think, Sir John, that I have not heard the rumours concerning your young knight bachelor. Have a care though. Your little expedition to the Pale of Calais might make him a fish in a barrel for Henry Tudor. But I'm sure I don't have to remind another old warhorse of such dangers.'

7

Sir Giles Ellingham repressed a shiver and pulled the coverlet up over his naked body. His bed mate, having already thrown on her chemise, was now pulling on her kirtle, smoothing it over her plump figure. She plopped down upon the bed again and pulled on her shoes.

When she stood up, she put her hands on her hips. 'Münze?'

Ellingham looked over to the man leaning in the doorway of the cramped, low-ceilinged bedchamber. 'Gaston, give her a couple of groats. My purse is moth-ridden.'

Gaston Dieudonné smirked, reached into his belt pouch, and produced the coins. A giggle sounded behind the Burgundian's back and he knocked away a slim hand that had reached around to dip into his pouch. 'The exchequer is in a parlous state, my lord. Something we need to discuss.' He held out one small silver coin – a *patard* – and the girl at the foot of Ellingham's bed glared at him, snatched it away, and pushed past Dieudonné. She grabbed her companion by the arm and descended the narrow staircase to the ground floor.

Ellingham rolled over. 'It's barely morning, Gaston. My head hurts and discussing money won't help it.'

'I will get us some bread and cheese. A sausage, if I can find one. We'll eat… and talk.'

-

By the time the Burgundian had returned, Ellingham had dressed into his black doublet and threadbare green hose. He was in the only room that was on the ground floor of the house, a gloomy, ill-lighted *salle à manger* which also served as living quarters and contained a brick-and-mud hearth, a roughhewn table, a cupboard and a few chairs. The youth poked about in the embers of the fire, stoking them up again. He threw on a few sticks of lichen-coated wood to coax it back to life.

Ellingham knew full well the money was running out. But he'd been frozen with indecision for months – seemingly just as much as his mentor and friend Sir John. Dieudonné had had some success at cards and had kept food coming, as well as the occasional whore or two, but Ellingham felt as if he was drying up inside, his entire self now turning to brittle clay that would soon crumble into dust. It was all so far from the promise of a year before, the thought of returning to find his siblings and perhaps his fortune as a son of the royal blood. Now, he was ashamed of his hubris. He had no money and no prospects. And it looked like Sir John Hawker didn't either. But the wily old knight still managed to pay their meagre rent from whatever stipend the palace had granted him.

Dieudonné placed a loaf of bread on the table and then thumped down a wedge of cheese wrapped in muslin. 'No sausage, my prince. Too early yet.'

Ellingham lifted a brown clay pitcher of small beer from the cupboard, the remainder of the previous day's ration. He pinched together two wooden cups and sat at the little table. 'I thank you, dear Gaston.'

'How was your lady? She had a comely face. Unlike mine.'

Ellingham winced a little. He didn't like discussing such things, even if Dieudonné appeared to take pleasure in it. Part of him didn't even understand why he whored. He was still bitter over the betrayal of Maria Hunyadi, now so many months gone by. He had lost his heart to her only for her to abandon them all in the Saxon lands of Hungary. Without explanation. Anger and loss still ate away at him and he knew he was adrift, adrift on a sea of shattered promises and regret. Only steadfast

61

Gaston Dieudonné, standing by him as a 'retainer', helped him to salvage a scrap of honour as a gentleman and knight in the eyes of the court at Malines.

'Give me your knife.'

Dieudonné flipped out his eating blade and handed it over, grip first. Ellingham sliced the cheese in half and stuck the blade in one chunk and pushed it back to the Burgundian.

'We have waited long enough, my friend,' said Dieudonné sympathetically. 'You have been patient and listened to Sir John's counsel. But you have not advanced your cause an inch in months. It is time to set a new course and you already know what that is.'

'Hawker is waiting for a pass from the palace. We need that to get into Calais.'

Dieudonné's lean face, sharp cheekbones unshaven for a few days, broke into a patronising smile. 'My good fellow, he does not seem to be pushing his suit very hard. Not for someone who claims to be a spy for the duchess dowager of Burgundy. It's only a pass of safe conduct. Not the keys to a kingdom.'

Ellingham looked at the table and chewed his bread. His head still hurt so he drained a full cup of beer. 'So what would you have me do? Join those German mercenaries who are infesting this place and every other town west of here? Sir John is only waiting for the best time. For the right time. I trust him.'

'Sir John is tired. We have both seen it. And he has lost interest in the cause. But can you blame him? He has a wife and child now. Why *should* he risk everything for the House of York? He can stay here and grow fat and old living on the Habsburg payroll. Watch his boy grow up.'

Ellingham twisted in his seat towards Dieudonné, scowling. 'He remains loyal. Do not speak of him that way. I know his measure. I know his hatred of Tudor, of Beaufort, the traitorous Stanleys.'

'You remind him of his past.'

The words sank deep, a stiletto thrust to his heart. He said nothing in reply.

Dieudonné spoke quickly and quietly, laying his hand on Ellingham's forearm. 'He has convinced you to remain in hiding. Convinced you not to reveal yourself to your aunt who lives up there in the palace. A woman who would embrace you. I swear it! We have waited too long. You should go to the palace and seek an audience. See that frog-eyed châtelain of hers.'

'You talk like a fool, Gaston. Why would she believe me?' He waggled the hand which wore a gold ring, a ring with an inlaid wild boar of silver. 'Because of this trinket? I think not. My wagging tongue would pave the way straight to her dungeon.'

'We have reached desperate times, my prince. If I believed that Sir John still held the will to meet his promise to you – to return to find your sister, to kill the usurper – I would have kept my wagging tongue in my mouth. But I cannot.' He reached down into his belt purse and pulled out a small blue cloth pouch no bigger than a starling's egg. Keeping his eyes upon Ellingham, a sly trace of amusement on his lips, Gaston Dieudonné opened it and pulled forth its contents.

Ellingham drew back with a start. 'Sweet blood of Christ!'

Between his thumb and forefinger was a single rough-cut ruby, still encased in a spidery armature of yellow gold. The last remaining Tear of Byzantium.

Dieudonné held it aloft, and even in the dim morning light of the single horn-glazed window, the gemstone shone and sparkled as if alive. '*This*, the Dower Duchess of Burgundy will believe.'

–

Jack Perry ran his tongue quickly across his lips, nervously, and thrust his right arm out sharply towards his opponent. An instant later he felt the pain of a blow to his left inside bicep and he flinched, stumbling backwards out of range. Jacob de Grood pursed his lips and shook his head. He twirled his quarterstaff in his hands and took his guard position anew.

'*Boy*, if you insist on learning sword and buckler you must learn to hold the damned little thing *outstretched*! If I had a sword in my hand your left arm would be lying on the ground now.' Jacob spoke in Flemish, intent on making Jack learn a language of the continent.

Jack groaned in frustration. He was determined more than ever to be a crossbowman. And he needed to master the art of his secondary weapons: arming sword and buckler. But he still wasn't used to wielding something the size of a dining trencher in order to shield himself and his instinct was to hold the buckler close. Which was obviously the wrong way to do it. 'It's hard to think about doing it right and then doing it!' he moaned.

'You shouldn't be thinking at all, boy,' said de Grood, exasperation in his voice. 'Let's do those exercises I taught you again – in German. Drop the buckler then throw me a blow – from your Vom Tag guard!'

Jack did as he was told, gripping his sword with both hands. The German names of the guards and blows he had learned. Silly names like 'from the roof' or 'boar's tusk' but it helped him to remember. This time, he was more successful. His outstretched blade deflected Jacob's counterstrike even though his own blow was caught by the quarterstaff. Jacob nodded. 'Better. Much better.'

'This German tongue scrambles my brains, Jacob. I was still trying to learn my French. Now this.'

De Grood chuckled and switched to German. 'Well, you'd better pick it up soon. You may be fighting alongside some of these landsknechts you see strutting around town. If you want to join a retinue you will have to speak the tongue. They'll beat it into you otherwise.'

Jack had seen these mercenaries that patrolled Mechelen each day. Dressed as gaudily as a Christmas mummer and puffed with arrogance, they maintained order in the town as they did in Ghent and Bruges all under the command of the Habsburg overlords. Jacob had told him most *landsknechts* were Germans

– but not all. They were a mix of Flemish, Burgundians, and others besides, even an Englishman or two he'd heard tell. If Sir John was to lead them into battle again, it was likely to be alongside these fellows. Jack knew he had to learn, and learn quickly. For weeks he had been training in the yard of Jacob's father, away from the gaze of others. He was improving, he knew that, despite Jacob's harsh bellowing. But he was also desperately bored by the inactivity of the last several months and sword drill was all he now lived for. He could not understand Sir John's reluctance to take to the road again. With spring on its way, some campaign would be likely called, and he wanted to be part of it. But John Hawker talked little of such things now.

Jack took up his guard again. 'Jacob… why does Sir John not speak of a return home? Or of fighting again? I've mentioned it to him, but he only growls at me to keep training.'

De Grood relaxed his stance and sighed. 'Boy… he has a family now. He is in no hurry to rush into battle yet. Not until he sees which way the wind is blowing. There will be a new rebellion in England, fear not. He hasn't given up.'

'But *I'm* his family too!' said Jack. 'And I am his squire. But we stay in this place day after day and do nothing. She doesn't want me skulking about in that little house. Nor Sir John, if truth be told. And that babe screeches all the day and night besides.'

De Grood put one end of his quarterstaff to the ground and leaned upon it, his eyes down. He made a grunting noise as he sometimes did when he was thinking. 'Well… you should stay here from now on. I will ask my father. But I warn you, the old bastard will put you to work. He's never liked idleness.'

Jack's face brightened. 'You would do that? I will work hard.'

De Grood laughed. 'He might turn you into a weaver! You'll have to trade your crossbow for a loom.'

Jack frowned. 'I'm not ready for that. Not yet. I'll not take up a trade.'

De Grood shrugged. 'It would be safer than a life on campaign. And far more money to be had. War is changing fast, my lad. Pike squares and more handguns… more cannons, by Christ. Camp discipline likely to kill you just as quickly as the enemy. Or the bloody flux! I'm beginning to think the odds are worse now than before.'

'Then why didn't *you* stay here and work for your father?'

De Grood smiled. 'Because I was young. Like you.'

Jack grinned.

De Grood cleared his throat, spat, and hefted his quarterstaff. 'Take your guard, boy! Show me I'm not wasting my time.'

8

Hawker smiled at his son who was happily bouncing in the arms of the nurse. He leaned over and touched the babe's head with a gentle caress, still, after all these months, almost unbelieving that he was indeed a father again. Chiara took him by both hands and squeezed tightly. They were standing outside the house, young Jack dressed in half-armour of breastplate and back, waiting across the narrow street and holding the reins of two mounts.

'You are the perfect merchant of Malines, my love,' said Chiara, lapsing into her native tongue and abandoning her French. 'Would that you would remain one from this moment forward.'

'It was not my lot in this life, Chiara,' replied Hawker wistfully, in his rough Venetian. He was dressed in his travelling clothes: a dark wine doublet, black hose, brown riding boots, heavy woollen cloak, and a black bonnet adorned with a pheasant's feather. His *cinquedea* dagger was hitched high up on his left hip.

Chiara's hands moved up to cup his chin. 'This is so hard, Giovanni. It brings the memory of when you left me before. It is not one I wish to remember. Not ever again.'

'It is different now. We are here… together. It is only two days' ride to Calais. In and out, I promise you. We probably won't even find who we are looking for. I suspect he has long disappeared, if for no other reason than his own safety. But I must honour my promise to Sir Giles. You know this.'

She nodded. 'I do. It was the price of my rescue. I cannot speak against it. But you must take all care… and return to me.' Her eyes held anxiety and love for him, mixed. She seemed to be searching his own, expecting a sign that all would be well. There was little Hawker could do to meet the expectation. He had no illusions about what lay ahead. He would be entering an enclave fully under Tudor rule. He could give no guarantees of his return. He enveloped her in his arms and kissed her full upon her mouth, a deep passion suddenly rising and blotting out his own worries for what lay ahead.

He released her, slowly, and smiled. 'The sooner I leave, the sooner I will return. Fare you well, my love.'

Hawker took up his reins from Jack. 'Mount up, lad,' he said softly, still dwelling upon the warm embrace of his wife.

Jack pushed up his barbute helm which had slipped down a little over his eyes. 'Yes, Sir John.' He launched himself up into his saddle and Hawker did the same. With a wave to Chiara, he followed Jack down the street and out, headed to the main square where the others would be waiting.

They were there, mounted and ready. Ellingham, dressed much as Hawker in civil merchant fashion, with his personal armed 'retinue' on either side: Gaston Dieudonné and Jacob de Grood. It would not seem unusual in such heated times for a wealthy merchant to be escorted by men-at-arms. Hawker believed they would receive few questions and the pass from the palace would put paid to any further doubts raised by Habsburg patrols.

Hawker slowed and drew up in front of Ellingham. 'A good morrow to you, Master Wickham. We have fair weather for our journey, it seems.'

Ellingham gave a slight bow of his head. 'And a good morrow to you, good sir. We wait at your pleasure, John Rede.'

Hawker looked over to de Grood and gave a nod. The Fleming flicked his reins and moved out, Jack turning his horse and following close on de Grood's cruppers, and Dieudonné

68

– a rather sour look of disappointment on his sharp face – following behind Jack. Hawker supposed the Burgundian's role as humble retainer did not sit well. Hawker had grown even more distrustful of the fellow of late, suspecting he was filling Giles's head with all manner of rash advice for the future. A spell as a man-at-arms, even if only a ruse, would put him back in his place, and rightfully so. Hawker fell in beside Ellingham and the party headed at a walk towards the west gate of the town.

They made the walls of Ghent well before the sun began to set, thus sparing them an interrogation by Habsburg guards looking for a bribe after the gates had been shut and barred for the night. They rode into the great city of grey spires, built upon English wool, and de Grood guided them to a hostel he knew well from older days. A group of about ten *landsknecht* mercenaries, short swords on their hips and leaning on halberds, eyed their progress to the centre square. They laughed at some muttered jest, all looking like peacocks for their ridiculous plumery and satins. Hawker relaxed when he and the others had ridden past, unchallenged.

The modest inn, a ramshackle house whose back wall was part of the western wall of the city, proved hospitable and discreet. Hawker, fatigued by the ride, bedded down after their repast while Ellingham and Dieudonné stayed up long into the evening. The next morning they departed at sunrise as soon as the gates were open. They made Roselare by midday and carried onwards towards the coast, the weather holding fair and clear. Rather than risk an arrival at Calais after dark, Hawker decided to make another stop for the night on the road near Veurne. Up again at cock-crow, they made their way west along the coast road, Jack jabbering like a magpie to Jacob most of the way with the Fleming grunting his occasional replies, a model of restraint. As the March sun rose to its meridian, the white walls of Calais appeared in the distance once they mounted the last of the dunes, foaming grey surf rolling into the beaches below them. The sight left Hawker unsettled. Despite his bravado, he knew he and Ellingham were walking into the lion's den. But it would be far more dangerous if they journeyed across the water that lay in front of them. He could see at least half a dozen cogs berthed along the jetty just outside the walls. One might be destined to take him and Ellingham in its hold, in chains, to face Henry's justice.

The lion's maw – the portcullis of the Lantern Gate – was open. And, as he expected, the sentries stopped their progress. The guards wore livery jackets with the emblems of the red-and-white rose – King Henry's new badge – embroidered upon them. A few of the others had the four-diamond badge of Giles Daubeney, an unshakeable Lancastrian stalwart and now the lord of Calais. The sight brought forth in him feelings of resentment, resentment for the defeat nearly two years earlier that had changed his world. He felt bile rise in his gorge as he handed over his pass when it was demanded.

The old soldier who perused it, snotty nose close to the parchment, frowned because of doubt or the fact that he could not read what was written. He turned to one of the sentries.

'Upstairs! Fetch the captain.'

Still mounted, they waited, horses snorting and pawing as anxious as their riders. Ellingham tilted his head up and studied the parapet above, then looked across to Hawker. The youth's face was taut as a drum skin, his eyes bright with nervous energy. The old sentry stared up at Hawker but said nothing. His companions tapped the butts of their pole-arms against the square paving stones of the bridge, already bored.

In a short time, an officer emerged from the doorway of the gatehouse and approached them. The sentry handed him Hawker's pass and stood back. The captain scanned the paper and looked up at Hawker.

'John Rede? An Englishman? Living in Malines?'

'Some of us do get further than Calais,' replied Hawker. 'My grandsire even got as far as Agincourt.'

The captain let out a small laugh of genuine amusement. 'Business with the Staple then, Master Rede?' He cast an eye over the men-at-arms of Hawker's party and then brought his attention back to Hawker. 'Go on in. But keep your escort out of trouble. We'll be watching.' He handed back the pass, Hawker saluted him, and the man waved them past.

They rode underneath the massive gatehouse and Hawker knew he was now on English soil for the first time in an age. They came immediately to the market square and on the far side was the wool guild – the Staple Hall, as it was called. Next to it sat an even grander edifice, the towering Council Hall. They dismounted and gathered together, Hawker's eyes searching the square. Hawker heard English and French carried on the seaside breeze as the many merchants and townsfolk went about their business. The glory of the carved stone buildings of state was permanently marred, covered by the white-and-brown excrement of the wheeling gulls, their incessant screeching reverberating through the square.

Hawker turned to de Grood. 'You and Jack take the Burgundian with you and go to Mother Richards' inn. It's rank... but inconspicuous. Get us rooms if there are any to be had and wait there. Dump your harness, but keep on your swords.' He handed over a small pouch of coins.

'I remember it,' said Jacob without emotion. 'The stew pot there gave me the shits for two days afterwards. But it will be easy to fit in with the rest of the rabble.'

Hawker could see that Ellingham was chewing his bottom lip as he listened. He lay a hand on the youth's forearm and spoke quietly. 'No one knows us here. And those who did probably think we are long dead in Venice.'

Ellingham nodded but said nothing.

Dieudonné edged closer to Hawker and Ellingham. 'I would join you gentles. Now.'

'Not as you are attired,' said Hawker, the menace in his voice clear. 'And not into this place. Go with Jacob, find a room and

71

change. We'll speak together later. You're under my command still and you would do well to remember it.'

Dieudonné looked at Ellingham and raised his eyebrows, expecting intercession.

'Do as he says, Gaston. We must all play our roles.'

The Burgundian looked at Hawker, rubbed his thumb and forefinger down either side of his mouth, and snorted. 'Very well, your honours. But poor Dieudonné is famished and needs food if he is to serve as a good man-at-arms.'

De Grood reached over and grabbed the Burgundian by the elbow. 'My lord?'

Dieudonné's smile was laced with disdain. He jerked his arm away from the Fleming and turned on his heels, yanking the reins of his mount. 'Very well, lead on!'

Hawker and Ellingham entered the guild hall. A babble of Flemish and English carried loudly up to the high, ornately plastered ceiling. More than a dozen merchants stood in small groups conducting their business: haggling over the sale of raw wool or complaining of the prices the Bruges weavers were demanding for their finished cloth. Hawker made some cautious introductions of himself and Ellingham, the latter remaining silent. Hawker told the merchants he represented a syndicate of weavers in Malines who were curious to know how Tudor rule would affect the market for their wares. After a few minutes, two English wool merchants invited them to discuss the situation over a pot of wine nearby. Hawker smiled and agreed and Ellingham too, clearly the junior partner.

Once ensconced in a narrow inn on the east side of the square, the wine began to flow and soon thereafter tongues loosened. Hawker paid.

'If I knew the answer to what you ask,' said one of the merchants, a chubby-faced fellow with thick, dark brows and a bulbous nose, 'I would command the market and be a rich man. Richer!' He chuckled into his pewter tankard.

His companion, a younger fellow with fair hair and a thin blond moustache, spoke up. 'Well, we do know a *little*. We're not fools.' He pushed back his blue velvet bonnet with its ostentatious peacock and pearl spray. 'If the Flemish can be convinced that we are moving more raw wool to France – or to Venice – well, they'll pay more to keep their share. It's as obvious as the nose on his face,' he said, jerking a thumb towards his companion.

The chubby one heaved a shoulder into him; a good-natured shove. 'That much *is* true, I warrant. But it won't happen. Henry won't sell out Brittany to the French – that's what they want – so he'll keep dangling the promise of trade to them if they behave. And the promise of war if they don't. The French noble houses are too busy warring amongst themselves to risk that too.'

Hawker leaned forward, shoulders hunched. 'But the king owes his crown to French support. Surely the French regent and council expect something in return? His loyalty, for a start.'

The moustachioed one wagged a finger. 'But he *is* king now. He can do what he likes. Sod the French.'

The chubby one took a drink and set down his tankard delicately on the trestle. 'Master Rede, you can tell your weaver friends in Malines that all will be well. No need to fear for the market. We might even come to some negotiation on terms to better those of Ghent or Bruges. If you are their man to speak for them. Who was it in the guild who sent you here?'

Hawker froze. His pause seemed to last forever. But Ellingham spoke up instead.

'It is Master Bertrand de Grood.'

The chubby one's closed mouth formed an 'o' and he nodded. 'I do not know him.'

The other nodded and raised his pot of wine. '*I* have heard of him. His tapestry work is well known – and sought after. He has a fine workshop, I understand.'

'That is just so,' said Hawker, recovering his composure. 'And he is well considered in the guild there. His counsel matters.'

A third merchant joined them, pushing the others aside and plopping down between them. 'Here you are! Went to the wrong hole. By Christ, those Flemish are a mean, stingy lot. They'll beggar you silly unless you're sharp! Who have we here?'

The moustachioed one introduced Hawker and then Ellingham.

'William de la Haye,' said the new arrival, giving a court bow. He then turned to the chubby one. 'Oh, bless my soul! Your ship's master is looking for you at the hall. Says he can't offload your cargo until he's paid. Buzzing like a wasp, he is.'

The chubby one groaned and drained his wine. 'Impatient fool. *I'm* still waiting to be paid by someone else! Come on, young James, lend me some muscle and let's meet the rogue!' The two rose and left, one pushing the other until they found the doorway.

De la Haye bellowed for more drink to be brought. The tapster complied and the merchant directed Hawker's and Ellingham's cups to be refreshed too.

'What brings you here to Calais, then?' he asked, raising his tankard to them.

Hawker made light talk about their quest to find preferable terms for trade for the guild. But he then quickly turned to being the questioner.

'It is said the Staple runs the town, not the king's men in the castle across the square.'

The man smiled, seeming to almost relish the statement. 'It has always been thus.' He was younger than Hawker, perhaps, but not by many years. His greying hair, long in the latest fashion, was wrapped around both ears. De la Haye wore a mantle of darkest blue, trimmed with marten fur, which showed fraying at the edges. It was not new. His eyes, a peculiar shade of green and slightly hooded, went from Hawker to Ellingham and back again. 'Better to let the Captain of Calais – whoever it may be – *think* he rules the roost.'

'And what of the prior Captain of Calais?' said Ellingham. 'Where is he now?'

Hawker nearly bit his tongue. The lad was far too keen to dash in before Hawker had taken the measure of the man.

De la Haye exhaled and rolled his shoulders forward. 'The royal bastard? Aye, well, you can imagine the post was not his for very long after Bosworth battle.' He shook his head forlornly. 'Truth be told, it was ever in name only. He was a boy when Richard appointed him. Still is… really.'

'Where is he then?' asked Ellingham.

Hawker shifted his feet under the table and bit the inside of his cheek.

'Where *is* he?' echoed de la Haye. 'Why, he's still here in Calais. Waiting for quite what, I do not know. If Henry had sent for him, he would already be gone.' The merchant must have noted Ellingham's eager expression. 'I would caution you against anything more than a simple curiosity. My lord Daubeney has many eyes and ears. It isn't wise to speak of the cause of the White Rose.'

'He is allowed the freedom of the town?' Hawker's voice was low, cautious.

'Yes. He spends most days at the inns. Pays his respects at Staple Hall. Goes to Mass near upon each day. He seems not to lack for food or warmth. Has a modest house off the square here.'

'You seem to know much about his movements.'

Ellingham looked into his wine. 'It sounds a sad existence. Lost.'

De la Haye studied Ellingham intently. 'Yet he lives. But, mark me, if there is another failed rebellion – like Lord Lovell's last summer – then it might grow more precarious for him. The king has a nervous disposition. As any tailor will tell you, loose ends are best dealt with sooner than later.'

Neither Hawker nor Ellingham said a word. The merchant took a swig of wine then pulled a small scrap of cloth from a pocket in the lining of his mantle. Concealing it in a cupped palm, he extended towards Ellingham, and slowly unfolded his hand. It was an embroidered badge, cut from a tabard. A silver boar, curling tusks detailed in golden thread. De la Haye closed his fist and secreted the badge away again.

'There are a few of us about still,' he said quietly. 'But hope grows fainter each month. Soon all will be forgotten, I think. We make new lives. Our past becomes but a dream. Imagined.'

Ellingham leaned forward. 'Has he no friends? A woman?'

The youth was showing more concern than prudent, thought Hawker, quickly scanning the chamber for anyone showing more than passing interest in them.

'I've said enough,' replied de la Haye. 'But if you would glimpse him, go to Saint Mary's at the eastern wall. He will be well-attired, mouse-brown hair and fair of face. He usually has a servant boy with him, trailing behind.'

'You have misjudged our passing interest, sir,' said Hawker sternly.

The ageing merchant smiled. 'I beg your pardon, sir. But I would say this to any new to Calais. Guard your confidences and guard them well.'

Ellingham looked over to Hawker and Hawker stood. 'It is time we took our leave. I thank you for the drink and we will no doubt see each other again over business in the Hall on the morrow.'

De la Haye nodded. 'Fare you well, gentles.'

They left the inn and went into the square.

'What is your plan now, Sir John?'

'I know what *your* plan is. But we must be cautious. We should go to Mother Richards' and see how the others fare. Then decide.'

Ellingham looked to the clock tower over the council house. He put his hands on his hips. 'It is nearly vespers. I am going to church. To Saint Mary's.'

Hawker shut his eyes. 'You will be the death of me.' He turned and fixed Ellingham with the look of an indulgent uncle. 'Very well. Let us be quick about it!'

9

Hawker and Ellingham walked briskly through the streets of the
enclave, the English crown's last remaining foothold in France.
A stiff breeze coming off the Narrow Seas rippled through
the tight alleyways, gaining force and whipping their mantles
about them. The steeple of what had to be Saint Mary's church
poked above the rooftops and they fixed it in their line of sight.
Hawker worried if the others had found space at the inn and
were keeping out of trouble. Jacob would be as stone. That he
knew for certain. Jack, the innocent, might be easily coaxed
into loose conversation unless Jacob kept him reined in. As for
Dieudonné – as unpredictable as a primed hand cannon – he
could only pray.

'I will go in and see if he has arrived,' said Ellingham, no
sooner than had they reached the tympanum and double oak
doors.

Hawker jerked him back by his arm. 'We both go in!'

The youth turned and knocked off the older knight's hand.
'You are not my master, Sir John. And if I choose to reveal
myself to my flesh and blood I will do so. Without your leave.'

Hawker grabbed Ellingham's forearm and leaned close. 'You
will get us killed! *All* of us. You have liberty to risk your own
neck, but think of Jack and Jacob. We know nothing of this
man, be he your blood or no.'

Ellingham's reply was cold. 'I am tired of being alone.' He
brushed past and went inside.

Hawker caught him up, eyes adjusting to the gloom. There
were very few at prayer and the priest had yet to arrive to

conduct the service. But Ellingham was well ahead of Hawker. He spotted straight away a fair youth with brown mousey hair to the shoulders, kneeling in prayer in the last pew to the left of the aisle. A young boy was next to him, seated. The servant was slight and blond-haired, around ten or eleven years, and obviously bored. He watched the altar and picked his nose. And Ellingham was already filing into the pew to join them.

Rather than bull his way, Hawker took station at the back, just behind them and within earshot. His eyes quickly took in the other worshippers. If John the Bastard had warders, they would no doubt be here already, and observing all. And though he was in church, he mumbled aloud a curse – at himself – for allowing the whole mad enterprise to find fertile soil.

He stepped forward to the rear of the pew as Ellingham kneeled, nearly shoulder to shoulder with the man who might be his half-brother. It would be difficult to hear any exchange, but he would have to try. It was pure luck that no one else was near them. Ellingham leaned in to whisper to the youth. The youth turned, looked at him intensely, and pulled back slightly.

'*Who* are you? I do not know you. Or anything of you.'

Ellingham raised a spread palm. 'I am your half-brother. By the same sire. And I have sought you out.'

John of Gloucester shook his head slowly, disbelieving. He then noticed Hawker looming behind. He stood and shook the lad next to him. He moved sideways to exit the pew from the other end, pushing his servant in front of him.

'I beg you!' said Ellingham in a loud whisper. 'Hear me out!'

Hawker stepped in front of the young man and held out his hand. 'My lord, he speaks the truth. I am John Hawker, knight and liegeman to your father.'

The youth stopped, eyes wide. He glanced back to Ellingham before facing Hawker. 'I do not believe you.'

Hawker could easily see that the two could be brothers. The same jawline, eyes, height. And they could not have been more than a few months apart in age. Ellingham leaned over the back of the pew. 'My name is Giles. Born in Middleham. This good knight has been my companion since Richard tasked him with my protection.'

The fellow's hazel eyes narrowed, still unbelieving. 'Stand away, sir!'

Hawker saw that the near empty church had taken no notice of them. Yet. But they would not have another opportunity if John Plantagenet bolted from them now. Hawker pushed himself closer. 'Hear your brother out. For that is who he is.'

John looked past Hawker, eyes darting. Either reassured no one was watching, or relenting at being cornered, he raised himself up and folded his arms across his chest. 'Be quick then with what you have to say.'

'This is Sir Giles Ellingham. Knighted upon the road by your father a week before he fell at Bosworth. Look upon him! You see yourself.'

'It is true, dear brother!' said Ellingham, jumping in, full of earnest enthusiasm. He had now come around the other side to stand close by. 'We would lead you out of here, if you wish it. It is not safe for those of our name. But we have friends.'

John of Gloucester tilted his head. 'The only ones in danger here are you, given what you say. I serve at the king's pleasure. And he has seen fit to give me twenty marks a year.'

'That will not save you,' said Hawker darkly. 'Not in the end. He is ruthless. If he changes his mind about your loyalty, well, then, what shall you do?'

'I've done him no wrong. Not talked of rebellion. It is *you* who endanger me with your presence.'

'John, come away with us,' said Ellingham. 'You take great risks living under his protection.'

The youth's face twisted suddenly, disgust flooding him. 'I do not know you! And I reject you. You bring only trouble with you.' He again made to step around Hawker.

Hawker placed his hand on the youth's arm. 'He wears the boar's head signet. He is your brother.'

Hawker became aware that a priest had entered and was observing intently. John became more agitated and pushed again. 'Out of my way, sir.' He looked upon Ellingham, the glance lingering for more than a moment. 'If you value my life and your own, for pity's sake let me go now!'

Hawker stepped back.

Ellingham's subdued voice strained. 'For the love of Christ, brother... *hear* us.'

Hawker noticed the servant boy was gone. 'Where is your page?' he demanded, gripping the young Plantagenet by the wrist. 'Where has he gone?' The youth looked at him as blankly as a village simpleton. His expression spoke of surrender and fear, mixed.

'He is not my page. And Calais is not a town. It is a prison.'

Hawker felt the blood in his veins grow cold. He quickly looped his arm through Ellingham's and wheeled him out the doorway, Ellingham protesting all the way.

'We must get out now!' said Hawker, his heart already beginning to pound harder.

'What do you mean?' said Ellingham, throwing off the older knight's guiding arm. 'We *are* out now!'

Hawker swept up Ellingham again, marching him forward. 'We must get out of Calais this instant! Before they shut the gates. Sweet Jesus above, the boy wasn't his servant. He was his warder!'

—

Jacob threw his portmanteau over the back of the saddle, ran the straps through and grabbed the reins of his horse and Hawker's. He trotted out of the narrow alleyway from the stables to the front of the ramshackle Mother Richards' hostel and shouted for Jack to hurry along.

Hawker, Ellingham and Dieudonné met them at the doorway, the latter mumbling a string of curses in French, while his head swivelled about looking for any impending attack.

'Mount up,' said Hawker, retrieving his reins from Jacob. 'Keep them at a walk! The boy has to make it back up to the castle at the western wall in order to warn them. We might just outrun them.' He prayed the gates were not already shut as darkness had begun to descend on them. They'd have no way out otherwise, locked inside with an entire garrison of King Henry's soldiers to contend with.

Ellingham looked lost. Hawker knew full well the reception they received from his half-brother had been like a knife thrust to the youth and the hurt plainly showed: a blank, middle-distance stare where there ought to be steely focus for their escape.

'Giles, come!'

Dieudonné darted forward and retrieved Ellingham's horse from Jack, bringing it around for Ellingham to mount. 'Come, my prince,' he said quietly, 'time to go.'

Wordlessly, Ellingham swung into the saddle and moved off towards the square with the others.

Jacob came alongside Hawker, but his eyes were focused ahead. 'What is your order, Sir John? If it comes to it. Do we fight? Or not fight?'

Hawker looked at him hard. His reply was soft spoken. 'We go down and take as many as we can with us.'

Jacob nodded. He then called over to Jack whose horse tossed its mane, side-stepping on the cobbles. 'Put your eyes back into your head, boy! And slow that beast! He *knows* you're twitchy – so he is too.'

They clopped down the street and reached the square where they could see the Lantern Gate looming, torches now alight in front of the open gates. The portcullis was not yet lowered, and Hawker whispered a prayer. Reaching over to his left hip, he eased out his long Italian dagger just an inch or so from its scabbard. He sidled up to Ellingham – who stared dead ahead – devoid of emotion. The other three fell back into line behind them: Jacob and Jack together, and Dieudonné last of all.

The gate and walls drew closer in view. Hawker could see the guards preparing, the oak bar for the gate already being manhandled from where it had been propped. 'If they stop us,' said Hawker, turning in the saddle, 'do *nothing*! If I draw my steel, then you let fly.'

Hawker's mount reached the wooden planks under the guard tower, the stone archway rising over them. The sentry held up his hand, his comrades blocking the way through. Hawker in turn held up his hand for his party to halt. Ten feet above, the iron prongs of the portcullis were suspended over Hawker's head. Another guard appeared to Hawker's left, emerging from the stairwell which led up top. It was the captain of the gate-house again.

'Your honours? Leaving already?'

Hawker touched his bonnet and nodded. 'We have concluded our business – sooner than expected – and wish to get back to Flanders for the morrow.'

'Aye, well you won't gain entrance again this eve if you change your mind. Not heard much of travellers choosing to journey in the darkness.' He smiled. 'The town has had trouble of late with visitors not paying their bills. Departing in a hurry and all.' The man's eyebrows raised.

Hawker smiled back. 'Are you accusing me of thievery?'

Ellingham's closed fist lightly punched Hawker's knee. Hawker turned and looked behind Dieudonné, whose horse was barely into the gate tower. He saw three men – tabards, helms and polearms – and one smaller figure with them, a boy. Striding fast.

The captain chuckled. 'Nay, my good sir. Just warning that we are cautious here. By necessity.' He waved off his men who barred the way with glaives.

Hawker touched his brim again and kicked in his heels. He and Ellingham moved forward and had barely reached the other side when the shouting began.

'Stop! Stop them!'

The captain turned to the newcomers and as he did so, Dieudonné reared his mount and collided with the man, knocking him to the ground. Jacob and Jack thundered past, Dieudonné close behind. Hawker wheeled and drew his blade and Ellingham as well. Jacob managed to deflect the thrust of a glaive with his sword, turning tightly upon the sentry to prevent him striking again.

'Ride!' shouted Hawker. 'For the love of God, ride!'

They followed the road, clods of earth flying under their horses' hooves, the jetty and sea mole on their left. The ground rose steadily as they ran parallel to the town walls. Behind them the shouting continued and a bell began clanging wildly.

They reached the flat upland overlooking Calais and Hawker reined in, signalling the others. In the fading light he could see a group of torches at the Lantern Gate, then mounted men.

Jack's horse turned and trotted ten feet back down the track. He twisted in the saddle, sword held high. 'Sir John! Let's bring the war to them! No more running!'

'Jack Perry, you dolt of a boy!' yelled Hawker. 'Get back here!'

'We can ambush them up ahead, Sir John! In those trees!' He was fired as hot as a poker in the flames, sword twirling in his fist over his head.

Dieudonné roared with laughter. 'The boy is a lion. A simpleton, but a lion.'

Hawker cursed loudly and trotted over to Jack. 'You will get your chance, boy. This is not it.'

Jacob pointed back down the road. 'They're following us out, Sir John,' he called, voice steady. 'At least half a dozen.'

'Look at me, boy!' Hawker placed his mount between the castle and Jack. 'You will get your chance. But you obey me always! Now, we *ride*.'

Jack swallowed hard and nodded, his face streaming with sweat. When Hawker turned again, he saw that Dieudonné was already well ahead, pounding up the road, Ellingham at his side.

10

He lay wrapped in her arms and at peace. It was late afternoon. When he had arrived back at Mechelen around midday he had handed off his horse to Jack, told the boy to go to Jacob's, and then entered his house. He had seized Chiara in a powerful embrace, kissing her face and drinking in her joy at seeing him return whole. Nicholas lay napping in his cot and he and Chiara stole away to their bedchamber, Hawker lifting her off her feet. She had laughed and scolded and then they tumbled together on the bed. Now, sated and tired, he ran over in his mind what had passed, and what was likely to come.

He had fulfilled half his promise to Giles. The adventure of Calais had left him saddened, not just for Giles's disappointment, but for his own. He knew he was losing hope, hope for a restoration of Yorkist fortunes. And he believed Giles was beginning to feel the same. His half-brother had rejected him utterly, probably informing on him to boot. Self-preservation was a powerful driver of men. John of Gloucester, bastard of the late king, had made his choice which side to take.

'When will you tell me what happened out there?' Chiara's voice was quiet, almost afraid.

Hawker's throat made a growling noise. 'I am still trying... to make sense of it, my love. We found who we were looking for. But he had no wish to be found. Sir Giles is... saddened. For his loss. As am I.'

Chiara let out a sigh. 'Need I ask? Did you come to blows there?'

Hawker turned on his side and faced her. 'We fled in haste. No blood was spilled.'

She draped her arm over his hip. 'I thank God for that at least. And you have fulfilled your promise to Sir Giles.'

'Half my promise.'

'Enough for him to realise it was a fool's errand. These are dangerous times for the blood of a fallen house. You knew that. So did he.'

'I no longer know his heart. If he still has the stomach to fight for York and for what is left of his house.'

'Where did you leave him?'

'He is with Dieudonné. They have probably slunk off to a tavern to lick their wounds and drown their disappointment.'

It was Chiara's turn to growl. 'I doubt very much that Frenchman – Burgundian – whatever he is, is disappointed. He's a clever fox and preens over Giles like an unctuous… *bah*.' She trailed off, exasperated.

Hawker knew she spoke the truth. 'I know he pursues his own interests through the lad. But it is a long gamble for him. The future for York is fast fading. The royal heirs are dead, in prison, or… hiding. Maybe hiding here.'

'So what will he do next? What will *you* do next?'

'I must find news from the exiles. Gain an audience with Lord Lovell. De la Marche will help me, I'm certain. There is rumour of a young boy they claim is Edward – son of King Richard's older brother, the Duke of Clarence. He is of the royal blood.'

Chiara groaned again. 'Your English politics. As bad as Venice!'

Hawker smiled forlornly. 'You can't possibly imagine. I remember when King Edward executed his brother, the Duke of Clarence. When they're not killing their enemies, they're killing each other. Now, there's nary a one left.'

Her hand moved to his stubbly cheek, stroking it. 'You must decide what *you* want to do next. Our coin is running low. You can *be* a wool merchant and not just pretend. You told me your father was one. You know the trade.'

He rolled on his back and looked at the ceiling beams. 'I have thought upon it, I do confess. I feel these old bones now more than ever. But the palace might have other ideas. I seem to still have some use to them. In what I have always done.'

'You are your own master, my love. And there will come a time when you will not be able to bear arms any more. What shall we do then?'

Hawker prickled at her words. Even if she spoke the truth. 'You think I can just lay down my sword and then haggle over the price of a wool bale or a wagon-load of cloth? If there is fortune still to be had at court here then I will pursue it with all my strength. I must keep a roof over us. Do what's best for our boy. And the money I take from the duchess is good coin indeed.'

'If not overly generous.'

Hawker rolled the coverlet off and got out of bed. His body was stiff from the saddle and his back cracked audibly. 'We should not have lain abed so long. The nurse will gossip. And I have much to do.'

Chiara pulled the coverlet up over herself. 'I do not doubt you. I never have. But I can see the suffering and worry in your face. About what lies ahead. And it frightens me.'

Hawker's chin dropped to his chest and he let out a sigh. Still naked, he sat down again on the bed and grasped her hand. 'My love, I will keep us all safe. You must believe me. And you must not worry. There is still promise to be found in this city!'

She squeezed his hand. 'I do believe you. And I am content to stay here and embrace it. Dress. I will see to the babe.'

He put on his white cambric shirt, pulled on braes and hose, and rummaged about the floor for his shoes. She sat up, watching him, and waiting for him to finish dressing, but she remained silent.

Hawker went down the creaking staircase and entered the hall. The Flemish nurse, a local woman that Bertrand de Grood had found, was holding Nicholas and she bowed curtly as the knight came in. Hawker reached out his arms to take his son. The nurse gave him a knowing look and smiled before handing over the child. Hawker wasn't sure just who the boy took after. He had never given much thought to babies or children – not since he had lost his firstborn all those years before – and the strange creatures seemed to change by the day. The eyes were bluish or grey, and very large. They stared up and held his gaze. A fine thatch of brown hair spiralled out, covering the child's crown. Hawker felt a flood of warmth that God had seen fit to reward him with a son after so long but, so too, did he feel unease and a faint heartache, an undefined longing, maybe for the uncertainty of a world changing far too quickly for him.

Nicholas screwed up his face, pained, but with no cry forthcoming. Hawker turned to the nursemaid.

'Give him here!' she directed. 'It's wind.'

A moment later Hawker's arms were emptied of the burden and he stood there, watching. Watching and feeling adrift on a sea of doubt for what lay ahead.

–

Gaston Dieudonné sipped his wine and observed his companion with interest. Sir Giles's disappointment was leaching away to leave a fine patina of bitterness in its place.

'Coward. Traitorous bastard.' Giles spat the words out as he stared into his drink. 'He would have betrayed me. Betrayed his own blood to save his skin.'

They were in a small brick-lined alcove in a low, vaulted undercroft near Saint Rumbold's church. An enterprising wine merchant had gained permission to set up a tavern in what had once been part of the bishop's demesne. Dieudonné had discovered it, found it bucolic, and noticed it was haunted by the young, affluent and handsome. Around them, lay clerics of lesser orders, lawyers and scriveners, all rubbing shoulders and drinking their fill.

'You are right, my prince. In every sense of the meaning of those words. But men act to save themselves in different ways. Some easy and some… not so easy. He has chosen the easy way. And dishonourable at that.' Dieudonné could tell there was another emotion stirring in the young man, just underneath the surface. Shame. Shame for being rejected, for being on the run. For being a by-blow scion of a fallen house.

Giles shook his head as if still disbelieving the situation he found himself in. 'We could have gotten him out with us. The fool. But he grovels and takes Henry's money instead.'

'And he has made his decision. Chosen his side.' Dieudonné lifted his eyebrows. 'Though… mark me, I would say it is a temporary solution for him at best.'

Giles grunted. 'Aye, to put his trust in Henry Tudor is like shaking hands with the Devil and thinking one has gotten the better bargain. Twenty pounds will seem paltry reward when he finds his neck on the block.'

'So then… *he* has made his decision. What will yours be?'

Giles looked at him, almost surprised by the question. 'My decision? I am waiting for Sir John to point the way. And still waiting.' He took a long drink from his cup and set it down on the trestle again. He let out a harsh bark. 'I'm like a boy halfway up a tree. Too uncertain to climb higher and afraid to climb back down. You must think me a poor excuse for a knight. For a man. Why do you stay?'

Dieudonné reached across and wrapped his long fingers around Giles's wrist. 'Because of my belief in you. My loyalty to you. My love for you.'

Dieudonné took heart that the youth did not withdraw from his gentle grasp, as he had done before. And it amazed him still, that only a little more than a year earlier he might have been willing to sell Giles to the Tudors. Indeed, it had been his whole plan to find his own fortune. A scheme he nearly succeeded in carrying out in Venice. Unforeseen events had interceded, true, but his own affections had slowly grown more ardent, transforming him – and changing his plans for fortune and favour.

'My dear Gaston, your friendship has upheld me these many months. We've fought together. Struggled. I am grateful you have stayed. Been steadfast.' And to seal his words he placed his hand on top of Dieudonné's. 'You remained after Maria Hunyadi betrayed me – betrayed all of us – and ran away. That was a time when I was broken. Unmanned by her.'

Dieudonné nodded his understanding. He could never tell the youth that it was he who had made Maria leave the company in the dead of night. He had intended to kill her, but relented, admiring her craft of deception. Instead, he had demanded she depart else he would reveal her true intentions and her thieving past to Giles. And Dieudonné had felt his influence grow stronger, week by week, on their journey from the Hungarian lands back to the west. His conquest was almost won, he could feel it.

'Adversity has sculpted you, my prince. Made you the stronger to face what lies ahead. And I will stand by you.'

Giles withdrew his hand and pulled his arm out from under Dieudonné's delicate clasp. He wrapped both his hands around the half-empty wine cup, massaging it. 'Hawker's ship is becalmed. We neither go forward nor back. And he is distracted now. Wife and babe. That is my fault, isn't it? For offering to return to Venice to fetch his bride.'

'I know I sound like the chiding crow. But I told you before, Sir John is getting *old*. Maybe too old for this game. Your loyalty to him has been more than admirable. But now is the time to go to the palace. Gain audience with your aunt. She will embrace you, I feel it in my bones.'

Giles looked intently at him. 'It is a risk. A risk that she will think me a pretender… a fraud.'

'Bah! You have the signet ring. And Hawker will vouch for you. He is sworn to your service by his oath to your father. Do not doubt yourself! Christ, you even have Richard's jaw. His hair… his lips.' Dieudonné resisted the urge to reach over and touch them.

'He would vouch for me,' said Giles. 'If he was called in after the fact. He would have no choice.'

'That is true. But why not first tell Sir John that you intend to go. I would wager that if he sees your mind made up then *he* will introduce you. That is the far better – far more certain way. Is it not?'

Giles frowned a little. 'He does have the ear of that old châtelain, de la Marche. It would be far better to be presented rather than walking in and demanding to be seen. I think you offer wise counsel, my friend.'

Dieudonné smiled. 'Then let us drink to it, shall we? You will bring a newfound joy to the palace. To the cause of the White Rose.'

Giles lifted his cup and smiled back. 'To the White Rose. And to our good fortune.'

The Burgundian drank and sat back. 'We will breathe new life into the cause. Be assured, I will stand at your side as long as you wish it.'

It was now Giles who reached across to grasp a forearm. 'To our friendship! And to the future!'

Their wooden cups clanked together and they drank them dry.

11

'You are right, Giles,' said Hawker, 'the time has come.'

They were sitting near the crackling fire that blazed in the hall hearth. Nearby, but not too near, young Nicholas Hawker slumbered in his wooden rocking cradle. Chiara had left the knights to their conversation, fully understanding the importance of Ellingham's visit.

Ellingham turned to look at Hawker, the surprise clear in his face, his eyes wide, and a smile blossoming. 'Sir John, I had expected reticence from you... your previous cautions... but my heart sings to hear your agreement.'

Hawker chuckled. 'Circumstances change. I never intended to deny you access to that path, I was waiting for the opportune time. And there are things afoot. You have heard the rumours.'

Ellingham nodded. 'Yes, but who is to know what is true? It is said another rebellion. But the last never caught fire, did it?'

Hawker shuffled his shoes along the woven rush matting and shifted his weight uncomfortably in the creaking, spindle-rigged chair, a triangular affair with an unravelling rush seat which had come with the accommodation provided by the palace. 'This time, better preparation – and more gold from the duchess – may favour the outcome. Lord Lovell is determined to take to the field again if he can gain the troops.'

'I pray that it might be so. So, you will introduce me again, to the duchess? As my father's son?'

Hawker lowered his chin slightly. 'I will introduce you to Sir Olivier first. He will know the best way to introduce you. He already knows who you are. A fact he's kept quiet about.'

Hawker watched Ellingham's face darken. 'He knows already? Then who else does?'

'The Tudors learned who you are while we were still in Venice a year ago. Word has leaked out now. But at least the journey to Wallachia removed you from their list of concerns. They must have spies here, but whether they know you are here now, I do not know.'

'But they surely know *you're* here. In the employ of the palace. It wouldn't take a scholar for them to deduce I am here too.' Ellingham stood and walked closer to the fire. He crossed his arms.

'That is all the more reason we throw in with duchess dowager. Learn what is being planned. I can no longer offer you the protection and guidance I have done. And what more can I teach you? We both know this. It is why you have come this day.'

Ellingham turned to face Hawker, his hands still wrapped about his elbows. 'And what of your other promise to me? To find my sister?'

Hawker looked up at him. 'After what happened in the past few days, I presumed you might have thought better of the idea. But, if you still have your heart set upon it, then would not a return with an army at your side improve your chances?' He had hoped Ellingham would give up on such a quest, fraught with high risk and requiring a journey across England, conducted in secrecy. Entering Calais had been dangerous enough. Returning to England, alone, unseen, would be difficult as every port was being watched by Henry Tudor's spies and officials. In Calais, they had experienced but a taste of what they could expect back in England.

Ellingham's voice carried a whiff of defiance. 'I have not decided yet, Sir John. But if you wish to withdraw your promise to me, then I will release you from it.'

Hawker stood up and put a hand on the youth's shoulder. 'Giles, first cares first. Secure your own position here before making any decision that would take you into the heartland of the enemy. I tell you truly, there are plans and schemes now that could change all. Let us find out together what course is the best. The wisest.'

Ellingham exhaled noisily, frustrated, but seemingly acquiescing. 'I understand your counsel. We must learn what the duchess – and the emperor – have hatched. But it's been near upon a year since we returned. I have accomplished little.'

'We've stayed *alive*,' said Hawker, smiling and giving the youth a gentle shake. 'No small thing given what we've been through. And change is coming.'

Ellingham did not smile back. 'When do we go to the palace?'

Hawker looked at him and nodded. 'I will go this day and find the châtelain. Arrange an audience for us.' He raised a finger towards Ellingham's chest. 'But Sir Olivier will decide the chiefest way to do this! We can make no demands.'

'I understand.'

There was a quiet yelp of awakening from inside the cradle which quickly grew into loud snuffling and snorts. Hawker stooped down and retrieved his son, bouncing the child in his tightly bound wrappings.

'He's as heavy as a goose already! Here, hold him!'

Ellingham's brow furrowed as he awkwardly accepted the burden, holding the child out almost at arm's length.

Chiara whisked in though, from just outside the chamber, and scooped up Nicholas before Ellingham could say a word. 'Giovanni! Sir Giles has no wish to be a nursemaid!' She threw Giles a smile and a courteous nod.

Ellingham unconsciously rubbed his palms. 'Then I will leave you now, Sir John. Thank you. I await your word.'

Hawker grinned, watching Chiara fussing over the child. 'It will be soon, Giles. Have no fear! I promise you.'

–

It was another two weeks before Sir Olivier de la Marche agreed to see Hawker, and the month of April well along. Hawker felt sheepish for having to put off Ellingham as to why they had gained no further ground with the palace. Hawker knew things were swirling at court. New intrigues. But he had not yet been allowed to share in any confidences. For now, he was nothing more than a poor beggar knight, a henchman who might be called upon when needed. And, for the moment at least, he was not needed.

A messenger called for him though on a Monday morning, yet another sullen *landsknecht*, tall, bearded, and sprouting three great white plumes from his felt cap. Hawker accompanied the soldier across the town and to the wide thoroughfare where the white stone palace lay adjoining an ancient church. Once inside, he was guided across the tessellated black-and-white hall floor and led to the gardens. He remembered these from over a year before when he and Ellingham had been given an audience with the duchess dowager. Now, the gardens were devoid of life: the French and Alba roses starkly bare, lavenders dried and shivering in the still somewhat crisp April wind which blew through the cloister. But he also spied some young shoots in the lavender and the blood-red leaves of new growth upon the rose climbers.

The *châtelain* was waiting for him, wrapped in a long black cloak and his head covered in a velvet bonnet of dark blue, a cluster of pearls set in gold upon his brow.

'A good day to you, Sir John.' The lack of warmth in his face matched the cold wind that blew around them both.

'Sir Olivier,' said Hawker, giving a court bow. 'Thank you for receiving me... finally.'

It was then that the *châtelain* let slip a small smile. 'There have been other priorities. All of which have outranked yours.'

'I am grateful that you can now give of your time. But would it not be better to meet inside? Preferably near a hearth?' Hawker grinned.

94

Sir Olivier's expression remained unchanged, his large protruding eyes blinking but once. 'I cannot see around a doorway to spy out eavesdroppers. Here, there are none. Let us sit over there.'

They moved to a stone bench near the far wall of the cloister. The *châtelain* sat and fluffed his voluminous cloak, clutching it about his chest and then hunkered down. Hawker thought he looked like a toad sitting on a rock.

'Your tale of Calais was not especially illuminating. I had expected more in the way of useable information.'

Hawker sat next to him. 'And I had expected to remain there for more than two hours. The circumstances were unfortunate... as I have told.'

Sir Olivier folded his hands in his lap. 'And how fares your bastard charge?'

'He has held his peace for nigh upon a year. But he is now desirous of seeking an audience with his aunt. And I support him in that wish.'

Sir Olivier sighed. 'Sir John, the lad might be better served by remaining incognito. He has come this far standing on his own. I have told the duchess nothing of him.'

'He would know his blood kin. And he is eager to serve the cause.'

'He is as poor as you. What can he offer?'

'To begin with, a stout heart and a sharp sword.'

Sir Olivier chuckled into his tucked chin. 'I see. But the cause is served by money and soldiers. Many soldiers. And your company has dwindled over the past few years, I understand.'

Hawker burned at hearing it. Yet it was true. 'He can raise men. Once they learn who his father was.'

'She is not overly impressed with you, Sir John. Richard's other Knights of the Body fell with him. You, somehow... survived the outcome.'

Hawker bristled anew. 'I was never a Knight of the Body. But I was there fighting... protecting his bastard son. Saving his

95

life. He would have joined his father in death otherwise, I can assure you. That is the oath I swore to King Richard.'

Sir Olivier's lower lip pouted and he nodded thoughtfully. 'Ah, well, that may put you in a better light.'

'And you might ask the same of Lord Lovell,' added Hawker. 'He managed to escape Bosworth too.'

'That is true. But he has carried on the fight. You – on the other hand – went to Venice, I seem to remember.'

Hawker clenched his jaw a moment. '*That* was also under the king's orders.'

The *châtelain* frowned. 'Best not to mention that episode again.'

'The jewel she thought I carried when last I was here? The basting her spies gave me on the street?'

Sir Olivier tilted his head and placed a finger aside his nose. 'Well, I have forgiven that. So then… we shall be granted an audience?'

'I will request it. Sir Giles has the right to ask. But I can guarantee nothing. And you should be aware of new developments. There is another blood relative arriving to see Her Grace. The Earl of Lincoln should make it here by the morrow with a small retinue. It seems he escaped England just as the noose was closing.'

Hawker sat back on the bench. 'John de la Pole.' He was Richard's nephew and his appointed heir should Richard die childless. Hawker had never met him and had not glimpsed him on the field at Bosworth. His arrival was more proof that a new rebellion was gathering strength.

'I imagine that Her Grace will inform you of her plans when she is ready. And tell you what she expects from you.' He looked out into the barren garden and smiled to himself. 'It seems they have found a new king. A boy king they have spirited out of England and taken to the Dublin Pale.'

Hawker turned. 'What? Who could that be?'

Sir Olivier swivelled around to look at Hawker. 'Does it truly matter? Whoever the lad is, they intend to pass him off as

Edward, the son of the Duke of Clarence, a true Yorkist heir. That will rally support among the Irish lords and the stalwarts in the north of England. Lord Lovell will lead an invasion by summer.'

Hawker swore under his breath. 'Edward the Sixth. But Henry Tudor surely has the real Edward already in his grasp. Ensconced in the Tower, no doubt.'

Sir Olivier laughed aloud. 'Who is to know? Or believe *which* boy is real and which is an imposter? Lord Lovell's lad will be a changeling. So it matters not.'

'Then this new rebellion is alive,' mused Hawker, half to himself. He rubbed his stubbly cleft chin and studied his shoes. He then turned again to Sir Olivier. 'Do *you* believe they can raise enough men this time to stand a chance?'

Sir Olivier arched a brow. 'With enough gold one can raise a cathedral to the skies. Or buy ten armies for one campaign season. The duchess will leave no stone unturned to end the Tudor usurpation. And this time, the emperor is fully behind her plans. He is worried Henry will join his French friends to invade Flanders. That must not happen. It is why I asked you to gain any intelligence in Calais as to English intentions.'

Hawker nodded. 'I have told you all from that expedition. You know how it fared.'

'Foolish of the young man to seek out his half-brother. You should have realised that if John of Gloucester was still in Calais then he was bought and sold.'

'The pull of family ties has no wisdom to it. Yet it is a powerful magic.'

Sir Olivier stood up and shook the chill from his shoulders. 'Await the summons. With the arrival of the earl, things may move with great speed.'

Hawker arose and gave a slight bow to the *châtelain*. 'Thank you, my lord.'

Sir Olivier tilted his head, his protruding eyes drilling into Hawker's. 'And tell young Ellingham to guard his tongue. In these times, death comes quickly and quietly to those who sing too loudly.'

12

Jack Perry watched the old weaver with fascination. He was seeing a picture painted in wool. Strand by strand, the shuttle of the loom was sent sliding and clacking through the tapestry, the weaver's gnarled fingers slammed the frame roller, and the whole process was repeated. Endlessly, it seemed. Beside the old man another loom clanked and slammed, its weaver hunched over on his stool, his ruddy face almost contorted in concentration, hands moving deftly, motion after motion. The yarns' strands twitched on their spools, the reds, whites, blacks, greens and blues all blending to create the scene of a stag hunt, half-finished but recognisable none the less. And Jack suddenly recalled seeing prisoners in Venice, chained to treadmills set in great wooden wheels which raised and lowered shipping cranes at port. This looked about as much fun.

Bertrand de Grood, master weaver to the duchess dowager, wrapped an arm over Jack's shoulders, and leaned into his ear. Jack couldn't understand the guttural Flemish and only smelt the strong onion breath of the man as he spoke. Jacob de Grood, Bertrand's only son, stood behind Jack and let out a laugh.

'He wants to apprentice you! Says he will make you a skilled weaver. Wealthy in time. If you learn well.'

Jack turned to Bertrand, nodded, and smiled awkwardly. He could think of nothing worse. Except the treadmill. 'I am a man-at-arms,' he said quietly. 'A squire.'

Jacob laughed again and translated for his father. De Grood the senior, shook his head sadly and clapped Jack on the shoulder. He spoke again, his voice dramatic.

'What did he say?' asked Jack.

'He said you will find your grave the quicker upon that path. Which is the same thing he told me. A hundred times at least.'

Jack frowned.

'Well,' said Jacob, 'you're not a squire yet. And a barely competent man-at-arms, by my reckoning. You may still take him up on his offer if you like.'

'Piss off,' said Jack.

Jacob tousled Jack's mop of hair. 'Then let's to the yard. Time to teach the pell a lesson. Or you can try teaching me one.'

They went outside to the long narrow yard. Down among the apple trees that grew at the back, the oak pell beckoned. Jacob had set it into the ground years before and it was now weathered, leaning and crow-pecked. Jack was sick to death of hitting it. Sick to death of endless practice. Had he not proved himself already in half a dozen skirmishes? He had even helped defeat a castle garrison and had killed its captain himself! He'd been with Hawker since he was probably ten years old. He knew only of encampment, the march and soldiering. Nothing else mattered.

'Need I put on my harness? The pell never hits me back now, does it?'

Jacob's eyes narrowed a little and his cheek scar twitched. 'No… but I can. Put on your armour. Helm too.'

'He won't go soldiering again, will he?' said Jack flatly.

Jacob huffed and put his hands on his hips. 'I'll tell you true, boy. I do not know. But we must stand ready. For when he finally decides what he will do.'

'There is no more company. There is only us.'

He watched as Jacob's rough and broken face seemed to sag a little. 'Take heart. He can raise another. If he chooses to.'

'Things have changed now. I can tell. What have we done since Easter last?'

Jacob frowned. 'You are sworn to him.'

Jack shook his head slowly. 'Jacob, I am not. Never took an oath, I did. Never was made a squire proper-like.'

'Sir John is a poor knight. But he is honourable. You would be hard put to find a better one.'

Jack hefted his breastplate and back and fumbled with the shoulder strap and buckle. 'I know that. I owe my life to him. I know that too.'

'Then, boy, you will take instruction. No carping. And you will keep saying your prayers at church, as will I. And we will pray for Sir John. Pray that he finds fortune… and purpose.'

—

Face flushed hot from his swordplay, Jack left de Grood's house to stretch his legs and cool down in the breeze that whipped through the tall buildings of Mechelen. He still wore his padded, thigh-length red gambeson now practically faded to pink, and his breastplate and back. He felt lifted, as he usually did after a heavy practice, muscles aching a little but blood pumping in his veins and skin tingling with sweat. He also wore his blade at his hip, the same he had carried back from Wallachia: a sturdy Saxon-forged arming sword with a simple cross-hilt guard. Heading towards the main square, he felt himself beginning to swagger, his sword hilt clanking on the edge of the breastplate. He may have had nowhere to go, nor had a master who cared much any more, but at least he could *look* like a proper man-at-arms.

All around him the huge, towering houses of Mechelen rose up, tiny alleyways breaking the wall of red brick, grey stone, and paint of alabaster white. As he neared a corner, a chorus of raucous voices drifted to his ears. He nearly careened into them. A group of a dozen *landsknecht* soldiers, part of the personal army of the Archduke Maximilian, were out on a carousing mission, singing and half-drunk. For a moment his heart stuck in his throat. They spotted him immediately and three broke off at a dash towards him, just feet away. Jack froze. He didn't even have time to put hand to his sword hilt for they were upon him in seconds.

One laughed and threw his arm and all his weight around Jack's shoulders while his comrade wrenched Jack's arm forward. They drew him into their midst, laughing and shouting in what sounded like Flemish or German to him – maybe both. He was carried along by the current, all an ungodly babble of strange languages and harsh cries. Jack's head was spinning with confusion. But he was not being beaten up. He seemed to be joining their parade. The fellow with his arm still wrapped about his neck kept trying to tell him something, but Jack could make neither head nor tails of it. At length the man gave up and rubbed Jack's locks briskly as if playing with a pet dog. Someone broke into a ballad and the others chimed in, singing along.

A few moments later they were standing near a stone archway and a swinging sign overhead marked by a rampant lion in red. They piled through the doorway, pushing, shoving and laughing, and Jack was again carried along by the sheer momentum of men eager to get inside wherever it was.

It was a tavern, long and low, heavy rafters looming overhead. A row of barrels on racks covered one side of the vast room and the rest was taken up with benches and rectangular trestle tables. The place already was half-full when they barged in and now it was splitting at the seams. Jack caught a glimpse of the burly innkeeper's face, eyes bulging at the new arrivals, but he was soon bringing clay flagons of wine to the *landsknechts*, the picture of calm and confidence.

Jack found himself wedged between two huge men. They both wore *mi-partie* hose and voluminous white shirts and red-and-blue leather doublets, 'pinked' with cut-outs of diamonds and moons. The sword quillons of the man on Jack's right scratched along his breastplate as they sat shoulder to shoulder. He leaned in and clearly was posing a question to him. Jack shook his head.

'I am English!'

The man laughed and repeated, 'Eeenglish! Eeenglish!' and began waving and pointing at Jack. Another across the trestle took notice and called over.

'You are an Englishman!'

Jack lifted his head higher at hearing his own tongue. 'Aye, that I am!'

'I am a Scot! And we are all friends here.'

Jack smiled and the man next to him slammed a cup of wine in front of him, instantly spilling half of it.

The Scot pointed to his chest, shirt half open and exposing a thatch of bright red chest hair, which matched his ginger beard. 'I be David Weems! Of Fife! Who are you then?'

'Jack Perry! Of Lincolnshire!'

'Well met! Drink!'

Without hesitating, Jack raised up the wooden cup and knocked back a gullet full of red wine. David Weems did the same and the empty vessel banged to the table.

'What brings you here to this place, Jack Perry?'

'I'm in the service of an English knight.' He was on the verge of naming Sir John but thought better of it.

'We serve the archduke. His father the emperor. His whole damned family if need be!' He studied Jack a moment, eyebrow raised. 'You look to be just a lad. But you're in harness?'

Jack raised himself up again. 'I've already fought battles. In the Hungarian lands. Taken a few knocks too.'

Weems made a melodramatic 'o' with his lips and gave a mock frown. 'Sounds like you've seen some heavy combat then.'

'Enough. Enough to know what I'm doing.'

'Oh, aye. I do hear you. How many summers have you seen, lad?'

'Fifteen. And what about you?'

Weems laughed. 'Cheeky sod, aren't you? I be twenty and five, though I cannot be certain.' He managed to get his cup refilled and it seemed the noise had quietened the more the *landsknechts* concentrated on their drinking. Jack was finding it easier to hear what the Scot was saying.

'So, tell me, English… how is the pay in service to a belted knight?'

Jack was loth to admit he received but a few coins from Hawker when it was needed. But nothing more. 'It's good enough.'

Weems wagged a finger. 'No amount is ever good enough! But we get four gulden a month and that be more than even a three-handed bricklayer will make. And if you're what the Germans call a doppelsöldner – a double-pay man – you get just that. But, by God, you'll work for it.'

Jack found his cup being refreshed. He picked it up and drank again. 'And what do the double-pay men do?'

'Hand-and-a-half sword. Or halberd. For cutting up the enemy pikemen. They do have to run around a lot more than us lot!' At that, he laughed. He pointed his cup towards Jack. 'If you're looking for good pay and some adventure, you could do worse than join up. We got rules, mind, but we still fairly well can do as we like.'

Jack smiled. 'So what are you doing in here? Guard duty?'

Weems chuckled and shook his head slowly. 'Cheeky little sod. Aye, guard duty. And enjoying the peace of Burgundy. When there's no campaign we do want we want. Within reason, mind. Like I told you, we have rules. And if you break them, aye well, then it's the noose.'

Jack was intrigued and intimidated by his new comrades. The boredom of recent days had disappeared like a fleeting summer downpour and he could maybe, just maybe, dream about sunnier times.

'What do you play with then?' asked Weems. 'That a good arming sword you have there? Ever handled a pole arm?'

Jack glanced down at his hilt. 'I know a little. Played with a glaive. But I'm a sword and buckler man. And a crossbowman besides.'

Weems stuck out a forefinger. 'Now that, my lad, is what our banner captain is looking for. Our complement of bowmen has dwindled this past year. You have harness. Weapons. Cock and balls. Just need to take the oath.'

Jack felt himself pulling back. It was becoming all too real for him. 'My lord will be looking for me. I must go now.' He managed to extricate himself from the giants either side but as he pushed himself up, both hands on the table edge, a large hand clamped down on his wrist. The German next to him, a man with pock-marked cheeks and a bulbous nose as red as a medlar, looked up and glared at him.

'*Bezahlen*!'

He'd heard that in Flemish from Jacob. The soldier was asking him to pay up. He felt his throat go bone dry and sweat instantly tickle his armpits. He hadn't a penny on him. The frightened look on his face must have been obvious for David Weems slapped a coin on the trestle and shouted something in German. The soldier released Jack's wrist and palmed the coin instead.

'So, Englishman,' the Scot said, leaning back on his bench. 'How much is that knight paying you to polish his armour?'

Jack could do no more than give a sheepish grin of embarrassment.

'Aye, then. If you fancy fair pay and loyal comrades, we've made camp outside the north walls, a wee stone's throw away. Look for our fähnlein – our company's banner – the blue and the red.'

13

The clanking of their gleaming harness and arms sounded magnificent. The guard of escort comprised two *landsknechts*, Jacob de Grood, and young Jack Perry: the Germans leading and Jacob and Jack following – side by side, in their wake. Behind walked Hawker and Ellingham, both dressed in the finest clothes they could find: some wealthy merchants' cast-offs. And at Ellingham's right walked Gaston Dieudonné, sieur de Liancourt, an exile from lands now under the heel of the French king. Dieudonné's finery matched that of the Englishmen, the addition of a narrow white heron feather spray in his mulberry wool bonnet somehow setting him off from the other two. Hawker's *cinquedea* bounced rhythmically at his side, Ellingham's Hungarian studded rondel dagger was cinched up high on his red leather belt. Both wore velvet bonnets of black, somewhat frayed at the brims.

Those people who congregated across the great square and the wide street thoroughfare leading to the ducal palace ceded passage like a parting sea as they approached. Giles thought perhaps it was too flamboyant a parade but Hawker reminded him that the look they cultivated would colour how they were received. If one looks to be worthless, then they are duly treated so. Once at the white stone archway to the palace they were halted. The Germans parted, Jacob and Jack moved to the side and the three were ushered into the high-ceilinged hall.

Giles had worked hard to convince Hawker to let Dieudonné attend too. Hawker had grumbled that the Burgundian was not party to their business, but Giles had said he had been part of the company from the beginning and deserved the honour. No sooner had they stepped over the threshold when a halberd barred the Burgundian's passage.

'Only the knights,' growled the captain of the guard, standing off to the side. 'Your comrade must wait outside with your men-at-arms.'

Giles watched Dieudonné puff himself up in outrage. 'Giles, will you let this oaf tell you who you may keep as your companion? Where is the châtelain?'

Hawker did not repress his satisfaction, a thin smile breaking momentarily upon his face. 'Wait upon us!' he scolded. 'Do not throw our audience into question.'

Giles placed a hand on Dieudonné's forearm. 'Gaston, I beg you, do not protest. Wait outside.'

The Burgundian narrowed his eyes and shot Hawker a look of disdain. 'Very well, my prince. I yield to your wishes.' With that he turned upon his heels and went out, infuriated, flapping his short mantle and stomping away like some posturing rooster in a farmyard.

Giles gave Hawker an embarrassed look. 'I know he is prideful but such treatment would hurt any man of his station.'

Hawker loosened his cloak. 'We are not here for his benefit.'

Sir Olivier de la Marche approached from further down the immense vaulted hall with the rolling gait of a man who had spent much time in a war saddle.

'Gentles! Welcome! Her Grace is ready to receive you both!'

Hawker made to move forward but a *landsknecht* stepped in front. The captain pointed to Hawker's dagger and then Giles's.

'I'm sorry,' said Sir Olivier, 'I should have reminded you. No steel in the presence of the duchess. You may leave your blades here.'

They were ushered past a receiving chamber and deeper into the palace where the rooms were smaller and more intimate.

Sir Olivier stopped at a set of polished double doors of oak and turned to them both. 'She is aware of who you are, Sir

Giles,' he said quietly. 'And, Sir John, I have explained your situation of recent years. I believe she is better disposed than previously.' He then swivelled his head towards Giles. 'But I caution you! Let her dictate the conversation. Say nothing rash.'

Giles nodded his assent but now was more confused and uneasy than before. Exactly what was he to say? Or not say? He could already feel his palms tingling with sweat. He was about to meet his paternal aunt. He realised he had never met any of his blood until his father had knighted him a week before the debacle at Bosworth. He feared rejection, but now – in the moment – he feared acceptance even more for what it might force upon his shoulders. The châtelain knocked once, paused briefly, and opened the doors.

She stood at the other end of the tapestry-filled chamber, rays of sunlight pouring through the tall windows which lined the room, motes of dust dancing and floating in the draught. Giles noticed two guards poised at the door behind where she stood. He and Hawker approached the small dais at a slow walk. From the brief audience of over a year before, he had forgotten how tall she was – as tall as he – and very handsome for her years. Her high forehead accentuated her large grey eyes, fine nose and alabaster complexion. She stood, hands clasped at her front, dressed in a flowing gown of brocaded gold and claret, alive with embroidered roses and acanthus. In widowhood, she still stood proud and commanding, a daughter of the House of York and regal in her own right.

Sir Olivier stood to one side and Hawker and Giles doffed their hats and dropped to one knee at her feet. Slowly, she reached out and held her right hand in front of Giles. He leaned in, gently grasped the long fingers, and touched them softly to his lips. She did not offer Hawker the same opportunity.

'I thought there was something about the young man who briefly walked with me in the garden all those months ago,' she said coolly. 'I spied something of familiarity in your face. Now the mystery is clear.'

'My lady,' replied Giles, his mouth dry. 'We did not conspire to conceal the truth from you. It just seemed… prudent… given our precarious situation. And you would have had little reason to believe me.'

She looked down upon him and nodded, perhaps satisfied.

Margaret then turned to Hawker. 'Sir John, you have found your way back here as well after your adventures in the east. Further word of your prior service to my brothers has been brought to me. More detail, shall we say. I was rash in assuming you had failed in your oaths to them both. Who knows? There might be yet another turn you could afford the cause. When the time comes.'

Hawker bowed his head deeply but did not reply. The duchess dowager half-turned and took a seat in the ornately carved and gilded chair behind her, settling the folds of her gown.

'You both may rise.'

Giles stood and watched her, hands clasped, looking to read her mood. But she had acknowledged him, even if only indirectly. He quickly realised she was remaining focused on his face, a look of inquisitive interest and an expression in her eyes that was almost hopeful in nature. She seated herself in an ornately carved and gilded throne.

She pointed at Giles's hand. 'I see you wear my brother's sigil.'

'Yes, your Grace.' He glanced over to Hawker. 'Gifted to me by Sir John, for it was given to him by King Richard. As a token of thanks.'

Hawker's eyes met Giles's, but his face was unreadable.

Margaret set both hands on the arms of the throne. 'Your father was a noble man and a gifted ruler. But he made more enemies than friends. And he made them more quickly than he could deal with them. There is a fine line between being bold and being impetuous. I fear Richard may have strayed too far into the latter. And my heart is still filled with sorrow for him.'

She had said it. He felt his chest flutter a moment. Her words still ringing in his ear.

'Alas,' she continued, 'my late husband, the duke, was of a similar disposition. It brought him to ruin as it did my brother. I would offer a counsel to you, Sir Giles. Guard the truth of your lineage well. I do not think revealing it to the world will benefit you greatly. Our enemy is ruthless beyond measure. And though you be a bastard, without claim, it would be no great thing for them to pursue you, merely to eliminate another branch of the tree. Do you understand me?'

He nodded. And he understood. He would remain in the shadows and never carry the Plantagenet name.

She looked over to Hawker. 'Do you not agree, Sir John?'

'Your Grace, it is what I have counselled these many months.'

'I have given you some mark of my favour since your return to Malines. That was for past service to the crown. Now, there may be more opportunity for you to gain further favour.'

'I remain fully in your service, your Grace. As does Sir Giles.'

She acknowledged his pledge with a deep nod. Her eyes flashed sternly. 'I mean to bring war to Henry Tudor. To root the stinking Welsh badger out of his uneasy hole and to destroy him. To that end, my Lord Lovell and the Earl of Lincoln are plotting an invasion. One that the Burgundian and Imperial treasury will support with men and ships. But there is much work to be done. Sir Olivier will tell you more. And of what you might do to aid the cause.'

She stood. The signal that the audience was at an end. Sir Olivier bowed low and turned to the Englishmen. 'My lords...'

Giles reached into his doublet and pulled out the small thing he had concealed.

'Your Grace, as a token of my affection and loyalty... I give you this.'

And he handed her the last Tear of Byzantium, glistening in his fingers, a rough ruby wrapped in golden wire like the strands of a spider's web.

She deftly plucked it from his hand, studied it a moment, and then looked at him gravely. Giles felt his heart rise up into his mouth.

'What was lost has now been found?' she muttered. And she looked over to Hawker.

Giles glanced at his comrade a moment and saw the knight's eyes were huge with surprise.

'No, my lady,' said Giles. 'It was taken in Wallachia. And it is the last of the treasure of Prince Vlad Dracula, scourge of the Ottomans and defender of the Faith. And, if it would please you, I would have it back as the seed to raise a lance of men in your service.'

Her line-thin eyebrows moved higher. 'You are full of surprises, Sir Giles. Your gift finds favour and is gratefully received. And it is now... returned.' She held it out again for him to accept. 'Therein must lie a tale worth telling about this little treasure. I will send for you again. In the not-too-distant future.'

The *châtelain* had by now flushed a deep red. 'Retire, my lords,' he said, *sotto voce*.

Hawker bowed and turned as did Giles and they rapidly made their way to the doors.

'How?' hissed Hawker. 'And for the love of Christ, why? She knew full well it was the Tear!'

Giles kept looking straight ahead as they re-entered the hall. 'It is *a* Tear. And it was Dieudonné's. His to give. He gave it to *me*. And it is as you said: I must look after myself now.'

Sir Olivier caught them up, huffing with consternation. '*Boy*, is your knowledge of French so poor that you do not know the meaning of rash? You are indeed your father's son!'

–

Gaston Dieudonné seethed. He'd wrapped his arms around himself, leaning against the outside of the palace far below the long mullioned windows above. He was practically trembling with anger, inflamed by a growing sense of abandonment. How could he not be granted an audience alongside Giles? He had, of his own free will, given Giles the gemstone. Foolish in retrospect as he had not insisted on some sort of promise that Giles would get him inside. It was beyond galling. Why hadn't Giles protested, *insisted* that he join them?

The Fleming and the simpleton of a boy stood apart from him, sharing some jest. De Grood reached over and gave a playful slap to Jack's helm. Dieudonné looked the other way. Had he not professed his loyalty – his love – for Giles? Now, for the first time, he was beginning to question how his little infatuation, maybe his lust, was making him forget his common sense. Instincts of self-preservation, honed over years, tossed out like shit from a chamber pot. He groaned aloud, filled with embarrassment. And his anger simmered.

Hawker was a boil that needed lancing. Giles had come far in the past months, sliding ever closer under his own wing, but still Hawker was there to pull the golden youth away. Had he grown weak and complacent? Too cautious? Perhaps his affections were dulling his decision-making. A year ago he would not have hesitated to eliminate a problem when it first raised its head, before it became a threat. Now, he questioned just how much he himself had changed. For the worse.

His eyes glanced down the wide cobbled thoroughfare to where the ducal palace blended into an ancient church, no more than twenty paces from where he stood. A group of well-dressed merchants conversed – too far for him to hear. But one of the group stood slightly apart and more noticeably, was looking in his direction. The man made brief eye contact then turned again to his comrades before again glancing over. Dieudonné unfolded his arms, looked down for a few moments, then walked to where de Grood stood.

'Enough of this,' he muttered loudly. 'I don't have to wait here with you. It is your task, not mine.'

De Grood looked at him dispassionately. 'You may do as you choose. I am not your keeper.'

Jack's eyes widened but he kept silent.

Dieudonné harrumphed and turned his back on them both, ambling slowly in the direction of the gaggle of chattering merchants. His gaze focused again on the lone man who had shown interest in him.

As the fellow's features came into clearer view – aquiline nose, thick lips and piercing blue eyes – Dieudonné instantly felt his chest seize in shock. He checked his pace and stopped, stomach tightening. He *knew* the man, and worse, the man knew and recognised him. He was staring right back, absolutely immobile.

He was a Frenchman like himself and, also like Dieudonné, a pretender of station, of loyalties, and of nations. Dieudonné had met him in Brittany when they both were in the orbit of Jasper Tudor in exile, worming their way into favour by doing whatever it took to be noticed. And both had followed Jasper and his young nephew, Henry, in their invasion of England, hoping for preferment and wealth should Richard's crown fall. While Dieudonné stood there, his eyes locked on the other, his first rational thought was as to *why* Armand Moreau was standing ten feet away in the main square of Malines. Moreau had been a spy for the Tudors as well as the French and if he still remained so, what was he doing in the heart of Flanders and Brabant – territory of the Burgundian enemy?

Dieudonné blinked rapidly a few times, his brain trying to calculate the possibilities. Moreau had either gone over to Burgundy or, more realistically, was still working for the French. Either way, Dieudonné knew he could not afford to let the man slip away. He had been seen. The threat was real. He started walking again, veering slightly away from the group but keeping his gaze locked on Moreau. Moreau interjected something to his comrades then they all moved off at a walking pace, rounding the next corner. Dieudonné followed. They had not gone far when Moreau said something else to his comrades and then turned back the way he had come. They carried on and Moreau began to walk steadily towards Dieudonné.

Armand Moreau placed himself in front of him, smiling. It was knifing distance.

'Gaston Dieudonné, sieur de Liancourt. Or has that title worn out its usefulness? I see that you remember me.'

Dieudonné gave a court bow, touching his bonnet and setting his heron spray quivering. 'I do remember you, dear Armand. But I confess I am surprised to see you here of all places. Have you wandered too far north?'

The man's eyes narrowed ever so slightly. 'I am exactly where I choose to be. The bigger question is why are you here? Seems you have made new friends.'

'Maybe we both have the same master still,' said Dieudonné playfully. 'You are no merchant. Nor am I. What would you say if I told you I could deliver up the outlaw Sir John Hawker? King Henry would pay a hefty bounty for that prize, would he not?'

Moreau looked past Dieudonné and then his eyes darted either side, checking for new arrivals. 'Hawker?' he sniffed. 'I think you have the heftier price on *your* head, my old friend. My lord Bedford did not take kindly to your murder of his servant after the victory at Bosworth. He was fond of that young Breton.' He raised a gloved forefinger. 'Ah yes... and also his two factors in Venice whom you brutally butchered. No, I speak wrongly. Three. If you include *their* servant.'

Dieudonné shook his head, smiling. 'The Breton... that was an accident. Play gone wrong. The others were Hawker's doing. You must believe it. I have been deep into his confidence these many months. My plan has been to find out all I can of the White Rose. To make myself useful. And I am nearly ready to offer the feast to your master. My master still.'

He was taking a huge gamble he knew. Moreau might be in the act of double-crossing the Tudors and here to offer his services to the Burgundians. Or may have already done so. Moreau looked at him with undisguised disdain. But he had not turned on his heels.

'You are foolish to be airing such fancies here in a public square. And I the bigger fool for giving you a hearing. And you've not mentioned the young sprig of the fallen tree. The one I saw you arrive in the company of. Would you deliver him up as well?'

Dieudonné reached over and was about to gently lay his hand on Moreau's arm when the Frenchman pulled back, taking half a step, eyes growing larger. 'Keep your place!' he hissed. 'You are being watched where we stand. I would never be so foolish as to entreat with you on my own. People have a way of ending up dead after a conversation with you, Dieudonné.'

Gaston Dieudonné feigned a look of hurt. 'What good would be served by taking young Ellingham? He is a bastard and no threat to Henry.'

He knew the stakes of this game would be raised sooner or later. Hawker was not enough. And the situation was moving faster than he could think through.

'Then what is he doing here?' spat out Moreau. 'Conspiring at the court. If he is no threat he would have stayed in England swearing fealty to his new king.'

'My dear Armand, he is of no consequence. But there is also real treasure to be had. From Hawker's journey to the east. A casket full of gems. Would that buy your confidence? Along with Hawker's head, of course.' He'd worry about finding a treasure later. For now, it was all he could do to draw Moreau into his own net.

'I must return to my companions. What sort of cow-brained scheme are you proposing?'

'We make plans for me to deliver Hawker up to you. You take as much of the reward as you wish. Just explain my absence to my lord Bedford. Tell of how I burrowed deep into the rebels' conspiracy.'

Moreau threw a rapid glance back to where his companions waited. 'If you are in earnest, Dieudonné, you will meet me this eve – at the Three Bells. I will give you my decision then.'

He made to turn and then looked at Dieudonné again. 'And do not think to follow me any further. It would not end well for you.'

Armand Moreau gave him one last narrow-eyed glare and then swiftly walked away.

Dieudonné watched him rejoin the group of four gentlemen, exchange a few words, and then all of them carried on. The Frenchman knew this day would be the most dangerous time for his survival. Moreau might already be playing him, but equally – if he was spying for the Tudors – Moreau's life was just as much in jeopardy in Malines as his own. Neither trusted the other, but both had revealed themselves. That was a vulnerability he could use if need be. He had no choice but to meet Moreau and see if he could entice him, despite the risk of being taken himself. He would worry later about how to lure Hawker into capture. And if worse came to worst, he would tonight find out where Armand Moreau lay his head abed. One always needed options.

14

Her face was alive with anticipation when he entered, her almond eyes, sea-grey, opened wide and searched his face for clues even before he spoke. When Hawker's thin lips broke into a smile, her face glowed anew.

'Tell me all, Giovanni!'

He swept her up in his arms and rocked her close to him. Burying his face into her hair, he spoke quietly. 'All will be well. The duchess has found favour with us. We may stay here. So long as I do her some small service from time to time.'

Hawker felt her head pull away slightly from the caress of his lips.

'Does that mean she wishes you to be her condottiere? To fight again?'

Hawker released her gently and looked into her face. 'My love, *that* duty now falls to Sir Giles. As is right and proper. He has offered to raise a small company in her service. I believe she is content to keep me closer to the palace. Counsel and such like.'

Chiara hugged him tightly. 'I have prayed for such news. That we might be free to live our lives in peace. Raise our son… a son you will live to see grow happy and strong.'

'Well then, I must put away my harness and take up the quill and ledger.'

She laughed a little, reaching for the back of his neck. 'I can do that as well. I did so before. We will not bother with wool! We will import the best silks from Florence. The only battle you need fight is with anyone else in Malines foolish enough to challenge our trade! Giovanni, I have already spied out how few merchants here offer such cloths. We will prosper, I know it.'

Hawker smiled and nodded. 'I believe you. But it will take gold to build such an empire. And what pension the duchess affords me is precious little to accomplish that.'

Chiara grimaced a little. 'But there is still *my* gold... what I brought out of Venice. And you must still have some you left with the Medici bankers. Your letters of credit?'

'There is not as much as you suppose, my love. It is there as a last resort for us. And as for your ducats, well, they are already fewer, are they not? For what comforts we enjoy now.'

She pulled herself up tall and gripped his shoulders. 'Then, we begin small and work hard. We can do whatever we wish! Find those who might wish to invest.'

'The palace might aid us in such an endeavour, 'tis true. But I am an old war dog. You will have to teach me the ways of the merchant. I usually bark when a honeyed tongue is required.'

She smiled up at him. 'I will teach you, husband. Have no fear.' She pulled him along by the hand to the best chair. 'Sit here a while. I shall fetch you a cup of wine.'

He did as she bade, listening to the soft crying of Nicholas upstairs and the singing of his nursemaid doing her best to quieten him. As soon as he sat, he relaxed, his legs and feet stretching out towards the glowing embers of the hearth. Chiara returned from the cramped buttery with his drink, placing it in his hands and folding his fingers around the cup. She knelt down next to him.

'And what shall become of Jack Perry? And your man Jacob?'

Hawker's chin fell to his chest. 'Jacob I will release from my service... if he chooses to join with Sir Giles. But perhaps, he too, has tired of war. I do not know.' He chuckled. 'But his father would be glad of it, I am certain.'

'But the boy... he is too young to decide where his future lies. He is devoted to you and will listen to what you tell him.'

Hawker sipped his ale, staring into the red, smoking embers. 'He believes himself a squire, though he be no such thing. I am a broken, poor knight and could never raise him to be what he desires. Would that I could convince him to become an apprentice. It would be a far better prospect than the life of a man-at-arms. I have no wish to see that boy butchered on a field in Flanders or Brittany. Nor in England. For that is next on the cards.'

'He *will* listen, my love.'

Hawker regarded her, pensive. 'He is already in love with killing, I fear. And I have made him. He has only ever known war. It will be difficult to undo the handiwork that has been done. Christ, forgive me.'

—

'Your pride was so dented that you could not wait until Hawker and I came back!'

Dieudonné gave a shrug. 'You know my nature, my prince. I meant no disrespect. But it was *I* who gave you the jewel to give. I should have been with you there. Standing alongside.'

Ellingham tossed his mantle to the chair in front of him. 'And I am grateful for the gift. It has done its work.'

Dieudonné lifted his head a little. 'She has accepted you? And the jewel?'

'Aye. Though I am to remain Giles Ellingham. By her command. But I will raise a company to serve the coming campaign. In England. And the ruby will buy me a few men at least.'

The Burgundian risked a smile. 'So then, she will grant you another audience? Perhaps bestow her own token of favour upon you?'

Ellingham nodded. 'I believe it is possible. She took kindly to me and did not resent the fact that I had concealed my identity when last we met.'

'That was Hawker's doing.'

Ellingham shook his head. 'At that time, Sir John's counsel was the right one. But time has moved on. Will you stand by me or sulk? I need you, Gaston. To build our lance with me. Find men. Money. Burgundy is throwing its weight and its purse behind a new invasion to be led by Lord Lovell – and the Earl of Lincoln.'

Dieudonné's ears pricked up even more. 'So, you are privy to the plans? When will they sail? And at which coast will they make landfall?'

Ellingham threw himself into the chair on top of his mantle. 'Ah, Gaston, I do not know. We are to be called back – to a council, I presume – to meet the nobles and play our part.'

Dieudonné's heart sank. A few morsels of intelligence might have helped his suit with Moreau. He had but little. And until he met the man again, he could not know if he was still a spy for the Tudors. He might have already double-crossed them and be in the service of France or Burgundy. Luring him into a trap. He felt his stomach churn and he clenched and unclenched his hands, nerves taking over.

'Are you well?' Ellingham sat up and leaned forward. 'You have flushed as red as a rose.'

Dieudonné swallowed hard. 'A bit queasy of that capon we finished this morning. I will recover. Shall we take some wine? It might settle my stomach.'

Ellingham nodded. 'That would go down easy now. I'm fair parched after meeting the duchess. I thought I would jump out of my own skin and could scarce believe I was there, in the palace and meeting her after all this time.'

'I will fetch us the wine if it has not soured.' He moved off to the small storeroom at the back of the house. In the dwelling next door, a man was beating his wife. Dieudonné could hear her anguished cries. A piece of furniture thumped, then more shouts. It elicited no sympathy but reminded him that violence could come to visit without warning. He could feel his heart pounding again. Too much uncertainty for his liking, this nagging fancy that at any moment an armed party of palace guards could pour through the front door, Armand Moreau standing behind them, forefinger pointing. He knew he had to keep his head, think his way forward. He had done it before. In Venice. And even before that, in France and Brittany. But he also knew his impulsive side, the darker nature that sometimes overruled him. He knew he must keep that beast in check to find his way out of the maze he now found himself in.

He carried the stoneware flagon into the hall where Ellingham sat, legs splayed, slouched in the chair, long russet-coloured gown in disarray. His green hose and codpiece were on display, distracting and annoying Dieudonné in his present mood. For his part, Ellingham looked to be far away.

Dieudonné handed him a cup of Rhenish red, just this side of drinkable. Ellingham looked up at him as he accepted it.

'You are behind me on all this, are you not, Gaston? You will help me build a company – in my own right?'

Dieudonné forced a fulsome smile. 'Of course, my prince.' He still burned a little at being cut out at the palace. He would make sure that did not happen again. And in the back of his mind he was still wrestling with how he could betray Hawker but not endanger Giles. It would not be an easy thing to accomplish. Nor had Giles done much to earn his protection. 'Why would I not stand by you?'

Ellingham sipped the wine, grimaced slightly, and took another sip. 'If my cousin Lincoln shares his confidences with me, then I shall be at the centre of the rebellion and earning a place in command. Do you not agree?'

Dieudonné smiled again. The Earl of Lincoln didn't know Giles from Adam. The youth was getting carried away by misplaced enthusiasm – or faith. 'Perhaps, yes perhaps. But one must tread carefully here, you understand. You do not know that Plantagenet prince. Not yet, at least.'

Ellingham's brows knitted briefly and then he had another drink. 'Yes, you are right, Gaston. Best not to seem too eager. Our friendship must grow. It will... it must.'

Dieudonné smiled again, sympathetically. 'You will triumph. Have no fear.'

They finished their wine in silence and then Ellingham stood. 'I must go pay a visit to Sir John. He was most vexed with my little surprise to the duchess dowager. I'm afraid I handled that rather badly.'

'Nonsense, it was yours to give... or not give. He will have to learn to accept you are a knight in your own right, not his retainer.'

Ellingham retrieved his over-mantle and threw it around his shoulders. 'Still, I must not let him fall into black thoughts again. He is already wrestling with his own worries. That I know for certain. Will you not come with me?'

Dieudonné shook his head slowly. 'Nay, I do not think that would aid your effort, dear Giles. Best you speak with him alone.'

'Then we shall sup later?'

'I am not quite myself this afternoon. I think I will take the air about the town. Clear my head.' He gave a little laugh. 'Who knows, I might venture beyond the gates!'

Ellingham's face showed a trace of genuine concern. 'Are you well enough? Perhaps you should take to your bed.'

Dieudonné laughed lightly. 'There is no better physik than a walk in the brisk air with oneself. I will be back by nine of the clock, rest assured.'

—

The brief purple haze of twilight had descended upon Malines, the sun passing below the tiled roofs and chimneys of the town and fast dissolving into night. Dieudonné made his way from their house near the south gate towards the centre, a lone presence among scattered groups of townsfolk heading to their home and hearth. The bright sun of the day had warmed the place but now the air was already becoming brisker with a chill descending.

He had stolen old workman's clothing earlier from an unattended wash line: a hempen shirt stained from years of wear, and a mid-length tunic of coarse, undyed beige wool. To these he had added a padded coif for his head and a dark brown cloak and hood, also of coarse, napped wool. His skinny legs were in green hose, feet shod in a pair of well-worn brown leather shoes. For his imminent rendezvous, he needed to look as ordinary as possible and as different as possible from the peacock he usually dressed like.

He hung about the side streets, waiting for darkness to descend totally. When it had done so, he made his way north, across the main square and stunted tower of Saint Rumbold's and into a less salubrious neighbourhood near the town walls. The Three Bells tavern he had known over the previous months. As he approached, he saw an iron brazier burning to illuminate the front, stuffed with bits of old wooden planks. A symbol of welcome to the thirsty of a cold winter's evening. Dieudonné lowered his chin, the front of his hood pulled down over his forehead, and walked through the wide-open doorway.

The place was full to bursting. His eyes scanned the tables and benches, lighted by cheap tallow candles. The burble of dozens of conversations buzzed in his ears, the occasional raucous laughter breaking the steady, underlying drone. He recognised Armand Moreau's heavy features quickly. The man was seated at a table near a window with five others. But Dieudonné noticed that he was not conversing with any of them. He was on his own, grasping his cup of wine and staring into space. That was a good start. Dieudonné went to the back where the barrels were arrayed, a long wooden rail in place in front of them. He put down a coin and gestured to a servant.

Cup in hand, Dieudonné made his way over and pushed through the gaps between benches. Moreau looked up and saw him, but said nothing. After some effort, Dieudonné made his way in and gently prodded a neighbour to slide over. The Frenchman sat down at the table directly next to Moreau and on his right side.

'I see you decided to come rather than run and hide.'

Dieudonné splayed his hands on the table and kept his chin down. 'I told you what I can offer. I am here to learn if you can offer something in return.' Their voices were low, the others at the table animated in their own conversations. Moreau had chosen the location wisely. No dark alleys for him: this place was stuffed with people and any violence would not be tolerated, with escape unlikely.

Moreau raised his cup and took a long drink. Dieudonné wasn't sure how long the man had been there but he could see the jug near the cup was nearly empty. 'I can promise you nothing, Gaston. Neither mercy nor payment. That is not for me to decide. If you wish to prove your loyalty, then an act of faith will be required.'

He had expected no less. But it made it sound as if Moreau was on his own in the town, working to gather intelligence with no one to report it to. He quickly scanned the crowd to see if anyone was showing undue attention to them. No one watched. 'I told you I can deliver Hawker. What more is there?'

'You will deliver him… and yourself. Then there are the stones you mentioned. That will help your suit, I'm sure.' Even in the darkened tavern, he could see how mottled Moreau's face was from drink, flushed and sweating. He had known him briefly in Brittany, serving in Jasper Tudor's retinue in exile. He'd never really liked the man, finding him oleaginous but without the charm needed to make oleaginous a tolerable quality. Just another climber who had hacked his way to a position of importance. If he was truly on his own, Moreau might need him to give himself up to help manage Hawker's transport. But it was more likely he would end up in a dark cell being tortured for what he knew of Plantagenet scheming in Flanders. So far, he was not liking the arrangements on offer.

'I will have to lure him out of the town. Someplace you can intercept us. Have you others?'

Moreau grinned at that, licking his fat lips. 'I will tell you what you need to know. Not necessarily what you want to know. There is a house here, in the town. Bring him that far and the rest will be done.'

'And you will get me out? Back to France? Or England?'

'My tale of good report will put you in good stead. I can promise no more.'

'That is precious little to put my faith in.'

Moreau shrugged. 'Gaston, I need but pass word to the palace – with a few details – and your safety in here in Malines will be even less certain than what I am offering. And even though you are a bad man, Gaston... you were very, *very* bad in England. Doing in that poor boy for reasons I do not wish to know and then running away with the enemy. Then Venice. Think of this as your act of contrition.'

There was an explosion of laughter at the next table and Dieudonné felt his chest almost seize with the shock of it. He swallowed, recovering his composure, and took a sip of his own wine. 'Is that it, then? Bring him to a certain house. Then help you spirit him out.'

'I can supply you with a draught to make him compliant. You can tell anyone he's dead drunk and you're taking him home.'

Dieudonné began to feel trapped. He didn't like the offer and Moreau was clearly closing off his exit should he decide to not play the game. If he could settle for just Hawker delivered, dead or dying, then he might have something worth risking.

'And what of the other. The young one.'

'Yes, I've given that more thought. We need him brought along too. Let the king and his uncle decide on his fate. You and I might be in for censure if it was found we let the young man slip away. Better safe than sorry, no? First him, then Hawker. Same day. They don't share chambers, so it's easily arranged.'

Dieudonné felt his heart begin to sink. 'You are sure of that? The lad is harmless as well as useless.'

'Not for the likes of us to decide, Gaston. You can find another bum-boy easily, no?'

Dieudonné lifted his cup to Moreau. 'Then let us drink to it.'

Moreau eyed him carefully, then raised his own and clanked it against Dieudonné's. 'I will show you the house later. Tomorrow, you deliver.'

Dieudonné smiled at him and touched cups again and drank. He leaned against Moreau, wrapped an arm around his shoulders and gave him a shake. 'I am in your debt, Armand! You have given me salvation.'

Moreau eased himself slightly apart and took another drink. 'You have yet to earn it, my friend.'

Dieudonné laughed – heartily – as if it was some good jest and then slapped Moreau on the back. Moreau shot him a look of puzzlement, but Dieudonné slipped his left arm over the man's shoulder and gently eased him closer. He looked him in the eyes, smiling. 'And you, Armand, have yet to deserve it.'

Dieudonné felt the man instantly tense but it was too late. Dieudonné's right hand and the stiletto it contained, moved like lightning. The square blade had a tip so sharp a barber-surgeon would have been envious. It slipped straight into Moreau's doublet below the breastbone, concealed by the table edge. The fulsome shove of Dieudonné's wrist sent it straight into Moreau's heart. The man jerked but once, stiffening, a stifled cry on his lips that others might hear as a repressed burst of laughter. With his arm still wrapped around Moreau's shoulders, Dieudonné gently brought his head down onto the table, wrapping a limp hand around the man's cup.

'You never could hold your drink!' said Dieudonné, his voice elevated slightly. And he sat there, finishing his own cup with one hand patting Moreau's back. He sat for no longer than a minute or two, already worrying that Moreau would begin to puddle the floorboards even though the stiletto left but a small hole. He concealed the stiletto again and stood, extricating himself from the bench. He grabbed the wine jug and announced he'd be back with more – but not too loudly. Keeping the hood of his cloak up, he slowly made his way through the throng to the door.

Once outside, he rapidly headed east through the streets, making his way to the outside rear of a church where he had stored a bundle of other clothing near the buttresses of the nave. He hurriedly changed, rolled up his old, worn clothes and moved to the canal that ran nearby. Once these were tossed into the water, they rapidly floated downstream. He then took the sticky iron stiletto and flicked it away into the canal where it plopped and sank. Dieudonné made a wide sweep of the town at a normal pace, heading east then turning west again before returning home.

He was deeply disappointed. It all could have worked out so perfectly had Moreau not been so uncompromising. But at least his stomach wasn't queasy any more. He had solved the chief problem.

Part III

A CONTRARY WIND

15

Sir Olivier's chambers at the Malines palace seemed no less grand than those of the duchess dowager, thought Hawker. High-ceilinged and finely plastered, the room held just a table and chairs and a fire at one end. Two great cupboards stood on the far wall bearing many pieces of silver plate and one huge, colourful ceramic charger, balanced precariously on the uppermost shelf. He and Ellingham sat side by side at one end of the great table. Sir Olivier sat at the head, and opposite sat Francis Lord Lovell and John de la Pole, the Earl of Lincoln. Never had he ever expected to be in such company. One a bosom companion of Richard since boyhood, the other two Plantagenet princes: one legitimate, the other a bastard. He was more used to receiving his orders in hushed tones, delivered in private closets, dungeons or kitchen hallways. What young Ellingham next to him made of it all, he could only guess.

The boyish earl leaned forward. 'Her Grace has told us to admit you to our confidence. Two loyal knights of our late sovereign. We welcome you.'

Hawker bowed his head briefly. The earl looked not much older than Ellingham. He had supposedly been at Bosworth Field, but Hawker had not glimpsed him there. The same for Lord Lovell. But here were both men again, now together in exile and planning to return to the fight against the Tudor usurper.

'Sir Giles,' said Lovell, 'I am sorry to be the bearer of sad news. Your father, Sir Thomas, departed this life some months ago. I expect you had no word of that.'

Ellingham blinked a few times. 'No, my lord, I had not received word.'

'I do not have the particulars, but I understand it was from natural causes.'

Hawker watched Ellingham. The youth seemed to offer little emotion, if any. But did Lovell know of his true parentage?

'As you were his only surviving child,' said Lovell softly, 'his estates are by right yours now. But Henry has nipped that in the bud, as you can probably guess. I thought you should know. It gives you yet another reason to join us. If you needed any other.'

'I have a bushel of good reasons to fight on, my lord.' Ellingham's voice was flat.

'We all received God's grace that we survived that day in August,' continued Lovell. 'We may now gather our forces again to give challenge and this time we shall have victory.'

Hawker knew that Lovell's little rebellion the previous summer had fizzled like damp gunpowder in a breech. 'It will take a sizeable army. The usurper has had over a year to build his support. Buy his loyalties using confiscated lands. How do you propose to raise the men?'

Lovell quickly glanced over to the young nobleman next to him. 'Ever the practical tactician is my old sword master!' He turned back to Hawker and smiled. 'We have managed to convince the duchess – and the emperor – to finance the expedition. They will supply over two thousand landsknechts as well as the ships and supplies.'

'With respect, my lords, that is not near enough.'

'No, it is not. That is why we sail first to Ireland. The Earl of Kildare will bring a few thousand more infantry and men-at-arms. It will be enough to make a landing in England. Once there, the disaffected will flock to the standard in the north. We make for York and then work our way south to London. We take Henry and his army where he meets us.'

'With a new king at the head of our column,' said Hawker without irony.

Lovell smiled and again looked to Lincoln. 'You are well informed, Sir John. Prince Edward, nephew to King Edward and King Richard, will be crowned in Dublin. He is already there, awaiting us. When the news is spread, the country will rise up.'

'You mean the son of the Duke of Clarence, the same who is held by Henry in the Tower?'

'*That* boy is an imposter,' said Lincoln, with more than a hint of irritation.

'I understand,' replied Hawker in a tone of mock apology.

Sir Olivier de la Marche cleared his throat. 'My lords, Sir John knows the situation being faced. We need not discuss it here.'

Hawker guessed that Lincoln had his sights on the crown in the event of victory and that whoever the ten-year-old boy was – changeling or real prince – he would not be wearing it for long.

'We trust Sir John and Sir Giles,' said Lincoln looking directly at Hawker. 'And we will not speak further of the coronation until the time comes. I would rather we would get to the matter at hand. The matter that concerns both these gentlemen.'

Hawker leaned forward and placed his elbow upon the table, clasping his hands. 'I would welcome that, my lord. To hear where we both might fit into the plans.'

'We need more scourers,' said Lovell. '*Prickers.* Men who might precede the invasion and raise hopes of the people. Those with retinues and lands. And we need them between Leicester and Bishop's Lynn all the way to Nottingham. You hail from Stamford. Sir Giles from Middleham.'

'We will give you gold to win hearts,' added Lincoln. 'Spread rumour of our numbers. Of our support. And once we have taken York and march south, you will then join us with whatever force you have managed to gather.'

Hawker smiled and shook his head. 'My lords, you take me for a much younger soldier. Sir Giles could lead such a party and cover far greater distances than I could ever manage.'

Ellingham sat up even straighter in his chair, the anxiety on his face growing. 'If that… is the role you ordain me for…'

'You are too modest, Sir John,' said Lovell with a laugh. 'You have scoured before. In the north when King Richard was still only Duke of Gloucester. You too, Sir Giles. Beating the hedges and chasing down Buckingham's rebels. I know. I was there, too. On the King's Council.'

'I assumed I would be more in the role of counsel in this enterprise,' growled Hawker. 'My days in the saddle are over now.'

'Surely not!' said Lincoln, sitting back. 'You're still hale and could beat half my men-at-arms in single combat. Besides, you've proven yourself at moving with ease in enemy territory, dealing with threats, and, most importantly, surviving them. How else could you have made it from Bosworth to Venice and back again? Sir Olivier tells me you and your company ventured even further, into the Hungarian kingdom in search of treasure.'

'We found little.'

'You found *some*. One stone in particular, I hear.'

Hawker said nothing. He knew neither man, in truth. He did believe that they were committed to toppling Tudor – their adventures over the past year had proved it. They had lost everything in England, just as he had. He detected a more visceral hatred of the Welsh bastard usurper in Lovell, still mourning the loss of his great friend, the king. As for John de la Pole, he seemed to have chosen his side rather late in the game, perhaps when all other options were closed off. But he knew his claim to the throne was far better than Henry Tudor's was. That might be incentive enough.

'My lords,' said Hawker, spreading his hands, 'I have no means to live off the land back there. No friends I may call upon. Did you forget all my years away in the republics?'

'Then begin in Lincolnshire. Old allegiances die hard. I am sure you will find succour there in some corner. It will not be for long. Our army will be advancing quickly after York. You can join us then, once the die is cast. What say you?'

Hawker crossed his arms. 'Well, I will consider it.' He looked over to Ellingham. 'But you would do well to give this man next to me the honour of command in your vanguard. He is deserving of it. Do not tie him to me. My small company has come to an end. He can lead and lead well.'

Lincoln smiled. 'I have no doubt of that, Sir John. My cousin has my affection and my trust.'

Hawker watched Ellingham's eyes widen a little. The youth gave a curt bow of his head.

'But,' continued Lincoln, 'I think he will serve greater purpose alongside you over the next few months. If, indeed, you decide you can serve the cause leading an advance party.'

'I will think upon it, my lord,' replied Hawker, giving a small nod.

'Good. And you will need to depart with all speed should you decide to join us. We will get you the coin you will need. Passage too, to a port where you might slip in unseen.'

'I think we understand, my lords,' said Ellingham, jumping in. 'Time is of the essence to lay the groundwork.'

'And utmost secrecy,' added Lovell. 'Sir Olivier has told us this day that a spy was found in a tavern nearby – dead.'

Hawker looked over to the old Burgundian knight. Sir Olivier seemed to tense his jaw. He nodded.

'Possibly. It was reported to the watch when the tavern master could not rouse him. Seemed suspicious because there had been no brawl reported. The man's only wound was from a narrow blade into his heart. It looks like an assassination.'

'Who was he?' asked Hawker, his alarm growing.

'We don't yet know. But he was new to Malines. Said to be French by those in the tavern. Asking too many questions over the last three days.'

'If he was in the service of the French – or the Tudors – surely your men would have taken him out.'

'Or he fell out with his own,' suggested de la Marche. 'We did not know of him. But we do know there are agents here in the town sniffing about. Have a care. All of you.'

Lord Lovell eased his chair back and stood. 'Then we leave it to you, Sir John, to make your decision. You have professed your desire to save the cause. This is your chance.' Ellingham stood and Hawker reluctantly followed suit.

Lincoln rose also and the two noblemen left together. Sir Olivier remained seated. He looked over to Hawker and sighed. 'I was with the late Duke of Burgundy. At Nancy. It fell to me to identify his body after the battle. Or what was left of it. It is something that forever lives in my mind's eye. I will judge you no less, Sir John, for leaving this war to younger men.'

'I will give you my decision soon,' said Hawker.

When they had left the palace, there was at first silence between them. They walked slowly across the cobbles, heads down. After a minute or two, Ellingham spoke up.

'I will not lie. I'm disappointed that you are averse to the opportunity they offer. We have talked much of the cause. Of fighting on. And now you seem to have given up on it all. You speak of giving your decision soon. You have already made it!'

Hawker slowed and stopped. 'My cause was you. And you have proved yourself. The king would have been proud of his son. It is time for you to lead your own company into battle. I must protect others now – those who cannot protect themselves.'

Giles's jaw went slack. 'And what will you do *here*? Living off the scraps of what the palace might be willing to throw you? You have no land, no property.'

Hawker exhaled heavily and lay a hand on Ellingham's arm. 'Giles, the old life is done for me. I barely survived our adventure in the Saxon lands. You saw that. I am growing slow. Easily winded. It is time for me to make a new life with what time the Lord grants me.'

Ellingham shook his head, as if unbelieving. 'New life? What will you do? You are a *condottiere*!'

'I have written to the silk weavers' guild of Malines. And to the wool men. With what money remains I will set up as a merchant. Bringing in cloths from Florence... from Lucca. Chiara knows the merchants there.'

The look of hurt in Ellingham's eyes was real. 'This strikes me hard, Sir John,' he said quietly. 'And I cannot envision such a life for one as you.'

'You will, in time, Giles. You should go home and draw up your plans. Decide whether you will go on your own and stir up the countryside as Lovell asks, or wait. Wait and sail to Dublin with the main force. Whichever you decide, I know in my heart you will persevere and triumph.'

Ellingham seemed to look off into the distance of the main square. He then turned, without a word, and walked away.

16

She leapt into his arms and wrapped her own around his neck like a love-struck maiden.

'Giovanni!' she said, squeezing him tightly. 'You have made my heart sing!'

Hawker gently grasped her arms and lowered her feet back to the stubble of the winter grass of the yard. 'Well, I told them I would think upon it, but I had already decided before I went to the palace. It is as I told you. We strike out anew. A different venture.'

Her face now had a sweet but determined cast as she looked up at him. 'And I will stand by you, my love. Your help-meet. We will succeed in trade. Here... or anywhere we choose to go. I can feel it in my bones.'

Hawker smiled sheepishly. 'Even if I know nothing of that trade?'

She placed her palm over his heart. 'I will teach you all that I know. And in Venice I did far more of the real work than that bastard I was married to. I have forgotten none of it. You were *condottieri*, Giovanni. You commanded hard men. You can easily command fat and gouty Flemish merchants!'

He did not know what would befall them. How could any mortal man? But standing there, holding her in the small, brick-walled yard, the breeze animating the budding branches of the old apple tree behind her, he felt such a surge of contentment and hope as he had never felt before. 'Then, Chiara, I will be your willing pupil.'

She laughed. '*That*, I am not so sure of. But for my part, I will work hard to master the terrible Flemish tongue. So rough.'

Hawker squeezed her again. 'But you and I – and Nicholas – we will speak Venetian together, no?'

'Always, Giovanni. Always. And –' her face brightened again '– who is to say where we might go next? What do you think of Florence? The Medicis would value a man of your experience. And we would be a long way from the reach of the doge.'

He looped his arm in hers and began to walk back to the house. 'Let us begin our journey with shorter steps. Malines will serve us well.' He paused for a moment. 'Sir Giles took my decision most hard. But, truly, he needs me no more. His aunt has acknowledged him and that was my hope.'

'He is his own man, Giovanni. And a good one. But it is time for him to stand alone.'

'Jacob will be pole-axed by my words. I know. And Jack. Poor Jack.'

'You must tell them both. The sooner the better.'

Hawker nodded slowly. 'Yes. I will go to de Grood's now. Before Sir Giles breaks the news to them.'

Chiara squeezed his hand tightly. 'I will be here waiting when you return. God give you strength.'

His company, now a tiny rump of the five lances of mercenaries he once commanded – one man-at-arms, a would-be squire, an errant knight and his sly companion – was this day about to be pronounced dead and buried.

–

The sound of clashing steel came to his ears as old Bertrand de Grood led Hawker through the maze of his ground-floor dwelling and out the back. Hawker only managed to catch about half of what the old weaver master was saying, but it was clearly a complaint about work, workers and, as usual, his son.

The long wide yard was neat except for the rear where Jacob had sunk a wooden pell into the ground for practice and where no grass now survived. Bertrand called down to his son and then grumbled something under his breath before turning back for the house. Hawker exhaled, took a breath and walked down to where Jacob and Jack stood. They had paused their practice and Hawker saw Jack's face already beaming at his arrival.

'Sir John!' called Jacob. 'You going to join us for a bit of sparring?'

'Not in my finest garb, old friend. Come, both of you, I wish to speak of... matters.'

Jacob rested his blade in the crook of his arms and nodded, his face registering perhaps what he may have expected. 'Of course, Sir John, let's go back inside.'

Jacob led them in and they climbed to the first floor living chambers of de Grood. Hawker passed by the bedchamber where he had lain wounded two years before after he'd been attacked. The memory was stirred afresh as he walked past. Jacob offered him a seat at the round wooden table and then found a jug of wine and some cups. He set to pouring while Hawker sat and regarded Jack Perry. The lad looked nervous, knowing that Hawker had news to impart. When Jacob had joined them and taken his own seat, he then raised his cup.

Hawker lifted his, stared into it a moment, then took a sip. 'I was once told that a poultice is best removed quickly – the pain of it much less than a slow pull.'

Jacob sat back and Jack's brow furrowed.

'I am disbanding the company. I am out of treasure and out of time. A wife and child must be provided for. There will be no more campaigning for me, Jacob.'

Jacob's lower lip rolled down as he digested the words and Jack winced as if he had been stabbed. 'Sir John... that is hard news indeed. I had expected it would come, sooner or later. These past months since we have returned, well... it is no surprise.'

'I must release you from my service. The better for you to sign with a new company, if that is your desire.'

Jacob chuckled. 'Release me? Lord, where would I go? No, if you sheath the sword of war then it must be time for me to do the same. Teaching this lad here his blade work, well, it has made me think *that* could be my new profession. A master-at-arms to the idle youth of this town, perhaps. I'd earn some good coin, I reckon.'

Hawker smiled wanly. 'That you would, my old friend. I am certain.'

Jack's visage had hardened, a scowl taking shape, his ginger-furred lip quivering slightly. He had still said not a word.

'As for you, Jack Perry,' said Hawker softly, 'I am not forgetting you or your good service.'

'Then why am I no longer your squire?' said Jack, his face mottling. 'Have I not served loyally? Fought by your side?'

'Hold your tongue, boy!' growled Jacob, pointing a forefinger.

Hawker raised his chin. 'You have done all those things. And I have looked after you since you were a stripling. I am not about to abandon you. Hear me out.'

The lad's prominent Adam's apple bobbed once.

'I know you have trained hard these past months. And that you were already blooded. That I understand. But change is on the air. Change in the art of war. The time of the old companies of arms is over. It is now about great armies and even mightier warlords and princes. I am old and have had my fill. If you seek out new employ – a new liege lord – you will find only sorrow at the end of that road. Meagre pay and sickness to boot. And death on the field will be the likely end of it all.'

'But you are my knight! My liege lord! And you have broken *your* oath. Not me.'

Hawker swiped his forehead, annoyed. 'Boy! You must listen to me. I want to offer you the chance to find wealth, to survive, find a wife when you are ready. And that chance is by trade. Jacob's father will take you as his apprentice. You will learn, prosper! I will pay for your indenture to him. You'll want for nothing.'

Jack's eyes glistened as he swallowed Hawker's bitter medicine. 'I am already a soldier,' he said hoarsely. 'And I will not sit on my arse at a loom every day. No matter how much you desire it.'

Jacob glanced over to Hawker with raised eyebrows. But he said nothing. He did not need to. Hawker well remembered Jacob's own youthful rebellion against the weaver trade demanded by his father.

'You must sleep upon it, Jack. Do not be hasty. I will be staying here in Mechelen too. For I am going into trade myself. A guildsman, God willing.'

Jacob's head tilted, eyebrows moving higher still.

Jack stood and placed his fingertips on the table. 'You've given me up as your squire. So be it. But I'm still a man-at-arms. I've proven it and it cannot be taken from me. Not even by you, Sir John.'

Hawker felt his heart ache. 'I bring hard truths to you. But know that I love you as my own. I would not counsel you for ill. I beg you to heed me. Think upon it.'

Jack gave him a court bow. 'If that is your will, Sir John, then I will do as you say. May I go?'

'You may go, Jack. With my blessings.'

When he had left, Hawker stared at the scarred table, playing with his cup.

Jacob gave a grunt of contemplation. 'He is more than a boy, Sir John, even if he is not quite a man. But he will not be broken by anyone. And he is already his own captain, whether we like it or not.'

–

Ellingham stood in front of the counter, arms folded across his chest. The goldsmith on the other side held a ruby encrusted in a golden cage between his fingers, and with a grunt, moved it closer to his right eye. The goldsmith's partner moved forward for a look and the one handed it to the other along with a glass lens.

'This gem is eastern in nature, I think. Somewhat Turkish, I might say.' The goldsmith's French was perfect. 'Do you know its provenance?'

Ellingham was hesitant to give too much information. 'Yes, it is from eastern lands. I know little else. What will you give me for it?'

The goldsmith pushed his silk skullcap up on his brow and contemplated the stone as his companion held it. 'I think we can give you nothing for it, sir.'

Ellingham's arms dropped. 'Nothing? It is worth a fortune surely!'

'It is only worth what someone will pay for it.' His companion shrugged and handed the stone back, then muttered something in Flemish. The goldsmith once again studied the gem. 'Your problem is that it is *too* valuable… and too ugly. A stone of this weight and one so crudely cut. It would take time to find a customer with any interest.' He handed the Tear back to Ellingham.

As it plopped into his hand it fell heavier than it had before. He had never expected the gem to prove such a problem and, sadly, it was his last remaining source of wealth. If it could not be sold, then to him it was as good as worthless. The goldsmith must have seen the consternation clear upon his face.

'If you need to rid yourself of it for some coin, you could always go to the Lombards – across town. You can pawn it with them and get something for it, at least. Redeem it when you have come into better fortune. That would be your best path, I am sure.'

Ellingham could say nothing, still stunned by it all. How was he to raise the money to retain and equip a troop of mounted men-at-arms? Pawning the Tear would no doubt provide just a fraction of what he would need to keep a few lances in the field for six months. He mumbled a thank you to the goldsmiths and left. There was probably another goldsmith in Malines, but he felt the result would be much the same. As for the Lombards, he'd have to pay for the luxury of pawning it, paying them interest for as long as they held it in their keeping. He was so dispirited he felt he could not even bother to try.

Gaston's gift had proven to be double-edged. And he'd probably be furious when he heard the news. But without gold, he was staring starkly at the option that Lord Lovell had presented: leading a much reduced company to England, maybe only him and Dieudonné, and stirring sedition prior to the invasion. And the duchess dowager would have to pay for that even. With heavy heart he set off down the street and back to his cramped chambers. Perhaps leaving the gem with Margaret would have been the best course after all. Was it too late to do so?

When Ellingham returned, he found Dieudonné peevish and already at the wine though it was mid-afternoon. Not much more than a day ago, the Burgundian had been buoyant at his revelation that Hawker was giving up command. Dieudonné had then regaled Ellingham with plans for their military success helping to lead the rebellion in England. This current opportunity was what he'd had been hoping for these many months: favour and patronage from great lords in a noble cause.

But now Dieudonné seemed nervous and anxious for no discernible reason. He looked up at Ellingham when he entered, eyes slightly wild.

'You're back. Well, what did you get? Enough to equip us all, God willing.'

'There were no buyers, Gaston. It is too valuable... and too ugly, they said. They told me I'd be better off pawning it.'

Dieudonné sat up and swore. 'They have given you a tale of nonsense! You should have pushed back and bargained. Christ! I should have gone with you. I would not have let them get away with it.'

Ellingham scowled. He didn't like being treated like a servant boy who'd failed at his task. 'There's clearly more to it, Gaston.

Maybe they knew of its provenance. Don't make me out as some simpleton. It *is* a big, ugly stone and one that few people could afford. I should have left it with the duchess.'

Dieudonné scraped his boots along the dirty floorboards and rested his elbows on his knees. 'I am sorry, dear Giles. Just annoyed for you. We will find another way to get the coin.'

'The town seems fretful to me. Those goldsmiths were on edge – as if privy to something I did not know. And the châtelain confided to us that the palace had caught a spy.'

Dieudonné's head snapped up. 'What? When was this?'

'Well, a dead spy, anyway. Found in a tavern with one knife wound. No one even knew there had been a murder. Thought he was drunk. The palace believes he was French.'

'So, just the one *dead* spy then? They've not captured anyone else?'

'I don't think so. At least, not as of yesterday. Do you think they are looking for us? Or maybe just me?'

Dieudonné stood up, agitated. He reached for the wine flagon on the table and poured another cup. He avoided Ellingham's gaze. 'If Hawker can't be bothered to gain more details then you must, Giles.' His voice seemed thick, maybe clouded by the drink. 'We need to know who is in this city and what they are looking for. Perhaps it is already time you go back to Sir Olivier and request an audience with your dear aunt.'

17

Hawker accompanied the finely bedecked merchant into the great Cloth Hall which lay at the top of the market square. Its unfinished belfry – like that of nearby Saint Rumbold's – looked sadly forgotten and bereft. Inside, thought Hawker, it was not much better. There was little of the golden embellishments of some of the other guilds and the cavernous space just looked like a hollow and empty barn. A whistling wind blew through the hammer-beam ceiling rafters. The merchant beckoned Hawker to a long bench at the side of the hall.

The entire place was lined with benches where business was being conducted in low tones. An occasional laugh echoed upwards, carrying across the stone-paved floor.

'My warden will join us, shortly,' said the merchant, the master of the guild. 'Please sit.' Hawker exchanged a few pleasantries in his rudimentary Flemish, optimistic that the guild had agreed to meet with him so quickly. Another man came in soon thereafter. A younger fellow, dressed sombrely, a flopping bonnet tilted across the right side of his head. As he walked, he rested his hand on the golden hilt and scabbard of a fine dagger.

'A good morrow to you, worthy master,' said the man, giving a court bow to him and then to Hawker.

'Sit, Johannes. This is the gentleman we discussed earlier, John Hawker.'

Johannes smiled politely and nodded. 'I remember our conversation.'

The guild master turned to Hawker. 'You of course understand we are not a tradesman's guild. You would not be eligible to belong to one of those as I understand you have no trade – other than war – and have never been apprenticed or made a journeyman.'

Hawker felt his right eyebrow begin to raise.

'You wish entry into the cloth merchants but, as I am an honest and direct man, I must tell you now – that will not be possible.'

Hawker stood up. 'You have yet to hear my plea. And you say it is impossible?'

'Sit, sir, please. I will explain.'

Hawker slowly took his place again on the bench. The warden Johannes was still smiling like a fool.

'The rules are quite clear and strictly adhered to,' said the master gravely. 'You have not been long resident in Mechelen, for one. We have always sought those gentlemen merchants who have roots here – ties of blood and family. From what I know you have none of these.'

Hawker began to quietly simmer, his face becoming warm in spite of the chill of the hall.

'We have on occasion made exception for a few very wealthy Italians from Genoa but, I can assure you, the fee for the privilege was extremely high. Something, I suspect, you would not be able to match. It also required the approval of the town council and the palace.'

'And what if I could meet that bar? Money *and* imperial assent.'

The master lowered his chin slightly. 'Ah, well, there is a strict limit to our numbers and, at the moment, our company is full. So, you see, there really is no way forward. I am truly sorry.'

'Truly sorry,' echoed Johannes, nodding like a donkey.

Hawker knew that these obstacles had been raised just for him. By someone with much more importance. 'And supposing I begin to import my silks anyway? You have no power to stop that.'

The master gave him a pained look. 'We don't. But the council does. And it will empower us to seize your goods. It is already the law of Mechelen. And Antwerp. And Bruges. If you were thinking of setting up business there.'

Hawker stood up slowly and squared his shoulders, fixing his eyes on the master. 'And, as men of business, I am sorry for having taken up so much of your time.'

The master appeared to draw back a little, probably half believing Hawker was about to pounce on him like a cat on a rat. But Hawker swept his long brown robe to the side and walked away purposely without a glance behind him. He was not going home though. He was going to the most likely source of this invisible portcullis that had been dropped down in front of him. The palace.

At the great studded oak door, a stone's throw from the market square, one of the halberdiers recognised him, saluted, and went inside to announce him. Hawker watched a church tower clock across the wide cobbled street and waited. At the quarter hour, a tiny golden figure emerged and struck a bell with a hammer, once. Hawker continued to wait, arms clutched and trying to slow down his breathing. He was still furious for the bucket of cold water that had been emptied on him.

Just as the half hour rang, the palace door creaked open and he was finally ushered inside. The guards led him along the passage he now knew well, down a corridor and into the more private chambers of the palace. At length, they stopped at one door, knocked, and then led Hawker in.

The room, eastern facing, was bathed in the bright sunlight of late morning streaming through the high cathedral-style windows. A single table draped with a tapestry was at the far end and next to it stood Sir Olivier de la Marche.

'Come in, Sir John. Approach.'

Hawker did so, hearing the doors close behind him. The halberdiers remained, watching. Hawker gave the *châtelain* a bow of respect, exhaling long and slow to calm his cauldron of simmering rage. 'My good lord, thank you for agreeing to meet with me with no notice. I am grateful.'

The frog-like eyes blinked and Sir Olivier smiled. 'You are a loyal servant of Her Grace. Of course I would see you. What is the cause of this urgency?'

'I've made no secret of my intentions to you, my lord. I wish to settle here. Raise my son here. Turn my attention to trade. I think I have deserved that opportunity after years of service to the English crown.'

'And?'

'It would appear my suit to join the merchants' guild of Mechelen has been stymied. Without entry, I would have no means of beginning business here.'

The *châtelain*'s expression did not change. 'We don't make their laws, Sir John.'

'But the palace can overrule them, can it not? Overrule the council and let foreigners in.' He knew that Sir Olivier was well acquainted with the little conspiracy. The man's lack of surprise was plain. It had all been arranged.

'What you desire would not be in the interest of the palace. Or the cause we all serve. Surely you see that.'

'I told you I have no wish to lead a company again. That is done. Sir Giles is younger and more deserving of such honour.'

The *châtelain* shook his head and wandered around the table. 'Why do you deny who you are? What you have been all your life? You became a knight. Sworn to service. Like me. Now you stand there and tell me you are a man of commerce?'

'I could be.' He cringed inside at the weakness of such a reply.

'You are a slayer of your king's enemies. You are a knight. You have fought in the field and – upon orders, I've heard – kill like a wolf in the dead of night. Of that I have no doubt. Not much more than a day ago you were told where your service to the cause of the White Rose lies. It is in England.' Sir Olivier stopped his wandering and jabbed with his forefinger.

'*You* know how to survive in the midst of the enemy. Spread fear. Spread lies. Money to coax loyalties. Lord Lincoln and Lord Lovell would not have asked you if they thought you were too old or too enfeebled to meet that task. Her Grace, sister to your late liege, expects you to meet that expectation. You would truly leave a brave but inexperienced youth like Sir Giles to undertake such a mission?'

'Sounds like you are resorting to blackmail, my lord.'

'I am appealing to your honour.'

He was trapped. And yet he could not deny what the Burgundian had declared. He was no merchant. He had always been a soldier. *Condottiere.* He'd been dreaming, wishing, that he could begin again here. But, deep in his heart, and right alongside his love for Chiara, was the knowledge that it was not who he was or would ever be. He leaned on the edge of the table with both hands and exhaled deeply, a sigh of surrender to the truth of his existence.

'I will undertake the task. But I have conditions.'

'Name them.'

'I would have you deed me the house my wife and child live in.'

The *châtelain* tilted his head slightly. 'Agreed.'

'Second, I ask for a pension for my wife in the event of my death. The sum of five hundred ducats per annum. Plus a subsistence she may draw upon from my departure until my return.'

Sir Olivier frowned. 'I will convince Her Grace to pay two hundred and fifty. The subsistence I can grant.'

Hawker nodded, feeling a weight lift from his chest. 'And I will not set foot on ship until I have those documents – signed and with seals affixed – in my hands.'

The *châtelain* approached him and extended his arm to cement the bargain. 'You should make preparations immediately. We will procure you passage and coin. Take only Ellingham and two or three men-at-arms.' He released

Hawker's hand. 'You see, we *can* do fair business here in the Burgundy lands. Lord Lovell will want to give you further instructions, I am sure. Be at the ready.'

'I would have your word as a gentleman and knight that you will see that my lady wife does not want until I return. She has no one else here.'

Sir Olivier nodded once. 'I give you my word, John Hawker.'

Hawker bowed and headed for the door.

The *châtelain* called after him. 'Sir John! You should know also we have captured another French spy. I suspect he's in the employ of the Tudors. He has yet to sing loudly but we have managed to learn he's been following Lord Lovell since his arrival. And… he's been shadowing Sir Giles too. We shall get it all from the rogue before long, but be on your guard. He may have other accomplices.'

Hawker bowed again and left the chamber. The two halberdiers led him along the corridor, the way he had come before. As they walked, he saw two figures coming towards him: a man and a boy who looked no more than twelve. As they drew closer, Hawker paused a step. The olive-skinned man, heavy-set and well-dressed, he recognised immediately. It was Sir Edward Brampton. A favourite of King Richard, Brampton was a Portuguese Jew who had converted in his youth to the Christian faith and who performed many royal favours, flitting among the courts of Europe. And it was this same man who had given him a fateful order to be fulfilled – on orders of the king – four years earlier.

Now, here he was in the palace at Malines. As the two passed him on his right, Hawker caught a look at the boy's face. And again, his feet slowed, his memory jarred as if by a blow to his head, loosening a fragment long dormant. Hawker stopped and turned. A few feet away, the boy turned back and regarded him through narrowed eyes. Brampton too, turned back and then laid a hand on the boy's shoulder.

Hawker stood there, frozen for what seemed an age. Brampton locked eyes on him for a moment, then guided the lad away without a word. Hawker could not bring himself to call after them.

He watched as the two receded down the corridor.

The memory of that night at the Tower of London poured forth. The two boys, the fraught escape along the walls, the lashing rain and the tossing wherry waiting for them on the Thames. One falls, the other – the younger – he heaves into the bouncing boat. Richard of Shrewsbury, the last prince.

The gloved hand of the German halberdier fell hard upon his shoulder, jarring him back to his present, a world away from the memory that forever haunted him.

'*Kommen Sie, mein Herr!*'

18

She had to be told first. He owed her that, at least.

He said nothing during their modest supper, and soon after he and Chiara went to bed, Nicholas in his cot next to them. When Hawker awoke a few hours later, he stirred and struck flint and steel to spark up a rush light near the bed. Its warm, golden glow illuminated her face where she lay and his heavy heart felt like breaking. The crow's feet at the corner of her eyes, the lines engraved upon her pale forehead, these reminded him she was no longer truly young, despite her vigour and beauty. And now, he would be leaving her to fend for herself and their miracle child. Again. She stirred from her slumber after not too long, rolled closer to him, and smiled.

'You're awake. I will make us some caudle. Warm and spicy.'

He smiled at her and nodded. He had no wish to tell her his news while lying abed for he knew the upset it would bring. 'I will go down with you.'

Chiara bent over Nicholas, checking to see that the child slumbered on. Then they both robed and went down the narrow staircase into the hall. The embers in the hearth still glowed cherry red and Hawker stoked them up again before tossing on a few sticks of firewood. Chiara, wordless, fetched the mulled wine and a small cooking pan. She sat near to the fire and was about to begin spooning egg yolks when Hawker placed an arm on her shoulder.

'We must talk first, my love. I have news to share.'

Even in the weak light she must have seen the cast of his face. She set down the clay pot and the pan and stood up. 'When you

153

arrived back this day, I saw you were quiet. I should have asked you then what was wrong.'

'I could not bring myself to share it with you... not then.'

'Sweet Jesus. What has happened?' She gripped his arm, searching his face. 'What have you withheld all evening from me?'

He gently pulled her away and then held her shoulders. 'I must go to war again. To England.'

She said nothing. Hawker watched the anger slowly blossom.

'Chiara... there was no other way. The palace has the guilds in its grasp. The duchess expects me to earn the coin I have been given... and pay for the roof that has sheltered us these months.'

When she finally gave answer, her voice was steady and measured, but sharply tinged with the pain of betrayal. 'You risked your life to save me. Endangered your men's lives. So, what was that all for? Tell me. We were making a beginning here. Mother of God! *I* was beginning to learn to make a life here. With our child. In this cold, damp city full of pinched faces and sour looks. Now, now you are to leave again. And this time you will also be leaving your son.'

He let his grip on her shoulders loosen. 'This is what I am. What I have always been. And it is all that I know how to do.'

'Is that all of it then, Giovanni?'

'I have done what I've done for you and Nicholas. It is the *only* thing I could do to keep you safe. You will want for nothing. This house is yours now. If I am slain there will be a pension for you in gold coin each year. For as long as you and the boy remain.'

He watched her wince.

'The palace has promised. It will be written, signed, and sealed by the châtelain himself. And Sir Olivier will support you with money from the moment I depart... until I return.'

She stood there, motionless, his hands barely touching her shoulders as if they were scalding hot. She swallowed hard and let out a breath. 'Swear to me. Swear to me that you tried to change your path. That you tried to convince them to release you. That is the only way I can accept what you say you must do.'

'I swear to you on my immortal soul, Chiara. There was no other way.'

She stared back at him a moment and then nodded. 'I am already grieving.' She gently pushed away, returning to the stairs. He was left alone.

Hawker felt hollowed out inside. But it was done. Now, he had to move quickly to live up to his part of the bargain. Though it was nearly midnight, it was time to dress and pay a visit elsewhere.

On the hearthstone, the little pot of egg yolks sat next to the unfinished caudle mixture in the pan. A rat lapped at the eggs, an abandoned bounty.

–

Ellingham was lying abed, but awake, when the heavy, deliberate knock on the door sounded below. He threw back the coverlet, jumped out of the bed, and began rummaging for his hose and boots. The knocking sounded again: three steady beats. It sounded like the pommel of a sword on the oak. Wearing just his shirt and hose, he managed to grab his arming sword and then bounced down the tight stairwell to the ground floor. He passed by Dieudonné's cramped little bedchamber to see the man hunched on the floor, cursing, and pulling on his own clothes.

'Gaston! Hurry!'

Quick enough, Dieudonné had his back by the time Ellingham stood before the door. 'Who goes there!' he shouted through the jamb. The Burgundian had moved back and stood in a two-handed guard with his sword, ready for any onward rush.

'It's Hawker! Open up! I am alone!'

Ellingham swore softly, stepped back, and threw the bolt from the door. Hawker came through, looking as dishevelled as he was but more fully clothed. The knight's *cinquedea* dagger jangled at his waist.

'Giles, I am sorry to disturb you at this hour. But we must talk.'

Ellingham's brow furrowed. 'Talk? What has happened?' He shut the door again and bolted it. 'You could not wait until morning?'

Hawker looked at them both. 'No. And sleep has fled me.'

'And now me too,' mumbled Dieudonné, sourly.

'Then we must talk, Sir John,' said Ellingham, nodding. 'Come.'

They went up one floor, into the solar, still illuminated by the dying hearth fire. Ellingham rested his naked blade alongside the fireplace and turned to Hawker. 'So, then. What has happened?'

'I have relented. Out of damned necessity. But relented, nonetheless. I've decided to do as Lord Lovell has asked. Lead a party to scour the countryside. Raise support for the rebellion. And I need men I can trust. Men I know.'

Ellingham felt his jaw go slack. 'But… you were most adamant, Sir John. You were done with it all.'

'I know that full well. But my situation has changed. I must look after my lady and my son. And leading this venture is the best way – only way – to accomplish that. My service will benefit Chiara. Immediately… and permanently.'

Ellingham threw a glance to Dieudonné but the Burgundian merely stood in the background, listening with interest but showing no trace of judgement. 'So, what are you asking?'

Hawker folded his arms across his broad chest. 'I would have you with me. We ride to Lincolnshire and points north and west. Jacob and Jack with us.' He didn't mention Dieudonné.

'Sir Giles seeks preferment with Lord Lovell. And with his cousin, the Earl of Lincoln. Joining the invasion force itself.

Leading it.' Dieudonné's voice was helpfully soothing, a polite point of order for Hawker's benefit.

Hawker ignored him. 'Giles, I would not employ those I have not the measure of. Not on a journey as fraught as this. I will be moving quickly – stopping at estates I know. Those who sympathise with the cause of York. Your cause. I need the company we forged.'

Ellingham spoke quietly, still surprised by the turn of events. 'Sir John, it is a forlorn hope. What can you accomplish there? How will you outrun all the sheriff's men? They will hunt you the moment they realise you've landed, stirring rebellion.'

'It is what has been demanded of me. And of you. Sir Olivier has told me that I should have you with me. Lord Lovell has assented.'

Ellingham took a pace back. 'I know nothing of this. I want to find out what the duchess dowager – *my aunt* – thinks of these plans. I will see her myself.'

'The plans are inscribed in stone, Giles. There is nothing you or I can do. And it may not be any safer here now. They have caught another Tudor spy. Sir Olivier told me they are working on him. But he has already admitted to having been trailing Lord Lovell. And you.'

Ellingham felt Dieudonné approach his side as soon as the words had left Hawker's lips. He had forgotten over the last few months that he might still be hunted by Henry's henchmen. Now the threat was real again.

'They will squeeze him dry soon,' continued Hawker. 'There could be a few more in his gang. I wish to sail as soon as the châtelain can get us on a ship. If word gets out ahead of us, then we will stand no chance at all upon landing on the Norfolk shore.'

'*Another* spy?' Dieudonné's voice was almost tremulous.

Ellingham had no reason to doubt Hawker's sincerity. And he knew full well the only way he was going to regain his honour and fortune was by the sword. He would have to fight on, whether it was with Hawker or with the invading army. Eventually, he reasoned, the two would meet up. If they all survived. 'You were privy then… to these… decisions? That I was to journey with you?'

'Giles, just what were you hoping for? Those lords need large retinues. How many men can you – or I – hope to give them? They know this. Our best purpose is to be their advance. To be swift and light the fires of rumour across the land.'

Ellingham looked down at the floorboards, his stomach fluttering with the sickening remembrance of the failed attempt to sell the ruby gemstone. He then turned to the Burgundian. 'What say you, Gaston? What is to be done?'

Perhaps it was the drama and suddenness of the offer, but the colour of Dieudonné's face had turned to chalk. He hesitated a little, risked a rapid look at Hawker, and then looked again to Ellingham. 'Sir Giles, if I may be so bold, the news that Sir John has brought us has changed the situation. Changed it completely. We should join him and make sail as quickly as possible.'

Ellingham felt his eyes widen, stunned by the turn-around of his friend. But perhaps that was the only way forward. If Dieudonné believed it so, and if Hawker did, what other choice was there? He took a deep breath and moved to the grizzled knight, reaching out and grasping him by both his muscular biceps, honed from a lifetime of swinging a sword. 'Sir John, I would be honoured to ride at your side again. Tell us when we sail!'

19

Jacob de Grood's laughter filled the room. His livid scar – from right lip to cheekbone – made his face appear almost maniacal, the mouth far wider than it should be.

'A good jest, Sir John! The best you have ever played! Retiring to your dotage was something no one who knows you could actually swallow whole.' He wiped his eyes with the back of his hand, shaking his head. 'How long have you been planning this then?'

Hawker found it less amusing. 'Since yesterday. They black-mailed me into this venture, but I've managed to twist their arms enough to be granted generous terms to my surrender.'

Jacob caught the seriousness of his master's tone and pursed his lips to force some decorum. 'Forgive me, Sir John. I should not have made light of things. What do you need of me?'

Hawker stared out the leaded window of the de Grood solar and at the blue sky outside. 'See to the mounts. If they don't look up to the journey then sell them and get others. And get Jack to see to all the harness and weapons we still have. Cleaned and oiled.'

Jacob growled. 'That lad. Haven't seen him all morning. He grows scarcer by the day. Boredom.'

Hawker turned. 'I put him in your charge, Jacob. The boy needs guidance.'

'With respect, Sir John, he's hardly a boy now. And I'm no nursemaid. I train with him every day – when he shows up.'

Hawker mumbled a curse under his breath. 'I will speak with him. I have left him alone far too long.'

'When do we leave?'

'The palace sent word to me this morning. We have passage from Antwerp. The day after tomorrow.'

Jacob whistled softly. 'That is half a day's ride north. We must leave here tomorrow if we are to make it. With the preparations and all... that is whisker close.'

'Aye, it is. Sir Giles and I will go to the palace shortly to receive our full instructions and take charge of the gold.'

Jacob smiled. 'For us?'

'No. For bribery and loosening tongues. Find Jack and get him to work.' Hawker stared out the window again.

'Sir John?'

Hawker looked again to his man-at-arms. To his surprise he saw that the Fleming's eyes had become moist.

'It gladdens my heart we fight together once again. It is what we have always been meant to do.'

–

The white palace nearly glowed in the bright sunlight of midday. Hawker and Ellingham waited patiently to be invited through the ornately carved doors.

'Why do you need him with you?' asked Hawker, seemingly beginning a conversation in its middle.

Ellingham understood though. 'Gaston is a loyal friend. A supporter.'

'He is out only for his own good. That has been clear to me for some time.'

'But he saved your life in battle. He might do it again, if given the chance.'

Hawker harrumphed. 'I'm surprised he is not here banging on the doors again to gain entry.'

'He is making ready for the journey,' said Ellingham, irked by Hawker's animosity. 'Said he had no need to take part. He is more concerned that we have what we need for the venture.'

'Noble of him,' said Hawker flatly.

The great doors squealed open upon their iron hinges. Two halberdiers emerged and beckoned them inside and, after divesting them of their daggers, ushered them down the long corridor that comprised the central hall. Ellingham nervously made sure his doublet was fully buttoned and pulled up his somewhat balding, blue velvet robe fully about his neck and shoulders. This time, they were led down stone stairs to the cellars, and in a brief moment of anxiousness, Ellingham worried they might be about to be consigned to the cells he knew must be there somewhere. But, once in the vaulted chamber, brick-lined and supported by ancient pillars of stone, they soon found themselves in an unusual room. It was covered in wall tapestries with a great round table at it centre. The stone floor was strewn with rushes and dried lavender, the sweet, spicy scent filling the air.

On one side stood the three men he had only briefly met before: Sir Olivier de la Marche, Lord Lovell and the Earl of Lincoln. Upon the table were six leather purses, each the size of a fist.

'Welcome!' said Lord Lovell, inclining his head politely. 'The hour has come. Shall we light the torch that you shall bear back to England?'

Hawker bowed his head smartly. 'We leave for Antwerp in the morning, my lord. I need you only to tell me which ship we seek out.'

'Good,' said Lovell, his enthusiasm brimming over. 'It is a large carrack, the *Artemis*. Her master is loyal and trustworthy. He will be waiting for you. He will make for Norfolk and Yarmouth. If it is safe.'

'The usurper will be watching all the ports,' said Hawker. 'I hope Yarmouth less so.'

Lovell smiled. 'He can't watch all of them equally well. And I made it out only weeks ago. Proceed west and north as you see fit. You are ostensibly merchants – with armed escort. Seek out those who you knew to be adherents. Tell them we are coming and that you are there to raise support.'

'Remember,' said Lincoln, jumping in, 'I hold estates in Norfolk and my father the duke may yet come to support our cause. If you feel too exposed to Henry's watchful eyes, ride to Norwich and his manor. He is resident now and you will find succour there.'

'In Lincolnshire,' added Lovell, 'we hear Sir Thomas Burgh at Gainsborough is sick to death of the usurper already. He may lend a sympathetic ear and could raise a sizeable array for us.'

Hawker looked from one noble to the other. 'So... I gather from this you will invade with a force in the east. As well as a force from the west. Sir Olivier tells me of the army the Irish lords are raising. And of a young king to be crowned in Dublin.'

The *châtelain* looked apologetically to Lord Lovell. Lovell looked annoyed for but a moment, then nodded solemnly. 'That is just so. My lord Lincoln and one mercenary army will land in the east and raise up his estates – with his father's help – and proceed to link up with the western army and King Edward once he lands. You will spread the word. I intend to take York without resistance and then move south. Henry will either challenge us in Nottinghamshire or Leicestershire – or else he will hole up in London. That remains to be seen. But we will crush him this time.'

Hawker nodded and placed his right hand over his chest. 'God give us fortune, my lord.'

'You are a stout fellow, Hawker. Richard of blessed memory mentioned you to me more than once. Said you were dependable. Discreetly effective.'

Hawker bowed again. 'I was honoured to serve him.'

Ellingham regarded John de la Pole, the young Earl of Lincoln. He was tall with shoulder-length dark blond hair and eyes of grey. He could not be more than a few years older than himself. His face was very fair, his form almost effete. Had he even seen much war? Had he even fought at Bosworth? He reckoned he himself – in the past year alone – may have seen more of battle. Was his own experience for this enterprise so easily disregarded? And why was Hawker being so servient? There were a hundred questions going through his mind, yet Sir John was content to bow and scrape.

'And I was honoured to be his son,' said Ellingham, his voice elevated.

Lovell's attention swivelled to him. 'I knew your father well. Since boyhood.' Lovell gave him a kindly if somewhat condescending smile. 'I was probably with him at Middleham when he sired you. When we were playing truant from Warwick's master-of-arms.'

Ellingham felt his face flush. 'I am only sorry I could not save him at Bosworth Field. Christ knows I tried. Sir John and I both.'

'Yes... I am sure you did.' Lovell's words were almost reluctant. Ellingham glimpsed a subtle look of amusement on Hawker's face.

'Dear cousin,' said Lincoln, speaking up again. 'Your valour is unquestionable. But be cautious in England. Not many know of your true parentage other than Henry and his cohort and you will be safer with it staying that way. The day will come though. Have faith and be patient.'

This time, Ellingham kept quiet and just nodded.

'Gentlemen,' said Lovell, 'I know you have little time to prepare.' He pointed to the bags on the table. 'Here is your coin. Three of silver and three of gold. For your expenses and for buying support – or silence. You will no doubt need every penny.'

Hawker looked at Ellingham and then moved to the table and lifted three of the leather pouches. Ellingham did the same.

'Godspeed to you both!' said Lovell. 'We will see you in England before long.'

'When might that be?' asked Hawker with an ill-disguised smirk.

Lovell looked at him sternly. 'That would be telling too much, Sir John. Even to you. Fare you well, gentlemen.'

Hawker walked briskly across the cobbled streets, *cinquedea* jangling at his hip. Ellingham kept pace at his side, not quite knowing where they were going.

'Am I alone in not understanding exactly what they expect us to accomplish?'

Hawker stopped and studied a small puddle of rainwater at his feet. 'Giles... they expect us to be captured and interrogated. We were just stuffed like Christmas geese – with false information – and are now ready for the oven.'

Giles's jaw dropped. 'What do you mean *false* information?'

Hawker's voice was barely audible. 'There is no eastern army. It is a ruse. They would be fools to divide the small numbers they have. The entire army must sail from Dublin – and land somewhere in Wales. I would bet my last shilling on it.'

'Blood of Christ! What are we to do then?'

Hawker looked at him and smiled grimly. 'We go anyway. But we will not march to their drum. We're going elsewhere.'

'They would *betray* us?' Ellingham could not bring himself to believe they would sacrifice him, of all people, to the Lancastrians. But if it was true, then he had been deluded of his own importance in the Yorkist family. He began to feel sick inside.

'Betray may be too strong a word,' said Hawker, resuming his pace again. 'They do want us to scour the countryside – while we're able – but getting captured would suit them just as well. They want Henry to divide *his* forces. If he thinks the invasion comes from two different directions, he may have no choice but to do so.'

'But they told us of the lords we might find support from,' said Ellingham.

Hawker exploded with a harsh, short barking laugh. 'Gainsborough never lifted a finger to help Richard, though Yorkist he may be. He is every bit as much a fence sitter as is the Duke of Suffolk in Norwich. We will find no help from either quarter.'

Ellingham hurried after the old knight. Sadly, it all made sense. They could be being used as decoys, a scented lure to attract the hounds. If true, they had been primed to play a far different role than the one they had thought. The three purses tied to his waist suddenly felt like millstones. And his glorious bloodline seemed to have accomplished nothing in convincing John de la Pole to take him along to lead the venture from the front. So what was Hawker planning on doing differently?

'Where are we going now?' he asked, feeling as if they were now caught up in some violent ocean current.

'To see how Jacob is getting on. And if he's found that laggard Jack Perry yet.'

They reached the house of Bertrand de Grood and could hear the arguing going on in the courtyard at the side. Jacob was bellowing at his father as he led a chestnut palfrey out of the stables to be tied alongside a black courser that was nosing at the weeds in the cobbles. When he saw Hawker and Ellingham approaching, he waved off his sputtering father like a man fending a dozen wasps.

He hurriedly tied off the horse and came over to them. 'Sir John,' he said sheepishly, 'Jack is gone.'

'Gone where?'

'He has taken all his armour… weapons. Even the crossbow.'

'He's ridden away?' asked Ellingham, incredulous of the news.

Jacob frowned and shook his head. 'No, that's the strangest part. He took no mount.'

Hawker swore softly. 'He left no word?'

'None of the servants know where he went. A few saw him go this morning.'

Bertrand de Grood chimed up from behind, but in such rural Flemish that Ellingham could not follow.

Jacob groaned. 'God give me strength. He's demanding I go out and find him. Blames me for filling his head with nonsense… and swordplay. Said the lad had been halfway to becoming *his* apprentice.'

165

Hawker reached up, tore the hat from his head and slapped it across his thigh. 'The young fool! He's on foot. He'll not have gone far.'

'But where to? And why?' asked Ellingham.

'He says I have forsaken him,' said Hawker quietly. 'He could not accept me hanging up my harness for good.'

Ellingham suddenly realised none of them had given much thought to their young comrade in the past months, once they had been safely ensconced in Malines. 'We must find him before he ends up in a ditch somewhere. Beaten and robbed.'

'He'd never end up in a ditch without at least a good fight,' said Jacob encouragingly.

Hawker said nothing for a moment, rubbing at his temples. 'He was never planning on having to go far. He told me yesterday that he was already a soldier.' He looked up at Jacob. 'Where are the emperor's soldiers encamped? The ones garrisoned here in the town.'

Jacob swore softly in Flemish. 'The landsknechts. Their camp lies outside the north gates.'

'Pray that we are not too late,' said Hawker. 'Let's mount up.'

—

The bare ground extended a few hundred yards beyond the north walls of Mechelen. Cleared long ago for defence, it was perfect for a garrison camp. A sea of dirty, brown linen bell tents spread out in front of them, surrounded by a rudimentary ditch and earthen berm. Fascines of hazel branches and willow buttressed the temporary fortifications and there was a muddy dirt track leading to the one entrance. It was barred with a felled tree set upon two sawhorses. Nearby stood half a dozen landsknechts leaning on glaives and halberds, the German 'land servants' of Emperor Maximilian and the scourge of the rebellious Flemish towns. They had brought the guildsmen of Bruges to their knees a year earlier, earning a reputation for cruelty.

And according to Sir Olivier de la Marche these men would be the core of Lovell's army going to Ireland.

'If Jack is in there, how do we get him out?' asked Ellingham, his horse skittish from the sound of raucous laughter and shouts from inside the encampment.

'We demand to see the commander,' said Hawker, dismounting. 'Jacob! With me!'

They approached the guards and Jacob spoke to them in German while Hawker and Ellingham stood back. One of the guards gave a shrug and turned to enter the camp. He came out a short time later with a man wearing gaudy hose and doublet and whose flat red wool cap was bedecked with plumes. Jacob gave him a court bow and repeated his questioning. He was met with little but scowls.

Hawker stepped forward, bulling past a young, spotty *landsknecht* who tried to bar his way. His German was far from perfect, but he knew it well enough.

'We are looking for an English youth. We think he is here to join your company.'

The officer smiled, whether at his accent or about Jack, Hawker could not tell. But he answered quickly enough, nodding.

'The Englishman? Yes, I was on the gate when he came. Brave lad and full of boasts in bad Flemish. He was taken to the warlord.'

Hawker set his hand on his dagger pommel. He knew that Martin Schwarz was the mercenary who commanded the entire company. And de la Marche had told him he had earned his reputation for ruthlessness in the field. 'The lad is my servant and I demand his return.'

The officer laughed. 'Your lad has left your employ today. He's taken coin in hand from atop the gun barrel. Been read the articles. He's ours now. So, you and your comrades can fuck off.' He whistled up the guard around him who came forward with pole weapons at the ready.

Hawker stared down the officer for a moment, laying his hand on Jacob's arm when the Fleming started to move forward. He knew full well that he could do nothing. Jack was no longer a boy. He was now a man, a man whom Hawker had moulded through battle since boyhood. A boyhood he himself had helped to rob him of. And Jack Perry had made his choice to follow the drums of war on his own.

20

In the sputtering of the rush light at the bedside table, Chiara could see his eyes, glistening and wet, as he stared at the ceiling. She knew he had held back all evening and it pained her to see his pain. She had never seen him shed tears, and this silent, simple revelation of the Englishman frightened her a little. He was vulnerable.

'I do not judge you for any of this, Giovanni,' she said, gripping his hand under the coverlet. 'You are condottiere and you always will be. I knew this years ago.'

'Did I ever have a chance to become someone else here?' he asked, voice rough.

She rolled over and covered him with her body as if to shield him from the world. 'You sought to do so, and I believe you with all my heart. We move on. When you return, my love, it will be to fetch me and Nicholas. We will all go to England.'

For a few moments there was silence between them. She had already accepted that he could not outrun his past any more than she could.

'I have failed Jack,' he said. 'How can I be a father to our son?'

She lifted her head up from his broad chest. 'You have failed no one! Jack Perry is a man now. And he is *not* your son. He was a man when he slew my husband as he tried to murder me. And he has proved himself a man many times since, from the tales I have heard. Do not sink into self-pity, my love!'

She saw Hawker close his eyes.

'I have steeled myself to face your leaving. And I am ready to go on here until you come back. But if you *dare* surrender to self-doubt, Giovanni Falco, I swear that is something I could never forgive of you. I need to know you will fight with all your strength and cunning. And that you will come to me again.'

She felt his arms envelop her, enclosing her in an embrace she sensed he needed as much as her. He held her tightly, his aquiline nose nuzzling her neck. 'I am sorry, Chiara. Sorry, that I could not win the war here. These scheming merchants. The palace. They have both outflanked me.'

She stroked his cheek. 'To hell with them all. We take their money now and later you will show them their folly when you return the victor. When you have helped a new king onto a throne.'

She could see his stubbly face break into a smile even in the dim light. 'I will fight for you, with all my strength and heart.' He kissed her tenderly, fell back to the pillow, and closed his eyes again. After a few minutes had passed, she realised he was fast asleep.

—

The orange ball of haze that was the morning sun shone down upon the street. It was the hour of Terce, and for Hawker, it was already too late a start. He held his son aloft and looked into his face, the animated cherub grinning back at him. He could see Chiara's features there, perhaps some of his own, but this he was less sure of.

A few feet away, Jacob de Grood stood in full armour, holding the reins to both their mounts. At the end of the row of houses, he could see Ellingham and Dieudonné, waiting for him. He kissed the boy once on his forehead, gave a silent prayer of blessing, and handed Nicholas back to the nurse. He turned to Chiara. She was not crying. Her face was uplifted, proud, silently urging him good fortune. Hawker swept her up one last time and kissed her full upon the lips.

'Keep the scrolls safe, my love,' he cautioned. 'The house is yours and the pension will see you through. If you ever have need of help, Sir Olivier is now sworn to protect you in my absence. I trust him.'

She smiled bravely. 'Then, so do I. May the Virgin protect you, my love!'

Hawker released her, a wave of foreboding sweeping over him as he realised it might be the last time he held her in his arms. He took up his reins from Jacob, mounted, and looked down on Chiara and Nicholas one last time. 'Fare you well!'

They trotted up the street and joined the others.

Giles smiled and nodded at Hawker. He was dressed in the same merchant's cast-offs as before, the glint of a breastplate showing underneath the cloak. 'Good weather for the journey, Sir John!'

Hawker nodded and his eyes drifted over to the Burgundian. He looked nervous, playing with the slack in his reins, eyes moving up and down the street.

'My lord Gaston,' said Hawker, 'what ails you this morning?'

Dieudonné's head swivelled back sharply to face the old knight. He wore full harness but instead of his helm – which was strapped to his horse's cruppers – he wore his velvet bonnet and gaudy plume. 'We should not draw too much attention to ourselves here. We need to be out on the road north.'

'That much we can agree upon,' said Hawker, nodding.

They passed by traders in the main square, already busy at their stalls. None paid them too much heed for they would have appeared just as two merchants – perhaps father and son – and two men-at-arms, off on a venture to Bruges or Ghent. Or Antwerp. The north gates were open and unattended, and they passed through and out onto the open road and grassy plain, copses of trees scattered here and there.

To their right, Hawker caught sight of the dozens of tents at the *landsknecht* encampment and instantly felt his chest tighten. He wondered how Jack fared in his new world. It was one even more unforgiving than the one he'd abandoned, that fact Hawker knew full well. He said a second silent prayer, this time for Jack Perry.

The road was smooth and wide, and Jacob set the pace at a canter. For the first time in many months, Hawker suddenly felt a surge of hope for what lay ahead. He was going home again, to roads, rivers, hills, valleys and fens he knew well. He would spread the word that a true king of the royal blood was on his way and that the days of the Welsh usurper were numbered. And he would take pleasure in putting to the sword those who stood in his way.

He had decided some time ago what the first destination would be. One he had yet to tell Ellingham. It would not be the false friends of the house of York suggested by Lord Lovell. He needed to find others he might depend upon.

They made it to the Cistercian abbey of Roosendael in good time, crossing the Nete by ferry. They rested and watered the horses on the far side, and Jacob shared out some bread and cheese he had in his saddlebags. Ellingham had said little thus far though they had ridden alongside. He knew the youth was probably still angered he had been told to accompany him on what might be a forlorn hope. And he could be forgiven for doubting this venture into the unknown. But Hawker already knew that if battle was joined in the coming weeks, it was the best chance for Giles Ellingham to make his name and gain his fortune.

Hawker proffered another chunk of bread to him. 'We'll be there by dusk. I promise you a better meal then. Why does Dieudonné keep throwing glances back the way we have come?'

Ellingham raised his brow. 'Had not noticed that. Perhaps he is just keeping watch. I told you he is worth having with us. Eyes like a hawk.'

Hawker nodded slowly. 'And the ears of a fox.'

Ellingham studied his crust of bread. 'What do you think awaits us?'

'In Antwerp?'

'No. In England.'

Hawker pulled out an apple he had secreted and took a bite. 'We will be as shadows. No one expects us and we will follow the lesser tracks, staying off the main roads.'

'You have a destination in mind, don't you? Not one Lord Lovell or Lincoln offered up.'

Hawker gave him a wry smile. 'We will follow our own path, Giles. I would ask your patience until we are safely at Antwerp and are ready to embark.'

Ellingham tossed away the last of his bread. 'Very well, Sir John. I know I have little choice in the matter. This is your venture... again.'

—

The man sat cross-legged on the cold stone floor. He knew he was somewhere in the bowels of the town hall of Malines. He'd managed to scrape up enough straw to make a seat for himself so his wet bottom was not on the frigid stones themselves. But a cold, damp backside was the least of his problems. Sitting hunched over, he contemplated the ruin of his hands. They had been turned to jelly by an ingenious tool of his torturer. The Flemish bastard called it the 'crocodile'. Clamped about his knuckles, with each turn of a wooden knob, the device had slowly begun to crush his fingers. After a day of such play, he had felt further silence on his part was no longer worth the effort. He'd confessed.

The recorder continued scribbling at his little wooden desk which was positioned beneath the only window to the outside world, albeit through a long, narrow tunnel of brick.

'You should have chosen a more believable persona,' said the recorder, twirling his quill. 'Claiming you are a Breton merchant when your accent is clearly Parisian was not the most convincing mask of a talented spy. You should have known we have a few Bretons here who would interrogate you.'

Pascal was past caring. 'What more do you want me to tell you?'

The recorder thumbed through his sheaves of paper. 'You were here to lend support to your comrade – who ends up being murdered in a tavern by someone he was meeting. And this man, this Armand Moreau, was shadowing Plantagenet exiles here. You have spoken of Lord Lovell. But why were you following the other English? This Giles Ellingham and his comrades. Are you in the pay of the French court or the Tudor one?'

Pascal was having troubling concentrating. His hands throbbed terribly, the pain running up his arms in continual waves of agony. He winced. 'Both.'

The recorder leaned forward, smiling. 'Elaborate... please.'

Pascal couldn't suppress the groan that emanated from him. 'I *told* you. I have gathered information for the Duc de Bedford... Jasper Tudor. He is interested in the movements of Ellingham. The mercenary called Hawker, too. They are declared outlaws in England.'

'So, who was your friend meeting with? Who killed him and where are they now?'

'I don't know who killed him.'

'Did you kill him?'

'No. I did not. I offered to go with him. He refused me.'

The recorder's tone became impatient. 'I am more than certain you do not wish my friend to come back in here again and give you his less than tender attentions. *Who* was he meeting?'

'Some French exile... passing as a Burgundian. He might have double-crossed the Tudors... killed a manservant after King Henry's victory and run away with Yorkists.'

The recorder scratched his nose with the quill. 'So... if this fellow was a turncoat, then why was Moreau meeting with him?'

Pascal sighed. He was very tired of it all. 'Moreau said he wasn't sure if he was still working in the Tudor or French cause. That he might have wormed his way deep into Yorkist confidences. Wanted to bring him back to our side. He is in Ellingham's company still.'

The quill tapped with irritation upon the oak writing desk. 'A name?'

Pascal rubbed the swollen lump that was once his left hand across his brow. He let out a weak laugh born of total surrender. 'Name? An amusing one… for a murderer. Dieudonné. Gaston Dieudonné.'

Part IV

THE DIE IS CAST

21

Jack Perry took the step that he knew would change everything. He crossed the threshold into the encampment of the German *landsknechts*, moving past the four halberdiers who stood guard at the makeshift gate. The soldier who led called back to him in a language Jack could not understand; harsh, guttural and commanding. Around him, the camp was both familiar and strange. Jack had been in the baggage train of Hawker's company since he was ten. He knew the ways of soldiers. The fights. The food. The camaraderie of the road. Proud boasts and, at times, blind panic. But they were English, and these men were not. He began to feel a sickness rising in his stomach when they approached the largest of the canvas tents. What if he had made the wrong choice?

The halberdier opened the tent flap and beckoned him inside with a grunt. There were several men gathered about one table, jabbering with one another. The halberdier announced him and they looked up. Jack understood one word that was spoken: *Englishman*. One of the men, a strange-looking fellow with a short beard but no moustache and with an outlandishly large bonnet, which flopped to the side of his head, spoke directly to him.

Jack was flummoxed. He stuttered in bad Flemish that he was English, then realised he didn't know the Flemish for 'volunteer'. He pointed to the sword on his hip and the crossbow slung at this back.

The officer laughed while a few of the others just shook their heads.

Jack managed to say he knew the Scottish soldiers, which he then rendered in French to stem further confusion. '*Ecosse!*' He then remembered the colours the Scot David Weems had told him of their banner: the red and the blue. '*Rot! Blau!*' he said hurriedly, but then he could not remember the word for flag.

One of the other officers said something to the bearded one who nodded in return. While Jack stood, sweating profusely in his breastplate, backplate, gambeson and barbute helm, one of the men left the tent and called out an order to the guard. For a few minutes he was the source of mirth, standing there confused and increasingly uneasy while the Germans joked. The tent flap parted again and this time two soldiers entered: David Weems and another. They bowed to the officers. Jack managed a smile at Weems, but the Scot ignored him. The bearded one spoke and Weems replied quietly.

At length he turned to Jack. 'You're a brave one, Englishman. Tell me what you want so I can tell *them*.'

Jack removed his helm and proceeded to do so as best he could, voice shaking.

Weems translated it into German. The officer spoke and Weems looked at Jack. 'He thinks you belong in the baggage train. You're a boy.'

Despite his fear, Jack began to bristle. 'Tell him I've already fought in battle. Many times. England. Hungary. Wallachia.'

David's eyebrows raised a little, but he turned and spoke. There was some muttering amongst the Germans and then the bearded one spoke to the Scot and pointed to Jack.

'You're in luck. The captain says if you can swear to your experience, he will take you on. They can use more cross-bowmen. And he says you're in our fähnlein. If it turns out you are a braggart and a liar though, you'll hang.'

Jack bowed to the officers, hardly confident but relieved he hadn't been beaten or worse.

'If you hadn't come armed and in harness, they would have thrown you out into the ditch,' added David quietly.

The bearded one beckoned him to the table.

An older soldier was seated on a stool next to him and he looked up at Jack. 'Name?'

Jack told him and the man wrote it down in a ledger of sorts. Next, the man spoke at him in rapid German as if reciting some prayer from memory. Weems approached and whispered into his ear. 'He is reading you the articles of war – or at least a short version of them. You will have to swear on them. And swear to serve the emperor.'

Jack found his throat catching when he tried to swallow. How could he swear to something he couldn't understand?

At length, a golden crucifix was slid across the tabletop by one of the other officers. 'Hand!' said the seated man, pointing at the cross.

Jack complied, laying his palm on the crucifix. The man looked beyond Jack and spoke to the Scot sharply. David leaned in again. 'You must speak now. Just say it in English. Say, "I swear it so to Almighty God". That should do it.'

Jack, stuttering mightily, said the words. The seated man grunted and then slapped a small gold coin on the table edge near to Jack, motioning for him to take it up. Jack palmed it.

'*Grüss Gott!*' said the bearded one loudly and all the others laughed. Jack managed an uncertain smile and backed away with a series of awkward bows.

The bearded one then gave some order to David and his companion and they raised their arms in a salute. David grabbed Jack's arm and pulled him away. 'Let's go!' he whispered.

'What did I swear to?' asked Jack, half stumbling across the wax-cloth floor of the tent.

'Never mind, lad,' said Weems. 'I'll tell you later.'

Outside the tent, Weems dragged Jack along and threw an arm about his shoulders. 'You have some set of bollocks, lad! I never thought you'd actually turn up after you left the tavern. But here you are! You've landed yourself in it now.'

Jack didn't quite know what to say. 'Thankee, David. For helping me.'

'Save that for later, Jack Perry. This here is Luke. Of Kirkcaldy.'

The other Scot had said not a word thus far and now merely nodded an acknowledgement of his introduction.

'So, I'm in your company now?' asked Jack.

'That you are. The blue and red. There are about four hundred of us. Germans mostly, some Flemings, and Helvetian confederates – Switzers – ones who need the money and don't mind fighting for former enemies. And then there's us. Eighteen Scotsmen. And one little Englishman.'

'What happens now?'

'I bring you to the feldweibel. He's our master – our sergeant – and he'll have a look at you and tell you where he wants you. You've got your bow, so you'll be in with the others and the few hand-gunners we've got. But I imagine you can bed down with us lot. At least until your German gets better.'

Luke finally made his voice heard.

'That's some fine harness you have. You might have to fight to keep it. Some of the lads don't have much of anything. Just warning you now, Englishman.'

He was a head taller than David and had thinner, black hair cropped short showing a few scars on his scalp and an almost saturnine countenance. He wore torn hose like David's and a filthy, ripped, doublet of madder-red wool. It was padded, with its stuffing spilling out at some of the seams. He looked like a moulting bird. And he wore a codpiece that stood as erect as a tent pole.

Jack nodded, not really knowing what to say.

They went deep into the sea of tents which seemed to extend as far as Jack could see. There was a gentle slope to the plain, which Jack knew led towards a shallow stream running parallel to the walls of the town. As they weaved around the tents and along what had become muddy tracks where the grass had been trudged away, Weems blurted out snatches of information, things Jack struggled to take in. He was excited and fretful not knowing what would be expected of him next. Around them he saw many men going about the business of camp: sharpening weapons, mending clothing, gambling, arguing.

'There are a third of us still billeted in the town,' said Weems, pushing a staggering, drunk *landsknecht* out of their path. 'The rest of us are here… in this stinking place. At least until we march off. We're told we're going to war again, but I don't rightly know whereof.'

'I know where,' said Jack.

David Weems of Fife laughed heartily and threw a glance to Luke. 'I see. So after you left us you must have gone drinking with the commander himself. You know the great captain, Martin Black?'

Jack shook his head.

'He is the obrist as the Germans call it. The commander who put this company together. Friend of the emperor himself. The fellow who pays us. So, Englishman, where are we going?'

'England.'

Weems stopped in his tracks. 'You hear that, Luke? Well, Jack Perry, save the story for tonight. And don't mention it again for now, understood?'

Jack nodded but Weems was still looking at him.

'That knight of yours? He told you?'

Jack nodded again and Weems grinned. 'He'll have your guts for running away.'

Jack thought of Sir John. What would he do upon finding he had left? He had wanted to leave a note but couldn't write and did not want to share his plan with anyone for fear they might tell on him. Now that he was knee-deep into his new employ, he began to feel it was *he* who had abandoned the old knight out of frustration and anger. It was dawning belatedly upon him that Sir John would have looked after him come what may. He had himself taken away that option.

They reached another group of linen tents, all various shades of shit-brown. High above on a makeshift pole flew the banner:

a nearly square flag that was just two horizontal stripes, red on top and blue underneath. There was a large clearing near the centre, an assembly point, reasoned Jack. And nearby stood a small group of soldiers, each one nearly a giant. They were all armed with fearsome-looking glaives and other pole weapons, short swords hung at their belts.

An officer was addressing them. He was dressed like the other officers Jack had already seen: gaudily and extravagantly like some strutting peacock. His multi-striped hose and green velvet doublet was covered by a mantle of fine wool trimmed in fur. A wide, flopping bonnet of black with three ostrich plumes covered his head. The *feldweibel*, no doubt. He saw the three of them approach and halted his lecture.

'*Was machen Sie, den!*' he bellowed.

Weems raised his hand to his brow and spoke, this time in Flemish. Jack managed to understand some of it. The sergeant turned his attention to Jack, looking him up and down.

'Armbrüste, eh?'

Jack answered 'crossbowman' and then repeated the German. He spoke in what Flemish he could assemble in his head and told him his name and where he had come from. The officer crossed his arms and listened.

'How many have you killed with it, boy?'

'At least a dozen, as I swear on my mother's soul.'

The sergeant laughed. He looked to be about the same age as Jacob de Grood, salt and pepper beard stubble showing. 'Englishman, eh? Well, we start teaching you drill tomorrow. What do you know of pike squares and hedgehogs?'

Jack didn't know much about pike, never having caught one, but he also heard the word for hedgehog which he knew – *igel* – and found his voice. 'Don't know pike but have eaten roast hedgehog once.'

The sergeant's eyes widened, there was a pause, and then a bellow of laughter. 'He is a jesting fool, this one! I will have to keep an eye on him. You Scots can have him for now until I get my gunners and bowmen sorted. The captain is beating me like an old mule about drill. So you better be there sharpish when you hear the drums!'

Weems pulled Jack away and they carried on. Jack could see smoke rising from a group of wagons at the far end of the camp. He could also make out barrels and crates, spits for cooking and a few women walking about. It was familiar to him: the baggage train where the sutlers and cooks lived and worked. They arrived at the tents where the Scots were encamped, and Jack was introduced.

'He's a wee one, isn't he?' said one brawny Scotsman. 'He'll have some trouble shouldering a pike!' Jack could hear a mixture of what he assumed was Scots as well as some English and a few of the soldiers approached to tell him their names and welcome him. A few whistled softly, tapping his breastplate and the spaulders which protected his shoulders and biceps. They milled about him, occasionally prodding or slapping his back until Luke raised both arms and called the little group to silence.

'I say it's time to give the Sassenach his first lesson!'

There was a chorus of 'ayes' and in the next moments Jack was roughly shorn of his armour and gambeson. One of the soldiers threw them into a tent and then he was lifted and his boots and hose were ripped off. He fought them as best he could, swearing away, but there were too many. His shirt was pulled off over his head and he was then carried bodily in just his braes, down and away to the end of the camp towards the shallow river. He didn't feel the chill of the air. His fired-up anger was keeping him warm.

The men began singing some song in Scots and Jack had now decided protest wasn't getting him anywhere. He saw what he knew to be a jakes for the encampment. The smell was already strong in his nostrils. He kept getting turned as he was man-handled, the scene forever changing as he was either up or down. But he caught sight of the running water of the river sparkling and then saw a channel had been cut to divert and fill a long trench parallel to it.

'He must be baptised in the midden!' yelled a soldier. It was then Jack understood where he was headed, and he began to struggle anew. Past the makeshift logs and supports that formed the planks and seats, the gang brought him kicking and yelling to the other side. A great pit of steaming filth about six feet deep was below him, a mix of shit, rotten food and river water. With two on his arms and another two on his legs, they swung him back and forth at the edge, counting each time. Each time he felt his body swing up, he rued his choice to find fortune on his own.

But the swinging suddenly stopped, and he was carried on, along the river bank, and to a group of tents that stood on their own. The soldiers were laughing and hooting like madmen and Jack now had no idea what his next humiliation was to be. One of the men rushed ahead and opened the tent flap and the others carried him inside.

It was lit by a few lamps and upon several fleeces sat two women in nothing but gauzy chemises, their long hair down around their shoulders. One was old enough to be his mother, her companion perhaps a bit younger. Jack was tossed into their midst, landing on his side before rolling onto his back. The ladies screeched with laughter, shooing out the soldiers with their combs. Weems was the last remaining. He tossed a silver coin to the older woman and then looked at Jack and grinned. 'You can add that to what you owe me for the tavern, Englishman!'

The younger woman giggled and straight away yanked loose the tie of his braes, pulling them away. Jack lay there like a hammered veal calf and blinked a few times. He had been a *landsknecht* for less than an hour.

22

Jacob de Grood raised his wooden tankard of beer to Hawker. 'To your health, Sir John! I'm pleased to be back in employ.'

Hawker shook his head. 'You know damn well you were never out of it.'

They had made it to the port of Antwerp just around sunset and without incident. There were many inns along the main quay and Hawker chose one that had several doors, front and back – if needs must. The stable alongside was also convenient and he'd made sure that Jacob had sufficient coin to keep the grooms loyal and attentive.

Jacob shrugged and filled his mouth with some more day-old rye and cheese. It was now late of the evening, most merchants and seamen drifting away, and the burble of conversation so quiet one could hear the logs of the fire crackling. They'd taken two rooms so that no one remained on their own. Hawker was tired. He'd not ridden that hard since the misadventure of Calais. He was now aching for a bed, even if it was a bad one.

Hawker had tracked down the master of *Artemis* as soon as they had arrived. Joris Smout was a taciturn seaman of few words. He'd told Hawker to be ready to board an hour after sunrise and that he intended to catch the ebb tide on the Scheldt. Smout would wait for no one. His ship was a good-sized carrack, three-masted and of wide beam. The ship lay at berth alongside the quay itself, which meant they would be able to run the horses up the plank of the gangway and onto the deck. The master had assured Hawker that he transported horseflesh often and Hawker hoped that he wasn't being too literal. He told Hawker he had several slings and lines to make them fast where they stood on the deck. Besides, the crossing would be no more than two days, he said. Hawker had no choice but to trust him.

Hawker took a drink and saw that Ellingham was still just as subdued as he'd been all the day. It was born of bitterness, he knew. Dieudonné, too, had little to say, and seemed to spend most of his time watching the main entrance of the tap room.

'You must be relieved, Giles, that we're here. All is in readiness. Have we not found purpose again?'

Ellingham looked into his beer for a moment. 'Purpose? I pray that it is so. But we were not the ones to set the conditions. If we are to sail into the unknown, tell me where you see us disembarking.' He lowered his voice a notch. 'If not to Yarmouth.'

Hawker pursed his lips and set down his tankard. 'Very well. You're deserving to hear more. We'll convince the master to take us past Yarmouth – up the coast – and make for the Glaven ports. Blakeney would suit us.'

'And why not where Lord Lincoln told us?'

'Because I do not care to risk a Tudor reception party at Yarmouth port. It is far too busy a place and Henry will be watching it constantly. Blakeney gives us a better chance at secrecy – and it's closer to where I intend to lead us.'

Ellingham slowly unfolded his palm towards Hawker.

The old knight ignored the sarcasm. 'We are going back to *my* manor. To Lincolnshire. My sister will aid us.'

It was now Jacob who stared into his beer.

Ellingham tilted his head. 'To Stamford? That did not go as expected two years ago. And you think she will welcome us again? Assuming, that is, she is even still there. Henry Tudor probably gave your manor to someone else by now.'

'And I pray that it is not so.'

'What are you expecting to find, Sir John?' said Dieudonné. 'Once we get there.'

Hawker leaned forward. 'Men who still believe in their rightful king. Men who would salvage their lost honour.'

'You have been away a long time, Sir John,' Ellingham said, his voice tinged with more than a little doubt. 'What if you find no one willing to rise up?'

Hawker sat back and raised his chin. 'I will not believe that. Even a dozen men in harness would give us the strength to travel the roads. And give us leverage with Lord Lovell once battle is joined. And I swear to you now, if this is to be my last battle then I will see it in the company of soldiers under one banner and not as a ragged band of outlaws.'

'I seem to recall you once said you would help me find *my* sister.'

Hawker felt the barb. 'I know that. I have not forgotten. And if God grants me the time I will honour that promise. But she is beyond the Severn – at Raglan – or else in London at the usurper's court. We don't know where and we stand little chance of getting to her as long as Henry Tudor lives.'

'So, then... it must wait,' replied Ellingham quietly. 'For victory. With an invading army we know nothing about. Nor where it will land.'

Hawker reached over and grasped Ellingham's wrist. 'Jesus, lad! You and I have travelled over half of Christendom together! And for what? Did we find what we were seeking? Our fate lies in England now. And this could be our last and best chance to find what was lost. No matter the odds.'

Ellingham leaned further over the trestle. 'And what did you lose, Sir John?'

'My land. My honour. And most painful of all... belief. In myself. And that is the greatest sin.'

Ellingham frowned a little and then looked down. 'I do understand *that* at least. There can be no future without honour.'

'Staying alive has a rewarding quality all of its own, my lord,' said Dieudonné archly.

'No, Sir John speaks a basic truth, my friend,' said Ellingham, half-turning to the Burgundian. 'Surviving without honour and respect is not living. I know this.'

'And that is why we venture forth now,' said Hawker, again gripping Ellingham's arm. 'Not because we know whether we will succeed or lose, but because we'll find what we have lost, come what may. My dear lady's future – and my son's – is secured by a knight's promise. A man I trust. But only I can secure my future. Let us do this thing together.'

Ellingham looked at Hawker and nodded. Hawker turned to Jacob, sitting grim-faced next to him. The Fleming evinced a crooked smile and then nodded to the knight.

Dieudonné sat back and feigned a yawn. 'My comrades, the hour is late and I must to bed. Until the morning then!' He rose, squeezed Giles's shoulder briefly, and then turned away.

–

Dieudonné did not go to bed, at least not straight away. He went outside and walked to the quayside to have a conversation with himself.

For months he had been hauling the youth onto his own shore – both adoring him and disliking him at the same time. In Malines, he had banished Hawker to the edge of relevance, out of Giles's sphere, and instead he had taken the place of the old knight. The youth had not yet found his way to his bed, but he was heeding Dieudonné's counsel, little by little. Ingratiating himself with his duchess aunt and on the verge of preference.

And then, the Fates intervened. Shut out of the visits to the palace, he had waited, anxious, to learn what Giles was being advised. The arrival of Armand Moreau soon thereafter had turned everything upside down. And the final cut had been the capture of one of Moreau's men, threatening his own exposure. This left him but one course: follow Giles back to England. And then hope for the best. Hope that he would ride in the midst of the Yorkist lords to victory – and patronage. It was a slender thread, he knew. But he still had choices.

Sailors were loading vessels in the darkness, illuminated by torches set in stands. Dieudonné watched their efforts, lost in his deliberations. A light breeze blew across the paving stones, refreshing him.

'Comment vas-tu, Gaston?'

Dieudonné rapidly moved to his left, out of the puddle of light while at the same time drawing his dagger. He wheeled in the direction of the voice and then slowly backed away from the quay to the warehouse side again. The spoken French had made him jump from his skin. His eyes tried to pierce the gloom to see who his visitor was.

'Come closer,' said Dieudonné, the dagger twitching in his hand.

To his surprise, the man did, following him into the deeper shadows. He stopped just out of reach and spoke quietly. 'My lord, I am here as a friend. Hear me out.'

'I have no friends,' rasped Dieudonné, spreading his feet evenly, ready to spring. 'Who are you?'

The man made no move to come closer. 'I was with Armand Moreau... and another. Did *you* kill him?' The words were almost a whisper.

'No, I did not. I left him alive – and drunk – in the tavern.'

'I am not sure I believe you. But I will. Otherwise my message to you is wasted.'

'How did you manage to follow me all this way?'

'I managed. I knew you would try and flee. Before the palace came for you. They have Pascal and he has no doubt been tortured for what he knows. What he knows of me. And you.'

'I know not of whom you speak, you corner-creeper.'

'But *we* know of you. We have followed you these past weeks. And the young royal bastard you lie with.'

Dieudonné debated jumping the man and killing him straight away. But something held him back. The fool was not here to take him in. He was here for something else. 'Speak your piece and be quick about it. Before I change my mind.'

'We followed the English lords to Malines. Our masters would have intelligence of their intentions. Then we found Ellingham... and you. The Duke of Bedford has not forgotten you.'

Dieudonné scratched his left thumb along the edge of his dagger, irritated. 'You are taking too long.'

The man started to come a bit closer, but Dieudonné extended his arm. 'Have a care,' he hissed.

'My name is Baudet. And I can tell you that you may yet redeem yourself. When you reach England. The king and his ministers – they are willing to pardon you, pay you – if you deliver up the outlaw and the bastard. I have been assured of this. It was Moreau's plan to tell you this himself. You would find grace and much favour. A new beginning. Search out the king's party when you return! Go to London!'

'So says you.'

'I am no longer safe in Flanders or Brabant. I'm taking ship too.'

Dieudonné chuckled darkly. 'Not my ship.'

'No, no. Another. But do not tarry here. The duchess will be looking for you soon if she hasn't already begun.'

Dieudonné had no reason to trust the man. By his height, bearing and voice, he was no soldier. He could easily end him and drop him into the river. 'Why have you risked coming to tell me this news?'

'Because I serve the House of Lancaster. As once you did.'

Dieudonné huffed to himself and waved his dagger. 'You may disappear now. And hurry, before I change my mind.'

The man said nothing more but turned and walked swiftly away down the quay. Dieudonné's head was now abuzz with worries – and many questions. He would be sleeping with a drawn sword at his side this night. Assuming he would sleep at all.

Joris Smout had been true to his word. Two hours after the sun had risen, the *Artemis* creaked and complained as the warps pulled tighter on the river side of the vessel. They were being towed away from the quay by oarsmen in a large wherry, into the swiftly flowing current. The bow of the vessel swung out and men on the quay helped give her stern a push. Hawker steadied himself as the ship listed a little, moving slowly in the wide Scheldt. Master Smout shouted and his sailors scampered and attended to lines and sails.

Jacob bounced across the main deck and joined him at the rail, having checked the horses were secure.

'Does my heart good to be in harness again, Sir John. But can't say I am glad to be going to sea again.'

'We will bear it, Jacob.' Hawker rested his elbows on the railing and looked towards the bow where Ellingham and Dieudonné stood conversing.

Jacob leaned next to him and looked out onto the river. 'And we'll need to get you and Sir Giles more armour from somewhere. Before things get too hot. Breast and back are not enough for pitched battle. But I don't have to remind you of that.'

Hawker followed his gaze. 'We have our helms too. The rest we shall find somewhere.' He paused for a few moments. 'What will happen to Jack?'

Jacob sighed loudly. 'I thought he was contented for the moment. Learning more sword craft. I swear I never expected him to run away.'

'He is young. Impatient for war. I should have foreseen it.'

'He has a good head on his shoulders. He's strong and able. And it is his life.'

Hawker looked down into the rippling brown water. 'I failed him. I was the father he never had. But, maybe, not the one he deserved.'

'Your paths may cross again, Sir John. He is bound for the same war as we. God willing, we will find him.'

Hawker clapped Jacob upon his back warmly, the Fleming's armour jangling.

'I only pray we will not need to turn pirate before this voyage is over,' said Jacob quietly. 'If this master wants to go to Yarmouth and nowhere else... well.'

Hawker looked at him and smiled weakly. 'Pirate? Why for? We have plenty of gold now to buy his loyalty. Enough to sail to Cathay if we choose!'

'And if he says no?'

'As you say. We have our swords.'

The *Artemis* picked up speed rapidly once they caught the ebb. The sailors climbed into the ratlines and began to unfurl the sailcloth, first upon the foremast. After half an hour had passed, they were well out into the main channel, sailing north by north-west, the spires of Antwerp becoming smaller in their wake.

—

As the *Artemis* rounded the first bend in the river, a lone horseman pounded up to the quayside, sparks dancing from his mount's shoes. His eyes saw two large vessels moored and several smaller ones. He reined in and trotted over to a group of seamen who were coiling the heavy cables that were strewn across the stones.

'You, there! Where is the *Artemis*?'

Two of the dock men stood and pointed out into the river. 'Long gone, now!' said one.

The messenger swore loudly and roughly yanked at his reins, jerking his horse around into a turn. He trotted to one of the nearby inns and dismounted. He threw his arms over the horn and the cantle, pressed his forehead into the saddle seat, and then he banged it, twice.

Sir Olivier de la Marche would be furious.

23

The *Artemis*, on a westerly course under far less than half its canvas, sailed along at a slow but safe speed in the darkness. The moon bathed the sea and the deck in a whitish light, nearly metallic in colour. The surface had been mercifully smooth out into the vastness of the German Sea and Gaston Dieudonné prayed it would remain so. He hated everything about ships and being upon the water. On the sea, there was nowhere to run, no choices other than surrender, fight or drown.

He had again come on the main deck to drink fresher air. The stern cabins of the carrack were cramped and stinking of musty damp. And, he had awakened to notice that Ellingham was not in his cot alongside him. He had his boots on already and he rolled out of his sling as the ship listed, helping propel him to the cabin doorway. De Grood was up too. Dieudonné watched him adjust the blankets that lay over the backs of the four horses. The Fleming patted the noses of each of them. Dieudonné could see their eyes were large and glistening, reflecting in the moonlight. They were terrified still.

Ellingham stood at the bow end of the maindeck, just before the forecastle stair. He was staring out over the waters. Dieudonné moved up next to him.

'I noticed you had arisen. Is all well?'

'I'm not seasick, if that's what you're asking. I just cannot rid myself of doubts. Doubts about this venture – this new course Sir John has set us on. Doubts about myself.' Ellingham's normally fluent and elegant French seemed strained and faltering.

'Do not doubt yourself, Giles! It is natural to be apprehensive when one sets out on a new course.'

Ellingham turned his head to look at him. 'I should have argued more forcefully in the palace when I had the chance. With Lord Lovell and the earl. *Pushed* myself into their consideration.'

'I am sorry I was not there to support you, but I was prevented from coming, as you know.'

'Yet even so… you urged me to undertake this instead, didn't you? Why did you change your mind from one day to the next?'

Dieudonné was caught off guard. He didn't like being blamed for things, much less than by Giles. For an instant, his anger surged, but he quelled it before trying to answer.

'My prince, it was clear that those lords would not consider you to stand at their side. You are too youthful and – in their eyes at least – inexperienced of major battle. This adventure is the only other throw. That we may stay in the game. Remain *relevant*. Until we join battle.'

Ellingham snorted. 'Inexperienced compared to Lincoln, my cousin? I've fought more than he has! For the past few years I've hidden away my identity, then, when it is revealed, it still counts for nothing. My aunt gave me only cold recognition. I knew not what to make of it.'

Dieudonné wrapped his arm around Ellingham's shoulder, but he felt the youth recoil underneath it. 'Giles, they have other princes. For now. Perhaps she sees that your role lies in the future – not to be risked now.'

'No. I am a bastard. Always. She has sent me away on this foolish errand instead.'

'It is not foolish. And it is the only choice. For now.'

Ellingham glared at Dieudonné such that he pulled back his arm from around the youth's shoulders. 'Sometimes, Gaston, I think you are as changeable as the wind.' He then reached into the concealed pocket of his doublet and pulled out the little duck-egg blue velvet pouch. Reaching for Dieudonné's hand, he pressed it into his palm and closed the fingers around it.

'You may have this back, for all the good it has done me. Maybe this stone is cursed after all.' Ellingham pushed away from the handrail and hurried back down the deck and around the mainmast. Dieudonné felt his face flushing despite the chill. He pushed the gemstone into his own pocket. A cold anger continued to well up, making him feel more distant from all around him. With it came a sense of disquiet – perhaps the detection of early rot – in something he thought had been a perfect and attainable goal. The conquest of Giles Ellingham.

It was bad enough that his love had been spurned, but it almost incensed him to think his loyalty had been questioned. Did the youth not think that he, too, was taking a gamble with his life? He himself was returning to a foreign land whose new ruler he had betrayed two years earlier. That was a risk that could not be laughed away. He felt a bitterness rise up in his mouth. It now seemed to be an all or nothing bet, like in a game of cups and balls. The House of York – or of Lancaster. He had to choose wisely because this late in the game, he might only get one chance.

–

Hawker was up with the daybreak, a hazy sort of light suffused by a sky of high cloud. From the high forecastle deck, he looked down on Jacob watering the horses, and the crew swilling the deck with buckets of seawater to flush out the piles of shit and puddles of piss. Despite the cloud, the weather looked to be holding fair and the wind was strong. The *Artemis* ploughed the waves, its bluff bow dipping and rising, and he could see the hazy coastline of England in the distance.

He thought about what lay ahead upon that shore. With luck, he believed they could make it to Stamford without being stopped by sheriffs' men. They would skirt the larger towns on the way, talking themselves out of trouble if they had to, or else a short sharp fight to decide it. The risk was if they ran into a retinue of some lord or a band raised for Henry, arrayed by local knights. That would mean flight – or death.

And what would he find upon returning to the old grange? Would Catherine welcome him? Harbour him, if needs be? He truly did not know. But surely the ties of blood would count for something. He still had a large sack of gold coins there, hidden. Treasure from his first foray into Venetian service. He had given Catherine another. He had looked out for her interests as well, had he not?

'So, there it lies.'

It was Ellingham, who had come up the stairs, catching him unawares.

'We've made good progress.'

'Does he know of our change in course?'

Hawker turned and gave Ellingham a wry smile. 'No, not yet.'

'You say we need keep our aliases once we're on the road. Rede and Wickham. Do you really think anyone will believe that ruse?'

'It only needs to be believed for as long as it takes us to get past an outpost or a patrol.'

Ellingham nodded. 'I suppose, I am more worried about the reception we will find in Stamford. What if Catherine is gone away? Or – forgive me – dead. Then what?'

'I won't lie to you, Giles. I cannot answer that. I can only hope that she yet lives and still runs the house. But I know in my heart she would never betray me. Or you. I ask that you have faith. And I know we will find others who will join us and fight when the time comes. As it will.'

Ellingham approached the rail and took in a deep lungful of air. 'Faith? I have not much else to my name. I slept poorly, Sir John. A hundred phantasms in my mind not helped by this god-dammed tub we sail in.'

'I know. We will both sleep better once on land. In a good feather bed, if we can find one between Blakeney and Castle Acre.'

Ellingham said nothing.

'Come with me. It's past time we had a conversation with Master Smout.'

They found him in the aftcastle, in heated conversation with one of his sailors who was manning the whipstaff, which steered the vessel.

'A word with you, Master Smout!' said Hawker in his heavily accented Flemish.

Smout swore, turned back to his man and issued a command, then pounded across the planks out from under the covered stern. 'What do you want?'

'I would know how far you reckon we are from Yarmouth,' replied Hawker politely.

The master, a stocky square-headed man, barefoot in his hose and padded jerkin, put his hands on his hips. 'By sundown – but we'll have to wait upon the tide to see whether we can go in straightaway. We get there when we get there.'

'I would beg you for a change in destination, sir. We do not wish to land at Yarmouth.'

Smout broke into a grin, his teeth ground to nubs from loosening knotted ropes for twenty years. 'You don't, eh? You may be English knights but to me you're just passengers. This is my ship. We are bound for Yarmouth, and that is where I am contracted to go. If you wish for elsewhere, you can get there from Yarmouth.'

'We need to go to Blakeney... up the coast.' Hawker looked him in the eye, feet planted on the gently swaying deck.

The smile melted from Smout's face. 'I know where it is... and I don't give a whore's crack for where you need to go.'

Jacob emerged from between two of the horses and slowly came up behind Hawker. He said not a word but gave the master a hard stare.

'Master Smout,' said Hawker, smiling. 'It is no idle request. And I can pay you handsomely in gold gulden if you will but land us there. You've already been paid for our passage. Now you get paid twice over. You can return to Yarmouth and land tomorrow.'

Smout's eyes flashed. 'And if I say no? The palace's orders were clear.'

Hawker raised his palms. 'What can gold not settle? Name your price.'

By now, four sailors had gathered behind Smout, knives in their belts. Jacob was wearing his sword belt, but not his armour. He stepped to Hawker's side, face expressionless. Hawker's hand moved to the hilt of his *cinquedea*, resting upon it. Ellingham took two steps back and set his feet at shoulder's width.

Hawker could see Smout was chewing on the inside of his cheek. Thinking. 'You already know that we will fight if we have to. And how would you explain that to the palace? Your precious passengers killed. I know what you have been ordered to do. And *you* know who we are.'

Hawker hoped that his bad Flemish, sprinkled with German, had made sense. 'Yarmouth is not safe for us any more. We will not land there.'

One of Smout's men made to move forward but the master lashed out and gripped his arm like a striking snake. The man moved back behind.

For a long moment he stared at Hawker. And then he let out a laugh so raucous and explosive that the horses flinched in their slings. 'Gold gulden solve many problems! Maybe it can solve ours, Englishman.' He raised a forefinger of warning. 'But I will be paid *now*. Not later. Understood?'

Hawker smiled and gave him an exaggerated courtly bow. 'Then let us make the transaction like two good Christians.'

Smout shook his head, smiling. 'Come with me. We'll strike a bargain and drink aqua vitae to seal it.'

Jacob whispered into Hawker's ear. 'And I will stand at your back.'

Ellingham looked over to Hawker. 'If I understood half as much as I think I did, we just averted a little war at sea.'

Hawker nodded and smiled at him. 'But be on your guard, just the same,' he said in English.

–

Joris Smout kept his word. The ship headed north by north-west, the coast of Norfolk four points on the larboard bow, a league or more distant. Hawker knew the man was seething underneath at his authority being challenged, but the gold had swayed him. Blakeney being on the north coast meant sailing around the county towards the Wash – the very route they had sailed leaving England two years earlier. It also meant many more hours at sea.

The winds stayed fair but their luck did not hold to the tides. By the time they reached the Glaven, the tide had ebbed. Smout dropped anchor and they waited until just before daybreak before entering the estuary on the flow. That last night Hawker had slept badly again, his Venetian dagger gripped in his hand upon his chest. Ellingham had fallen asleep upright in his tiny bedstead, clutching his arming sword, his back propped against the cabin wall. Hawker had taken the precaution of wedging a bit of wood into the jamb of the cabin door to prevent it from being fully shut. Smout might have easily trapped them by shoving a marlin spike into the hasp, locking them in.

But with the morning sun and the crisp air, the fears of the night were dispelled. Smout paid them no heed, busy with the delicate task of navigating the channel into Blakeney port. Jacob and Dieudonné had donned full armour again, Hawker and Ellingham their breast and backplates. Three seamen fended the ship with long poles and the *Artemis* finally rubbed noisily along the rope bollards of the pier, shuddering slightly. Hawker saw Jacob make the sign of the cross before untethering the horses.

'Burgundian! Make yourself useful!' Jacob cried in French. 'You're not a lord yet.'

Dieudonné grinned but his eyes were filled with an intensity that screamed disdain. 'I am here to serve,' he replied sarcastically. He looked after only his own horse though, loosening the sling it was in. The saddle was sticky and damp with saltwater and he cursed.

The gangway was put in place and the section of railing lifted out.

Smout stood, arms crossed, and watched as his passengers led their unsteady mounts carefully down onto the dock. Hawker turned and looked up at him. He saluted him with a gloved hand and doffed his bonnet. Smout gurned, and then spat over the side.

Hawker took Ellingham by the elbow as they walked their horses across the quay. 'We must mount up now and get out of the village before the customs men come.' He could see a group of officials gathered at the far end, one holding an enormous ledger, shouting at one of the others.

'Agreed!' said Ellingham.

Hawker signalled to Jacob and Dieudonné, who then both put feet to stirrups and hauled themselves into their saddles. Hawker looked about the quayside, searching for watchers, and then mounted as did Ellingham.

Hawker led them out, single file, down the dirt track towards the church and the main road south. Ahead, the landscape was an undulating coverlet of rolling fields of greens and browns, isolated stands of twisted pine trees, all the land gently rising towards where Fakenham lay, miles distant. It was as he remembered it, as a far younger man. He found the main trade road and it soon widened enough for them all to ride two abreast. He looked over to Ellingham. The youth's face was set hard with worry. For himself, he felt strangely light-headed, looking out on the countryside he knew well and had been away from for so long. He would bring Chiara and Nicholas here, one day.

He called across to the young knight who was staring blankly down the road. 'Lift up your heart, Giles! We have finally returned. It is the middle of May!'

Ellingham gave him a dejected look. 'God has seen fit to deliver us. Now we must see what else he will bestow.'

Hawker managed a light laugh. 'You carry too much upon your shoulders. No man living can know His will. We endure… and take what joy we can each day. For me – this night – it will be a bed of goose down, if God wills it.'

Ellingham shook his head slowly and couldn't suppress a grin. 'You truly do not know where we're going, do you? Tell me it is so. No great stratagem. No plan of engagement. We're like dandelions, blown by the winds. And it doesn't bother you. Ever.'

'I have a nose for making the right choice when I need to. And I chose to stand by you.'

Ellingham paused for a moment, then nodded. He resumed his watch of the road ahead.

The morning wore into midday. They passed a few wagons bearing barrels, bound for the Glaven ports. And one, piled high with what Hawker recognised as bales of wool, tightly wrapped in muslin, probably from Fakenham market and headed for Flanders. The sight of it brought a sudden melancholy to him. A childhood memory of riding along on one such journey, buoyed by the soft bundles over every rut and hole. A lifetime ago. Of a sudden, he found himself choking with emotion. He coughed once, suppressing it, and wiped the back of his hand across his mouth.

They stood to the side and let the wagon pass by.

Hawker could not keep his eyes from it though. Ellingham took the lead, not waiting for him. Then Dieudonné trotted to catch him up. Jacob came alongside Hawker.

'Sir John?'

Hawker looked up.

'We make a halt?'

The old knight shook his head. 'No.'

It was then he heard Ellingham cry out a warning.

Hawker wheeled his horse and looked past the others. Up ahead, a hundred yards, there was a party of half a dozen mounted men. God had revealed to him His first test of faith.

He drew his arming sword a few inches from its scabbard and threw back his mantle over his right shoulder.

24

A week had passed in the blink of an eye and Jack Perry's head was still spinning.

The army encampment, which to him had at first seemed lazy and disorganised, had proven to be an illusion. In reality, it was a beehive of useful toil with layer upon layer of complexity underpinning it all. From the finely bedecked officers in their satin sashes to the lowliest dirty and ragged *landsknecht*, an unspoken hierarchy ruled everywhere. A separate army of cooks, clothes merchants, armourers, ditch-diggers, errand-runners and harlots lived cheek by jowl with the soldiers to meet every conceivable need. Jack even saw a priest administering one day and the next a chiurgeon sewing up a man's bicep with catgut and needle.

And the training had begun for him in earnest on the second day. It was unlike anything Jacob had prepared him for, a style of fighting wholly unknown to him. For one, he had never seen a pike before. It was like a long-spear but far longer – over fourteen feet – with a narrow, sharp but un-barbed steel head. The easier to stick into someone and then pull out again, said David Weems. In England, Jack had watched from a distance the clash of armies at Bosworth, but this seemed far, far different. The *landsknechts* formed into tightly packed squares, row upon row of pikemen. The first row or two would point their pikes ahead to the enemy, the rows behind had theirs raised to the sky.

Small groups of crossbowmen and hand gunners would linger on the flanks, able to shoot and fire and retreat inside the safety of the square when in battle. The front ranks also held the 'double-pay men', the long-sword and glaive- and halberd-bearing soldiers who would dash out on command and try and penetrate the enemy formations. Jack understood the idea was to create a massive 'hedgehog' of these long spears, that would move across the field and defend itself by staying together as one. And although Jack was seeing them train in groups of dozens, Weems assured him the squares could grow to be enormous: five hundred men or more in each, banners fluttering in the centre, booming drums and shrill fifes sounding the commands.

And Jack had already been tested. The sergeant had pulled him aside his first morning and made him spar with a double-pay man. It was to prove he was what he claimed to be. Jack had taken up guard with his sword and buckler outstretched as Jacob had drilled him. The veteran grinned through the entire sparring, probing with his *katzbalger* − 'cat-scrapper' − a sort of short, round-tipped arming sword most of the *landsknechts* seemed to carry as their side weapon for fighting close in. The man also had a small round shield, which he feinted with, poking it out to lure Jack to strike. But Jack's method was steady, cautious even, and he hit the shield only to force the soldier to respond. Jack then quickly converted the blow with a simultaneous side-step and brought it to a halt near the man's neck. The double-pay veteran laughed loudly, shook his head, and the sergeant waved a halt to the sparring. It was enough.

'Not bad for a boy!' the officer told him. 'Now back to the others in the square!'

Unlike Weems and the Scots, he was not destined to be a pikeman. His practice amounted to running about with his crossbow while the others practised marching and turning on the flanks. There were only about ten crossbowmen in his *fähn-lein*, and a dozen gunners. Most were Germans and Confederates from the Alps and he struggled to understand them. Flushed with embarrassment at their frustration with him, he did his best to emulate them and at least match their accuracy while shooting at targets. He knew he had to master their tongue or he would be lost. In confusion, it might even cost him his life.

'I knew not a word of their blasted tongue,' reassured Weems, one evening around the fire outside their tent. 'But one picks it up quick enough... stops you from getting hit on the head!'

Jack found it easier to understand the Scots than the German, but he took the point. He'd learn it, and learn it fast. He was already grateful that Weems had taken him under his wing. The fiery-bearded soldier from Fife seemed to be held in high esteem by the others and it was no bad thing to have such a man as a friend. His comrade Luke was also from Fife and they had joined up together, having left the retinue of some Scottish nobleman and run away to Flanders.

'Pay was always late,' said Weems, speaking into his beer, 'garrison duty was boring and cold. We'd heard there was better pay over here. Dependable pay.'

'And the fighting?' asked Jack.

'We've beaten up a fair few apprentices and their masters in Bruges and in Ghent in the past year,' replied Luke. 'Thought we'd be going southwards by now though. To a real battlefield somewhere. Maybe you will turn our luck, eh?' Luke was a taciturn fellow at the best of times it seemed, but he had slowly begun to warm to Jack. He had taken to jesting with him more than insulting him, which was a start.

After a few days he'd gotten the pace of life in camp: up with the light, then bread and cheese or sausage to break the fast, drills, and later a more substantial bowl of stew from the sutlers' wagons at the far end of the encampment. Evenings would be spent gambling over cards and dice, listening to the one or two *landsknechts* who played lute, fist-fighting or visiting the harlots' tents.

And though Jack had his hands full with coming to grips with his newfound trade, his mind frequently wandered back to that first afternoon when he had found himself in the arms of a very willing woman. He felt sheepish about it now, the not knowing quite what to do. But she and her companion had taken charge and he found glorious revelation in an act he knew to be sinful but still somehow couldn't understand why when it felt so good. And he wanted more.

Weems wagged a finger at him the second time he brought up his desires. 'Look, lad, you will beggar yourself in no time if you frequent those tents. Same for dicing. But, with the dice, at least you don't have to fear for your cock festering. Go slowly!'

Jack contemplated that and didn't mention the matter again.

Even with his lack of experience, Jack had begun to notice the mood of the encampment changing after his first few days. Weems told him that rumours were sweeping the camp about where they were destined for and when they would leave. Jack had heard enough from Hawker to know they were headed for a ship and to Ireland. He had only told Weems, and Weems had not yet spread the news.

Weems lifted his square chin, eyes narrowing. '*Ireland?* You said England a few days ago.'

Jack frowned to himself. The politics of it all were beyond him. 'Something about a new king being crowned in Dublin – a boy. The rebel lords intend to raise an army there and then sail over to England to battle King Henry. The landsknechts are part of that army. That is what my knight told me.'

Luke looked downcast. 'That is a long way from here. A *long* time at sea. I hate boats.'

'Jesu,' mumbled Weems. 'He's right. Maybe a fortnight on ship. And then you say we will sail again – to England?'

Jack nodded.

'Christ help us. I'd rather march to France and scrap with them!' He shook his head and then looked at Jack. 'Maybe your wish to spend your gold on harlots isn't such a bad idea. While we all can.'

And the soldiers were drinking more and not just at night. The provost and his men could often be seen hauling away men for brawling. Drill alone was not enough to quell the disquiet and boredom. Nor deter those who had a streak of badness. On the seventh day, Jack heard the sergeant bark the command that dismissed his square of pikemen, double-pay men and bowmen. In the rapidly dissolving ranks and files, he sought out Weems and Luke, both balancing their great pikes upon their shoulders. But before he reached them, two Flemish pikemen intercepted him.

'You there!' said one of them. 'I like those spaulders you wear. A crossbowman doesn't need armour like that. Fancy a wager for them? I'll put up this here Tyrol dagger.'

Jack wasn't about to give up his shoulder armour – part of the armour he'd been gifted in Hungary. And it was a boldfaced lie that he wouldn't be needing it. Most of the soldiers had only a breastplate and back, their heads topped by a close-fitting skullcap of iron. Arms and legs were bare of armour. With his far better harness, Jack already stood out awkwardly from most of them.

The pikeman balanced his haft of ash in the crook of arm and shoulder and flipped the dagger out with his free hand. 'A very good piece. More use to you, boy.'

Jack shook his head and started walking again, throwing his crossbow over his shoulder. They followed him, bellowing that he was rude and not a game comrade. He felt a hand on his shoulder and he spun around.

'I don't want your poxy dagger!' Jack blurted in his bad Flemish.

'Then I shall fight you for it!' said the pikeman. He was not much taller than Jack but he was older and had a face full of knife scars. His companion laid a hand on his shoulder and said something that sounded like he should leave off. The pikeman swore, fixed Jack with an evil glare, and then turned away.

Weems had witnessed the last moments. 'Have a care, Jack Perry,' he said. 'He's a nasty one. Stay away from him.'

Late that afternoon, Jack and the Scots made their way down to the collection of tents where the cooks and camp followers lived, near a sharp bend in the river. There were many wagons and field kitchens there, great iron stew pots simmering over makeshift uprights and poles hacked out from cut-down trees. It was almost a town in itself, existing solely to feed and supply nearly two thousand men every day. For a couple of *pfennigs*, one could have a large bowl of stew with whatever the sutler had managed to throw in that day: goat, sheep or pig.

Weems and Luke had wandered over to another kitchen in the vain hope of different fare while Jack waited in a queue with his bowl in front of a great cauldron from which a burly sutler and his buxom wife took turns ladling out stew. The line moved forward. Jack could smell the pot from where he stood, a distinct smell of pork and God knew what else wafting over him. He shuffled forward again, used to the monotony after a week of it.

He thought again of Sir John and Jacob and how they might have reacted to his running away. He felt bad that he knew not how to write a message. Nor could he have risked telling anyone to tell them later. And there was guilt in him too for the manner of his leaving. But it was far too late to go back now. The penalty for desertion was death. He had desired adventure and escape from Mechelen. He had now found it.

He felt fingers rap at his shoulder, the lames of his armour tinging with each tap. He turned. It was the Fleming pikeman again, and two of his comrades.

'If you won't play fair like a good comrade-in-arms then we'll treat you like a peasant! I'll take what I want!'

Jack felt himself go flush with the challenge, his cheeks instantly going hot. 'Your face looks like you've lost most of your fights,' he stammered. 'I'd move off if I were you.'

Jack heard the sutler call out to move up. He turned his back on the Fleming and took two steps, holding up his wooden bowl. There was a grip on his forearm and he was swung around again to face the Tyrolean dagger a few inches from his face.

'I'll give you a few of the licks I have then, shall I?'

Jack pushed him back and he came on again but the sutler's great wooden ladle came down between them. The man barked out a command in German and then shoved the ladle into the Fleming's chest to push him back. Jack stepped to the side and saw the brown stew drip down the Fleming's breastplate. A curse exploded from the Fleming and he went for the sutler like some lunatic. The German, wide-eyed and surprised by the attack, struck the Fleming in the head with his ladle, which rang loudly off the man's skull-cap. The pikeman in turn swept the dagger in a wide arc and Jack watched the sutler lean backwards as the blade passed by him. The pikeman paused and the sutler stood there, almost frozen, his hand across his throat. Jack saw lines of red appear between the man's fingers and when the sutler pulled his hand away there was a torrent of blood.

Soldiers around the cauldron suddenly gave way. Some cried out. The sutler's wife screamed and the sutler himself sank to his knees and then gently rolled over onto the muddy ground. Two big double-pay men grabbed the Fleming and began to beat him; the man's companions had already made themselves scarce. Jack dropped his bowl and backed away into the milling group of excited soldiers. A finely bedecked soldier came trotting over to join the scene – another sergeant it seemed by his dress.

The Fleming flopped like a landed fish on the ground, all the fight gone out of him with the realisation of what he had done. Jack watched him dragged away by the double-pay men and the sergeant. Before they disappeared from sight, he saw another officer join them, the one he knew to be the provost of the company, a fearsome bear of a man who kept discipline and detained those who broke the rules and their oath. The Fleming was set up on his feet again and led off, meekly submitting. His friends were nowhere to be seen.

Jack was shaking and hurriedly went to where he had last seen the Scots looking for a meal. He found them sitting on a log and shovelling stew into their mouths like pigs at a trough. He excitedly told of what had just happened.

'I knew it would not end well,' said Weems, wiping his mouth with his doublet sleeve. 'The fool got it in his head he needed what you had and would not take no for an answer.'

'You'll get to see something special now, Englishman,' said Luke of Kirkcaldy.

'What do you mean?' asked Jack, already nervous that he might be implicated in the brawl. 'Will they arrest me, too?'

Luke waved his hand. 'No. If they were going to they would have plucked you out straight away. You were just nearby. Right?'

Jack nodded, not completely convinced.

'They pretty much let us kill who we like – when we're allowed to,' said Weems. 'But murder in the camp, well, aye, that is the biggest sin of all.'

'What will happen to the Fleming now?'

'Imbecile,' mumbled Luke. 'It's evil, it is. Killing the man who feeds you every day.'

Weems resumed eating, his spoon clacking into his bowl. 'There'll be a trial now. Maybe tomorrow. There must have been many witnesses.'

'There were,' said Jack. 'But I was the one who he was trying to fight. They might single me out.'

'Nay,' said Weems. 'There's no way to dress that pig up. He drew steel and went for the sutler. You didn't. Just keep your mouth shut.'

Weems handed Jack his empty bowl and told him to get something to eat for himself. He was still shaking when he paid his silver penny and sat down again with the Scots. But the food warmed him – whatever it was – and he became calmer. The Scots worried that the Fleming's comrades might come for Jack, so they advised taking to the tents earlier than they normally did. Jack slept fitfully, dropping off and then waking, fearful he might be hauled out of his rude cot and taken away. But there was nothing but the snoring and farting of his comrades and eventually he drifted off out of exhaustion, and slept until the morning.

As they arose and dressed, poking about the remains of their campfire, word came from the tents near them that the trial of the Fleming would begin today. There was some astonishment and a great deal of anger, said Weems, for murdering one of the camp followers was deemed very bad behaviour – even for a *landsknecht*. Before the sun had risen too far, they heard horns and drums coming from the assembly point at the centre of the encampment. And a short while later, one of the sergeants made his way through the tents, announcing there would be a 'pike court'.

Weems nodded when he heard. 'I thought that would happen. He'll get no lengthy trial, not that one. Not for what he done.'

'What then? Tell me.'

'Tell you? Lad, you can watch it for yourself. We all get to go see it.'

—

They assembled at midday to the slow, steady beat of drums. The banners of the two *fähnlein* that comprised their company flew at the centre of the open field. Jack let Weems and Luke push through the hundreds gathered to get a better view of what was taking place. There was a long table set up and two sets of benches. Jack instantly recognised the bearded one – the *landsknecht* officer who had sworn him into the company – seated at the centre of the table. He had on a wide black bonnet sprouting a dozen pheasant feathers and a blue feather from a more exotic bird that Jack did not know.

Weems pointed him out. 'He is the obrist, lord of the company. He serves directly under Lord Martin the Black.'

'Martin Schwarz?' asked Jack.

'Aye, as he is named in the German. Knighted by the emperor. And see the double-pay men take their places on the benches? They will judge the Fleming's guilt.'

These two were dressed in their gaudy clothes, each topped with some sort of extravagant hat. They all wore their short swords at their hips. Sergeants stood alongside, bearing halberds. When all were assembled, three of the trumpeters let their horns blare. The Fleming was led out of a nearby tent, stripped to his linen shirt, his hole-shot green hose, and low shoes. Even from the distance Jack was standing, he could clearly see the ashen face of the man, eyes wide in fear as he was led forward to the table.

'He will get *our* judgement,' said Weems quietly.

Jack still didn't understand what that meant. At the table, the *obrist* made some announcement – probably the charge of murder – and proceeded to call two other soldiers to the table.

'Those two will put the arguments, such as they are,' explained Weems. Jack watched as one began an oration to the two benches of double-pay men. It was the strangest sight Jack had seen in his young life. A group of soldiers seemingly dressed in motley, all bright colours and feathered plumes, listened intently while one of them bellowed and pointed at the accused. He launched into a spirited tirade, almost leaping about in his anger at the crime. After a few minutes he beckoned to a few soldiers standing nearby. These men brought forward the sutler's widow. Before they could stop her, she had broken free of their guiding arms and rushed the Flemish pikeman. She beat him with her hands and fists and he did little to defend himself before the guards pulled her off. She then kneeled upon the ground in front of the *obrist*'s table and pleaded for justice, hands raised. Finally, a double-pay man came over and helped her rise, escorting her back to the side-lines and the camp followers who had accompanied her.

The soldiers around Jack began mumbling their approval and shaking their heads at the baseness of the crime.

The second *landsknecht* officer to orate came on and bowed to the *obrist*. Many of those around Jack wandered off, bored with it, only coming back a while later. It went on for some minutes. Jack thought it was not a very spirited defence, but he felt his stomach wamble at the thought of this army magistrate calling him out as a witness, or worse, naming him the cause of the entire affray. He felt himself break into a sweat all over and then that caused his skin to itch from the woollen hose he wore.

'Sweet Jesu, David, what if they call me up there? What would I say?'

Weems put an arm around his shoulders. 'Worry not, lad. They won't. And if they did, I would go up there with you.'

Then, it was time for the accused to plead his case. Jack dug his fingernails into his palms as he strained to listen to the pikeman. He was dreading to hear the word *Englishman* spoken. But from the snatches that Jack could catch, the man was pleading for leniency and not making accusations. He, too, fell to his knees and cried out, imploring the benches of veterans to let him live. And, very unexpectedly, Jack felt sorry for the poor man, reduced to begging for his life. All the result of one moment of blind rage. The soldiers around Jack began to shout and hiss and eventually the pikeman was hauled to his feet again and led back several paces.

The *obrist* spoke to the men on the benches and the deliberation began. It did not take long. One veteran from each of the two benches came forward and went to the *obrist*. They spoke briefly and then the commander called for the accused to be brought forward again. Glorious in his purple-and-black doublet, hose and fur mantle, he slowly stood and made the pronouncement against the accused.

The pikeman crumpled and had to be held up by the two guards on either side. A great cheer went up among the hundreds of soldiers. Horns began to blare a fanfare. And then Jack watched in confusion as some of the soldiers, pikes pointed skyward, walked forward and into the centre of the clearing. There were at least one hundred of them and they took station in two lines, three deep, facing each other at about ten paces distant. The standard bearers of the two *fähnlein* brought the banners to one end and took station there: the red and blue of Jack's company and the black-and-white stripes of the other. The provost came next, followed by the guilty and his escort of halberdiers.

Weems again wrapped an arm around Jack's shoulders. 'This is the justice of the landsknechts. You will not have seen the likes of it before, Jack Perry.'

The provost spoke quietly to the Fleming and then beckoned him with an outstretched arm. The man had regained some of his composure now that the sentence had been passed upon him. He nodded and then began walking between the two lines. Jack could see he was calling out to those on either side as he passed, pausing briefly to say a few words to those it seemed he knew. The Fleming walked to the end and then walked back again, calling out to others. Occasionally, some of the cordon would call out to him words of encouragement.

'What in hell's name is happening?' asked Jack, craning for a better view.

'He is asking for the forgiveness of his comrades,' said Weems gravely. 'And he is receiving it.'

The Fleming stood next to the provost. He began reciting his *Pater Noster* and some around Jack prayed aloud with him. Many blessing themselves. And then the drummers began their cadence, and the pipers joined them. Jack watched as slowly every pike was lowered to the horizontal at about waist height. The provost struck the Fleming thrice upon his right shoulder. Jack saw the man lower his head and then break into a run down the length of the lines. As soon as he did so, the dense thicket of pike heads pierced him, again and again. Blotches of red quickly spread on his white linen, ripped to tatters in moments. He stumbled and made it halfway before he fell to the ground. The pikes thrust at him again and again until he stopped thrashing. Jack's jaw went slack.

'*That* is what murderers in this army get,' said Weems. 'Just remember – you only can kill when they tell you that you can kill!' He clapped a stone-still Jack on the back. 'Come on, let's go to the tents. I stole some good cheese from a store wagon before all this and I'm hungry again.'

25

Hawker and Ellingham manoeuvred their horses into the lead, Jacob and Dieudonné falling in just behind.

'Let me speak! Do nothing rash,' warned Hawker quietly. At a walking pace they drew closer to the men approaching. They were unarmoured, from what he could see at distance. They came on two by two, those in the front looked like merchants but the ones following might be men-at-arms wearing cloaks. Hawker's eye saw they were all riding nothing better than rounceys; not a war horse could he see among them.

The road was wide enough for four or five abreast and Hawker kept his party on the left, so that their sword side would be facing the potential enemy. The new arrivals showed no sign of alarm and Hawker reined in. He raised an arm in greeting.

'Hallo! You are bound for the coast then?'

One of the men, a young fellow and obviously well-fed, answered as his party reined to a halt.

'We are. Have you just arrived?' His demeanour was cautious but relaxed.

Hawker rapidly sized-up the others. Although armed, none seemed to be wearing harness and they looked to be what he had hoped: a party of traders headed out to sea. At their rear was a rider-less horse loaded with bundles.

Hawker gave an open smile. 'We had a good crossing. We have come from Antwerp. Looking to do business in Fakenham and Swaffham.' He noticed the others were eyeing Jacob and Dieudonné a little nervously.

'Then I wish you good fortune on your journey,' said the merchant, ready to give spurs to his horse.

'And to you,' replied Hawker. 'You may find Antwerp too busy to your liking though, if that is where you are headed. There is a rebel army taking ship even now to land here. They have a boy king and the Earl of Lincoln leading them. A good-sized force of Germans and Burgundians too, by the look of them.'

The chubby fellow's eyes widened. 'An invasion? Coming here? To Norfolk?' His companions started jabbering and Hawker tried to speak over them.

'Gentlemen, I do not know where they plan to make land-fall. I merely saw them making ready at port. A few thousands, easily.'

The man touched his hat in a farewell but said nothing else. He flicked his reins and the party moved forward, still chattering excitedly about the news.

'Are you sure that was wise?' said Ellingham.

'Why not? They are headed the other way and we are here to start rumours, aren't we? We must earn our keep, no?'

'We were lucky they weren't sheriffs' men otherwise we would not have gotten away so lightly.'

'They will spread the good word when they reach Blakeney. But we will be nowhere near Fakenham nor Swaffham.'

'Ah, Sir John!' said Dieudonné from where he was, close to Ellingham's flank. 'I must profess admiration for such spirit. Just as I would have done!'

Hawker gave him a hard look. 'I am pleased to have your approval, my lord Gaston,' he replied in French.

'So… to Castle Acre, Sir John?' asked Jacob, throwing a glance backwards just to check on the progress of the merchants.

Hawker nodded. 'We can make it there by nightfall. The road is wide and flat and a canter while the sun is high should do us all some good!'

Ellingham folded his arms across the bow of his saddle. 'So even de Grood knows where we're going? Where exactly *do* we take lodgings?'

Hawker smiled. 'At the Cluniac priory. They are discreet, welcoming to visitors and the monks like good food. You'll find little in the way of fasting there. And their house was begun by Burgundians so even Gaston might find a hospitable reception.'

–

The abbot of Castle Acre Priory welcomed them warmly and needed to know nothing more than that they had come from Flanders.

'You have found your way to our door after a long journey and your destination is not our concern,' he had told them, a broad smile on his face, bald pate of his tonsure glistening in the candlelight.

He saw that they were bedded in the lower level of his own lodgings and set a novice to wait upon their needs. He did not join them in eating for the priory had already taken their evening meal in the refectory, but Hawker's company dined on fresh carp that night from the abbot's stock pond, cooked in a parsley sauce and served with leeks, cabbage and the last of the winter's apples.

The four of them found themselves alone at table in the vaulted chamber, a good fire crackling opposite and cots and coverlets already set out for them near to it. Jacob helped himself to another chunk of bread and filled his pewter tankard with more ale.

'You knew of this place all along then?' Ellingham, now sated, looked across to Hawker and gave a smile of approval.

Hawker took another swig of his ale and nodded. 'I never had any intention of revealing our presence to any innkeeper or tavern master. Here, we are safer. Sanctuary should we need it. And between Castle Acre and Stamford there are two more abbeys. I have chosen the route already.'

'How do you feel? To be back after so long?'

Hawker raised his eyebrows. He had not expected Giles to ask such a thing and, indeed, was embarrassed by it. He had choked with tears briefly that day at unbidden memories and even now felt his own history weighing heavy on his heart. 'It is bittersweet, to be sure. But I pray we will find good reason to be happy in due time.'

Dieudonné stood and walked to the hearth. He prodded a burning log with the toe of his boot. 'I believe I will go outside to take some air,' he announced in French.

'I wouldn't wander beyond the abbey walls,' said Hawker.

Dieudonné laughed lightly. 'You think Henry Tudor is watching us already, do you?' He bowed and went to the door.

Hawker cast a knowing glance over to Jacob, who, after a few moments, rose from the bench and followed the Burgundian outside.

Ellingham shook his head slowly. 'When will you ever trust him? We've been halfway to Constantinople and back! Has he not proven himself again and again? He is prickly, I will grant you that. But he is loyal, too.'

'I have never understood his motives for joining us. I still do not. If he is who he says he is – of some noble house – then why stay with us all these months? After Bosworth the other Burgundian mercenaries who survived returned home. He clung to us like a lamprey.'

'He is… a conflicted man.' Ellingham's voice was quiet.

Hawker lowered his chin. 'Conflicted? By what decision?'

'By his nature,' replied Ellingham cryptically. He said nothing more.

Hawker scowled. 'Aye, well, you seem to understand him better than I. But until our war is won here, we tread with care. We are on our own.'

'I know that. We both risk much to be here.'

They were on the road again after dawn, having arisen to the sound of the monks chanting Lauds. Dieudonné felt peevish, borne of a restless sleep. Riding west, the land was flat as far as they could see. They descended from the rolling pastures of Norfolk down into the Fens, crossing the River Great Ouse at a ford and carrying on into the 'Wells'. No one took notice of them, and as they delved deeper into Fenland, they saw scattered groups of men cutting peat turves and loading them onto carts, others fishing in the many small meres that dotted the landscape. Vast fields of bulrushes nodded in the breeze and though it was May, a chill still lingered on the air. Dieudonné realised that Hawker had intentionally taken lesser roads, some no more than a rutted track the width of two horses.

The sun was sinking in the sky when Hawker called a halt to rest and water the horses. 'We should make Thorney Abbey by nightfall,' he announced to them all. 'We've made good time. It cannot be more than fifteen miles.'

Ellingham dismounted and adjusted his sword belt while his eyes scanned the landscape. 'This is not the way we came when we fled at Bosworth.'

'No, it is not,' said Hawker. 'We are much further south. More remote and fewer prying eyes.'

'It is a sodden, waterlogged shithole,' said Dieudonné, taking off his cloak and throwing it over his saddle. 'I see a pond there,' he said, pointing. 'This beast needs a drink and I need a piss.' He grasped the bridle and led his mount off the track and into the grasslands. The others dismounted too and stretched their legs.

Dieudonné wandered, armour jangling, his boots squishing and getting tangled in the long grass. He cursed. Cursed at the terrain and cursed at himself, for part of him no longer knew what he was doing in this place. He kept his eye on the pond, drawing ever closer and prayed it was not some stagnant pit of brine water. Although he had not slept well the night before, the monkish fare had gone down very well indeed. But dry bread and stale cheese had not improved his mood this day and he was both irritated and hungry. Giles had grown colder towards him ever since they had argued on ship, and he was both hurt and angry that his love for the youth had remained unrequited these many long months. And he was beginning to ask himself why he persisted in the quest. Was it infatuation turned to madness?

He entered a wide patch of dark green moss blanketing the ground leading to the mere. It was like walking on a mattress, his feet sinking and then springing up again. He felt his horse baulk at the unsteady footing and he swore at it, yanking the bridle. After a few moments the horse would move no more and he released the bridle with a curse, slapping his breastplate in frustration. He stormed forward, intent on relieving himself. His mount could go to hell.

Dieudonné took a step, lost his footing in the spongy stuff, and his left leg jerked forward to steady himself. But his foot found no purchase. He fell forward and plunged through the thin, quaking coverlet of sphagnum which covered the mere. And he sank.

The shock of it fully enlivened him. He thrashed and kicked. He kicked again and his head momentarily broke the surface. He gulped for air but sank again almost immediately. His feet found purchase on the bottom, the water and moss at the top of his head. But the weight of armour and gambeson underneath held him down, and try as he might to haul himself back, Dieudonné suddenly realised that he would now drown. The rust-brown water swirled around his face and then he felt his boots being sucked down into the mire of the bottom. He sank a few inches deeper.

Panicking, he scrabbled at the buckles of his harness, desperate to free himself, but his hands could only fumble. By now, his lungs burned and he fought to keep from expelling his last breath. He suddenly felt something at the back of his neck, a rough push, and then he was being hauled upwards by the lip of his steel backplate. His head broke the surface, he sucked in a breath, and then he screamed. He was being yanked backwards through the moss. He felt firmer ground underneath him and looked up to see the face of Jacob de Grood peering down at him.

'*Verdomde dwaas!*'

Jacob bent down and hauled him up into a sitting position. 'If you wanted a drink, Burgundian, you should have asked!'

Dieudonné did his best to stop shaking. Embarrassment swept over him, his panic subsiding. He rolled over, hands sinking into the moss, and he brought his legs forward on all fours and staggered unsteadily to his feet. The Fleming did not help.

He saw Hawker and Ellingham coming forward too, gingerly making their way through the treacherous moss.

'Gaston!' cried Ellingham, finally reaching him. 'Whatever possessed you? You're lucky Jacob chased after you.'

Dripping and sodden, Dieudonné turned to the Fleming. 'I owe you my life, de Grood.'

Jacob's face remained unmoving, but he gave a curt bow of his head in acknowledgement.

Hawker frowned at the scene. 'I would not have taken you for a fool of such rashness in unknown country, my lord. But the Lord seems to find favour – you're living up to your name. Can you ride now?'

Dieudonné's voice came out rough. 'I am ready.'

Why had it been the Fleming who had saved him from death? The oafish fellow had never liked him or trusted him, and that he knew very well. Why had not Giles been at his side? Inside, he could feel a new anger welling up, born of shame. With a second chance at life, suddenly a veil had been lifted from his eyes.

26

The abbey on the Isle of Thorney rose up like some great ship upon a calm sea. Surrounded by fenland, it could be seen for miles around, an unmoving vessel built of stone whose mission was the salvation of souls.

Hawker and his companions wound their way along the narrow causeway and then up the gradual slope which led to the abbey walls. The wind blew strongly across the marshes, shaking the rushes. Hawker saw that Dieudonné was now shivering almost uncontrollably in the saddle. He'd been in his sodden clothing and harness for hours since his dunking and now the sun was setting fast beyond the abbey. The temperature was dropping again.

They rang the bell at the gates and were ushered into the courtyard by two monks.

'We are travellers heading west,' said Hawker, dismounting. 'I pray you still offer hospitality to outsiders. One of our number has fallen into the marshes and requires care.'

The monk, clad in black robes, took Hawker's reins. 'We do, sir. But I must inform the abbot.'

'I know him,' said Hawker. 'Father Murcot will welcome us.'

The monk shook his head. 'I am afraid that Father Murcot died a few months ere our new sovereign took the throne. Richard Holbech is our abbot now.'

Hawker realised at once this meant that Henry Tudor had appointed him. He would have to be careful.

As Ellingham's horse was led away, Hawker whispered to the youth. 'The abbot may not be a friend. We must yet be wool traders. Wickham and Rede.'

Ellingham nodded. 'What of Gaston? He is looking in a bad way.'

Hawker saw that the Burgundian was ashen and nearly swooning. 'Jacob, help get him down. And from now on – no English or French. Just Flemish.'

Jacob nodded and helped pull Dieudonné down to the ground. The monks on watch called over to a group near the cloister walls for assistance and three other monks came running.

'Take this traveller to the infirmary, brothers,' said the one monk who looked the older.

The Burgundian, barely half-sensed, gave no opposition and he staggered off, buoyed by the brethren.

'If you follow me,' said the novice, 'I will show you where you can wait before the abbot meets with you.'

Ellingham shot Hawker a worried look.

'We are grateful for your hospitality,' said Hawker. 'Lead on.'

The remaining monk, no more than a lad but fully tonsured, led them to what Hawker remembered as the guesthouse, very near to the monks' refectory. It held half a dozen beds, a long trestle table, a rush-seated stool or two, and was otherwise shorn of any comforts. The walls were white-washed plaster and a large brass crucifix stood on a cupboard at one end of the chamber. Their portmanteaus were taken from their mounts and brought to them quickly. A short time later a monk arrived with a pitcher of ale and several wooden beakers.

'The dean comes to see you momentarily, but please, refresh yourselves.'

Hawker threw off his cloak and took a bench. Jacob began unbuckling his harness and Ellingham paced.

'Have a drink, Giles.'

'I should look in on Gaston.'

'You need to have a drink. The brothers will look after the Burgundian. I'm sure it's nothing but a chill from his mishap. They'll warm him up well and pour some aqua vitae down his throat. He'll be right by morning.'

Ellingham frowned, went to the table, and poured himself some ale and then filled two more. 'So then, what *do* we tell the abbot?'

'The same as in Calais. It need not be a complicated subterfuge. I will put some flesh on the bones. Enough to get us food and lodging for the night.'

'He is a Lancastrian, then. This abbot.'

'I'd wager on it. I hadn't counted on Brother Murcot being dead. He was not even as old as me.'

'Age means nothing to Death. We all know that.'

Jacob stretched, untied the tapes of his sweat-stained gambeson, and drained his cup. 'The mattresses look fine by me, Sir John. I will keep my mouth shut and sleep until you need me. By your leave.' He put his finger to his lips. 'And no more *English*.'

A monk with a close-cropped white beard entered, hands tucked into his sleeves. 'I bid you all a good evening and welcome,' he said, looking at each in turn. 'Who leads this company and what is your business here?'

Hawker stood. 'I am John Rede, a wool trader of Calais.' He had thought first to say 'Malines' but thought better of it, given King Henry's greatest antagonist was the Duchess Dowager Margaret. 'And this is my venture partner, Richard Wickham. My Flemish man-at-arms is here with us while the other is in your infirmary. Fell into a mere this afternoon.'

'Of the latter I have already had report,' the prior replied. 'I am Father James. And the abbot has told me to see that you are all comfortable and that your injured man is looked after.'

Hawker and Ellingham both gave a bow. 'We are grateful for the welcome,' said Hawker. 'We are bound for markets west and would not have intruded on the abbey were it not for our man falling ill.'

The dean pulled one hand from the voluminous sleeves of his habit and raised it to stop further explanation. 'It is no matter. As travellers you are welcome.' He seemed to study Hawker for a few moments.

Hawker, too, thought he must have met the monk on a previous visit. Thorney lay but six leagues from his house and lands and he would occasionally visit and give alms. It was how he had met Abbot Murcot before Bosworth. If this man recognised him, their jeopardy would be double.

'Have you been this way before, Master Rede? You bear resemblance to someone I once met. But he was of this shire, I believe.' The monk's face was a mask of neutrality, his grey eyes giving nothing away.

'I have never come this way before,' said Hawker, a faint smile on his lips. 'But the quality of the sheep fleeces of Leicestershire and the hundreds of Rutland are renowned. It is what has brought us so far across the German Sea.'

'As I said, your business is not of concern to us here. You are welcome to stay until you are well enough to continue your journey.' He looked as if he was about to turn to leave, paused, and then continued. 'And the abbot wishes you and your companion to join him in breaking bread this eve, in his lodgings. Your man will be served food in here.'

Hawker nodded.

The dean gave a bow. 'You will be sent for later.' And he turned and left the chamber.

Jacob whistled softly and went to throw a log on the dying fire in the hearth. He bent down and managed to stoke it up into good strong flames again.

Ellingham looked at Hawker and the knight thought the youth looked more haggard than the day's travails merited. Ellingham shook his head slowly. 'We must play our parts well, Sir John. Our necks might depend upon it.'

Abbot Holbech hoisted his silver goblet towards Hawker and Ellingham. 'I welcome you to the abbey. To your good health!'

Hawker and Ellingham raised their goblets and drank.

'How is your man-at-arms now?' asked the cleric.

Ellingham quickly glanced to Hawker then offered a reply. 'Your brothers thought he might have an ague of the marsh water, but so far a fever has not appeared upon him. I believe he will recover well enough.'

The abbot nodded slowly. 'I am relieved to hear it.'

Two novices entered with the first remove of broiled white-fish.

'We are Benedictines so I am afraid you will find little in the way of red meat in this house.'

Hawker smiled amiably. 'We are thankful for such good food as it comes, whether fish or fowl.'

The abbot said a short grace in Latin and then the platter was served up and they began to eat. The abbot tore off a huge chunk of white bread from a large round loaf that sat upon the table.

'Tell me, Master Rede, how long have you made Calais your home? I hear it is a lonely place.'

'I have not found it so as one may take ship here when required. Besides, my good wife waits for me and keeps a fine house in the centre of the town.'

'And you, Master Wickham? How do you find living on an island surrounded by the French?' The abbot laughed at his little joke.

'I am content there… for the time being. I am sure I will return to live in England one day.'

The abbot nodded as he considered the answer. He then lightly peppered Hawker with queries of mild interest, nothing too probing but enough for Hawker to be on guard. The abbot would be waiting for him to be caught in a contradiction. The conversation was interrupted by the second remove's arrival. Hawker's eyebrows raised when he saw it was a roasted capon practically the size of a lamb. It came upon a platter of roasted and boiled root vegetables and onions, sprinkled with sprigs of rosemary.

'Gentlemen, please do help yourselves to this magnificent bird!'

Hawker felt he had to steer the talk his way lest Ellingham slip upon his words. 'My lord, how fare your tenants these days? What is the mood of the shires hereabouts? I speak of the late wars that afflicted us so cruelly.' He hoped his words were sufficiently neutral.

'We are relieved of the outcome here, I would say, Master Rede. Are you asking whether the people support their new sovereign, our lord Henry?'

'I am in no doubt that they do, my lord. You see, I only enquire as to the effect on trade this past year and I look forward with hope to a better year in the months ahead. Master Wickham and I are both glad of the new reign and that it has ushered in a just peace for all.'

The abbot smiled. 'Wise words, Master Rede. The king himself placed me in this seat and this house serves him with heart and soul. As serve we do the Almighty Father.'

It came as no surprise to Hawker. And he knew there would be little truth coming from the abbot that denied local support for the Tudor usurper. Holbech was suspicious and no doubt would report to the sheriffs any travellers he suspected of being Yorkist spies. They would leave as soon as daylight allowed them to do so. Thorney was no safe haven.

'There are those in the past month,' said the abbot between mouthfuls of his drumstick, 'who say rebellion is in the air again. We have found these to be lies spread by a few malcontents. The king has ordered that magistrates are to hang those found engaging in such rumour mongering.' He waggled the drumstick towards Hawker as if to reinforce his point.

Hawker nodded sagely. 'As is right and just. Such falsehoods are bad for trade. Which is bad for the kingdom. Bad for us all.'

'Who would wish to return to the days of the child-killer? The Hog of York. The Lord has delivered us of him.'

Ellingham blinked and stuffed more chicken into his mouth then took a deep swig of wine.

The abbot turned the conversation to Hawker's wife in Calais, probably with more interest than was proper for a monk. Hawker humoured him with descriptions of her beauty and wit. When the abbot in turn asked Ellingham of his wife, Ellingham demurred saying he had lost his love to the Fates. Hawker thought it time to end the supper.

'By your leave, my lord,' he said, leaning back and patting his stomach, 'we have had a tiring and challenging day of travel. We will beg your pardon and take our leave now.'

'I fully understand, gentlemen. I will offer up prayers for your safe onward travels.' He spread his hands and smiled benevolently.

Hawker thought how good it would feel to put his sword through the abbot's fat belly. One day, he might get the chance. Outside and down the stone steps, Ellingham spat on the ground.

'The man is a pig. I burned inside when he spoke that poison of my father.'

'Bide your time, Giles. And keep your head. We have much to do before battle is joined.'

Gaston Dieudonné lay in his low bedstead, staring at the unpainted bricks of the vaulted ceiling over his head. The brothers in the infirmary had stripped him down, placed him in bed, given him two pigs' bladders filled with hot water, and covered him with warm blankets. The thick, goose-down pillow crunched reassuringly as he eased his head back further. He had been spoon-fed a porridge by a handsome youth of a monk, finely featured and smelling of fresh lavender. The fellow knew some French and Dieudonné found it sweetly alluring as

231

the monk struggled to find his words, smiling and apologising when he got them wrong.

When he had finished his bowl of porridge, Dieudonné had reached over and grasped the monk's wrist, thanking him. The youth had blushed fully, but then covered Dieudonné's hand with his own. He held it there for more than a lingering moment and then rose from his stool and left.

Now, it was dark. He was the only one in the infirmary and a small hearth nearby glowed red with burning sea coal. The ceiling reflected the colours of the fire and Dieudonné stared, his mind drifting back to a hundred experiences of his past two years. He thought about all the choices he had made in that time – both good and bad. And those he now relented.

He saw someone enter the room. It was a brother bearing an iron lantern. As the man drew closer, Dieudonné saw that it was the young monk, Brother Timothy.

'I have come to see if you have been able to sleep,' he announced quietly, taking a seat next to Dieudonné's bed and placing the lantern on the floor. 'If you are having difficulty, I have brought a draught for you… to hasten sleep.'

Dieudonné pushed himself up a little. 'That is most thoughtful. I have not been able to sleep for hours. It was a terrible day for me. I nearly drowned.'

The monk patted him on the shoulder and ran his hand lightly down Dieudonné's bicep. 'I understand. Take this.' He reached into his cowl and pulled out a small vial. 'It is a tincture that will help you. The taste is bitter, but it is only a small sip to swallow.'

Dieudonné held it out between thumb and forefinger. He paused and looked at the monk whose upper face lay in shadow. 'Brother Timothy, I have not been truthful. My nights have been plagued for days now – long before my mishap yesterday. I have longed for restful slumber for too long. Might your apothecary not give me more of this elixir? That I might take with me upon the road.'

He heard a grumble of indecision emanate from the monk's throat. The youth leaned in closer. 'It is a strong medicine, I am told. One needs but a small amount and too much might cause one to never wake again. I do not know that I could obtain more.'

'I beg you. I would not ask if I thought I could manage without such a thing. Just enough for one week. That is how long we remain upon the road west.' Dieudonné reached over and placed his long-fingered hand upon the monk's thigh and let it rest there. 'I need your help.'

Brother Timothy let out a small sigh. 'I will see what I might be able to obtain. Come morning. Now... take your draught.'

Dieudonné gave his thigh a squeeze and then put the thin glass vial to his lips. It was very bitter. The monk took the vial away and stood. 'God grant you slumber,' he whispered, touching Dieudonné's forehead. He lifted the lantern and was gone. Dieudonné leaned his head back and stared towards the ceiling. He thought about the coming days, his prospects, and his unrequited affections. And before he realised it, he had drifted away.

—

The abbot of Thorney Abbey did not see them off in the morning, nor did the dean. Two servants led their horses out of the stable and brought provisions. Two by two, the four made their way out of the gates and down the winding path leading to the causeway below. Ellingham rode nearly knee to knee with Hawker.

'Will they send for the sheriff?' he asked. 'I was not sure if the old dean had recognised who you were.'

'I don't know. I suppose much depends on how much they believe in redemption of the soul. Forgiveness.' He then grinned at Ellingham. 'But who knows, the dean might be a Yorkist!'

233

By late morning, they had entered the tail end of Lincolnshire, the landscape changing to undulating plain and wooded copse. Hay was rising in the fields, sheep grazing in others. Hawker's heart lifted at the familiar sights, the old stone bridge on the Welland, the ancient square tower at Tallington. These were things he had not expected to ever see again and for a moment he forgot that he was a man without land or rights and still outlawed by a sullied crown.

At midday they came to the manor house that was no longer his. It looked much the same, stone walls crumbling, the roof of the grange a patchwork of tiles and bad thatching. The pond was as stagnant-looking as ever. He could have left only yesterday. So, it seemed his sister had done little to make improvements. And, for the first time, he seriously entertained the thought that she was no longer there.

They rode into the courtyard and reined in. There was no sign of anyone.

'Wait here,' said Hawker to the others. 'And stay in the saddle.'

He dismounted and went to the door. Turning the ring, it opened, unlocked. He went inside the modest, hammer-beamed great hall and saw a servant girl setting the table with pewter. She turned, gave a gasp, and darted out towards the kitchen.

Hawker stood in the middle and took in his surroundings. His coat of arms had been white-washed away from the plaster of the hearth's chimney breast. The stained glass of the large mullioned window remained untouched though. He looked at the table and recalled the night after Bosworth battle, the conversation, and the plan to flee England that had been hatched right there. A decision and a course of action that would send him across Europe and back. So much had changed – and so little.

Catherine entered the hall and stopped. She looked at him but seemed almost not to see him. As if he was a figment, a ghost. Hawker softly spoke her name.

Her hand flew to her mouth. He began to move towards her, but she burst into a run and threw her arms around him. 'Brother! God has delivered you!' She pulled back and regarded him, still only half-believing. 'You great fool! You're alive!'

Hawker smiled and held her by her shoulders. 'Catherine... to set my eyes upon you once again. I never thought I would get the chance.'

She stepped back, shaking her head. 'You should never have returned. You *must* know that. Listen to what—'

He cut her off. 'I will not be staying overlong, I promise you that. There is much about to happen. Things I must tell you.'

Hawker gripped her wrists. 'I have Sir Giles with me. Jacob de Grood and... one other. We need shelter for a few nights... food and drink. And...' He paused. 'Sister, there is much I need to tell you. Things you must prepare for.'

The cast of her face had slowly changed as he spoke. She gently broke free of him, her eyes searching his haggard features.

'And just what do you expect me to tell my husband? I am now *married*!'

Part V

LIES AND DECEPTIONS

27

Jack Perry fought his stomach and won. His heaves subsided. He was not seasick but the stench of those around him who were was overpowering. The *Grace of Margaret* gave another shudder under a swell that swept the hull and the ship almost seemed to jump sideways like a skittish horse. Slings and nets swayed wildly and men groaned across the lower deck. Poor Luke of Kirkcaldy was being held over a bucket by David Weems, so weak that he could barely support himself. Jack's arm was wrapped around David's midriff, steadying both Scots as the vessel rolled again dramatically.

Luke had nothing left to give. David rolled him onto his side and patted his head. 'That will teach you to eat double portions at sea!' He pulled a rank woollen blanket over this comrade. 'Keep breathing through your mouth.'

Jack wiped his sweating brow with his filthy linen sleeve, his stomach threatening him again. 'Let's go up. I can't stand it down here any longer.'

David nodded and they made their way topside, bouncing and clinging to whatever they could find, and then up the stairs to the deck. The ship was a great three-masted carrack, and fully laden with men, horses, weapons and supplies. They were part of a flotilla of six vessels that had left port a week before. Now, a week out, Jack had no idea where they were in the vastness. The sky was clear blue but the white caps on the water told the story of an angry sea. Looking forward, he could make out the sails of just two other ships of the fleet, maybe a mile in front. Jack took a great lungful of fresh sea air as he held onto a thick line near the mainmast. A sailor gave them a foul look and gestured that they should be below. None of the army were to be on deck. Jack didn't care. He wasn't some rat to skulk in the stinking darkness of the hold.

David shook his head forlornly. 'Thought my last voyage would be my last!'

Jack laughed. 'And I thought I had sea-legs! Maybe I will get home someday. But that means taking ship again. *After* Ireland.'

'I don't even know where Ireland is.'

They both laughed and drank in the clean air, revelling in the wind. Somehow it seemed safer on deck, seeing the ship holding its course despite the elements and the seamen unfazed by it all. All had been a whirlwind of commotion after the trial and execution at the encampment. The day after, Lord Martin Schwarz had ordered the march of the army to Ghent. All two thousand of them, plus a few hundred followers in the wagons, had thronged the road leading west. The army stayed one night at Ghent only, terrified townsfolk locking their doors and shutters for the duration. The next morning they headed north to the coast to a small fortified town and port, which no one knew the name of. They took the place entirely over for two days before being herded onto the ships, bound for Ireland. Most of the soldiers had little idea where they were going or why. That mattered less. They were going to battle.

Jack spotted one of the provost's men forward of the main mast making his way towards them. He had not yet seen them.

'We'd better get below again. We'll get beat otherwise.'

They made it below deck and found the few feet of space on the planks that they had made theirs. Luke was rolled into a ball – passed out – and the other Scots sat hunched in their own private miseries. David and Jack sat next to each other leaning against the bulkhead.

'I never asked you,' said Jack, 'what made you become a soldier? To end up here.'

Weems sighed, hands on his knees. 'I was a thief when I was about your age. Not a very good one, mind. I'd steal whatever I

240

could and if there was a riot happening over anything – sawdust in the baker's loaves or water in the milk – then I'd be there with fists flying. And grabbing what I could afterwards. I was lucky I didn't get branded. Or have my nose slit.'

'Well, that is something we have in common. I was a thief too. And a runner for a gang of sturdy beggars.'

'I reckon it is no surprise, Englishman. Thieves becoming soldiers. I came from a family of noble birth – just the wrong side of the family. The side that got lost. But I never expected to have one of your lot as a comrade. A bloody Sassenach.'

Jack smiled. 'Sir John found me after my father had turned me out. Took me away to serve in his company. Looked after me.'

David's vomit-smeared face turned towards him. 'And so why are you here? My recruiting speech at the tavern?'

Jack looked down. He hadn't meant to bring up the subject. Now it filled his head. 'He stopped bothering with me. Didn't even curse me out any more. He had a son. So things changed and I got bored. I ran away.'

'I was plucked off the street by a man who knew a brawler when he saw one. When I told him my name, he said he would make me a man-at-arms. He took me to his great house and I trained. Got me harness and sword. But I only ever saw battle once with him. At Berwick.'

Jack nodded. 'So you have seen war?'

'War? It was against *your* lot. Your King Richard bested us and we ran like rabbits. After that it was back to garrison and guard duty. Escorting my knight's wife and her ladies to market twice a month. So, finally, *that* fool –' he gestured towards Luke '– and me… we legged it to a ship and ended up in Flanders. Next I knew we were beating up townsfolk in Bruges.' He let out a harsh laugh. 'Just like old times.'

By evening the seas had calmed again. Jack risked punishment a second time by stealing onto the main deck but the cool, clean air was enough to merit the risk. In the bright moonlight, he saw a long line of dark clouds against the horizon which stretched as far as he could see. Fearful it was a giant storm on the way, he asked a sailor on watch what the clouds meant.

The man's face scrunched in confusion at Jack's poor Flemish but eventually he understood. He shook his head and hissed. 'Not clouds, you fool. Ireland.'

–

In the morning, they were awoken by the rapid tattoo of drums on deck and shouts of the sergeants below deck. They were made to dress, get into their harness, if they had any, and await orders to disembark. Jack's first view of the city brought an amazed grin to his face, which by now was covered in the fine blond hair of a scraggly first beard. He stood dumb on the deck, jostled by dozens of others, his eyes drinking in the sight of some great cathedral, which rose up in front of him. Jack saw they had moored directly on the quay of a wide, brown river and that gangways had been set up and parts of the ship's railings removed. It was a great city to his eyes (having now seen several), hundreds of houses surrounding the cathedral like chicks clustering around a hen. Outside the walled city and along the opposite bank, verdant green fields and pastures covered the landscape.

Tall Luke, still white-faced and wraith-like, wobbled his way next to Jack and David.

'*Jesus!* Is that where we're goin'?'

It was and it wasn't. All the *landsknechts*, whether they were still ill or not, were herded off the ships and assembled along the quayside. The officers barked at them and the drums banged away. After the men, the next to be unloaded were the bundles of pikestaffs. With much confusion and shouting, the first company had managed to assemble in rank and file. Led by half a dozen double-pay men with halberds as well as the standard-bearer, it set off for the city gates. The second company was then formed, Jack and six other crossbowmen in the lead, the

Scots pikemen further back in the ranks. The drums sounded, the sergeants yelled, and they too set off for the walled gates of Dublin.

They slow-marched under the stone archway and entered the city. Throngs of townsfolk cheered their progress. Strung out for a few hundred yards, the clanking mass of men and pikes made their way through the main thoroughfare, deeper and deeper into the city. Jack couldn't stop grinning. He had never been in a parade before, and a feeling of immense pride flooded his chest. The *doom-doom* of the drums reverberated off the tall houses and filled the street with its beat. Directly in front of him, three gaudy and colourful halberdiers strode forward with exaggerated movements, much to the pleasure of the crowds. People pointed at their huge, jutting codpieces.

Jack adjusted his grip on the stock of his crossbow, which he carried over his right shoulder. More townsfolk filled the street, huzzahing and waving. He caught the eye of a few wimple-clad ladies and smiled at them. They giggled and jostled each other, one chastising another. Jack could see that they were soon to pass in front of the great cathedral. Already the bells were chiming in welcome.

The German next to him shouted above the din. 'Which grand house will we be quartered?' and he gave a laugh.

Jack had understood the German, just. He was getting better, thanks to old Jacob and his lessons of the past year. They marched on past the cathedral and wound their way clear across the city until Jack spotted more walls and another gate. And they continued straight on and through it. Following the company in front, they made a slow wheel out into the wide, shorn fields before them. It looked to be a market green. Beyond this was a row of less grand houses that stretched for what seemed a mile. Jack realised their shelter would be the tents once again. Whenever they arrived.

They were allowed to break ranks and their sergeants announced that the cooks would be setting up shortly to feed them. They were not to re-enter the city without permission. Disobedience would be met with the strictest punishment. So they waited, lying upon the ground.

'My body still feels like it is moving,' remarked Weems, spread-eagled and looking skyward.

Jack knew the feeling.

'I'm hungry,' said Luke, also staring at the sky.

'No wonder there,' said David Weems. 'Your belly has cast up its accounts these last seven days!'

An hour later the fires were started. The quartermasters had reached agreement with the town bakers and loaves of bread now went around along with great kegs of beer on the backs of wagons. The grumbling slowly subsided as stomachs were filled again. As more and more camp followers and sutlers arrived, the field came to resemble an encampment. Shit-pits were dug, bell tents were thrown up, green patches of mildew showing from a week at sea. By late afternoon, things had returned nearly to the way Jack had seen them in Flanders. A sense of ordered chaos prevailed.

Some of the army might have been quartered in the town. To Jack's eyes it did not appear that the *whole* of the army could possibly be camped out on the green. What no one knew was how long they would be staying. They weren't here to fight in the Irish lands. It was for England they were ultimately bound.

As the sun was beginning to set, Weems nobbled the older of the sergeants – his skill of the German tongue being the best – and tried to learn what was going to happen in the days ahead.

'Balthus says we will be here some days,' Weems told the small group of Scots. 'There is an army of Irishmen coming to join us for the venture.' He pointed over to Jack. 'And you, *English*, you are going to get a new king crowned. Right here.'

Jack frowned at his words. He didn't understand. Who was to be crowned king in Dublin? Jacob had talked about a new rebellion to overthrow Henry Tudor but nothing about a new king to take Henry's place. Those things were always Sir John's business, gobbets of intelligence that never seemed to get shared with him. His ignorance burned him a little, anger rising again, making him feel his decision to run away was the right one. He wasn't really running away from anything. He'd been left behind.

He crossed his arms. 'Don't look to me! I'm always the last to know!'

The Scots roared at that and then they trudged off to get a hot meal from the communal stew pot. After eating, a quiet descended upon the camp. The provosts and their baton-wielding assistants roamed, looking for troublemakers. Jack noticed the harlots had already set up their tents and custom was brisk from the soldiers who had been cooped up for so many days and nights. He decided against making a visit himself, found a noxious blanket, and rolled up on the ground in his tent.

The next morning, before breakfast, Weems suggested they get a shave from the ladies for a *pfennig* and Jack agreed. He had only a small leather haversack of belongings: one bone comb, braes, and one extra shirt and two pairs of hose. He rooted around, pulled out what had to pass for clean linen, and dressed. The women were more than happy to oblige the two of them, and their deft fingers, razor and scissors made quick work of Jack's sparse facial hair, shaving him clean again. His barber kissed him on the top of his head and sent him on his way, telling him to come back for more than a shave next time. Jack felt good in himself again, even if he did not know what lay ahead. How could anyone, really?

He had only been back to the tent for a short while, joking with the Scots who were polishing their harness and short swords, when a party of officers approached, led by Balthus, their veteran sergeant.

There were two double-pay men and the provost. They stopped and the provost's voice boomed out. 'Where is the Englishman?'

Jack understood at once and his blood froze in his veins. Slowly, his arm rose up over his head.

'Come with us!'

Jack threw a forlorn look at Weems who seemed as pole-axed and slack-jawed as he, and then moved forward on shaking legs. The provost nodded at him and then looked him up and down. 'You Englishman?' he asked. Jack nodded dumbly. The provost turned to Balthus. 'We need to dress him properly. Find him a doublet and good hose! Then bring him to the gate.'

Jack's head spun. Had someone sworn against him? The executed Fleming's comrades? He could not think of anything he had done wrong. Then, he remembered he had been out on deck against orders. He'd been seen! Balthus pushed him forward and brought him to the nearest sutler's wagon. The old veteran hurriedly ordered up a pair of bright woollen hose – one leg green and the other red – and a doublet of dark blue with ribboned sleeves. Finally, the sutler produced a codpiece looking like a purple turnip. Balthus paid, tossed the armful of clothing over and told Jack to strip and dress again.

Jack hurriedly complied, pulling on the clothes and awkwardly doing up the many laces while others watched with curiosity. Pulling on his shoes again, he stood and was then ordered to put on his breastplate and back, and to sling on his sword belt and scabbard.

'Hurry! Otherwise we both get bollocked!' ordered Balthus, guiding him forward with a gentle shove to his back.

Two halberdiers met them at the south gate and he was left to their custody. Jack wondered why he needed new clothes if he was to suffer some punishment. And he had been left with his weapons too. It all made little sense to him, but then again he understood very little about these Germans. One enormous soldier on either side, he was escorted up the same high street he had paraded the day before. They came to a tall house where several soldiers stood guard. Jack was led inside to the dark hall and then upstairs to the main solar.

Even before he had reached the top of the stairs, he heard one voice bellowing. A rough, guttural variant of the German tongue he had already heard spoken by others. It was almost unintelligible. Jack was led into the chamber. There was a long table covered by an expensive-looking rug, a heavy cupboard and a few chairs. Three officers stood there, one was seated with a quill in hand. The *landsknecht* who had been shouting looked at Jack and then addressed the halberdiers. 'English?'

One of them pushed Jack forward. He assumed he should bow, and he did so, as he had seen others do. The officer's eyes drilled into him. He was not an overly large soldier, but he looked well-fed, his raven hair well kempt and flowing down to his shoulders. Jack could not guess his years, but lines of age had already crept in around his dark eyes and his wide mouth. A slightly bulbous nose gave him the look of an intemperate drinker, yet his intensity belied no such weakness. But it was his fine dress that told Jack this was someone of importance.

'Englishman?' the man barked in English. And then he switched to German. 'And I'm told you speak German? Do you?'

Jack seemed to understand only every other word, but he got the gist well enough. 'Yes,' he answered, first in English and then in German.

The officer smiled and laughed a little. 'I suppose you do… after a fashion… I am your commander – Lord Schwarz.'

Jack nodded and then nervously touched the back of his hand to his forehead as he had seen other soldiers do occasionally.

'There are two great English lords arriving in the next day or two. My English is bad. To tell the truth, I have none. My French is pretty poor, but I suppose they might speak that a bit.'

Jack stood frozen, not knowing whether he should reply or just nod. Some words he understood, others just floated over him.

'You are a crossbowman, I'm told. I am putting you in my bodyguard. You can interpret for me when I ask you… For Christ's sake! Tell me you understand what I'm saying!'

Jack stood bolt upright. 'Yes, I understand, my lord!'

Schwarz looked at the other two officers. 'I hope you haven't pulled me a simpleton out from the ranks!'

They both gave a laugh and then Schwarz joined in. He turned his attention back to Jack.

'What is your name, boy?'

'I am Jack Perry. Jack of Stamford!'

Martin Schwarz smiled and then gave a bored wave of his hand. 'Very well. Get him back to camp, collect the rest of his harness, and tell his captain we are borrowing him when we need him.'

Jack was led outside and handed over to the same two halberdiers. They walked him back down the street and Jack saw the people stop and watch with interest, curiosity, and maybe even admiration. Jack matched the cadence of the soldiers on either side, and slowly, a smile came to his lips and remained there. He lifted his chin high and thought about what David Weems would say. Jack Perry was a squire again. And this time, to a great lord!

28

'You lying little bastard!' David Weems shoved Jack backwards with both hands. 'It's *me* who speaks better German! And they put you in Martin the Black's guard?' He spat on the ground and shook his head.

'I didn't ask for it!' protested Jack, hurt at the reaction of his new friend.

Luke gave Jack a mournful expression of disapproval. 'You've put yourself into the shit now, Sassenach. You won't have a straw basket to hide under up there with that lot. You'll be in the thick of it, my laddie.'

Jack stuttered, dumbfounded. 'He knew I was an Englishman! What was I supposed to do? Refuse an order?'

Weems waved his hand like he was swatting a fly. 'Bah! You had better get the rest of your harness – before somebody steals it.'

They heard the drums sounding to signal assembly for pike drill. Jack, dejected, went to his tent and collected his meagre belongings. But he was leaving the only friends he had now, something he had not thought through earlier. He put on all his armour, heaved his haversack over a shoulder, grabbed his crossbow and pouch of quarrels, and left. But Weems was there again just as he was about to head back to the walls.

'We were just becoming comrades… brothers. I was angry and spoke harshly. So then… I wish you well. Besides, you might find your way back down here before too long.'

Jack smiled. 'You might be right. Fare thee well!'

Weems clapped him on the shoulder. 'Get along!'

Hurrying back across the churned-up fair green, Jack saw many more soldiers arriving south of the town walls. An army of wild men, by their looks, numbering in the hundreds. They were sadly dressed in coarse woollen cloaks of pale brown or madder, sandal-shod, and bare-legged and even barefoot in some cases. Their long hair was matted and ill-cut, and they carried weapons more suited to tilling a field than fighting a battle. These were the Irish *kerns* he'd heard about. Servants and serfs of the great Irish nobles who had been sent to join the rebels. As his eyes scanned their ranks further, he saw many had spears, two-handed axes, bills, and a few with long swords. But nary a one even had a helm upon his head nor was there a breastplate to be seen — either rusty or shiny.

They seemed a bit lost, standing in groups and talking excitedly, probably wondering if they were to sleep in the damp open air upon their backs or if tents might arrive somehow to ease their misery. Perhaps their lords would also supply them more harness when the time came. But they were coming in great numbers and that was no bad thing, thought Jack. For he knew the *landsknechts* were not so numerous. More than that, he remembered well the size of the two hosts at Bosworth Field, both sides heavily armoured and well-equipped. He had no head for figures but, almost instinctively, he knew they needed greater numbers. He prayed more would flock to their banners once they landed in England.

He turned away and carried on to the south gate. This time, no escort was required as guards were getting used to his face. He returned to the townhouse and reported to a double-pay man standing out front. That soldier led him to the older officer — the scribe — whom he had spied earlier upstairs. The taciturn German barked at him to follow, and he was led into the bowels of the great house and out towards the back. Beyond the kitchens was a stone chamber and here he was told he would bivouac.

'Take a bed not slept in and report to the others in your guard.'

And that was all he was told. Two crossbowmen wandered in and introduced themselves. He could hardly understand a word. Theirs was a form of the German tongue even more undecipherable than that spoken by Lord Schwarz. He managed a few words, told them his name and pointed to one of the beds. He later learned the men were from Swabia, deep in the heart of the mountains and forests of the German lands. Somehow, he managed to understand enough and learned that there was not much for any of them to do at present other than to escort the commander whenever he walked the camp. They were not ordered to practise drill but had decided to hone their swordplay amongst themselves anyway to fight the boredom. Over the next few days, slowly, Jack settled into life among the Germans.

On the few occasions that Lord Schwarz ventured out to inspect his army, Jack formed a cordon with the other cross-bowmen and at least one hand gunner. There was always a throng when he walked about, and Jack's new comrades patiently told him tales of Martin Schwarz and the emperor. That he had as a young man been a shoemaker's apprentice in a place called Augsburg but longed to be a soldier. He'd proved himself in the emperor's service against the Burgun-dians in the seventies and on many other battlefields, rising to command his own *fähnlein*. Eventually, his fame and rising wealth enabled even greater command and brought him to the personal attention of the emperor. Then, with the German emperor inheriting the Burgundian kingdom, Martin Schwarz's skills had been needed in Flanders. He had become the most famous mercenary captain in the north of Europe and Jack Perry was now his bodyguard.

It had been almost a week since Jack had begun his new duties. One morning, a double-pay man came in and told him to get upstairs to the 'captain' as he was needed immediately. When Jack burst in, nearly breathless, he saw Schwarz standing in all his silken brocade finery and speaking with two high-born men. Jack heard the French tongue passing awkwardly amongst them. When Schwarz saw him, he beckoned him over.

Jack approached and bowed. Schwarz hastily explained in French and then told Jack in German he should speak English to the two lords.

Jack nodded and bowed again. 'I am Jack Perry. The Lord Schwarz commands that I help translate for him.'

These men were dressed as finely as the German and Jack knew they must be either great Irish lords or English Yorkists. They were both young, one perhaps a bit older than the other. They both had perfect, flawless features like the bronze effigies lying in repose which he had seen in churches. These were not ordinary men. They were high born. It was the older one who spoke first.

'Well, Jack Perry, you may tell Lord Schwarz that we have spoken with the Earl of Kildare and he will send at least three thousand men here to us in the next seven days. His younger brother will command and join the venture. Can you manage that?'

The other noble looked at Jack with a raised eyebrow. 'Whatever are *you* doing with German infantry?' He turned to the other. 'Most amusing. Look how he garbs himself!' Jack realised the nobleman wasn't really expecting an answer. He could now feel his stomach begin to roll. The noblemen seemed to be getting along perfectly well in their bad French and his presence seemed hardly warranted. But he bowed and turned to Schwarz and did his best in halting German – probably more Flemish than he realised – to say what the Englishman had just told him.

Schwarz nodded and then asked about the coronation of the boy king. Jack turned again, still ignorant of just who these Englishmen were, and told them what the German had asked. And so it went, for several minutes, Jack scrambling and wracking his brains to find the right words, stumbling from time to time. To complicate matters, Schwarz sometimes spoke over him in French, to which the English responded in French. Jack's head swam.

His ears burning red with self-doubt, he did his best. He learned that a Yorkist princeling, a boy, was with the two lords, ready to take the crown. They named him 'Edward' but Jack knew nothing more. One of the lords was the Earl of Lincoln and it was he who said the coronation would be the following Tuesday. The other – the older one – agreed and added that the ships would be ready to take them across the Irish Sea in the next ten days. He said the townsfolk of Dublin would not tolerate an army their size for very long and that he wished to embark by the end of May, weather permitting.

Schwarz had said his men were ready. But he asked where the landing would be. Lincoln at last referred to his noble companion.

'My Lord Lovell has chosen northern Lancashire – a deep port near the Abbey of Furness. We won't be challenged.'

Jack had never heard of the place. But he duly told Schwarz who in turn shrugged, telling them it was no concern to him so long as they could land unopposed and that a few more thousands of men would be waiting nearby to rally to the banner. Lord Lovell assured him that supporters in the north would come and in great numbers.

Schwarz asked the first objective in the north. Lord Lovell replied quickly, 'York.'

That was a city Jack *had* heard of, though he had never journeyed there. The audience was soon ended after that, with the two English lords remarking they now had business with the archbishop. Preparations for the Christchurch to be made. They bowed and left. Jack stood off to the side waiting for further orders. Schwarz turned to his subordinates but then noticed Jack was still standing there.

'Off you go!' he said with a wave of his hand. Jack turned and he heard the German call after him. 'You did well, boy!'

Food was better in the bodyguard, and that Jack knew for certain. He and his few comrades dined on what was brought to the house by the local butcher and baker after Schwarz and his officers had had their fill. Meat pies and sausages, pottages and good bread and cheese. This at least partly offset his loss of the Scots and their banter. Their accents were not easy but still far easier to understand than the Germans.

The day after Jack had served as interpreter, it happened that two double-pay men in Schwarz's guard fell ill. One was dead by the following day of a fever caught on ship and the other was taken away from the house not to return. That left only one. Jack got to thinking. Plucking up his courage, he went up to the solar where Schwarz and his companions drank and talked. He entered and saluted. Schwarz looked up and frowned at him, dark features contorting and his caterpillar eyebrows beetling.

'What is it?'

'My lord,' said Jack bowing, 'your pardon, but your guard has lost two men to sickness. I know two very dependable and loyal halberdiers. They both speak English, which you may find useful in the coming days.'

Schwarz mumbled something that Jack could not fathom. The great captain looked over to his scribe and then back. Jack held his breath. Schwarz leaned back in his chair and shook his head in astonishment.

'For one so young and foolish to be so bold!' He looked at one of the other officers. 'Should I have him whipped over a cannon?' The man laughed and Schwarz glared again at Jack. 'Who are these men? Do they now trail a pike or are they double-pay men?'

Jack cleared his throat, hoping he had understood the question. 'They are in the red and blues. Pikemen now. But in Scotland they were halberdiers and men-at-arms to a great lord.'

Jack could see the German press his lips tightly together and he prepared for a salvo. But Schwarz turned to the old scribe. 'Are we down two men here?'

The scribe nodded. 'I have not yet filled the billets. What do you want to do?'

Schwarz turned to Jack. 'You swear by these men, do you? Because I'll have all of you whipped if they're discovered to be sluggish and idle oafs!'

Jack stood bolt upright. 'I swear to it, sir. They are good men.'

Schwarz made a harrumphing noise and turned again to the scribe. 'Take the Englishman, find his obrist, and have him bring the Scots here. Put them down for three gulden a month, not four. They'll not be double-pay men until I test their mettle.'

—

Gloomy Luke of Kirkcaldy hoisted Jack up by his midriff and off his feet. 'You crafty Sassenach bastard!'

Weems' head swivelled around, taking in the appointments of the room in the great townhouse. 'If I'd known you were this much of a friend I'd have kicked you out of the tent sooner, Jack Perry. We might have been in The Black's personal guard a week ago!'

'You better know how to swing a halberd,' warned Jack. 'He says he'll have our guts if you don't.'

Weems held out his hand. 'Don't worry none on that account. We've both shouldered a pole-axe and a lochhaber axe and they be as good as a halberd.'

The two Scots had been floored by the suddenness of their rise, having never expected to even see Jack Perry again except from afar. Weems now swore his never-ending comradeship and Jack said it was in return for David having given him protection back in Mechelen. With their new money, the pair of Scots had visited the sutlers and fitted themselves out in new hose and doublets – padded ones that they could use under their armour. Now, taking their position in front of Lord Schwarz and his entourage, Jack and his crossbowmen behind, they would set off through Dublin and then out into the great encampment.

The Swabians seemed friendly enough after a few days and took well to the presence of the Scots. Jack became more confident in his bearing, happy in his heart, and skilful in his swordplay. He had his comrades again and, so it seemed, the confidence of a great lord (even if he was not considered much more than a trained monkey). Schwarz's scribe told the men of the guard that the new English king was to be crowned on the morrow and that they would be escorting the Lord Schwarz to the cathedral.

The May sunshine continued as it had for the last week, warming and uplifting. People had begun to gather early that morning in the high street and all around the Christchurch cathedral, crowds building right up to the appointed hour. Children shouted and ran without restraint, cut-purses weaved their way through those deep in conversation, and much of the nobility had now gathered and entered the great stone edifice, eager to see the coronation of a new king to challenge the Tudor usurper. The archbishop had sanctified the proceedings and those who wished to remain in favour, Lancastrian or Yorkist, would be wise not to ignore the occasion. Some Irish lords, however, defied the Earl of Kildare and would not come, nor would their bishops and prelates. Already, before the crown had been lifted over the boy's head, lines had been irrevocably drawn.

Jack, waiting outside in his cordon of *landsknechts*, saw a few dozen retainers in white harness, splendidly arrayed, arrive and dismount. This was the escort for the boy king in the company of Lords Lovell and Lincoln, as well as the Earl of Kildare. He saw a boy dressed in regal satins – a boy of no more than ten – mounted on a white palfrey. But it was time for Lord Schwarz and his contingent to go inside. Luke and David led the way with three double-pay men, all bearing halberds, Jack and his comrade bowmen followed behind Schwarz and his captains, and two hand-gunners followed behind them.

Trumpets blared and the robed clergy processed up the nave. Jack stood in the south aisle, he and his fellow guardsmen stationed around Lord Schwarz and his officers. The cathedral was filled with the high and the low, all waiting for the entry of Edward, soon to be a boy king. He now wished that he had asked Sir John more about the rebellion and who this Yorkist was. There was no one he could approach to ask who might actually know. He didn't dare speak out of turn. Some people started shouting out the name of 'Clarence', but this made no sense to him. Who could Clarence be? Still more seemed to be calling out for 'Warwick'. All he could do was watch the pageant unfold.

He fidgeted with his bow, trying to adjust the angle he carried it in his arms. Pointless, in reality, as he and the others had been forbidden from bringing their pouches of crossbow bolts with them into the cathedral, nor had the gunners brought match or powder. They were present only as ornaments to the great captain. There was a renewed and even more eager blast of trumpets and David and Luke, standing in front of him, both craned to see the entrance of the new king.

Jack twisted around, trying to get a look around the massive stone column that blocked his view. And then he saw the young man walking up the aisle, robes of ermine and silk placed upon his shoulders at the porchway. He got a clear view of the procession as it passed, headed towards the choir. The magnificently attired archbishop began intoning and there was much ceremony, none of which Jack could understand. After some minutes, though, it appeared that something was amiss. There was a lull in the ceremony and Jack could see the archbishop looking around and then whispering to some of the clergy.

Schwarz and his men started chuckling. Jack heard the word 'crown' but couldn't make out anything more. He then saw

Lord Lovell appear to his left, entering the transept, looking anxious and turning his head this way and that. He must have seen Jack because he stopped, looked at him, then beckoned him over with a silent call. This was risky. He was supposed to stand where he was, but for a nobleman to order him to attend could not be ignored either. He shot a glance up towards Schwarz, then quickly slipped to the side before his Swabian comrades could object or stop him.

'Jack Perry!' said Lovell in a high whisper, grabbing him by his shoulder. 'You can do a great service to the kingdom right here as we speak. Look there!' He pointed to a votive statue of the Virgin high up on a plinth in the corner of the transept. 'We need to borrow that crown that is upon Our Lady. Quickly, can you clamber up there?'

Jack saw it was too high. He bit his lip a second and then thought of something. 'A moment, my lord!' Jack became aware that the chorus had broken into song to keep the crowds guessing. He spotted where Luke stood. Not so close to Schwarz or his men and furthest to the left of them. He might be able to pull him away.

Jack sidled up to the Scot. 'Luke, I need you! Come with me!' The Scot looked surprised, shot a look over to the captains, and then shouldered Jack with a shove. 'Get away, you fool!' he hissed.

Jack grabbed him by his arm. 'Lord Lovell demands it. Look, over there!'

Luke twisted his head and then saw the now enraged noble, beckoning urgently. 'Ach, aye then,' he said quietly and then side-stepped a few paces until he was behind a stone column. The two of them reached Lovell and Jack hurriedly explained their task.

Luke gently rested his halberd against a wall and pushed Jack towards the statue. 'I will boost you up!'

Jack looked over to the guard and saw a wide-eyed David Weems silently mouthing to them, no doubt demanding they

258

get back into line. The lanky Scot leaned down, cupped his hands and Jack put a foot in them like a stirrup. Luke heaved himself up, Jack threw his hands out on the wall and rose up, higher and higher while the Scot grunted underneath. Jack could feel Luke's arms wobbling with the effort and his own legs were moving wildly as a result. He wasn't sure if it was a sin to be pawing at the Virgin, but he had no choice in the matter, desperate to gain a hold and to stop himself from tumbling to the side. Flecks of blue paint came off as he scrabbled at the statue, stretching with his right hand to pluck the golden crown from her brow.

'Hurry!' hissed Lord Lovell, standing off to the side.

Stretching as far as he could, he looped the coronet off the statue and gripped it tightly, calling to Luke to let him down. His feet once again on the flagstones, he handed it over with both hands to Lord Lovell.

Lovell took it and then gestured with it towards both Jack and Luke. 'You have done a great service to your new king this day! I will not forget it.' And with that he turned on his heels and drifted as surreptitiously as he could back towards the archbishop and the boy who stood dumbly still. Jack just managed to catch sight of Lovell swiping a square cushion from off a pew and then placing the coronet upon it, before the nobleman disappeared beyond a pillar.

Luke, standing next to Jack, whispered, 'We'll probably hang for this.'

'Come,' said Jack, tapping Luke's breastplate. 'Let's work our way back into the guard before they notice.'

The Swabians glared at him as he elbowed back into the line. One of them uttered what was no doubt a curse. Jack decided to worry about it later. His eyes again focused on the narrow view he was afforded of the coronation. A gilded crown of tin in hand, the archbishop of Dublin dropped it upon the blond head of the boy, and instantly a great cheer went up around the cathedral.

More cries of 'Warwick!' echoed and with less than total solemnity, the ceremony seemed to unravel then and there, Lovell and Lincoln's armoured retainers surrounding the new King Edward and ushering him out along the centre of the nave, people cheering around them. Jack watched Martin Schwarz as he turned to his companions.

'Bah!' exclaimed the great captain. 'The emperor would have roared seeing this circus! Let's get out of here.'

They filed out and before they peeled off to return to the townhouse, Jack caught one last glimpse of his new king, Edward the Sixth, being carried aloft and paraded up the high street on the shoulders of the tallest man he had ever seen in his life. A week later, and Jack could still see – in his mind's eye – the expression of absolute confusion and uncertainty on the poor boy's face.

29

It was John Hawker's turn to be surprised. He took half a step back, mouth agape and words failing him. Catherine nodded.

'You are... married,' said Hawker, struggling. 'When? To whom?' He looked off into the middle distance as if trying to guess the answers himself.

She crossed her arms. 'John, he is a *good* man. A knight of Lancashire. He was made lord of the grange and your holdings half a year ago. From the beginning he said I could remain here, but, later, he asked for my hand.'

Hawker looked like a gasping codfish. 'But... sister... you have no dowry.'

'He married me out of love. Is that so difficult to believe?'

He frowned, shaking his head. 'No, dear sister. Forgive me. I am happy for you. Yet if he is the one who owns my house then it must have been Henry Tudor who gave it to him. He is of Lancaster, isn't he? It *must* be so.'

She nodded. 'That he is, brother. His name is Edmund Blodwell and he is as old as you. He fought for the last Henry, under Warwick's banner. While you fought for Edward. I told you when you last left here that I would find my own way. Now I have.'

Hawker snorted a laugh. 'You have landed upon your feet like a cat thrown from a window. Where is he now?'

'You're lucky. He is away in London for a few days, but I expect him back the day after tomorrow. You and your men must be gone by then. Do you understand that?'

Hawker looked out the leaded window at his comrades still sitting mounted. Ellingham's concern was clear even through the thick glass. He seemed to be arguing with Dieudonné, gesturing and pointing. 'I understand, Catherine. I would not put you in danger. Give us time to replenish... I have a few things secreted about here that I must fetch.'

She raised a thin eyebrow. 'More treasure?'

'Of a sort. I gave *you* the remainder of the coin though. Which I hope you buried as I suggested.'

She didn't answer. She followed his gaze out the window. 'For God's sake, John, bring them in!'

Hawker went outside and led the company in. Catherine eyed each one in turn as they offered her a greeting.

'Jacob de Grood,' she said, looking again at the Fleming, 'you remember where the buttery is. You may go and fetch the ale there.' Turning to Ellingham, she inclined her head. 'Sir Giles, you look older than when last we met.'

Ellingham smiled. 'Many miles betwixt then and now.'

She looked over to Dieudonné. 'And you, sir, I have not met before.'

Dieudonné gave a bow of his head and answered her in English. 'Gaston Dieudonné, Madame... sieur de Liancourt and late of the Duchy of Burgundy.'

She continued to study him for a moment, her grey eyes drilling into him. It was Dieudonné who looked away first. 'I have told Sir John that I may only host you for one night. It is no longer his house. He will explain.'

Ellingham and Dieudonné looked at Hawker.

Catherine continued. 'I will see that food is prepared for you. The girl will show you to your chambers. Please, refresh yourselves and return to the hall when you are ready.' She clapped twice and a young servant appeared from around the corner. 'Show these gentles to the guest chambers.'

Ellingham gave Hawker a confused glance and then followed the beckoning servant. Dieudonné gave Hawker a sly smile, bowed discreetly, and left.

Hawker remained. 'What has brought your husband here then, to Lincolnshire?'

'We have a new neighbour. He has been tasked by them to improve upon their manor. It is Margaret Beaufort.'

Hawker swore. 'Where?'

'At Collyweston. She is turning the place into her little palace.'

Hawker looked at the floor and ran his hand over his forehead. Collyweston was not two leagues away. And of all the people who might end up on his doorstep it would have to be the mother of the usurper.

'She is not there yet,' said Catherine. 'And I doubt she'll inhabit it before another year has passed.'

Hawker looked up at her. 'War is coming here, and soon. She may never get to enjoy her new palace.'

'So then, it is as my husband warned. Rebellion. You should not have come back. You have yet to tell me where you have been these last two years but, surely, it was safe. Why risk your life in this kingdom again?'

Hawker smiled and laughed softly. 'Safe? We fought our way to Venice and beyond – and then back again. I would have stayed in Flanders. But, you see, I am now married too. With a young son. And I am here because I have no choice. What I do here is buying them both safety and freedom from want. Forever.'

Catherine suddenly looked like she would cry. She came to him and took him by his rough hands. 'I sorrow for you. That you had to part from them. You must tell me more. What is her name? Her heart is surely breaking in your absence.'

'She is called Chiara, a Venetian lady. Our son is Nicholas.' Hawker's eyes scrunched up, the reminder stinging them with tears. He nodded. '*They* are my treasure. I will tell you all, dear sister. I promise.'

'I understand now,' she said quietly. 'You are seeking a chalice. A chalice of grace... forgiveness. Atonement.'

Hawker did not reply. Jacob returned, bearing a large painted jug and juggling several wooden cups in the crook of his other arm. Hawker rapidly swiped his nose with his forefinger and cleared his throat. 'What kept you, man? I am fair parched!'

They sat at table as the sun swept very low through the great leaded window of the hall. Hawker took his place next to Catherine; opposite sat Ellingham, flanked by Dieudonné and Jacob. As bowls and platters scraped across the scored oak planks, it was too obvious that conversation was lacking. Catherine – Lady Blodwell – decided she would coax it herself. Their spirits seemed so low that they might even draw the life from the guttering candle flames.

'Gentlemen,' she said. 'None of us know what lies ahead. But we have bread and wine here this evening. We give thanks to the Lord and lift up our hearts even though they be filled with troubles.'

'A goodly a prayer as was ever, my lady,' said Ellingham. 'For generous fare and hospitality. And I am sorry if we are poor company. Uncertain futures have a tendency to make for melancholy.' He glanced over at Hawker as he delivered the last.

He *had* aged, she thought. Well beyond two years. What had he been through? Her brother had told of intrigue and battles in Venice and then some misguided quest into the Hungarian lands from which they barely escaped with their lives. Sir Giles bore no outward scars of his battles but she was certain the wounds inside him had not yet healed. Two years prior he had seemed much the same: distracted, sad, and with a heavy burden on his shoulders.

'I have not seen old Piers yet,' said Hawker, pulling a leg off the roast chicken.

'He died last winter, brother. A bad fever and the flux took him.'

Hawker dropped the meat onto his plate of pewter. 'Ah, so it is not just us who are the bringers of melancholy. He was as lazy as the day is long. But I had known him since I was young.'

'And speaking of those absent, where is young Jack?'

Hawker rested his forearms on the table edge and looked at his plate. 'He has joined the army of the Germans – in Flanders.'

Catherine put down her goblet and turned to Hawker. 'He is but a boy!'

'No longer,' replied Hawker. 'He is his own man now. I was too late to convince him not to take their oath. But our paths are likely to cross again. That same army is on its way here.'

Catherine looked over to Ellingham. 'I mourn for him already. But is this true? A German army of mercenaries?'

Ellingham nodded. 'It is. Paid for by the Burgundians and led by the Earl of Lincoln and Lord Lovell. They are gathering more loyal forces in Ireland under the Earl of Kildare.'

Catherine turned to Hawker. 'This is the news you told me of. Where will they land?'

Hawker didn't answer.

She smiled and took a breath. 'You do not trust me.'

'If you do not know then you cannot tell. I would not put you in danger.'

'Very well. So why are you here and not with the other rebels? What peculiar business are you on?'

'We ride ahead to stir the pot, sister. Spread rumour and coin where it will help win friends. Once the invasion has begun we will join up with the main host. In the meantime, Sir Giles is Master Richard Wickham and I am John Rede. We are wool merchants of Flanders – Calais.'

Catherine began to titter. 'You're spies? *You*?'

'If I may do anything to confound the usurper and cause him a sleepless night then I will do so.'

'Then you should know, my husband has told me much. The king watches the ports and his spies are in the north and west too. Already Henry and his advisors have taken station at

Kenilworth Castle for the Whitsun time. Messengers come and go there daily, Sir Edmund has said. They have issued orders that all those spreading rumour will be apprehended by the magistrates and set in the pillory. Spies will be hanged. Tudor eyes are everywhere. Even here at Stamford.'

'This is to be expected,' growled Hawker.

'Where, my lady, is this Kenilworth?' Dieudonné spoke for the first time.

Catherine smiled, amused by his broadly accented English. 'Why, it is in Warwickshire, my lord. It lies perhaps two days' ride, west and south.'

Dieudonné nodded and smiled back. Unreadable.

'Brother, know that the king has already issued the commissions of array. Men are coming to his standard from the south and the west. You will find little sympathy hereabouts for the House of York. You should go north while you can.'

Hawker resumed eating. Catherine scanned the other faces. De Grood was watching John, his brow furrowed, Ellingham stared into his cup, and the Burgundian gentleman seemed to be deep in his own thoughts.

'Sister,' said Hawker quietly, setting down his knife, 'what exactly does your husband know of me?'

She turned in her chair to face her brother more directly. 'Of course, he knows you were attainted. He learned that when he was awarded your property. He claims never to have met you. The blood-letting *here* is what damned you, not that you fought for Richard at Bosworth. That under-sheriff and his men you slew.' Catherine repressed a shudder at the memory of it. How the quiet grange had been turned into a butchery. 'Whatever became of that burly knight you were with? Sir Roger.'

'Dead.'

She nodded. 'That does not surprise me.' In truth, Catherine was amazed – but thankful – that her brother still lived, in spite of his misadventures. But he could not stay. Those times were over. Her life had changed now and for the better after years of sorrow. She loved Blodwell, for it had not only been his ardour for her that drew them together. They met because of the land and a pile of legal writs, but their hearts tied them together soon enough. Widow and widower, both childless. 'You should know that I told Sir Edmund that you were defending your house – and me – when the sheriff came. That they drew their swords first. He believes you are a man of honour. But someone who made a bad decision. As to your whereabouts… the last he knew you had fled to Flanders and then south. A mercenary again.'

Hawker grunted. 'Then I am consoled.' He took a long swig from his wine.

Catherine scowled. 'So then, what is your plan? Sir Edmund returns soon. Take what you need but for the love of God, you must leave before he arrives.'

'Fear not, we will be on our way north. We will take a few provisions to keep us upon the road. I can even pay for them. But I needed to see you. This place. Even if it is for the last time.'

She felt herself blushing. Was she too harsh on him? But it was dangerous for them all – and for her – if they remained, stirring trouble. 'This was your house. I am glad you have come. Glad to see your company again. It pains me to tell you to leave, but that must be the way. You know this.'

Ellingham spoke up. 'My lady, we have no wish to place you at risk in your house. I am grateful that you have given us a roof this night, at least.'

She smiled at him, still feeling herself flush. 'I pray for better times that you might visit again and not in secrecy.' In her heart though, she knew such times would never come. What is done is done.

–

Hawker had them all bed down in the same room. It had been his bedchamber once and with the addition of a few low trundle

267

bedsteads, it served its purpose. Jacob stayed down near the hall that he might sleep lightly and keep half an eye open for surprises. And Hawker slept soundly despite the uncertainties, almost as if his body knew he was home again. They awoke at first light to birdsong outside. Ellingham heard Hawker arise and then he got up, the ropes of the trundle creaking under him.

'Where is Gaston?'

Hawker shrugged. 'He was not abed when I awoke. He is probably already in the kitchen, looking for food.'

Ellingham dressed and looked out the leaded window onto the courtyard below. 'I can still see how it looked then, Sir John. The bodies. Your sister's cries.'

Hawker joined him. 'Giles, it was forced upon us. Had we not fought we would both be dead by the noose or the axe. Do not dwell upon it. We are yet the masters of our fates.'

'Does she know who I am?'

'No, I never told her. And now, she must never know. For your sake.'

'I am almost forgetting it myself now.'

Hawker put a hand on his shoulder. 'I need your help to retrieve something outside. Come with me.'

They went downstairs and into the large hall and out the front entrance. Hawker led him to the opposite side where the stables were and there, built into the grey stone of the grange, was what looked like a chapel.

'Are we to pray, Sir John?' asked Ellingham, following Hawker through the small archway. 'It seems a bit late for such things.'

Hawker laughed lightly. 'No, but you may if you wish. I am here to regain something I put here for safekeeping.' There was plenty of light from the six tall, narrow windows of the private chapel. Hawker proceeded down the centre aisle and stopped halfway. A large rectangular flagstone was there, bare of any inscription.

'Your father? Surely we are not here to take him.'

'Fetch me that lever bar over there.'

Ellingham did as he was bid and handed it to the old knight. Hawker jammed the flat end between the stones and leveraged up the corner of the flagstone. 'Here, lend a hand and help me lift it!'

The two of them managed to move it and flip it on its long end. The hole was shallow. Inside was a long canvas sack covered in mould. Ellingham drew back.

'It is no corpse, I promise! Help me shift it.'

They dragged the sack out, reeking of mustiness and damp earth. The distinct clatter of steel could be heard. Hawker sat back and opened it. Reaching in, he pulled out a long-tailed sallet helm as black as night and brass-riveted. 'I hid this in here before the journey to Leicester – and what happened later. It is an entire harness. It was one I had made after Tewkesbury. When I was knighted.'

Ellingham looked from the dark helm to Hawker. 'But why? Why now?'

Hawker sighed. 'To remind me of where I have been. And what I was.'

'Sir John, I do not understand.'

Hawker grunted and lifted himself up. 'Never mind.' He then gave a short, harsh laugh. 'Pray that I still fit into it!' He pulled out a rolled-up piece of fabric from inside the helm, tied with tapes. He smiled to himself.

'What is it?' asked Ellingham.

Hawker unfurled it and held it up. It was a knight's pennon, plain bleached linen embroidered with a golden anchor and a hawk's head. It was spotted with greyish mould but still was recognisable. He looked at Ellingham and smiled again. 'I will bring it. Who knows, I might have need of it once again.'

–

By mid-morning Jacob de Grood had re-packed Hawker's sable armour and placed it in the stables near the horses. The other portmanteaus of leather and the canvas sacks of Ellingham's armour were there too. For his part, Jacob did as he was told, waiting in the stables for them to depart and munching upon an apple.

Hawker prepared to take his leave, not knowing when he might return, if ever. As he had done two years before, he met with Catherine in her chamber upstairs. Ellingham he had left below with Dieudonné. The two seemed more remote from each other and from him in the last few days. Hawker knew the heavy cloud that hung over all of them dictated their mood. And what real hope could he give them?

'Where will you go now?' Catherine asked.

'West. Maybe north. We'll lie low until the invasion comes. And then… I must fight. Do not forget where I told you the last sack of gold is buried in the chapel. You are the only other that now knows. If the worst befalls me, will you see it gets to Chiara?'

She took both of his hands. 'If God grants me the power, know that I will. But I pray you will return. And know, too, that my love for you has never wavered. Nor will it. But I give you one last plea, brother. Return to your wife and child as soon as God allows. They are more precious than any personal honour. Remember that!'

Hawker embraced her. 'I am happy for your happiness, dear sister. You have long deserved it. I pray to God we shall meet again. But what I do next, I must do. For them above all. And then for me. But… it must be done.'

The sound of horses made Hawker pull back from her. Catherine rushed to the window.

'Dear God. It is Sir Edmund and his men.'

30

Hawker pounded down the winding stone steps to the hall, hoping that Ellingham and Dieudonné would already be there. All the while his mind was racing to come up with a ruse to mollify Blodwell long enough for them to take their leave.

Dieudonné was pressed alongside the carved stone window when Hawker entered, face set grim.

'We are discovered.'

Ellingham rushed to join him. He dared a quick glance out the pane and then swore. 'Four men, two are men-at-arms.' He turned and saw Hawker. 'What now?'

'It is Sir Edmund,' said Hawker. 'Quickly, both of you! Giles, over here to the table and sit! It is to be our travelling names and I will do the talking.' He pointed a finger at Dieudonné. 'Gaston… you must play the man-at-arms again. Do not fail us. When they arrive, I will tell you to go to the stables and assist Jacob with the horses. Understood?'

The Burgundian pretender glared and for a moment said nothing. He then gave a nod. 'Of course, Sir John. Understood.'

Hawker shifted his riding cloak to conceal his dagger and then sat opposite Ellingham. Dieudonné remained standing near them at the head of the table. It was only moments later the door opened. In walked Sir Edmund and another. They instantly froze, seeing they had guests.

Hawker slowly rose and doffed his hat and Ellingham followed suit immediately. Hawker bowed his head. 'Sir Edmund?'

Blodwell's surprise was stamped full upon his face. 'I am, sir. And who might you be?'

Hawker tapped his chest. 'I am John Rede, a wool merchant of Calais. My companion is Master Richard Wickham, my partner in trade. We came in search of Master Francis Hawker.'

Blodwell and his companion, a younger gentleman, walked closer. '*Francis* Hawker?' said the knight. 'He is dead many years. What is your business?'

Catherine emerged from the stairwell. 'Husband! You are returned! These gentlemen were in search of my father – or those who run his trade. They have sadly been misdirected as the wool trade is long over with my father's death. They are about to resume their journey now.'

Blodwell put his hands on his hips. He was greying but hale-looking, tall and broad shouldered. His small button nose looked misplaced upon the rest of what was a strong-featured face. 'Leave? No, these gentlemen must have food and drink to set them right for the road. Where is our scullion gotten to?'

Catherine bowed to her husband. 'I will see to it!'

Hawker bowed again. 'You are most gracious, my lord. But we must be on our way to continue to our next halt. We are sorry we have intruded on your house and good lady.'

'Nonsense!' bellowed Blodwell. 'If you have come from across the Narrow Sea then I would hear any news of Flanders or Calais. Besides, you must be curious as to news in these parts. Please, I beg you, do sit!'

Hawker looked over to Ellingham, who himself looked to be ready to run for the door. If they made excuses now, Hawker reasoned, it would arouse suspicions. Better to proceed softly and bide their time. He shot a reassuring nod at Ellingham and spread his palm out low on the table and tapped it once. Ellingham blinked.

'Aye, we would not be so churlish as to refuse your hospitality, my lord. We thank you.' He took a seat and Ellingham did the same.

'This is James, my bailiff at Collyweston,' said Blodwell. 'Work upon a manor there, you see.' He beckoned to James to sit and then took a seat himself at the head of the table.

'One of my guards… Gaston,' said Hawker, lifting a hand towards Dieudonné, who gave a curt bow.

Catherine returned with the kitchen girl and a pitcher of ale and cups. Hawker saw the look of absolute terror in her eyes. She glanced at him as she passed and he saw her give him a pleading expression. Hawker instantly understood she wasn't afraid for herself – or for him. She was afraid for Blodwell. That he would kill him.

The ale was passed and the servant made eye contact with no one else.

'The wool trade, you say? Damned poor these days, as I gather,' said Blodwell, lifting his cup. 'Where to next then, Master Rede?'

Hawker took a drink. 'The market is poor. But we hope for better days. So much uncertainty now. We will journey to Stamford for the night… and then, make for Leicester.'

'Leicester,' repeated Blodwell thoughtfully.

The serving girl brought in bread and cheese and some kind of cold savoury pie. She set it all in front of the master of the house. Catherine took up post at the archway leading to the kitchen.

'We will first speak to the wool merchants of Stamford at the guildhall,' said Hawker cheerfully. 'Make a few friends I hope! Then on to Leicester.'

'What do you make of tales of a rebellion? Have you seen anything on your journey, Master Wickham?'

Ellingham sat up straight and cleared his throat. 'Rebellion? We have seen no sign of one. In Calais we are as if on an island. We hear only what news comes from the ships.'

'But, of course, rumours of war one does hear upon the road,' added Hawker. 'That the Yorkists are landing east or west. No one seems to have any more truth than the next. But such rumours are bad for trade, which is bad enough now. I am sure the king has preparations in hand.'

Blodwell grasped the big knife that sat upon the platter and began cutting into the pie. 'The king is well served in this respect, rest assured. The main army will gather at Coventry. He himself is at Kenilworth for Whitsun feast.'

Hawker pouted. 'Aye, well, he must know where the rebels will land then. And be ready for them.'

'Henry knows full well they have an imposter in Dublin who they wish to make a king. It is laughable. But, by all accounts, they will set sail soon, if they haven't already. No matter. I expect them to be just Irish levies and a few mercenary Germans that Margaret of York has gulled into service. The western ports are watched. We are ready.'

Hawker nodded as the platter was passed to him. 'War is bad for business,' he said, lifting a wedge of pie. 'I pray that His Majesty will have a quick victory.'

Blodwell smiled. 'Bad for business… unless one is an armourer, no?'

Hawker forced a light chuckle. 'Indeed, my lord. How many men have assembled?'

The last vestige of a smile fled from Blodwell's face and it became unreadable. 'How many men, you ask? Numbers?' He paused and then smiled again, showing his teeth. 'Enough.'

Hawker managed a few bites – the pie sitting like a lump of lead in his stomach – but Ellingham took only his ale. 'My lord, we thank you for this refreshment, but we must be on our way.' He turned to Dieudonné, still standing stiffly nearby. 'Gaston, go out to the horses and make ready.'

Dieudonné glanced over to Blodwell before returning his attention to Hawker. 'Yes… my lord.' He gave a curt bow and left.

'Ah, well, I will spend a few hours with my dear wife,' said Blodwell, gesturing expansively towards a silent Catherine. 'Then I must go pay call to my tenants.'

Hawker swallowed what was left of his pride. It was galling to have to listen to Blodwell talk of *his* tenants and *his* manor. Galling to eat *his* food and imbibe *his* drink. All had been lost. All but his honour.

'Yes…' Blodwell continued. 'The estate here is in parlous condition. No work done in years. The previous lord was Catherine's brother, John Hawker. A renegade Yorkist knight. Outlawed. God knows where he is now, but he was no husbandman of his lands. And he fled leaving it all to my dear lady to manage. Blaggard.'

Hawker shook his head in feigned disgust but his ears burned. 'I wish you and your lady good fortune in the coming days, my lord. And so, we must now take our leave.'

Blodwell eyed him sternly and then nodded. 'Fare you both well.'

With Blodwell at his back, he made his good-byes to Catherine. 'I thank you, my lady, for all your hospitality.' He then silently mouthed 'goodbye' and turned for the door. Ellingham gave a bow and followed.

—

Dieudonné entered the stables and looked for the Fleming. At first he saw no one but then de Grood popped up from one of the stalls, naked blade in his hand. 'What in the name of God is going on out there?' The words were in halting English.

'What is going on, you ask? Hawker's brother-in-law has just come home and he's talking his way out of trouble. He hopes.'

'*Godverdomme*,' de Grood said, his voice falling low.

Dieudonné went to his mount and rechecked his saddlebags. The Fleming kept prattling on but his own mind was elsewhere.

'Just make things ready. That's what Hawker said.'

As they had from Saint Paul, the scales had fallen from Dieudonné's eyes. Hawker's fate was sealed, if not today, then soon. Since his fall into the mere, he could not rid his mind of the promise of the Frenchman at Antwerp. That he would be forgiven by the Duke of Bedford and by King Henry. But only if he delivered up who they wanted. He could do better than that. He had a gift. A Tear of Byzantium.

And now, now he was so close to friendly aid. Kenilworth not more than a day and a half ride. Sir Edmund clearly believed that Henry's forces would be more than a match for the rebels and their Irish peasants. He could now see that the advantage had shifted to Henry Tudor. Where were the uprisings? The riots against the crown? The idea of somehow revealing Hawker to Blodwell in the next few moments, before they mounted up, swiftly entered his mind.

But just as swiftly he realised that Blodwell had not enough retainers to be certain of overcoming Hawker and Ellingham – and the Flemish oaf. No, he had to bide his time. Until he was closer to the king's forces. Or a sheriff and his men. He could not afford to wait *too* long. Hawker would head north, no doubt, after telling Blodwell they were going west. And the north was for Yorkists. Dieudonné knew he was balanced on a precipice. But he had been many times before. And survived.

Hawker and Ellingham burst into the stables, and Ellingham threw open the big door. 'Mount up!' said Hawker. 'I am in the lead.'

They trotted out into the courtyard and rode past the front of the grange. Sir Edmund and his wife stood side by side and offered a wave of farewell to them. Hawker returned it. Dieudonné watched Hawker take a long, last look at his manor, before he touched his spurs again to his horse's flanks. They trotted down the track leading out to the road, Dieudonné at the rear. The last of them.

Sir Edmund Blodwell watched his guests ride off. Catherine looked down at her feet to the worn sandstone stoop then turned to her husband.

'That was generous of you, my love, to look after travellers such as they. In these difficult times, no less.'

Blodwell cupped her chin with his hand. 'It was the Christian thing to do. But, my love, you should be more careful of letting strangers in. There were not enough retainers here, you know. I worry for you. And I won't let it happen again.' The last he delivered with more steel in his voice than loving admonishment.

She blushed. 'Let us continue our meal, husband.'

Blodwell nodded. 'I will be in shortly.' Catherine entered the house and Blodwell called over to his bailiff, who rushed to his side.

'I need you to ride for the magistrates in Stamford. But overland – through the fields. Do you understand?'

'My lord?'

'If they are wool merchants then I'm a blind tinsmith.'

31

Jack Perry of Stamford weaved his way like a drunken man across the wispy beach-grass of a field overlooking a hulking castle that he heard one of the English call Piel. They had poured off the ships in their hundreds, desperate for dry land under their feet again. The carracks had managed to stay together across the tossing Irish Sea for the two days it took them to make landfall in the barren north-west. The harbour at Piel was deep and with battered but well-constructed wharves, allowing an easier disembarkation. Jack looked out ahead to see a sweeping view: undulating fields and stone walls, and in the near distance, a great stone building. Further beyond, hills and mountains rose against the horizon. The sun was high in the sky, afternoon upon them. He had no idea where he was.

A steady wind whipped across the peninsula. Until wagons were procured, the Irish and the mercenaries were forced to carry supplies inland. Lord Schwarz and his officers had remained to order the troops and get them moving into the interior while it appeared that Lord Lovell and the earl had ridden off towards the great pile of stone that lay about a mile distant. Jack tried to count their numbers. Four carracks had disgorged their soldiers and horses now. Jack reckoned a few thousand soldiers milled about the fields, some still heaving their guts, others gathering their weapons – guns, pikes, spears and bows – which had been placed aboard. A double-pay man sent by Schwarz had told Jack while still on ship that he and the Scots were to re-join their *fähnlein* temporarily until his lordship required them again. Jack stood with Luke and David, listening to the muttering and insults they had to suffer upon their return to the ranks. It was not the beginning Jack had expected.

'They'd better not reduce my pay,' mumbled Luke, slinging his heavy satchel.

David Weems laughed. 'You'd better keep your head down or you won't be around to collect it!'

They began their march inland to find a place to make camp. Schwarz and his officers were already mounted and moving ahead. The two complete *fähnlein*, banners unfurled, set off, and behind them followed the two or three thousand uncomplaining Irish foot soldiers of the rebel army. In the rear, those camp followers brave enough and needy enough to make the crossing followed on: sutlers, cooks, carriers, diggers and harlots, lugging their wares and supplies upon their backs and in bundles on their heads.

Two dozen mounted and armoured knights – more of the earl's retainers, probably – thundered past them, moving off to follow Lord Lovell and his mounted contingent. And, of course, the new boy king. The few glimpses Jack had had of him since the coronation made it all the more strange: the boy seemed expressionless and was carried on horseback in front of a rider – never mounted by himself. Jack mused if he might really be some sort of great wooden marionette, like ones he'd seen at the Stamford Fair.

Just a few miles inland, they were ordered to make camp for the night in open fields. The weather was warm but they had no tents yet. They huddled as best they could, taking a lesson from the bare-legged Irish *kerns* and using their voluminous woollen cloaks as makeshift shelters. Jack watched a few of them running after a lost sheep in the distance. They managed to bring it down with a thrown spear and dragged it back to their encampment. The sun had dipped into dusk by the time food was given out to the soldiers. Mouldy bread and cheese, some dried meat. A few barrels of ale were rolled in as well. It was meagre fare and Jack's heart sank. Someone said the abbey that lay in the distance and where the noblemen were staying the night would supply food on the morrow. Jack replied he wasn't going to hold his breath.

The following morning the march resumed. Lord Schwarz, arrayed in blackened armour and wearing a crimson cloak, rode at the head with his entourage. They marched for miles, each soldier wearing all the armour he possessed, even if it was just a breastplate and iron skullcap. The ground became more broken and hilly, rising steadily as they headed towards the mountains in the east. On the second day, as afternoon wore on, he heard a great cheer go up behind him. On both sides of their column, a mounted host passed at a slow trot, men-at-arms, knights and squires all in harness of good order, a few pennons snapping in the never-ending wind. Shouldering his crossbow, Jack called over to them.

'Where are we going?' he shouted. 'And how far is it?'

A man-at-arms veered closer to the marching files of the company. 'You speak English!'

'I am English!'

The man laughed. 'We are bound for York. Still many miles, my son! You'd better hope your feet hold out.'

He *cluck-clucked* to his horse to pick up the pace but Jack called out again. 'Who do you serve?'

'We are under Sir Thomas Broughton! More are coming!'

That, at least, heartened him. That others were heeding the call to arms. The host was growing slowly but surely. But the fells became steeper and the cursing around him greater. A few hours later they made camp near a village called Kendal. Somehow, wagons, which had been bought or stolen, caught up to them, bringing the cooks and food as well as tents for the two *fähnleins*, though not nearly enough for all the men. Fights broke out, and the provosts barked, making the soldiers sleep practically stacked upon each other. The *kerns* though, continued to huddle outside the stone houses and walls along the road, despite the chill of the night. They were hardy souls, keeping to themselves on the march. There would have been little understood if they had tried to fraternise, thought Jack, the Irish speaking Gaelic and the other soldiers Dutch and German.

Jack had never walked this far in his life. Under Hawker, he had always been in a wagon or mounted on his own horse. His feet ached but he had a good pair of boots and he felt himself becoming accustomed to the pace with each passing day. Once the food had caught up with them, the Germans began to joke and sing. They pressed on, following a course that weaved through the dales betwixt fell and moorland along a solitary road eastwards. Down they marched into the valleys of Wensleydale, where the going was easier and the road better. At Middleham, Jack saw more horsemen arriving to join their force, a few hundred at least, and cheers echoed from the walls of the castle. After a brief halt there, the army shouldered arms again and carried on.

A few miles down the road, Jack saw they were halting and fanning out across the grounds of what looked to be an enormous church abbey. The drums sounded the halt and word went around that they would be making camp here for the night. The Germans went about erecting the small number of tents they had, pulling them off the wagons while the cooking fires were started.

A bowl of gruel in his hands an hour later, Jack watched the sun sink behind the tower of Jervaulx Abbey while he slurped up the mix of oats and turnip and whatever meat had been thrown in. The Scots sat gathered in a circle, quiet as they wolfed their food, and Jack wondered how close they were to York, a great city he had heard much of from Hawker.

'We should go see if the Irish have stolen any more sheep to sup upon,' said one of the Scots, scratching at the fulsome set of whiskers sprouting on his throat and cheeks. 'We can barter some of this shit in exchange.'

Weems laughed. 'Aye, you do that, Duncan, you calf-headed sot. *You'll* end up in their cooking pot!'

Luke and Jack chuckled, and Duncan laughed along too. Jack had just finished the last in his wooden bowl when the provost and his man came to them. They all scrambled to their feet.

'The Englishman?' demanded the provost.

Jack stepped forward, stomach already churning.

'Come with me. His lordship demands. Ready yourself! You're a slovenly disgrace!'

David Weems leaned over to Jack's ear and hastily whispered, 'Don't forget your comrades!'

Jack wiped his face, put on his helm, and retrieved his crossbow, pouch of quarrels, buckler and haversack. He rapidly followed a few paces behind the provost and saw they were headed for the abbey. They proceeded into the warren of stone buildings, around the cloister, and through a great portico. They climbed the wooden staircase outside to the upper floor of the house and entered the archway. Jack swallowed when he saw a great retinue of lords assembled there, most in armour and all shouting, faces red with enflamed passion.

The provost took Jack's bow, grabbed him by the shoulder and propelled him forward towards where Lord Schwarz and his men were standing. As he moved across the great chamber, he saw they were arguing with Lord Lovell and the Earl of Lincoln. And then he knew why he was there.

Schwarz looked over at Jack's approach. 'Ah! He's come!' the Augsburger said loudly in German. 'My Englishman who can sort out this babblement!'

Jack raised his hand to the brow of his barbute helm and then gave a curt bow. 'My lord!'

'Tell these nobles,' said Schwarz, pointing, 'that I want to know where all the promised troops are! We have barely four thousand here. They said we'd have thousands more flocking to the standard. I am still waiting, God rot them!'

Jack's head spun, first trying make sure he understood what Schwarz had said and then figuring out how to tell the English lords. They were both puce with anger, eyes wide, and Jack knew if he got things mixed up it would be his neck stretched.

Jack bowed to Lovell and Lincoln in turn, and then did his best.

Lovell swore under his breath as he listened. 'Tell the German he is under our command and that more men *are* coming. *Have* already come, damn him!'

Jack interpreted for Schwarz and was met with a salvo of curses. 'We are advancing so quickly there is no time for others in the countryside to assemble and join our host! Tell them!'

Jack did so and was met with a derisive laugh from Lovell. 'Boy, you may tell Lord Schwarz that if we linger here we will have Henry Tudor poking us in our arse within a day or two. We must keep moving on to York!' The young earl, although seemingly more angry than Lovell, was content to let him do the arguing.

Schwarz's reply was not much more than a growling of swallowed words that Jack had trouble understanding. 'He says... I think, my lords... that the Duchess of Burgundy had promised him more support than he sees here now. But, being paid, he will fulfil his contract. Come what may.'

The Earl of Lincoln nodded, but Lovell looked at Schwarz with a jaundiced eye. 'Tell my lord Schwarz we will hold him to it.'

Jack bit his lip and spoke his broken German. 'He says, that you are a noble man who honours his contract.'

Schwarz pouted and then gave a nod of acknowledgement. 'Then we move on to York. Tell them.'

The English lords bowed and moved away to the long monks' table at the head of the chamber where they retrieved their wine goblets. Sitting there, on his own, and looking glum was the new boy-king. He pushed his cup back and forth from hand to hand, occasionally looking up to search the faces of the nobles and gentlemen around him.

Schwarz grunted and looked over to Jack. 'I think I keep you in my retinue from now on. I may need you again with these fellows.'

Jack gave a court bow. 'And my Scots comrades who also served you? May they return?'

Schwarz's eyes widened and he turned to the young officer next to him. 'Christ! The bollocks on this one! You should pay attention to him. He's going far!' He looked back at Jack, eyes stern, shaking his head with either admiration or disappointment. 'I haven't altered their pay yet, so they might as well earn it. Call them back to the guard.' He then turned to the officer again. 'Get this boy a mount so he may ride tomorrow.'

Jack broke into a grin. Schwarz noticed and poked a finger into Jack's breastplate. 'When battle comes, boy, we fight together – every man – on foot and in the squares. Don't forget that!'

–

Where he had laboured and marched for miles in ignorance before, now Jack Perry was aware of each piece of news arriving from fore-riders and 'prickers' of the Yorkist rebel army as it moved south, finally joining the Great North Road. He felt good to be on horseback again, even if he was dead last in the entourage. David and Luke, halberdiers once again, had to march behind, but were still cock-a-hoop with their reinstatement in the captain's guard. And Jack knew he had made firm allies of them.

But now, five days since they had made landfall, Jack began to catch wind of darker portents. The worst came when once again he had to assist the *landsknecht* commander with the noblemen. Schwarz's explosive reaction to the latest intelligence made Jack's heart sink. Word had just arrived that the mayor and aldermen of York would bar entry of the new king – and fight if necessary if the rebels lay siege. Lurking around the edges of the great captain's table, he caught the mood of the Germans: one of disappointment and betrayal, but also a fatalistic determination to fulfil their promise.

The army marched on. At a halt near Bramham Moor, a few miles west of Tadcaster, scouts brought word that some four or five hundred of the enemy were on their way from York under Lord Clifford. The English noblemen sought a conference with Schwarz and Jack again did his service.

Jack duly told the Germans that Lord Lovell was advocating an attack with his mounted men upon Lord Clifford's force that afternoon, so as to catch them in camp at sunset.

Schwarz's eyes widened. 'You mean to divide our strength! Go off and raid while we carry on south into Henry's main army?'

The Earl of Lincoln backed Lovell's strategy. 'If we leave them be, they will take us in the flank later when we can ill afford it! We must strike them now and send them packing.'

'Then tell them to do it and be quick about it,' muttered Schwarz to Jack, waving his hand dismissively. 'We will need every man we have when the main battle is upon us.'

When the English had left, Schwarz remained with his officers and they continued their dark conversations. Jack stood by long enough to hear what they were saying – though much of it went past him at the speed of a flying arrow. Schwarz caught him eavesdropping and ordered him away.

He returned to the stables of the inn that the Germans had paid for. The two flag companies – or what remained of them after the losses through sickness over the past days – were camped out on the moorland across the road. Weems was eager to hear whatever the news was from Jack.

'There is a smaller army bearing down on us from York,' Jack explained. 'Lord Lovell means to take his horsemen and surprise them. Tonight.'

Weems took a breath while Luke shook his head with concern.

'They plan to raid them and hopefully send them running back north. Then they will re-join us on the road south.'

'Well, Christ's blood!' said Weems. 'What if they don't?'

Jack sat on a pile of straw and folded his arms around his knees. 'The great captain isn't happy about any of it. The officers are saying the Irish have no armour and no bowmen. It will be down to us and the pikemen to take on the enemy.'

Weems nodded. 'Well, for the love of God, they're right about *that*. They're practically naked. Spears, mare spikes and long daggers won't be much good against cavalry and bowmen. It *will* be down to us.'

'And Lord Lovell's army too,' reminded Jack. 'We have the other armies of the northern lords.'

Luke stuck out his lower lip. 'Aye, and they are mostly mounted. We're the ones on foot if it goes ill. How fast can you run? My feet are already blistered.'

Weems leaned in towards Jack. 'What is the news of King Henry's army? How many does he bring north?'

Jack looked up. 'No one seems to know. Not yet at least.'

Weems stood straight and gave a harsh laugh. 'I'm thinking it's better to live in ignorance as a soldier than to know the truth. Maybe your promotion wasn't such a good idea after all, Jack Perry.'

Jack gave a shrug. He had already come to believe the same. 'Let's go find something to eat. I'm starving.'

32

Hawker guided them north by north-east, through the Deep-
ings and then straight north along the old Roman road which
would pass through Bourne. They rode hard for two hours. The
countryside was low and flat as far as they could see. Ellingham
felt as if the road would go on forever, never-ending, and that
he would be a wanderer the rest of his life.

After midday, Hawker slowed the pace to a walk to rest their
mounts and they chanced upon a small stream near the roadside
from which all might slake their thirsts. As the horses drank,
Ellingham stared down the length of the well-rutted and square-
cobbled track they had just ridden, knowing they would be
hunted sooner or later. He turned to Hawker, who stooped to
cup his hands with the fresh water.

'Tell me more about this old squire you hope will take us in.'

Hawker drank, wiped his sleeve across his whiskered face,
and stood up again. Ellingham heard the man's knees crack.

'James Mainwaring. More years upon him than me. His liege
lord died at the Battle of Barnet and he never bothered finding
another. Said he didn't need one. And he never picked up a
sword again, as far as I know. Ignored Richard's call to arms so
wasn't at the downfall. But he's a loyal man and, I hope… still
a Yorkist.'

'You hope?'

Hawker walked back to his horse and checked his bundled
armour was secure.

Ellingham noticed that Dieudonné was staring down the road they had come, as he had been doing all morning. 'You believe we were followed, Gaston?'

The Burgundian didn't turn to face him. 'Not yet, my prince. Not yet.'

—

The house of James Mainwaring lay outside the town of Bourne near to Bourne Wood, the tower of the nearby abbey just visible through the chestnut trees which clustered around the manor and outbuildings, all just blossoming with yellow catkins. The manor was built of stone and thatch, tall narrow windows on either side of a massive studded oak door. Hawker rode to the entrance, the others followed single file, and Hawker alone dismounted. He handed his reins to Jacob and banged upon the door. A dog began to bark inside.

A young male servant in a workman's apron opened the door cautiously.

'Is your master at home? Tell him it is Sir John Hawker come to call.'

The lad looked past, saw the others, and then looked to Hawker again. 'Wait here, my lord.'

The door closed quietly and Hawker took a few steps back on the flagstones. After no more than a moment, the door swung open again and out stepped an older gentleman, short, rotund and balding, his long grey locks flowing to his shoulders but his pate shining and pale. He wore a long green velvet robe, open, and fraying badly at the hem, his stomach overhanging his belted jerkin to the point the leather belt disappeared under his girth.

'Christ's nails! It *is* John Hawker!'

Hawker gave him a mock bow. 'It is. I am glad to see you are hale and well.'

Mainwaring tilted his head and grinned. 'And I glad to see you not dead and buried. As some have said.'

'My comrades and I must beg your hospitality, James. If only for one night. We journey north to York.'

The old squire rubbed at his nose. 'Is the town inn not hospitable enough to your liking, Sir John?'

Hawker nodded slowly. 'It doesn't take much to see we are travelling incognito. We would rather stay out of Bourne, if it can be helped. You are no fool, James, and I'm sure you can guess why.'

Mainwaring looked at Ellingham and then the others. 'A gentleman… or two. And a man-at-arms. I would say you are either looking for trouble or trying to avoid it.'

Hawker pressed his lips tightly for a moment. 'Probably both, my old friend. Will you help us?'

Mainwaring's eyes seemed to narrow in concentration and there was silence. But then he nodded. 'Come in. Young Hugh will see to your horses.' He half-turned to the carved stone archway and yelled. 'Hugh! Get back out here, lad!'

Mainwaring led them into his house and to his modest hall. 'I trust you were not followed,' he said, signalling for them to take a bench at the table. A large wolfhound loped into the room and stood its ground, growling at the newcomers. 'Heracles! You behave! This is a knight of the realm. Or at least the realm that once was.'

The beast lowered its ears and padded around the table to take a place underneath it, his eyes warily following the intruders. Hawker introduced his comrades and Mainwaring took time to look at each with a curious intent. A serving girl brought in a large clay pitcher and some tankards and he directed her to begin pouring.

'I won't ask your business, Sir John. I can guess it readily with the news of late.' He himself took a seat and pulled over a mug of ale across the well-scored planks of the table. 'I take no part in the struggles these past years. The royal court knows this – whose ever court it is – and they leave me be. I'm no use to them anyway. My retainers are striplings or withered folk like me. But I confess, I am surprised to see you dicing still.'

'I do what must be done. And no more.'

Mainwaring snorted a little. 'And you have done much already, John Hawker.' He looked to Ellingham. 'And what of you, Sir Giles? Irreconcilable with our new sovereign?'

Ellingham looked at him and then to Hawker. 'He is responsible for the death of my father. That is reason enough.'

Mainwaring's bushy brows raised. 'A blood debt owed. I understand such a motive.' His head swivelled down the table to where Jacob and Dieudonné sat, far apart from each other. 'A Flemish man-at-arms and a Burgundian. Curious company, Sir John. Would have thought your contingent would be larger for the task at hand.'

Jacob looked up from his ale suddenly upon hearing himself mentioned. Dieudonné merely gave a weak smile.

Ellingham didn't trust Mainwaring. Hawker was banking upon old friendships, but much time had passed. Loyalties shift like sand. The luxury of being left alone by the king usually demanded a price and he did not yet know what that price was nor if it had been paid.

'What is the mood of the county?' asked Hawker. 'Will Lincolnshire rise to fight Henry... or fight with him?'

Mainwaring laughed, a bitter bark of false mirth, and then took a drink. 'Nobody cares any more. And those that will fight will do so only because they must. Like you. Folk are not willing to risk what they already hold. Better the devil they now know. If you seek to raise a force in these parts, Sir John, you will find stony ground.'

Hawker said nothing and Ellingham's heart fell further.

The company became silent, the only sound was Heracles under the table worrying a large hambone. Mainwaring leaned towards Hawker and tapped him on the forearm. 'Come, you and Sir Giles. Perhaps I can cheer you up.'

Ellingham got up alongside Hawker and glanced over to Dieudonné. The Burgundian's face was a dark cloud for he had been judged, once again, as a retainer and not a knight.

290

Ellingham threw him a nod to acknowledge the slight, but Gaston only raised his mug to his lips and drank, avoiding eye contact.

Mainwaring led them through the kitchen and down a few stone steps to a small chamber at the back of the manor. It was a modest armoury. Two full suits of plate armour stood mounted on wooden frames and a rack of various-edged weapons was next to them.

'Both of you! Take what you fancy! I have little need of weapons or harness these days. Might end up doing myself more hurt than anyone else!'

Hawker went to the rack and immediately grasped a war hammer. It had a haft of ash four feet long, its iron head blunt and serrated on one end, the other a vicious spike. 'I would be grateful for the gift of this,' he said.

Mainwaring smiled. 'It is yours. And it is a good choice. I reckon the host you will be facing will be heavily armoured. Difficult work for a blade. May it keep you alive in the days to come. And what of you, Sir Giles?'

At his waist he still had the blade gifted to him by the woman who had bewitched him in Hungary. It was a handsome, well-made arming sword and tapered to a needle point. A reminder of her, both good and bad; memories he could not part with. His eyes scanned the rack of swords, flails and hammers but his desire for anything else was gone. 'I have what I need, Master Mainwaring. But I thank you.'

Mainwaring looked at him thoughtfully for a moment and then nodded. 'You are comfortable with your blade. That is good. I would venture only to give one piece of advice, young man. When battle is joined... stay mounted.'

Ellingham found it a strangely curious quip and his creasing brow probably gave it away. Did the old man mean he should not be unhorsed, or did he mean it would be easier to flee if the fight turned for the worse? Either way, it was unlikely. The English way of war was to fight on foot – nobles and soldiers alike.

They returned to the hall and Hawker tossed the war hammer to Jacob. The Fleming grinned and shook his head knowingly. 'I will stow it on your saddle, Sir John.'

More food appeared and they resumed eating. Hawker and Mainwaring talked of years gone by, old adventures, and wives lost to death. Ellingham found it all far from enlivening or encouraging. As the afternoon waned, Mainwaring left them to themselves, offering up the manor to them and telling them their bedchambers were ready whenever they chose to retire. The serving girl, Mary, brought forth more wine and then more platters of meat, bread and cheese. It was as if Mainwaring was giving them a last supper.

Candles and lanterns were lit for them. Both Jacob and Dieudonné wandered off and Ellingham was left to Hawker's sombre company.

Ellingham broke a long silence. 'We will be outnumbered, won't we?'

Hawker looked up, his face hard-set. 'I won't lie to you. It is likely. And I think Mainwaring knows it already.'

'What of these Irishmen? Germans? Surely others will have joined here in the north.'

Hawker took a drink of wine. 'We know there were some two thousand Germans. Not enough on their own. The Irish? Brave, no doubt, but if they're peasant levies what battle experience could they have? As for companies from the north, we must wait and see.'

Ellingham leaned forward, anger rising. 'For the love of Christ! Can you not hear yourself? Are you resigned to defeat? To riding to your death?'

Hawker's voice was quiet and measured. 'I am resigned to what God ordains. And I will fight with all my strength and determination. If one believes in the Cause still, then one must fight. That is why you are here.'

'So why are you here? Tell me that.'

'You know why. They held my wife and son to ransom.' Hawker raised his cup again and took a long swig. 'And I have paid it.'

'I know you far better than that.' He could feel his blood rising, frustrated with Hawker's wine-soaked, maudlin self-pity. 'It isn't enough. You could have left Flanders. Chiara and you. Returned to the republics. Florence. Milan. But here you are. Here *we* are.'

'I have done many things in my life. More than a few of them unworthy things. Sinful.' His voice was now so low it seemed he was speaking to himself.

'Then that is for your confessor. We have all done things we regret.'

Hawker looked at him and he at once saw the great sadness, even emptiness in his expression. 'I have confessed. I have been scourged. But some sins require more penance than that.'

Ellingham suddenly felt Hawker's grief enter him as if by possession. It flooded him with muffled despair. 'Sir John... we are all both light and darkness. Not all of one or the other. You *saved* my young cousins at the Tower. *You* did that.'

'I may have saved one. And to what purpose? I shall never know.'

'Your sins are absolved.'

'I have violated holy sanctuary. Caused men to be led to their deaths. I willingly murdered when I was told to do murder. All for my liege lords. And more than once. I was a knave, Giles. Not a knight. Make no mistake of that.'

Ellingham's jaw went a little slack. He'd known Hawker for two years, not a lifetime. The man he knew was just and forthright, but he remembered also how quickly Hawker had stabbed Contanto in Venice. The rage. How the hardness in him often overshadowed the Christian. He began to understand.

'So, you see, Giles, I will let God decide my fate. If I can save a friend from Death then I will do so. If I can guarantee Chiara and my son a life, then I will do what must be done.'

Ellingham swallowed. He could only nod.

It was then that Dieudonné returned, with Jacob hectoring him from behind.

'Always too eager to be on your way!' said Jacob, sneering. 'He's already checking his saddle and bags. Just when we have had the best fare in days.'

Dieudonné ignored him and walked to the table. 'If I am to play the fool – a groomsman – then I shall play it. Is that not right, Giles? We need not more than two knights in this company.'

'Sit, Gaston,' said Ellingham, annoyed. 'Have some more wine. Settle your humours.'

Dieudonné took the pitcher of wine and refilled Ellingham's cup. 'I will fetch us some more,' he said in French, laughing.

'At last,' muttered Jacob, 'he is useful.'

The Burgundian went out to the kitchen and after a short while returned with the pitcher. He poured for Hawker and then Jacob before tilting his own cup close and high-angled to the lip of the vessel. 'To your health!' he said raising it up. 'And to our little company of the White Rose.'

They resumed their drinking. But after the cups were drained, Hawker's eyelids began to drift downwards. 'I must retire. Tomorrow we set off for the north.' He looked over to Ellingham. 'And... this day I have said too much.'

Jacob staggered after him, from fatigue or from the wine, leaving only him and the Burgundian at opposite ends of the long table.

'So, my prince,' said Dieudonné softly in French. 'What shall we do now?'

–

Listening to the youth, Dieudonné found it more and more difficult to disguise his hurt, his blossoming disdain, with *bonhomie* and empty smiles. This royal bastard's betrayal and spurning of his devotion – his love – was bad enough, but now realising as he did the precariousness of his situation, the choice had become clear. They were not some spearhead of a Yorkist reconquest of this kingdom – they were on the run for their very lives. He listened, he smiled, and remembering how he had shed tears, alone, at the youth's rejection of him. He burned with shame. Such feelings were hard to conceal, and it must have become clear to Ellingham.

'Gaston, what are you dwelling upon?'

He smiled again, a smile that was more wistful than cheerful. 'I am thinking about the future, my prince. And what comes next. For me, it is bed. Goodnight.'

Dieudonné got up, bowed, and went to where the girl Mary had showed him he was sleeping, a small servant's room on the ground floor and near to where the other servants stayed. He could hear the Fleming in the trundle bed next to his, snoring deeply, breaths coming slowly, with great gasping pauses. That was good. He was no apothecary but he knew from experience that the draught the monk had given to him was a powerful one. Hawker and the Fleming had equal doses in their wine and he could only hope that neither would ever wake again.

He lay on the low, creaking bedstead, fully dressed in his gambeson and boots. In the dark, he looked up towards the ceiling and let his thoughts drift, waiting for time to pass. He would not sleep. After what he thought were a few hours, he rose and went back to the hall. The great hound was not there, and he assumed it had gone off to sleep with its master. The first hurdle passed. The risen moon afforded enough silver light for him to make his way to fetch his weapons, quickly buckling on his scabbarded blade and his dagger. He then went up the winding stone staircase and entered the bedchamber of Hawker and Ellingham. As he had hoped, Hawker was barely breathing, sprawled upon his mattress. He had managed to only remove his doublet before lying down in his shirt, hose and boots.

Dieudonné woke the youth, who started from his slumber, reaching for his dagger.

'No fear, my prince!' he whispered. 'I must speak with you now. My heart lies heavy.'

Ellingham pulled himself up in the bed. 'If it is so then we must talk, Gaston.'

'Not here. I must take the night air. Clear these thoughts from my head. Come with me.'

Ellingham was drowsy but complied, hastily throwing on his clothes and pulling on his boots. He clapped on his woollen cloak and followed Dieudonné down the stairs, quiet so as not to disturb the old squire.

'What could not have waited until the morning?'

Dieudonné sighed but did not halt his progress. 'I could not sleep. Not with the weight upon me. I need to confide in you. You alone. There is betrayal in the air.'

He led Ellingham outside into the warm night. The moon, though a waning one, still shed copious light across the courtyard. He could feel his heart starting to pound. His choice had been made, irrecoverably, but now was the time to do the deed. He would only get this one chance. 'Let us to the stables. We can speak freely there.'

Ellingham shook his head and pulled his cloak about him. 'You are most strange, Gaston. What conspiracy are you proposing?'

But Dieudonné had already set off across the yard, the strange but familiar scent of chestnut trees filling his nostrils. Timing is everything, he said to himself. He gently opened the door and left it open after Ellingham passed him, moving inside. His dagger he had now drawn from his belt.

'Gaston, it is dark as pitch! Let us go back.'

With his left hand seizing the back of the youth's collar, he jerked Ellingham back and brought the heavy pommel of the dagger down sharply upon his head. Instantly, he felt Ellingham's legs give way, a loud groan emanating from him. A second blow brought him down completely to the straw-covered earthen floor. Without pausing, Dieudonné yanked both of the youth's arms behind his back and set to tying his wrists with a cord he had whipped out from his belt. He rolled Ellingham over and shoved a rag into his mouth. Ellingham was moving on the ground, writhing slowly, senses dulled by the blows. The sliver of moonlight that shone upon him proved to Dieudonné that he was nearly senseless but, luckily, not dead.

The horses were ready. Grunting, he heaved Ellingham up, limp as a doll, and threw him over the saddle, facing backwards. Somehow, he managed to seat him, legs hanging over each side. He then lashed him securely to the horse, tying his bound wrists to the back of the saddle's cantle. Dieudonné could hear himself breathing heavily now, rushing to the stable doors and easing open one of them wide. With one hand holding Ellingham's confused mount at long rein, he then hauled himself up into his own saddle and kicked his horse forward. The short, sad parade came out of the stables and with a glance behind to make sure his prisoner was still mounted, Dieudonné kicked his horse forward again and they set off at a fast trot down the road.

There was enough moonlight for him to see the road and to follow the way they had come. There was no other choice: he did not know this country. He would make for Stamford – to Sir Edmund Blodwell's – with his prize, and his story. And then to his old liege lord, Jasper Tudor, Duke of Bedford, bearing the gift of a Tear of Byzantium and a Plantagenet bastard to go with it. But he was already worried these might not be enough.

33

The weather did not favour Gaston Dieudonné. The clouds rolled in across the flat landscape, low and dark, and the moon disappeared beyond them. Even with his eyes adjusted to the darkness, he could not see the road well enough and he knew he would have to make a halt. Ahead he saw the outline of a farmstead, one they had passed on the way to Bourne. Carefully, Dieudonné threaded his way down a sloping track and to the house.

Ellingham was conscious it seemed, groggy but alive. Dieudonné pulled the rag from the youth's mouth. Ellingham's head lolled. The Frenchman – 'Burgundian' no more – loosened his sword in its scabbard and went and banged upon the door of the house.

It took some pounding but after a few minutes the door creaked open and light spilled out. A short man of ruddy hue poked his face out.

'What be your business at this hour!'

Dieudonné squared his shoulders. 'The king's business! Open your door!'

The door opened wider and the farmer, wearing nothing but a long linen shirt, stepped back, pitchfork in his hand. Looking beyond him in the red glow of the low-ceilinged room, Dieudonné saw a middle-aged woman, wrapped in a coverlet with her hair undone standing near the hearth. Near her, an old crone was seated on a low, woven rush chair.

'I have a prisoner with me. An enemy of the king. A rebel and spy.'

The farmer said nothing, and the Frenchman hoped his poor English was understandable. He saw the farmer lift his head to look outside at the slumped figure still on horseback. He took another step backwards into his house and then gave a nod of approval.

Dieudonné managed to get Ellingham unhorsed and then half-dragged, half-carried him inside. He placed him down on a bench at the small square table in the centre of the room.

'Where are the rest of your men?' asked the farmer, a deep scowl on his face, and pitchfork still in his flexing hands.

'They have gone on ahead,' Dieudonné lied. 'Fetch some water for us.'

The farmer nodded to his wife who went out and came back with a pitcher. 'May I tend to him?' she asked.

Dieudonné roughly lifted the youth's chin, his hair was matted with dried blood and he could see a large lump on his crown. Ellingham's eyes began to focus on him. He was rising up from the depths. Dieudonné looked at the goodwife and pointed a long finger at Ellingham. She came over and gave him a drink and then set to daubing his face with a cloth.

'What do you want of us?' said the farmer.

'We will be on our way when the sun rises. You need do nothing else.'

The old crone, wearing nothing but a long smock, barked out a laugh from where she sat. She was spinning yarn now, a wooden drop-spindle dangling between her feet.

The farmer kept his guard and said nothing while his wife cleaned Ellingham's face and head. Dieudonné watched, his emotions roiling. Disdain and anger, hurt and shame, it all coursed through him, his very body tingling.

Ellingham looked up. 'Why?' he croaked.

'Because you do not know the meaning of loyalty. You do not reward it. You do not recognise it. I would have given you all that and more.' His words in French were thrown out like daggers.

'You have betrayed us,' said Ellingham. 'Hawker was always right to suspect you. I was a fool.'

Dieudonné laughed. 'I kept you alive! Hawker too! It was you who betrayed *me*. Spat at my affection for you.'

'Who are you, Gaston? You have lied for so long. But I thought I knew you.'

Dieudonné swept up a wooden cup in his hand and took a swig. 'I am French. Yes, I can tell you that now. And when we first crossed paths, I was in the service of Jasper Tudor. I tell you that freely because it does not matter any more.'

Ellingham's eyes filled with tears. 'All these months. All we have been through. And now you sell me like Judas.'

Dieudonné opened his mouth but words could not come. He stretched out his open hand, as if gesturing to a wayward child. 'Me! You say I betray *you*? I betrayed myself. My liege lord. For you. And now we are on the edge of an abyss. The White Rose is a lost cause, you poor fool.'

The farmer shuffled across the wooden planks of the floor. 'You are not English!' he said gruffly. 'That is the French tongue!'

Ellingham looked over at him. 'Yes, he is a Frenchman. But I am an Englishman. And he is a liar.'

Dieudonné wheeled on the farmer and put his hand on his sword hilt. 'I serve King Henry. Remember that, man!'

The farmer looked at his wife but held his ground. The old woman laughed again as she spun, her hand deftly twirling the spindle.

'I should have seen through your treachery,' said Ellingham, in English. 'Jacob's comrade – Jan Bec – he discovered you, didn't he? When we fled after Bosworth. You murdered him on ship and pushed him overboard.'

Dieudonné's jaw dropped in exasperation. He raised his hand up towards the ceiling. 'He would have ruined everything! I was left with no choice. I had joined with the company. With *you*, Giles. You had taken my heart! And then you spurned me!

You are a spoilt child who cannot understand the meaning of devotion.'

'Murderer,' replied Ellingham in English, his head dropping. 'Traitor.'

The farmer worked his way over to his wife and pushed her behind. 'I do not know who you are, Frenchman. Where are the king's men? Who is this man you hold?'

'Can you not see?' shouted Dieudonné, flecks of spit flying out. 'He is a rebel!'

'He is a boy,' said the farmer. 'I think you should leave my house.'

Dieudonné smiled and tilted his head. He drew out his arming sword and let it fall limply at his side. He began to tap the blade against his leg.

The farmer hefted the pitchfork. 'Get out of my house.'

Ellingham pushed himself up, swaying, hands still bound.

Dieudonné moved to push him back down on the bench and the farmer sprang. Back-pedalling, the Frenchman managed to raise his sword in a guard, catching the tines of the pitchfork. But the farmer pushed forward, pressing the sword against Dieudonné's breastplate and they grappled, stumbling about and each trying to throw over the other.

The old woman began laughing again and as Dieudonné wrestled, trying to throw the farmer off balance, he saw her get out of her chair. He then saw the flash of a short blade in her hand. She waddled to Ellingham, grabbed his bound wrists, and sliced the cords in one cut. Dieudonné gave a cry and shoved the farmer backwards, freeing his sword. But Ellingham bulled into him, a desperate cry of wordless rage pouring forth from his mouth. They tumbled to the floor and the Frenchman rolled just before the farmer's pitchfork descended, leaving the youth between him and the farmer.

Dieudonné grunted and pushed Ellingham's scrabbling arms off, raising his blade just in time to meet the prongs of the pitchfork. He twisted his wrist, locking his blade in the pitchfork, and stood up, roaring his defiance. But Ellingham was again on his feet too, tackling the Frenchman and sending them both slamming against the door. The crone's mad cackling seemed to be droning out everything else. Dieudonné pushed Ellingham away and sent his fist flying into the farmer's face, staggering him backwards. He then jerked open the door and ran outside. Ellingham followed but tripped and fell.

Dieudonné turned and raised his blade. So be it. No one would have Giles if he could not. The youth was on all fours, crawling forward, his neck bared. The Frenchman took a step closer and raised his sword up higher. Then the farmer charged again, a cry on his lips. Dieudonné parried the thrust and clipped the farmer's head, nearly severing an ear. The crone's high-pitched laughter filled the air. She stood in the doorway, eyes bulging, the knife waving in her hand. The farmer went into a crouch, his weapon levelled for another charge. Dieudonné heard the barking of dogs and the shouts of men from across the road. He knew now he had missed his chance. He took a few steps back, gave a cry of frustrated rage and then vaulted into his saddle. He jerked the reins and kicked the horse into a startled run into the black of the night.

One must always have choices – that was his motto – but Gaston Dieudonné now knew his choices were two: flee, or seek Tudor mercy.

–

When he entered the farmhouse, Hawker swore softly. Ellingham sat on a bench, head wrapped in a bandage. But he was alive.

'Are you the king's men?' asked the farmer, his head bandaged as well, and blood seeping through the wrappings.

Hawker looked at him and grunted, 'Yes.'

'Which king then?'

'Does it matter?'

The farmer said nothing. Hawker, clad in his armour the colour of jet, went to Ellingham and laid a hand on his shoulder. 'Are you whole enough to ride?'

Ellingham looked at Hawker, his face screwed up tight in puzzlement and pain. 'He betrayed us all. All these many months.'

Hawker nodded to Jacob to help up the youth. 'I was the one who was blind to treachery. My heart told me, but my head did not listen. I am sorry.'

Ellingham's eyes wandered off, straight ahead, as if he was seeing it all over again. 'He spoke of *my* betrayal. Of him.' The youth then turned to Jacob. 'And it was he who killed poor Jan – on ship.'

Jacob's hard face showed no emotion. Hawker shut his eyes a moment. His blindness had cost them much. 'He has revealed himself. Now we know where we stand.'

They walked Ellingham outside to the horses, Hawker moved slowly, his head still a little dizzy and aching from whatever drug Dieudonné had slipped into his wine. He went to his saddlebags and retrieved a pouch of coins. He moved to the farmer and placed the entire sack in the man's hands. It was payment deserved. 'For your trouble. And your wounds.'

'War is coming again, isn't it?' said the farmer.

Hawker winced at his words, knowing the truth. 'I pray that it does not find you.'

The farmer lifted the sack in his palm and nodded. 'I thank you.'

Hawker saw in the doorway the man's wife and an old woman. The goodwife still looked ashen and shaken from their ordeal. The old woman was smiling and nodding. Addled in her brains, no doubt, he thought. But then Ellingham walked over and gently took up the old woman's hand, bent down and kissed it. Her smile grew wider.

Jacob walked Ellingham back to his horse and helped him mount.

'Where do we go now?' Ellingham asked as Hawker led his horse to the front. Hawker looked up at the youth. He appeared wan and weak but more too – Hawker knew the lad was deeply wounded in his heart, his self-confidence sapped away. He would need time to heal, but Hawker feared there would be little of that to be had.

'We go back north. But we'll get you fit again first, at Mainwaring's. And then we must ready for battle. There'll be no more skulking in this shire. We are going to war.'

–

Gaston Dieudonné was led under escort, stinking of sweat from nearly two days in the saddle, hell-bent to make it to Leicester. His sword and dagger had been whisked away from him on arrival. The three men-at-arms surrounding him peeled off to one side and he felt himself being poked in the leg by the haft of a polearm from yet another guard behind him. He had embarked upon a terrible gamble with his own life and he had but one card left to play. He sank down to one knee and looked up at the man who stood a few paces ahead.

Jasper Tudor, the Duke of Bedford, brother and uncle to two kings, lowered the letter in his hand and regarded the dishevelled wretch in mismatched armour who kneeled before him.

'You claim to be Gaston Dieudonné, once a man in my service. I would hardly recognise you now, I think, if you are who you claim to be. Speak.'

'My lord, I remain in your service. I swear to you. And I was told in Antwerp by your agent that I would find forgiveness – and service renewed. If I came. His name is Baudet.'

The duke walked over to a small table and lifted a goblet and wine ewer that had been placed there. 'Baudet, yes. Then, sirrah, you will remember there were conditions attached.' He was probably as old as Hawker, taller though, and still very hale by the look of him. His robes were of heavy blue brocade trimmed in ermine, his golden chains of office draped over them. Shining black cordwain riding boots peeked out from under the hem of his skirts. 'Where is the rest of your company? Where is the bastard?'

Dieudonné bowed his head. 'My lord, I had him not two days ago. My prisoner. But peasants managed to free him. I barely escaped with my life to come here.'

Jasper Tudor gave Dieudonné a look of disgust. 'So these peasants managed to pluck out the little French thorn that is Gaston Dieudonné. And here you are… with nothing but pleas for mercy. *Begging.*'

'My lord, I do bring you something.' Dieudonné fumbled for the small pouch that hung from his belt. He brought forth the only thing that was concealed there and held it out, as his offering.

Jasper Tudor plucked it from the Frenchman's open palm and held it up. 'So, this is the Tear of Byzantium. So much fuss for such a dull gem. I grant you… it is large… but crude.' His fist closed around it. 'I will consider it partial penance for your sins.'

The duke took a drink, glanced out the window of the inn, and then sat in the great carved chair next to the table. 'There remains the matter of your past misdeeds. You stand accused of vile murders. Your desertion from my service near upon two years ago. These merit swift trial and punishment.'

Dieudonné felt his bollocks shrivel. He sank to both knees, head down.

The duke pointed a forefinger, at him. 'Look at me, you knave! The king has the power to pardon if I request it of him. And this I may consider. But only if you undertake the rest of your penance.'

'Command me, your Grace. I beg you.'

'The rebel army has landed in the north. They are coming south. If you can find the York bastard again – then you may find redemption from your king. I would think a creature such as yourself would have little trouble in finding him again. He will seek to join the rebels. Find him. Bring him to us.'

'I swear I will do as you say, my lord.'

'And I swear a promise to you here and now – if you dare attempt to run again – I will have you executed on the spot. Because you will have an escort with you from this point forward. Prove you are still a man worthy of my service. And the king's mercy.'

Dieudonné nodded and swallowed with some difficulty, throat dry. He was shamed. And this shame made him seethe with loathing all the more. Not just for himself, but for those who had belittled him, robbing him of his honour. And most of all for the one who had spurned his affection and loyalty. His ardour. He would redeem himself now. Or die trying.

Part VI

PENANCE AND REDEMPTION

34

The evening sun had finally melted away, leaving only a faint glimmer of twilight on Bramham Moor. Campfire flames danced, dotted around the field, and the low rumble of hundreds of soldiers in conversation around Jack Perry carried across the air.

He and his Scottish comrades had eaten what food they could find. A few hundred mounted men of Lord Lincoln – and Lovell – had ridden off before dusk to find Lord Clifford's force of Tudor loyalists, supposedly making camp not more than a league away at Tadcaster. Before the moon had risen high, Jack heard the sound of trumpets approaching and turned to see many torches bobbing in the distance. The raiders had returned. Soon enough the strong smell of lathered horseflesh floated to them, the pounding hooves vibrating across the soft ground.

From the cock-on-the-hoop noises of the riders and the laughter and singing, Jack knew them to have been victorious.

'Let's get back to the captain's encampment!' he said to Weems and Luke. 'Before he sends for us. We can find out what happened the quicker there.'

Weems made a sour face. 'Why bother? There will be no scraps for us, I can tell you that for certain.'

Jack went alone. He was allowed entry into the roped encampment, and he sought out Schwarz and his retinue. His arrival caught the captain's eye and Schwarz motioned for one of the officers. He came to Jack and handed him a metal contraption – a winding gear of some sort. Jack took it and looked at it, not knowing what to do.

'It is a *crannequin*, you dolt! The captain has sourced them for all the crossbowmen of his guard. Learn how to use it by morning.'

The officer turned and went back to the gathering leaving Jack standing there somewhat bemused by his new orders. But before he could turn and leave, the English lords arrived seeking an audience with the mercenary captain. Jack was immediately whistled for to come and assist with the interpreting, even though Jack knew that Schwarz's knowledge of English had got better.

'We've sent them packing back to York!' said a beaming Earl of Lincoln. 'Took their baggage train too for our trouble.'

Jack saw that Schwarz's joy was muted. He told Jack to ask if any prisoners had been taken and whether they'd been interrogated.

Lovell smiled. 'They were too busy running naked in nought but their hose to stop and yield to us. We cut through them. Cut them all down.'

Schwarz returned a smile, one laced sardonic. 'So, we still don't know the disposition of Henry Tudor's main army. How many were there at Tadcaster?'

'Five or six hundred men,' answered Lord Lovell. 'A small force, but one that won't be bothering us again for a while. We can proceed south with our flank unchallenged.'

Schwarz waited until Jack had haltingly translated it all. He then nodded slowly. 'We should send out our fore-riders to meet Henry's coming up from the south. We need to know more about what we are up against. Numbers.'

Lovell raised a palm to silence the Bavarian. 'My fore-riders and spies are already well ahead of us. They will be bringing intelligence soon. Have no fear of that.'

Schwarz grunted at the reply. 'Aye, well, I will send out riders too. In the next day or so. I'd rather hear about the strength of my enemy from his own men squealing under a hot iron.'

The English laughed at that and cups of wine went around. But Jack knew from eavesdropping the day before that his

German captain was uneasy. There had been no plunder allowed for the two flag companies, no rest for several days, and the penny-master was already worrying about the pay coffers running dry. Time was not on their side.

–

They were up with the sun. The drums rolled and rattled, the pipes gave their shrill call, and the march southwards began anew. They purposely marched along the main road, and through towns and villages, beating the drums and hoping to raise their numbers. A few dozens of men joined them – mainly farmer lads looking for money or adventure – but there were no more great retinues from northern noble lords flocking to their banners. The Irish who remained, and some number had fallen ill by the wayside now, were yet hardy and courageous for everything material they lacked.

The *landsknechts* might be better fed and watered, but even these were beginning to grumble. Jack reckoned they had marched some twenty miles a day since they'd landed and the pace was beginning to tell. Soldiers argued more, sang less, and the provost marshal's baton fell upon many more heads. Men growled, and so did their stomachs. They needed victory in battle – and soon. Luke of Kirkcaldy became even more morose. 'By the time we meet the enemy we'll be nought but skin and bones,' he said, half to himself.

By mid-week, they had marched down through Pontefract and then on to Doncaster unopposed. On Thursday they passed through Tickhill and by afternoon had made it to Worksop town. Word came that Lord Lincoln's fore-riders had spotted armoured horsemen they assumed to be Henry's. Lord Schwarz demanded to field a contingent to pursue them and he and his personal guard would go with them. While the bulk of the rebel army continued its march, Jack was again given a mount and he soon found himself riding hard, one of two hundred men, keen to take the fight to the Lancastrians.

He wore his breastplate and back, shoulder spaulders, gauntlets and leg armour, which went to his knee. He still possessed the Italian barbute-style helm he had obtained in the East, giving him the look of an experienced veteran of faraway wars, while his crossbowmen comrades were uniform in their Burgundian armour and open sallet helms. At his waist he also still wore the arming sword given him under Hawker. He had quickly mastered the *crannequin* contraption, which he found spanned the crossbow effortlessly by cranking its handle. He would probably have to shoot from the saddle, a feat he had never done before, but this would let him do it quicker and with more ease. He could no longer afford to sit on his arse and pull the string with his hands while his feet braced the bow prod. The crossbow now was spanned where it hung over his shoulder, and he needed only set a quarrel into the channel and take aim when the time came. If it came at all.

As they rode along the country roads, Jack thought of Sir John and Jacob and wondered where they were now. He had been thinking more and more of them both over the past days, his conscience heavy with guilt for having forsaken them. And although he felt that the old knight might be proud if he could see him, he knew full well that he had been dishonourable in abandoning Hawker. That Hawker needed not the services of a squire any more was poor reason to run away. His anger and frustration, held in check for so long, had finally gotten the better of him and he regretted it bitterly. He prayed to God for forgiveness and for Sir John to find peace in his life in Flanders. For his part, he was now deep in the fight for a new king, a path that had only one direction open. Despite the friendship of his newfound Scottish comrades, deep down he felt he did not belong and that he never really would. But it was far too late for such misgivings.

Lord Schwarz and his officers rode behind Jack and the contingent of crossbowmen. They were covered by more than a dozen members of the guard, men with demi-lances and swords. The remainder of the fore-riders were double-pay men with swords who knew how to ride, as well as mounted men-at-arms who served under the English lords. The pace of the ride varied, at times a canter while at others they would take rest at a slow trot. There was little time for banter amongst them and Jack did not really understand these southern Germans very well anyway, some of whom still resented his presence among them in the guard.

They had been in the saddle for a few hours and, from his vantage, Jack could see Schwarz looking agitated, arguing with his officers. They had found nothing to justify this adventure thus far, despite driving deeper south towards the bulk of the Tudor armies, which were no doubt gathering force. But shortly thereafter trumpets sounded and the entire contingent began to spur their mounts and head towards the great wood Jack could see a few miles distant, a forest that stretched across the horizon.

Jack's horse dutifully followed the others and he had little to do but hold on as it pounded across the fields. Far out ahead, his keen eyes made out a group of horsemen – armoured men – making for the woods ahead. Enemy fore-riders. The Germans and English both spurred their horses into a gallop, closing the ground. King Henry's men must have realised they would not make the cover of the forest in time and they began to break left, wheeling so as not to be caught from behind. In front of him, Jack saw two faltering Lancastrians knocked from their saddles by the lances of Lovell's riders. There were nearly a hundred of the enemy Jack reckoned. Both groups of horsemen now wheeled and slowed as they entered into close combat.

Jack slowed enough to stop from bobbing in his saddle and brought up his bow. Steadying his horse while trying to load a quarrel into his bow, he saw a rider in full armour coming straight for him. Jack raised the bow, frantically trying to steady it as his horse nervously shifted underneath him. At no more than ten feet, Jack squeezed the lever and he clearly heard the metallic *ping* as the bolt pierced the breastplate of the man-at-arms. The Lancastrian tilted to the side drunkenly, his mount carrying on past Jack. Jack dropped the bow on its sling and kicked his horse into movement. The swirling *melee* was making it difficult to sort friend from foe. Jack finished cranking his bow again; more horsemen were closing on him. Two were swept away by Germans driving their lances into them, a third kept coming and Jack panicked, dropped his bow and drew his sword. The blow that he parried jarred his whole arm, but he found himself striking back, even though his blade just slid from the man's armoured shoulder.

A quick exchange of blows brought neither of them hurt, their horses circling each other. But around them, the superior rebel numbers had begun to tell. A fully armoured English man-at-arms approached from the far side and brought his sword crashing down on Jack's opponent between the man's helm and shoulder, wounding him badly and tumbling him from his saddle. Jack moved off, taking in what was happening around him. Many were on the ground dead, some lay motionless over their saddle bows or hanging upside down, feet caught in stirrups. A few still fought on but more than a dozen managed to flee into the forest. It was clear though. Victory was theirs.

Jack sheathed his sword and finished spanning his crossbow in case more of the Lancastrians decided on a sally from the trees. He saw a few of the enemy taken prisoner and brought to where Lord Schwarz and his retinue had taken station in the field. The double-pay men shouted for the meandering troops to gather and slowly the horsemen gathered into a loose formation in case of further attack. Jack trotted over to Schwarz and his officers and approached, saluting.

'My lord,' he said, 'do you wish to question the prisoners?'

One of Lovell's squire gentlemen arrived and halted. 'You speak their tongue, lad?'

Jack nodded.

Schwarz barked at Jack to move closer and Jack saw where dismounted *landsknechts* were surrounding two Lancastrians, both looking bruised but not mortally hurt. Their helms were off and they stood, blinking in the strong sunlight, faces sweaty, and probably wondering if these were to be their last moments alive. Jack dismounted and approached. He bowed to Schwarz. The captain, bare-headed and with sword drawn, smiled. He looked to the squire who had now been joined by Lovell's other lieutenants. 'My Englishman will interrogate these prisoners!' he shouted in German.

Jack hurriedly told the English what was said. The squire frowned. 'And who are *you*, boy?'

'I am Jack Perry of Stamford. I am with these Germans. One of them.'

The squire laughed. 'Would make a cat speak! In truth?'

'Ask these prisoners who they serve! Demand their strength!' Schwarz bellowed at Jack.

Jack moved to where the prisoners stood. Two Germans pushed them to their knees and Jack found himself in the unusual position of commanding men who might be themselves knights or squires.

He did his best to sound his authority, hoping he wouldn't squeak. 'Which lord do you serve? Answer me!'

One of the men, the older of the two prisoners, spoke up immediately. 'We are Lord Woodville's retainers.'

'How many horse have you?'

One prisoner looked to the other. The older replied again. 'We number two thousand.'

Jack translated for Schwarz.

'Ask them more! Where is King Henry's army? Get numbers from them or we kill them here and now!'

Jack crossed his arms and demanded answers as best he could. It was hard to see the poor fellows quivering, voices shaking once they found the courage to speak up.

'The king is at Nottingham,' croaked the older soldier. 'Many thousands have gathered. The Earl of Oxford... six thousand, I think. Lords Strange and Stanley have six thousand more, we are told.' He looked directly at Jack. 'I beg you. Spare us, sir.'

Jack turned to Schwarz and told him all. If the German was struck by the news, he did not deign to show it. Jack quickly glanced over to the English gentlemen squires who stood looking at the prisoners. Their faces were set hard as stone.

Schwarz tapped his naked sword rhythmically on the side of his leg armour and chewed the inside of his cheek. He was silent for a few moments. Jack heard the younger prisoner begin to whisper the *Pater Noster*. The German raised his sword and pointed it towards the north.

'We have ten thousand at our heels and *more* are coming. And we are bringing fire and sword to you all from the north. We have driven your Lord Clifford and his army. We have driven *you*. And now we will drive your usurper king from his throne.'

Jack knew the numbers were a bold lie. He quietly did his best again to translate to the terrified men-at-arms while the Englishmen there listened too, mouths agape.

Schwarz moved closer and bent from the hip, drilling his eyes into each of the prisoners. 'You go tell your masters *that*! We are coming!'

The prisoners looked to Jack and began gushing their thanks upon hearing the English words. Schwarz gave orders for the men to be stripped of their armour, set upon horses and released.

He then turned to his comrades. 'There! It's finished,' he barked. 'Those two miserable wretches will spread the word for us. Now, let us get back before our two companies get overly anxious and desert the standards.'

Jack exchanged looks with the English squire and his companion. All understood the import of what had been said by the prisoners. King Henry's forces were *still* gathering strength and – if these beaten Lancastrians were telling the truth – the rebel army was already heavily outnumbered. Their chances of success now hung upon a very slender thread indeed.

35

Ellingham rubbed at the wound on his scalp, the lump still there despite the wych elm salve applied by James Mainwaring's maidservant. It hurt far less than his pride.

Hawker pinched the bridge of his beaked nose. 'You mustn't reproach yourself. It is I who bear the guilt for all this, Giles.'

Ellingham felt he was beyond feeling any sense of guilt. He was deeply ashamed and deeply disillusioned. 'Why, Sir John? Why did he do it?'

'Why? Because he turned again. You said he was in service with Jasper Tudor when he joined us after Bosworth. He lied then. I imagine his game was to turn us over when the moment came. He tried it in Venice but it went wrong for him. I cannot fathom why he stayed with us so long. His treachery was there all the time and I would have seen it if I had only listened to my guts and not my head.'

But Ellingham did know why. Gaston's professed love for him. Something he had pushed away, rejected, pretending he had forgotten, all despite knowing the Frenchman's appetites. He had been a fool to think it could be ignored. That unrequited affection had festered and finally burst forth into betrayal. Yet the depth of Dieudonné's deceit and his murderous knavery, that still beggared belief. And despite all they had been through together as a company across Europe, despite that he had saved Hawker's life and his own at least once, Dieudonné was now prepared to sell them to the Lancastrians. And to their deaths.

Mainwaring waddled into the hall and heard their conversation. 'Food is as good as physik, young sir! You should eat while you can.' He pulled the platter of cold pies and ham closer to Ellingham. 'I must say, I never liked the look of that Frenchman,' he growled. 'Always watching, never speaking.'

The sentiment was not a help. Ellingham said nothing.

'We must take our leave and soon, James,' said Hawker. 'We've been here a day and a night and every moment we remain places your household in danger. I would not put it past Dieudonné to attempt to lead a party straight back here.'

'They've left me alone since they took the throne,' said Mainwaring. 'I'll play the addle-brained old man if needs must,' he laughed. 'Go on, eat and drink before you take to the road. You have trials ahead and will need your strength.'

'Your kindness won't be forgotten,' said Hawker. 'You are a good man… a rarity in this world.'

Mainwaring laughed again. 'Aye, well, you didn't know me in my youth. But there's none left alive to gainsay you! Now, mark me, Sir John… I've sent Hugh down on horseback to the crossroads to keep watch until you set off. He'll beat that horse bloody to get back here in time and warn us if soldiers are coming.' He looked at Ellingham and frowned. 'Lad, you can't let your ill humours undo you. Search your soul later… see a priest if you must. Now though, you must ready yourself for what comes your way.'

Ellingham nodded. 'My heart tells me that too. Fear not. I will heed you.'

'Good. I know that King Richard would not have bestowed spurs upon you if they had not been earned.' He gave a little bow of his head and walked away. 'I shall go ready a couple of my crossbows. Just to be safe. Good angles of attack from my window upstairs if any king's man doesn't leave when I tell them to.' And he let out a harsh laugh again.

Ellingham turned to Hawker. 'I am ready. I would rather be in armour and setting out than sitting here doing nothing. Where will we ride?'

'It is time for me to do what I have taken payment for. Stir rebellion and fight… come what may. We go north. Make our way to Grantham and see if we can learn where Lincoln and Lovell's army now lies. If the king is in Leicester or Nottingham, and Lord Lovell has made good progress, then it is likely that battle will be joined in Nottinghamshire or Lincolnshire. We won't have far to go. I pray they've had success in raising men as they've marched south.'

Ellingham felt a little jealous of Sir John that he had a reason to fight on: his wife and son's future. What did he have, though? In the end, there seemed nothing he could call upon but vengeance. Vengeance for his father's fall and the end of his house. And for Gaston's betrayal. It would have to do.

Jacob entered the hall and came to them. 'The horses are ready, Sir John.'

Ellingham knew that a new fire for revenge burned inside the Fleming now that the man knew his old comrade Jan Bec had been murdered. And all the remembered warnings of Jacob de Grood concerning Dieudonné, each unheeded, did not make Ellingham feel any better. His own blindness had nearly cost him his life. Could he trust his instincts ever again?

'Very good,' said Hawker. 'Sir Giles says he is well enough to don his harness.'

Jacob nodded and smiled. 'I am glad to hear it. He is made of stern stuff. I will help him if he wishes.'

'Boldness and speed may buy us the time to reach the Yorkist army,' said Hawker. 'If we can raise a few men ourselves between now and then, so much the better!'

–

Giles smiled to himself despite the throbbing of his head wound, pressed by the weight of his sallet helm. They, probably the smallest company of soldiers in England, were trotting along the road north out of Bourne, destined for Corby Glen. Jacob rode in front, bearing Hawker's pennon upon an old lance given by Mainwaring. And close behind rode himself, and Hawker at his side. Hawker's black armour – *tête au pied* – gave the old knight a new menace, and slung along his saddle was the war hammer he had accepted of the squire. A few farmers on the roadside watched them ride past, their faces painted with confusion or amusement. Ellingham couldn't help but remember the size of Hawker's company just two years before – and that of his own. It had come to this now.

The village of Corby Glen lay about two leagues north-west of Bourne. As they rode into the centre where the market cross stood, the place appeared rather empty. A small herd of sheep bleated noisily in a paddock, some farmers walked by with hoes and spades, a few children ran past them, excited to see soldiers. Jacob twisted in the saddle to look at Hawker and the old knight nodded. They halted.

'A fire wouldn't even raise an eyebrow here,' remarked Jacob. 'Shall we push on?'

Hawker looked around him, towards the parish church, and then up the road ahead. He snorted and then looked at Ellingham. 'Scarce pickings, by the looks of it.'

Ellingham felt almost giddy with the desperation of it all and the ludicrousness of their predicament. 'Perhaps better luck in the next town,' he said, not really knowing what else he could say.

A man leaned over a low stone wall and called over to them. 'Are you knights?'

Hawker flicked his reins and moved closer. 'We are. What else would you know?'

'War's coming. I know that much.'

Ellingham saw that the man was probably his age, short and broad-shouldered. He wore a stained jerkin and an equally stained linen coif upon his head.

'Are you king's men?' the man asked.

Hawker smiled down at him. 'Which king might that be?'

The man smiled back. 'Matters nought to me. You offering pay for service?'

'I am. But you would need weapon, harness and horse.'

The man stuck out his lower lip and nodded, contemplating that. 'I've got me a horse, my old gaffer's helm and a rusty bill. Might have a dagger.'

Hawker sat back in the saddle. 'Have you ever fought in battle?'

The man grinned. 'Nay, sir. Never.'

'You're with us,' said Hawker.

Ellingham's jaw fell and de Grood let out a raucous laugh.

36

Hawker had an acorn with which to grow his oak. William Tice was the first recruit to the standard and Ellingham hoped they'd have time enough to gain a few more before battle was joined. Hawker paid William a month's wages after the man had sworn an oath to serve him until the death of either intervened. The man may not have been a soldier, but if he could swing a threshing flail he could swing a polearm, said the old knight. William Tice had no farewells to deliver so had retrieved his rusty weapons and a tired-looking rouncey gelding and swung into the saddle to ride at the front alongside Jacob.

Two hours later they reached Grantham. Hawker told them he knew the town well from younger days and when it had been strongly Yorkist in King Edward's time – even while the rest of the county had shown ambivalence to its rulers.

'And what will we find here?' asked Ellingham, both worried and sceptical as they wound their way up the high street.

'A good bed, at least,' replied Hawker. 'And perhaps a few more men to join our little company.'

'And if the usurper has already placed a garrison here? What then?'

Hawker shrugged his shoulders. 'Well, there'll be no bed tonight.'

The old knight led them to an ancient inn midway through the little town. A golden angel's head looked down on them as they rode beneath the stone arch and into the large courtyard of the place.

'Your father stayed here once, Giles. It is where he received the Great Seal of the kingdom.'

Ellingham said nothing. His eyes scanned the courtyard buildings for signs of armed men but there seemed to be only grooms and other servants. Some of these paused and watched them ride in, one man darting inside. A few moments later a stocky fellow in a great leather apron came out and approached.

Hawker dismounted but told the others to remain in the saddle. 'We are looking for rooms and fare for the night,' he said confidently.

The innkeeper gave a little bow seeing the knight's pennon flapping in the breeze. 'That will be easily arranged, my lord. Stabling too.'

Hawker nodded and undid the chinstrap of his sallet helm. 'Have you any news of rebellion? Of a rebel army on the move? And if King Henry's army has moved against them yet.'

The innkeeper licked his lips quickly and absently wiped his hands on his apron. 'Rebellion? Aye, word arrived last night from travellers. Battles in the north. The king's fore-riders bested and driven south. But I hear York city did not open its gates to the rebels. The Earl of Lincoln continues south and the king gathers strength at Nottingham. The city is in uproar.'

The failure to gain entry into York aside, the news heartened Ellingham a little. Lincoln and Lovell had indeed landed and made progress. But he still had no idea on their numbers nor how many soldiers Henry Tudor was managing to assemble.

'And what do you make of the mood of the people here-abouts?' asked Hawker.

The innkeeper chuckled nervously. 'The mood? Folk are keeping to themselves as they always do. Will you be staying just the one night? And are you off to join up with King Henry at Nottingham?'

Hawker smiled. 'Just the one night.' He didn't answer the second question.

The innkeeper's eyes took in Ellingham and Jacob, and then went back to the knight in blackened armour. 'Very well, good sir. I will get the grooms to take care of your horses and I will see to your chambers. May I know who it is we have the pleasure of hosting?'

Hawker did not hesitate with his reply. 'I am Sir John Hawker.'

The innkeeper bowed again and returned to the stone inn.

Ellingham winced inwardly at hearing Hawker's response, his mount fidgeting underneath him. 'That was reckless, Sir John. We might find rather an unwelcome awakening tonight.'

'It matters not,' growled Hawker. 'Not any more.'

They were about to lead their horses to the stables when the sound of a lone trumpet echoed across the yard. It was a short fanfare, delivered quickly and badly. Jacob was the first to bound back into the saddle and Hawker threw on his helm and buckled it. 'Giles, mount up!'

Hawker led them, single file, at a quick trot out again into the street. They went a hundred yards and veered right down another street where Ellingham instantly saw a great stone cross rising up. A market square. Hawker stopped just before they reached the edge of the square. At the base of the market cross were half a dozen men, armoured and mounted. A herald stood in his stirrups and began speaking in a loud voice, which carried well across the cobbles.

'By the authority of John Skipworth… knight and commissioner for the Parts of Kesteven! It is commanded that all fencible men, footmen and horsemen are to assemble here tomorrow to take service with the king's army for one month!'

There was already a number of townsfolk gathered with more arriving every moment. The herald, who wore breastplate and back, but no helm, signalled to the trumpeter nearby and after a second blast, he repeated his exhortation to the crowd in his exaggerated and formal style. 'Assembly will be at the hour of Terce! Bring your own weapons and harness! Bring food for four days!'

Ellingham saw Hawker reach down to his waist and draw his arming sword.

'Sir John!' said Ellingham in a croak. 'What in God's name are you doing?'

Jacob pulled alongside Hawker and hefted his lance.

Hawker raised his sword to rest against his shoulder. 'Our battle begins now.'

Before Ellingham could utter another word, Hawker kicked his horse and went forward, speed increasing to a fast trot across the cobblestones. He made straight for the Lancastrian herald. The man froze at the approach, not knowing who it was coming at him or even why. Hawker gave him no time think further. As soon as he drew alongside he threw a mighty blow straight into the herald's chest, tumbling him out of the saddle and sending him with a metallic crash onto the mud and shit-strewn stones of the square.

Hawker made for the next nearest opponent and soon all was a mass of neighing horses and shouts of, 'Treason!' Jacob unhorsed a second Lancastrian man-at-arms before the man knew he was even there. Ellingham found himself in a furious mounted exchange of sword blows with another, and William Tice, who had dismounted, was doing his best to harass the remaining Lancastrians. The Corby Glen man was darting about like some street clown, threatening to pull them off their horses with the hook of his bill. He finally succeeded in grabbing a Lancastrian and hauling him down with his bare hands.

It was over in a flash of whirling steel and baying cries of alarm. The six Lancastrians were down: dead, or wounded and yielding on their knees to the mysterious knight in black. Jacob, grim-faced, raised up the pennon-tipped lance and Hawker began shouting to those of the crowd who had not fled the scene.

'A Warwick! A Warwick! Your rightful king has landed and is close by! Prove you are still men of the House of York!'

There was stunned silence across the market square. Hawker walked his horse around, patting and calming it after the affray.

His eyes scanned the faces of the crowd, old and young men, boys and women. 'Have you forgotten who gave you this marketplace? King Richard! Show me the men of Grantham have not abandoned their true king! Fight the Tudor usurper!'

Jacob had by now dismounted with sword in hand, kicking away the dropped weapons of the enemy. The herald was trying to pull himself along the cobbles but Jacob put a boot on his back to halt his progress. Ellingham was breathing hard from the fight and half expecting to see more soldiers arriving at any moment. But there was now silence in the square except for the echoing hoof-clop of skittish horses.

Hawker swore, swung his leg over and dismounted, armour jangling as his feet hit the cobbles. He walked towards a group of townsfolk and threw open his arms. 'Who will join Sir John? I am a knight of Lincolnshire! I fight for the rightful king of this land! Who will join Sir John Hawker?'

Ellingham grew more anxious watching the old knight exhort the small crowd. But to his utter amazement, two young men pushed their way forward. 'We will! For Warwick! For York!' And then another three came from the opposite side of the square. 'A Warwick!' they began to chant.

In the end, there were seven men who came to Hawker's pennon and swore oaths. The rest of the townsfolk faded away into the side streets. Ellingham had never witnessed a miracle before, but this was the closest to such a thing that he had ever beheld. A man came forward, bowed to Hawker, and introduced himself as the mayor. He begged Hawker not to remain in the town lest he bring down the wrath of Henry upon them.

'I will consider it,' Hawker said playfully, 'if you place these my prisoners in the gaol and leave them until we have taken our leave. But that will not be before morning and not before we sup at the Angel.'

The mayor blinked rapidly, swallowing visibly. He nodded his agreement. Ellingham swore softly in amazement. The four of them had taken Grantham from Henry Tudor. And this time at least, John Hawker's reckless, brazen boldness had succeeded.

–

Jack Perry wasn't sure where he was. He heard one of the English men-at-arms say it was Nottinghamshire still, and that they had bypassed Newark-on-Trent – held by Henry's men. The glorious afternoon summer sun was still high in the sky as the *landsknechts* crossed a shallow ford on the Trent, splashing through the cold, thigh-high waters and then ascending a grassy, sparely wooded slope to yet another open plain. They crossed in their thousands over the course of an hour. When Jack and the Scots reached the high ground, the vista before them was brown furrowed farmland and verdant meadow, flowing downwards. In the distance to their left, Jack saw a village, its houses and their long, hedgerow-lined plots extending towards the fields. An old church stood off by itself nearby.

The rebel army poured forth onto the summit of this plain, filling the plateau for over two thousand yards. Jack heard a blare of trumpets and then the rapid, signalling tattoo of the drums.

'So then,' said David Weems, 'this is where we make camp. Another night under God's canopy. Let's hope it doesn't piss down.'

A large group of English mounted troops rushed past, heading towards the village to occupy it. Jack raised his hand to his brow and looked out across the landscape. 'I think this is where we will stand. Make our fight.'

Weems laughed. 'And what makes you say that, Captain-General? Have your wee bollocks grown a bit in the last few days?'

'We have the high ground here. We know King Henry's army is near. It makes sense, that's all. I *have* been in a few battles already, you know.'

'Have you now?' said Luke of Kirkcaldy, his voice dripping with irony.

'Look left,' said Jack. 'We anchor one flank on the village.' He then turned and pointed with his forefinger. 'To the right, down there, it drops off down a slope into a wood and then down to the river we just crossed. The enemy can't get around us from that side.'

Weems gestured with his thumb over his shoulder. 'And behind us is a godawful ridge and then a river. So not much chance of getting out again without a few scratches. We *have* to go forward.'

Jack frowned. It was true.

The Irish *kerns* flowed around and past them on both sides. There were also a few wealthy Irish contingents he had become aware of. They were armoured and better equipped, some rode even. But their numbers were far, far fewer. The two German companies, knitted together through iron discipline, had fanned out and begun to make camp in the orderly way Jack had grown accustomed to. Pikes were stacked at the ready, positions taken where they could quickly meet the call to arms.

A dozen donkeys laden with bundles trundled past. Jack recognised the load they carried: sacks of stale bread and groats for porridge, no doubt, assuming they could get water to make it. Food had gotten scarcer with each passing day. He'd kill a Lancastrian just for a good wedge of cheese. But, as it turned out, he managed better than that. A *landsknecht* double-pay man in mud-stained, drooping finery found him and ordered him and the Scottish halberdiers to report to Schwarz, who had now commandeered a house in the village along with the English nobles and the little king. They would be spared a damp night under the stars.

But the food and warmth came at the price of bitter knowledge. Jack entered the house he was led to – the largest on the street – and went through to where Lord Schwarz stood, surrounded by his provosts and quartermaster. He saluted and stood, waiting.

Schwarz turned to him. 'Good, he's here. Englishman, come with me!'

Without another word he stormed out of the chamber and up a narrow staircase to the next floor. Jack waited for the senior officers to precede him and quickly followed. Upstairs, in a large gabled roof space, Jack immediately recognised Lords Lincoln and Lovell and half a dozen of their knights and squires, in animated discussion. Behind them and seated at a table he spotted the boy king, all by himself. He looked small, almost waxen and unmoving, like the life-sized effigies Jack had two years prior glimpsed in a Venetian cathedral.

The German captain cursed loudly and beckoned Jack closer with an agitated wave of his hand. He had already begun conversing with the nobles in broken English, German and some form of French that Jack could not comprehend.

'Tell them, lad. Tell them I am displeased. Ask them where the rest of the troops are. What was promised to me!'

Jack once again did his best.

Lovell, conciliatory, tried to placate the mercenary. 'My lord, we have moved so quickly, how would you expect more to have joined? Our fore-riders have just told us the advance guard of the enemy — a few thousand, they reckon — will be here by morning. If we can best Oxford's men first, then Henry's reserves will lose all heart. We will break them. I swear it!'

The young Earl of Lincoln, in full white harness, fair hair and face dripping with sweat, added his own contribution. 'What would you do now, my lord? Go back? Offer surrender?' His demeanour was one of exasperation, the barely masked anxiety pouring out of him along with his sweat.

Schwarz's reply was almost resigned. 'My lord, I have given my word to the Duchess of Burgundy. I will hold to that, come what may. My men will earn their pay. I pray yours do as well.'

Sir Thomas Geraldine, leader of the Irish men-at-arms and levies, demanded his men take the vanguard. Schwarz ranted that such a thing was madness for those so unarmoured. It should be the phalanx of pike that form the wedge of the van, he countered. And so it went on. They debated deployments, who would go where, the depths of their line, where the Irish should be positioned, and many other things that Jack knew he had not translated correctly. By the end of the council his shirt and hose were sodden with perspiration. The gentlemen bowed one to another, wished each other good fortune and a few hours' sleep. Schwarz and his men went back downstairs but Jack remained, almost transfixed by the presence of this new king who sat so lonely. While the nobles made more plans and sent out new orders to their captains, Jack inched closer to the table.

'Your Majesty...' he whispered, bowing slightly.

The boy looked at him without much interest. 'Hullo.'

'You are king now... King Edward. But they do not confer with you?'

The lad gave Jack a wan smile. 'My name is John,' he whispered back. 'Who are you?'

'Jack Perry. Of Stamford town.' He did not know what else to say.

'Jack Perry, they keep me well enough and say I will soon have a throne to sit upon.' He paused, as if catching himself from saying something else. The boy suddenly looked afraid. 'God keep you, Jack,' he said softly. And then he glanced down at his folded hands.

'You there!' came a hoarse shout from a knight nearby. 'Get back downstairs to your men!'

Jack hurriedly left, leaving the boy named John to stare after him.

Back with the Scots, who had taken over another house nearby, Jack took some villager's rope-cot bedframe and blanket after they supped. Together all in the same room, they bedded down for what napping they might get.

'What is this place called?' asked Luke.

'East Stoke, a farmer told me,' replied Weems. 'They won't forget us soon, I reckon.'

330

'We fight a proper army tomorrow,' said Jack quietly. 'The Earl of Oxford's army first. They were at Bosworth Field.'

'Bosworth Field? Don't know that battle.'

Jack sighed. 'I'm saying they're well-blooded soldiers. Led by a soldier.'

There was no reply for a while. Then Luke spoke up. 'The Germans will have us up for Mass in a few hours. I shall make my confession and take the sacrament if they let us.'

'Aye,' said Weems, 'best to take what grace we can get. I welcome the fight. I'm tired of walking.'

On his straw mattress upon the stone floor, Luke of Kirkcaldy laughed, then could not stop himself, dissolving into a fit of hysterics. David Weems succumbed and joined in, and then Jack did too.

His few dreams that night were disquieted and before he knew it, he was awakened by cock-crow. It was still dark. Just as he had managed to arise from the creaking rope-slung cot, the drums started their steady beat, the call to arms. It was beginning.

37

Ellingham's skull didn't hurt much any more. But the pain he did feel went far deeper than his bloodied scalp. He had begun to think his life was worthless now, over, with no prospect for achieving anything, let alone a measure of happiness. He'd spent a night tossing with worry in Grantham, buried those worries deep once he had arisen, and then helped Hawker to muster his new troops for battle. Leaving the town in the afternoon and riding north by north-west on the main road, by the time the sun had dipped low in the June sky they found themselves in a tiny village in Nottinghamshire, a place called Hawksworth and not much more than a crossroads with a few houses and barns. Jacob de Grood barked orders to their little band, telling the men to go into the nearby churchyard, dismount and take rest. Ellingham could clearly hear bars slamming into place behind the doors of the cottages that lay opposite. Not a soul came out to greet or challenge them.

Hawker and he were the only ones still mounted. The others were watering their horses at a wooden trough near the church entrance. Hawker walked his horse up the road past the church and then turned it and walked back down, watching either side of the street. Ellingham waited until the old knight had rejoined him.

'Sleep out here tonight? In the open? You heard what those men from the abbey told us not an hour ago.'

Hawker was unmoved. 'Men need to rest. We can't ride in the dark.'

'With Henry's army a stone's throw from us?'

They had met upon the road that afternoon three servants with a mule and cart returning to the Grantham Greyfriars. They had told of a great army now on the Fosse Way out of Radcliffe. The king had crossed the Trent and was coming north. They said the rebel army was near Newark now and that battle would be joined in the next few days.

'The enemy needs to sleep too,' said Hawker, his words a flat mumble. 'We will shadow them come morning and get ahead of their march. We'll find Lincoln's army soon enough if we stay on the Fosse.'

Ellingham nodded. Hawker's sense was cold, but sound. They could do nothing else. He dismounted, tied his horse to a young tree in the churchyard, and observed the men as they did their best to take comfort upon the lumpy grass. There were a few graves about, long flat slabs to mark them, incised crosses upon them. Two short monument stones surmounted with carved quatrefoils stood at awkward angles, having sunk into the spongy ground. The little stone church sat stark and lonely, just beyond. Ellingham untied from his saddle a cloth sack with some food and walked further into the yard, passing the eight levied men as they settled down on backsides and haunches to take their repast. He found a raised lump of turf – probably yet another grave – and sat down upon it.

Hawker followed and joined him, awkwardly seating himself with a clanking of his armour, legs outstretched in front of him. They would be living in their harness for the foreseeable future, both a comfort of protection and a burden.

'Do you really think I would ride blindly into the path of destruction, Giles? A wish for death?'

Ellingham smiled. 'You have far more experience of war than I. But I confess I had a nightmare last night of meeting Lord Lovell and John de la Pole – and they commanded ten men, a few rusty spears and a donkey.'

Hawker shook his head, snorted a little, and stroked the peak of his sallet helm. 'I won't lie to you. We probably will be outnumbered. We can only pray it is not by much. But we have every chance of beating the usurper if our hearts stay true. Henry Tudor rules by fear. His men have no great love for him. Our hatreds – our vengeance, will sustain us, Giles. And sustain all who will fight him on the morrow. You can believe in that.'

The Grantham men were eating the food they had brought, talking quietly, and seated in a wide circle on the grass. Jacob leaned against the wall of the church, Hawker's lance and pennon still resting in the crook of his arm. He seemed to be staring off into the distance, lost in thought.

'These men… do they know what they're doing here? Where they are headed?' said Ellingham quietly.

He watched Hawker's eyes move to where his men sat. Some had breastplates and helms, some only padded gambesons. Their weapons were bill hooks, long daggers, one badly notched arming sword, and two rusty falchions that probably belonged to their grandsires. Four of the eight claimed to have fought at Bosworth, the other four were brave enough to admit they had never been to war. Ellingham yet hoped they might be better equipped before they had to fight the enemy.

'*They* know why they are here,' said Hawker. 'Some for the pay… for adventure. A few for revenge perhaps. It is enough that they are with us and I pray their courage holds out.'

'They've put the fear of God into the villagers around here at least.'

Hawker let out a little laugh, leaning back against the lichen-spotted stones of the church. They sat together for a time, neither speaking, Ellingham chewing his bread and cheese and sipping a bit of wine, nearly soured.

Ellingham stared at his bread a moment. 'You have saved my life many times, Sir John. Something I have never given you proper thanks for. I am sorry for that.'

'The debt – if there ever was one – was repaid by you tenfold. You delivered to me my wife and son. That is something I will never forget. Something I will be forever grateful to you for.'

There was silence between them again for a minute or two.

'It seems a lifetime ago we rode at Bosworth Field,' said Hawker. 'You have become a captain of men these past two years. Your father would have been proud. I am proud... for what it's worth.'

It was Ellingham's turn to laugh, tinged more bitter than mirthful. 'And what have I to show for it? What will we have tomorrow? Or the day after?'

'You have fought. You have won. Lost. Seen half the kingdoms of Europe. Loved. All these things have you done. And all are a certain treasure of a kind. Experience gained. A life lived. As for tomorrow, wait until God shows us the way.'

Ellingham turned to look at him. 'You are resigned then? To whatever will happen.'

Hawker didn't answer his question. Another long silence prevailed as they sat side by side watching the hazy red orb of the sun sink further away. At length, Hawker spoke again.

'There is something I have not told you. My reluctance to do so was only because I am unsure myself as to what I saw.'

Ellingham leaned forward, arms on his knees. 'What is it?'

'Back in Malines, more than a month ago... when I was at the palace, I saw a figure. At least I believe I saw him. It was the young Richard – your cousin, the son of King Edward.'

'And you didn't tell me this? You saved him from the Tower three years ago and now you say he is with the Duchess in Flanders?'

'I glimpsed him but only a moment... but I saw the boy's face. And I recognised the man who was with him. Sir Edward Brampton. One of your father's trusted men. The same man I believe it was who instructed me to take the boys from the Tower.'

Ellingham swore under his breath. 'Then in whose name do we fight this rebellion? Who is this boy king Francis Lovell has tucked under his cloak?'

'He is no one. Olivier de la Marche called him a changeling. Someone to take the place of the young Earl of Warwick, still a prisoner of Henry in the Tower. If Lovell and Lincoln fail… if *we* fail… there is yet another rightful heir to the throne. We must take comfort in that. We must.'

Ellingham tilted his head back until it touched the rough stone of the church wall. 'I wish I shared your certitude,' he said quietly. The wine had calmed him, made him drowsy. He noticed that the sky had slowly turned a glorious purple, the tincture of a royal mantle.

'I will take the first watch,' said Hawker, half to himself.

Ellingham, settled in against the stones and began to drift away as the night finally descended upon them.

He awoke with a start to see the burnished, shaved pate of a priest looking down on him. It was daylight, and as he jumped so did the cleric. The man held out his hands. 'Peace! Peace! I come to offer you and all your men the holy sacrament.'

Ellingham groaned, every joint aching underneath his armour. His head wound throbbed anew. He rolled over and pulled himself up using the wall of the church. When he turned again he saw that he was the last to awake. Hawker and de Grood had let him sleep the night through. He walked unsteadily to join the others.

'You are all off to war!' said the priest, flapping like a hen. 'Cleanse your souls before it is too late!'

Ellingham ignored his pleas and found Hawker readying his horse. 'You should have let me take the watch.'

'I was jealous of the depth of your slumber,' said Hawker smiling. 'Thought at least one of us ought to have a proper rest.'

'Which direction then?' Ellingham untied the reins of his mount, the animal grunting its displeasure at being taken away from its grass nibbling.

'We make for the Fosse Way, due west and about a league away. I mean to spy out Henry's army for myself and see what we're up against.' He shouted to Jacob to mount and Jacob duly ordered the lance of soldiers to do so, barking out the order in his heavily accented English.

William Tice approached, leading his little rouncey. He stopped and bowed curtly. 'Sir John, I spied a group of horsemen in the distance, out along the road we came in on. Too far for me to make out if they were soldiers. But they're gone now.'

'Well done,' said Hawker, nodding. 'We'll have to keep our eyes sharp both front and back. There will be fore-riders about from both armies. You take up the rear guard, William.'

The man tapped his fingers to his brow and turned his horse to the rear of the rapidly forming column.

The priest had followed Ellingham to where Hawker stood. 'You are a knight, sir? And are these your men? They require the benefit of holy sacrament.' His manner was respectful, but there was more than a little insistence in his tone. His duty as a cleric was at stake.

Hawker bowed his head to the priest and smiled. 'They are my men. But we have no time to take Mass with you. Bestow a blessing if you feel inclined.'

The priest puffed himself up. 'You think it right to camp on hallowed ground but scorn the need for absolution?'

Hawker's brows knitted and Ellingham wasn't sure if he was reconsidering the priest's offer. Then, the old knight nodded, almost to himself, and reached into his belt pouch. 'Will you take an offering, then? In gratitude?' He pulled forth a small black rosary, took the priest's wrist, and then dropped the rosary into the man's upturned palm. Hawker closed his fingers around them. 'It came from Rome... the Holy See, many years ago. I would see it have a use again. In this place.'

The priest opened his hand and looked at the beads and tiny crucifix. He stuttered a reply. 'Good Sir Knight... this was not my intention. I have enquired for your soul's salvation – not my gain.'

'My soul? Aye, well, it is in sore need of salvation. I have sinned much in this life. Shed blood in holy sanctuary... taken the lives of innocents. Led men to their deaths. I confess this to you freely, here and now. So... pray for me if you can. That is all I ask in return for this gift.'

The priest swallowed, looked at Hawker and then Ellingham. His brow furrowed but he said nothing. After a few seconds he nodded. When they had all mounted, Ellingham watched as the priest stood at the head of the column, made the sign of the cross, and spoke a benediction. Hawker bowed his head in thanks. It unnerved Ellingham a little to see the old knight so suddenly penitent and the thought entered his mind that perhaps Hawker believed this was his last chance to unburden himself of the invisible but heavy load that he carried. He watched Hawker cross himself, a slow and deliberate votive gesture with his black gauntlet, and then the knight urged his horse forward.

They set off at a slow trot.

After half an hour they came to the Great Trade Road which led north and south. The flat rolling meadowland stretched for miles and a short time after they had turned onto the road heading south, they saw what Hawker was looking for. A vast glinting array of metal some mile or more away, dazzling in the morning light. Jacob said he would ride to take a closer look. The Fleming kicked in his spurs and shot off into the meadow, parallel to the road. He soon disappeared where the ground broke, sloping downwards. Ellingham sidled up to Hawker's horse.

'How many do you reckon?'

'They're spread wide on either side of the road. I can see that from here.'

Jacob returned a few minutes later, hooves pounding. He reined in fast, his mount wide-eyed and snorting from the run. '*Godverdomme!* Five thousand, if I'm buggered! Maybe more. Most in good harness, head to toe. Not levied men – they're men-at-arms in the main, Sir John.'

Hawker looked to Ellingham. 'Well, now we know about the enemy. Let's find *our* army.'

Turning, Jacob led them off again, heading north at a canter, Hawker's tired and stained pennon flapping still on the end of the Fleming's lance. They had ridden for some four or five miles when the tower of a church could be seen dead ahead. Hawker, riding side by side with Ellingham just behind Jacob, pointed to it.

'The village of Stoke.'

They made another rise and as they did so the air was rent with the sound of two massive explosions of cannon fire. They pulled up sharply and looked across the fields to their left. Ellingham swore softly at what was now before them.

Two great armies were arrayed across the field, parallel to the road, their lines askew north to south and stretching for what seemed half a mile. Thousands of men, but numbers nearly equal. The furthest side – the rebels – must have initially held the higher end of the gentle slope but the two great lines had now collided into locked battle. Ellingham heard the clash of steel, blade upon blade, and the guttural cries of men in lethal struggle, an endless, deep murmuring which rose up to the sky, filling the air. He looked over to Hawker and saw the old knight's face was set hard as he gazed out across the field. The battle of Stoke Field had already begun.

Ellingham instantly knew – as Hawker did – that the enemy upon the road behind them was *another* of Henry's armies. And now he and Hawker were between the two of them.

38

Boom BOOM.

Jack Perry flinched. The serpentines – small cannons – belched forth their fire from somewhere beyond his vision, the explosion reverberating across the field. All he could see in front of him was row upon row of pikes pointing to the sky – a forest of ash and steel.

Looking between the files, a hundred yards ahead, he could just glimpse the wide front of the enemy, the sun reflecting off their armour. The *landsknechts* were deployed in an immense square, fifty men wide and some fifty deep, the colourful standards held by their ensigns in the middle of the vast formation. Jack and twenty other crossbowmen were grouped just inside the square – thirtieth rank and second file – the easier to move outside and shoot once the order was given. Handgunners were at the ready on the opposite side of the square. The drummers and trumpets were also at the centre of the formation along with the flag and Lord Schwarz. The front three ranks of pikemen had already levelled their weapons while the remainder stood ready, a giant hedgehog of spikes.

Jack looked again for David Weems and Luke. He sighted them standing further inside the square, clutching their halberds and straining to get a look at what was coming. He had a clearer view to his left, outside the formation. Hundreds of Irish warriors dressed in their voluminous woollen cloaks, some having shed them to wrap about their waists leaving themselves bare-chested or in their raw linen shirts. They raised up their short spears and daggers, goading the enemy across the field.

Further beyond them, out front, mounted men-at-arms in full harness stood ready, gleaming in the morning sun. Jack could feel his heart pounding. The waiting was the worst of it. But the cannon fire signalled that fighting was now underway. The answer from the Lancastrians came quickly enough.

The air was filled with a great swishing noise like a swarm of wasps and an instant later came the sound of clattering arrow shafts among them, the pinging of arrows on armour, and the scattered cries and screams of those struck. The cries to Jack's left were more numerous and to his horror he saw row upon row of the *kerns* fallen to the ground, long arrow shafts protruding from their prostrate bodies. That had been but one volley.

Without respite, a second volley came raining down among them, some landing vertically from above but a few coming straight on. More men groaned and cried out, more fell. Although Jack had fought in battle before he had never been subjected to a hail of death from longbows. He was grateful for his near full armour, better than many of those around him who wore just a helm and a breastplate. Again he watched, almost frozen, instinctively hunching his back as the arrow shafts clattered among them. The drums sounded a different staccato tattoo and immediately the double-pay men began barking orders.

'*Armbruste! Vorwärts!*'

Jack began fumbling for a quarrel for his bow from his slung pouch as he shuffled through to the outside along with the other crossbowmen. Led by a halberdier, they scuttled out and formed a line as quickly as they could. Jack tried to single out a target in the line of the enemy longbowmen but they were all just a mass of colourful tabards and glinting steel. He judged the distance, angled the crossbow upwards, and when the order came he loosed the bow. He didn't wait to see the effect as he was already furiously cranking his mechanism to span the weapon again. Some of his comrades cheered so they must have dropped a few of the enemy. Jack began to hear the explosions of the hand-gunners on the far side of the *landsknecht* square. But these were sporadic and far and few between.

Jack dropped to one knee and laid a quarrel into the crossbow. Before he could loose it, another volley of arrows came arcing in. He heard a shaft *swish* past his head and at the same time a great collective groan punctuated by a few screams came to him from further left. The Irishmen were taking the worst of it, unarmoured as they were. Jack cursed, levelled his bow at an archer who was standing further ahead of his comrades, and pulled the trigger. He was rewarded with the sight of the archer spinning in place and dropping like a sack of flour. Again, the German crossbowmen furiously worked their weapons to reload. But in the next moments, the Lancastrians loosed volley after volley which the mechanical crossbows could not match. More were falling around him and he knew it was only a matter of time before a shaft found him.

The officer yelled for them to retreat to the square and Jack mumbled a quick prayer, dashing back to the relative safety of the formation. Three of the crossbowmen did not return. Breathless, heart pumping, he jostled back into place in the line. A halberdier grinned cheerfully, nodding his support to Jack. They were just standing – not advancing – and being dropped in ones and twos by arrows. He knew well enough his army held the high ground but that was of little use if they were picked apart by longbowmen. And there seemed to be hundreds of them.

As if whoever was issuing orders had heard him, the trumpets and drums sounded. It was the order to advance. Jack heard the jangling sound of hundreds of men as they began moving, slowly but steadily, down the gentle incline and ever closer to the enemy. Another whisper of wooden shafts came pouring into them all. Jack heard a crash from somewhere around him. Another casualty. It took only a minute to reach the Lancastrians and an almighty roar went up on both sides as the lines crashed together. Jack could see and hear the clacking wood of the great pikes jabbing at the enemy. The yells and taunts. The steady, comforting beat of the drums. He could feel the momentum around him as the front ranks of the square surged, fell back, rippled, and surged again into contact with the halberds, bill hooks and spears of the other side. Mercifully, the arrows had stopped coming. It was now a battle of hand-to-hand blows and the din of crashing steel grew and grew.

For the moment, Jack could do nothing but hold his ground and wait until it was his turn to draw his sword and heft his buckler. The phalanx of the Germans held firm, a wedge of steel pressing into the vast array of the enemy. He could see a mass of men to his left: the Irishmen were pressing forward with spears and great axes. He moved forward a few more paces, following the man in front of him. And for the first time, Jack Perry felt they might win the day after all.

—

'We ride wide – through the village!' shouted Hawker. 'Reach our left flank and join them from behind!'

Ellingham kicked in his spurs and followed Hawker and Jacob de Grood down the road and into Stoke. Behind him, the new recruits dutifully kept pace. Entering the village, Ellingham saw the place was deserted. The sound of gunfire echoed from the meadow beyond the row of houses. Hawker slowed, making sure of what lay ahead on the narrow high street. Ellingham figured if they rode the length of the street, which lay parallel to the battlefield, they could then enter the high meadows and find the rear guard.

They were in single file, moving at a fast trot when Ellingham heard a scream and a shout from behind. His eyes took in the sight all at once: one of their men had been struck with an arrow, the man next to him yelled the alarm, and just behind the last of Hawker's men came a group of riders – men-at-arms – bearing down at a canter. Ellingham jerked his mount around and drew his sword. Hawker and Jacob, further up the road, were now pounding back to join him. The armoured Lancastrians beat down and unhorsed two of Hawker's men before Ellingham could reach them. Ellingham rapidly counted nine of the enemy and then found himself parrying the furious blows of a rider in rusty Milanese armour. There was a flash on the far side and Ellingham saw Hawker's blade bash the man's helm, toppling him out of the saddle.

The sounds of the swirling fight – neighing beasts and shouting men – echoed off the cottages. Hawker's untrained soldiers – none of whom were used to a mounted combat – were quickly being defeated. William Tice had already been knocked out of his saddle but was up and wielding his bill hook. Ellingham saw him plunge the weapon into the belly of a horse sending it and its rider to the ground. Before another moment had passed, Ellingham was parrying another vicious sword cut. He jerked his reins to manoeuvre around his opponent's flank and then caught a glimpse of the man's face. It was Dieudonné.

Another rider's mount, rearing up, careened into them both and Ellingham's horse stumbled and went down on its front legs, causing him to roll forward and out onto the road. He stumbled to his feet, still gripping his sword, only to find that Dieudonné had been unhorsed as well. The Frenchman let out a battle cry and came for him. Ellingham held his sword in both hands and backed up rapidly as he was rushed. The clash of their blades rang out.

Dieudonné was florid and wild with rage, eyes wide. 'Yield to me! Yield to me now!'

And he came on again. A flurry of blows pushed Ellingham back further and the next he knew his sword went spinning out of his grip, hands and wrists stinging. He crouched down and then darted the few yards to a gap between the houses. Staggering into what was a narrow cobbled twitten, he scrambled to draw out his dagger.

Dieudonné was on his heels, a stream of French curses on his lips. The twitten wasn't long and Ellingham wheeled, dagger arm extended. Dieudonné closed the distance, his face contorted with hatred.

'You! Either alive or dead – I win my freedom, my prince. Yield. I would see you kneel to Henry Tudor.'

Dagger against sword was little contest. But Ellingham had to tempt him to take a swing.

'You are as base a creature as ever was,' he hissed. 'Betrayal is foul but to betray a *friend* – a friend who you once loved, that makes you less than a man! You have no soul!'

Dieudonné's dark eyes went wider still. 'You betrayed *me*!' And he stepped with his leading leg and threw a straight edge blow that barely missed the wall of the cottage as it arced, seeking to take his head. Ellingham caught it on his dagger quillons and the force nearly shattered his wrist and forearm. The dagger flew away. Ellingham bulled forward in the same moment, head down, and they both went sprawling onto the cobblestones.

Their armour scraped and screeched on the stones as they scrambled furiously for advantage. Ellingham outweighed the Frenchman, but not by much. In a burst of energy born of desperation he managed to get on top of him, straddling him. Dieudonné hammered at his head and chest with his gauntleted fists but Ellingham went for the man's throat. There was no purchase though for his gauntlets to find under Dieudonné's high gorget. The Frenchman thrashed, bucked and grunted, but Ellingham was well braced, legs spread apart. He somehow managed to get his thumbs under the rim of Dieudonné's open-faced helm and he pushed hard. The Frenchman's chinstrap tightened and Ellingham leaned in with both arms, the helm rising up and off Dieudonné's forehead. He strained, hearing his own cries over those of the Frenchman. Dieudonné's face went even redder, eyes bulging.

Ellingham strained with all his might. The chinstrap held. Dieudonné's hands were on both his forearms, pushing. But Ellingham felt the grip weaken until it became almost a strange caress. A surrender. Dieudonné's eyes bore into his, but Ellingham now saw that those eyes were looking through him. Past him. He was gone. Ellingham pulled back as if he'd been scalded.

'*Why*?' he cried out, spittle flecking the dead man's face. But he knew the answer.

He emerged from the twitten, shaking. Bodies lay strewn in the street, a dead horse lying on one of them. Hawker, his armour speckled with blood, came towards him.

'Thank Christ! Are you whole?'

Ellingham nodded. 'Gaston is dead.' He saw that all of their attackers were either killed or fled, but there were only four of their own surviving other than the Fleming. Jacob passed behind Ellingham, entered the twitten, and emerged moments later. He clapped Ellingham on the shoulder and then went back to his horse.

'You saved me the chore. But I am envious. Jan Bec thanks you.'

Hawker's visor was up, his face ruddy and streaked with sweat from the brief fight. 'Then justice is delivered,' he said, voice gruff. 'Mount up. We have a battle to join.'

Ellingham could clearly hear the heavy clash of steel, the shouts and the cries drifting from across the meadows. The occasional detonations of handguns. He hefted his sword in his grasp and retrieved his horse, its flanks still quivering from the action. He soothed it and then hauled himself up into the saddle. Hawker nodded at him – some recognition of what he had just done – and then remounted. They rode up the high street and to where the houses ended. A small stone church lay opposite. Hawker gestured to the left and they ascended a grassy bank, which led to an open field. Ellingham saw the great host arrayed and almost immediately they were met by a charging lance of armoured riders who were covering that flank from surprise.

'Warwick! Warwick!' Hawker cried out. Jacob rode just behind, the knight's pennon still clinging determinedly to the

346

spear it was tied to. The Yorkist retainers slowed and challenged them.

'I am Sir John Hawker!' shouted the old knight. 'Take me to the earl! I have urgent news!'

A few men-at-arms separated from the lance and escorted them along the rear of the lines, the ground rising gently upwards. A wooded copse lay ahead. As they approached a large group gathered under the oaks, Ellingham turned to look out on the battlefield. The Yorkist line was now a wedge, unmoving, pressed not just on its front but also on the sides. Beyond, he could see more Lancastrian troops entering the field from the Fosse Way and taking up new positions to bolster the existing line. Worse still, he saw that hundreds of Lancastrian archers were taking up positions on the right flank a hundred yards from the battleline, unopposed.

Despite the daunting scene unfolding before him, in his mind's eye, he could still see Gaston's contorted face. The vision would not leave him.

He followed Hawker at a quick trot and they reached the command post where he saw both the young Earl of Lincoln – John de la Pole – and Lord Lovell arguing heatedly. Hawker trotted up and they and their retinue turned to confront them.

'By the Virgin!' said Lovell. 'I did not expect to see you again, Hawker.'

The Earl of Lincoln inched his horse forward. 'This is all you bring with you?'

'What I bring,' Hawker growled, 'is news. And it is not good. Henry's main army is moving onto the field, not a mile away.' Hawker pointed with his sword down the slope. 'What you fight here... *this* is but his vanguard. And you have not even broken them yet.'

Ellingham saw a young lad, perhaps twelve or so, mounted on his own behind them, looking frightened and lost. He was dressed up in fine doublet and hose, a light riding cloak and a velvet bonnet of rust red. He seemed not just frightened but awkward, unaccustomed to either riding or fine clothes. This must be the new king in whose name he was about to hazard his life. The boy's presence did nothing to fire his confidence, even as an imposter.

The Earl of Lincoln turned to Lovell. 'I told you this! We must commit *now*! Before it is too late and we are outnumbered.'

'Our Germans are holding!' retorted Lovell, gesturing towards the great pike phalanx below.

'But they have not yet broken Oxford's line,' said Hawker. 'If you don't do that soon then the enemy will prevail. You will be outnumbered by thousands!'

Lovell looked out across the battle. 'So many archers,' he mumbled. 'How did he assemble so many?'

'This is England,' said Hawker, his voice flat.

The Earl of Lincoln cursed. 'We must push their flank with a charge. Relieve the centre and help the Irish before they crumble from the arrow storm. I am issuing orders now.'

Lord Lovell, grim-faced, exhaled loudly and nodded.

'I will go with you,' Ellingham announced. 'We push them back.' It was as if he was hearing someone else speak in his voice.

Lincoln, visibly enthused and fired up, looked over to him, smiled broadly, and gave a formal bow of his head. 'I would be honoured to ride with you, cousin.'

Ellingham seemed to realise then that it was John de la Pole, the Earl of Lincoln, who was to be king if victory was theirs. He had been Richard's favourite, his nephew, his appointed successor. He was no bastard. And any man risking his life in battle was not about to let some changeling boy take his rightful place. After all these past months of fraught toil and danger, Ellingham now found himself where he had wanted to be: in a rightful battle for the White Rose. But it was not as he had imagined it. He nodded slowly at the earl. 'Then, cousin... let us gather your host and pray God that it will not be for nothing.'

Hawker looked at him long and hard, as would a father proud of a son.

'Will you ride with us, Sir John?' asked Ellingham.

He saw Hawker look out on the phalanx of pikes which was heaving, moving like a wave breaking again and again against a sea wall. Face set grim, the old knight tightened the rein of his skittish mount. 'I will. But first I must find someone.'

Ellingham followed his gaze. 'Jack Perry.'

'Jacob and I will search him out and see if he yet lives. Giles… God go with you. I will find you on the flank if I can.' Hawker raised his hand in a salute to him. There was now a look of almost amused self-confidence in his eyes. Like the Hawker of earlier days. 'You have come far, my friend. Fare you well!'

Ellingham didn't know what reply to make. He too raised an arm in salute and Hawker turned his mount and re-joined Jacob and the ragged survivors of his hastily formed band of retainers.

Lord Lovell's frown followed Hawker's horse. 'Who is this Jack Perry?'

Ellingham nodded to himself. 'He is Sir John's squire. Gone missing.' But in truth, he knew, it was more like a missing son.

'Dark fellow,' muttered Lord Lovell. 'Our paths crossed many years ago. Far and few since, though.'

The Earl of Lincoln flicked his reins, impatient. 'Enough of this! You stay with the king, my lord. Sir Giles and my men ride to the left. We will break their flank soon enough. Pray the Germans hold out!' He kicked his spurs in and shot forward.

Ellingham still could not rid himself of the image of Gaston Dieudonné's dying moments, which now suddenly flooded back to him yet again like a haunting ghost. He slammed his visor down and followed the Earl of Lincoln down into battle. But he saw before him Gaston's hate-filled face, contorted by the bitterness of unrequited love.

39

He was in the eye of the storm, near dead-centre in the great square of pikemen. Jack Perry juggled his crossbow and *crannequin*, jostling the Swiss crossbowmen on either side. He cursed as his winding mechanism jammed for the second time. Lord Schwarz, his officers, the standard bearers and the drummers, clustered together just in front of him.

Row upon row of pikemen stood firm, their long pikes raised skyward. Halberdiers were interspersed here and there among them. At the very front where the enemy was being engaged, Jack could hear the *clack* of poles, and the rolling, never-ending sound of hundreds of men yelling in battle fever. Where he stood though, waiting again for orders, there was a sense of false calm, but quiet anxiety was thick around him nonetheless. The square shuffled forward a few paces and he kept up. He'd already dashed outside the relative safety of the formation to twice to take aim and engage the enemy. It was a deadly gamble each time. A rain of enemy arrows drove him and his comrades back into the square.

Both David Weems and Luke of Kirkcaldy had been standing within hailing distance. They shouted encouragement to one another as they waited to move out. A lanky double-pay man, white ostrich plumes waving in his bonnet, came walking through the ranks, bellowing for the halberdiers to move forward into action at the front. Jack saw David turn towards him and smile. 'See you later! Or in London!' he cried out as he hefted his halberd and moved through the files. Dour Luke gave him a nod, wishing him good fortune, and followed Weems. And that was the last he saw of them.

He lost all sense of time. It could have been minutes – or an hour – since the battle had begun. Jack did not know whether they were winning or losing. There was no way he could tell. A great whispering *whoosh* sounded overhead and a rain of arrows fell among them. Some had come from above, others shot straight through the formation. Jack heard several men screaming. A pikeman near him groaned, then swore loudly and plucked out a shaft from his arm. He'd been lucky that it was nearly spent when it struck him.

Another volley of enemy arrows came into them. This time they were far thicker. More screams echoed around him and moments later excited cries came from where Schwarz had been commanding. He was no longer visible. Jack moved and craned his neck to see. *Landsknechts* were yelling and milling about where Schwarz had stood, some bending and kneeling down. Jack's chest suddenly tightened as if he too had been struck. Lord Schwarz had fallen. The other officers tried to instil order but like rippling waves, the confusion and chaos held in check now threatened to break free as the realisation of what had happened began to spread.

A bearded double-pay man, face purplish from shouting, pushed into the crossbowmen. He smacked the helm of one of the Swiss and swore. 'Get out there! All of you! Give them back some pain!'

Jack hefted his bow, rummaged in his pouch for a quarrel, and hurriedly followed after the other ten crossbowmen. They emerged and saw around them a sea of dead and dying. The Irish had largely fallen back, dozens of brown woollen heaps were scattered across the field like so many grazing sheep: the unlucky who had been struck down. Jack knelt on one knee and looked at the line of Lancastrians which seemed closer than ever. They were slowly advancing. Heart pounding away in his chest, hands shaking, he somehow managed to lay the bolt into the bow, raised it to his shoulder, and chose his victim. In just those seconds, somehow, the enemy had closed the distance and now was barely a stone's throw away. His fingers squeezed the lever and the muffled *thwack* of the release sounded in his ears. He saw his target fall. It was the last bolt he would fire. The enemy was upon him.

Groups of wild, bare-headed, half-naked Irish warriors ran past Hawker, unheeding of anything except preserving their lives. Hawker reined in. The field was strewn with hundreds of bodies, arrow shafts protruding skywards. He now understood why the Yorkists had ceded the high ground. At distance, they were facing an arrow storm. Better to begin the close fight and stop the deadly rain. Ahead of him, the lines to the left of the German mercenaries seemed to be slowly dissolving. Further beyond, new lines of Lancastrian soldiers were entering the field from the Fosse Way, and taking positions. And there were more archers with them. It was worse than he had feared over the past weeks. The promised uprising in England had been stillborn and the Germans and Irish levies were not enough to tip the scales.

There were clumps of English: armoured Yorkist men-at-arms, armed with glaives, bill hooks and pole-axes, forming desperate defensive circles, their numbers too small to build long, unbroken lines. Hawker had seen routs before and this was fast becoming one. Groups of riders, Yorkist and enemy, now engaged on the periphery, close to the enclosures of the village, charging in with lances, spears and swords.

Hawker looked over to Jacob. The Fleming did not have to voice his assessment. It was clear upon his face. Hawker urged his horse over to the four remaining men he commanded. He could see most were petrified with fear, eyes huge.

'I give you all a choice! You're released from my service. Keep what I have paid you and go back home.'

The men exchanged nervous looks with one another.

'William Tice,' said Hawker. 'You've proved your service. Lead these fellows back home.'

Tice shook his head, the sweat glistening on his brow and cheeks. 'I'll earn my pay, Sir Knight,' he said. 'I've nothing else to do.'

'You will find something. Go.'

His face scowled with indecision but then, thinking upon the odds, he nodded. Tice raised his hand in a salute and then jerked his reins. His mount turned and shot back up the slope. That was all it took. The other three remaining recruits followed him in an instant.

Hawker wheeled his horse and scanned the formation of the *landsknechts*. If Jack was a crossbowman still, he might be able to find him, even among the hundreds.

'We take the horses down to the last of their ranks,' Hawker said to Jacob. 'I will dismount and go in.'

Jacob's eyes went wide. 'This is madness! How will you find him?'

Hawker didn't bother to answer. He moved off down the slope and towards the shifting phalanx. Already, the flanks were weakening, turning the once rectangular formation into a throbbing ball of confusion. Still numbering what must have been well over a thousand, they held on. Hawker reached the rear pikemen who were already aware of the mortal danger they were in. They were half turned to the left, ready to lower their pikes against any Lancastrian advance up their flank. Hawker dismounted and handed his reins over to Jacob. The pikemen and halberdiers paid him little heed as he waded into their midst, seeking to reach the three standards that were raised high near the centre, still waving proudly with defiance.

Bodies were everywhere, struck down with arrows, and wounded men lay in agony in the trampled grass and mud, shot through thighs and arms. It took Hawker what seemed an age to push his way through the cursing mass of Germans. Some looked at him with surprise in his head-to-toe black armour. Others swore and pushed him back. But the centre grew nearer and the sound of the drums louder. Then, a great whisper of shafts filled the air, the sound of their wood clattering and bouncing off of armour all around him. Men cried out. Hawker could see a cluster of soldiers about the flags, some kneeling others standing and shouting. Pushing through, Hawker saw what looked like a senior commander being cradled by another man. He'd been struck in the throat, blood pouring from him.

A great clatter of pole weapons reverberated along the front. Hawker could just see the great phalanx parting, tearing itself into two like a rent garment. As the gap widened, halberdiers jumped forward to engage the Lancastrian spears and bill men who surged with their advantage. Like a miasma, panic began to set in, rolling up the ranks, the long pike-shafts shivering in uncertain hands as men jostled, backed-up into those behind them, or dropped and ran. Some *landsknechts* rapidly shifted their positions – screamed at by their sergeants – and moved to defend the dying commander and the standards. To the left of the banners and the drummers, Hawker spotted a group of crossbowmen kneeling to reload.

Before he could reach them, they had sprung up again and a dozen of them dashed off to venture outside the pike square to take their shots. For a brief instant, he thought he saw the distinctive raised ridge of a barbute helm – Jack's helm – when all the others were rounded skullcaps. He pushed on, following them out the side of the formation. Lancastrian 'harriers' – fast-moving sword and buckler men and glaive wielders, were already moving to pick off those who had fallen out of the defensive square. Three made for the crossbowmen. Hawker broke into a trot. He cursed himself loudly, already feeling winded without having even thrown a blow.

'Jack! Jack Perry!' His voice croaked with hoarseness and he knew as he yelled he could not be heard above the din around him. The Lancastrian line of men-at-arms had moved up now, pinching from both left and right. Hawker could see them creeping forward, just a dozen yards away from where the crossbowmen crouched. He heard the crossbows loose their bolts and at least three found their targets. But the fast-moving 'harriers', wearing studded jacks and gambesons, had already set upon them.

Hawker recognised Jack immediately. Before the pole-axe-wielding Lancastrian could thrust the lad, Hawker had pushed Jack aside with a shove of his shoulder and knocked away the soldier's haft with arming sword. The man recovered and immediately lunged, but Hawker stepped inside and let his blade fly, striking the soldier's light helm with a ringing blow and dropping him senseless. A second lightly armoured Lancastrian attacked and the sword glanced off Hawker's shoulder. Hawker rounded on him, and blocked his next blow, sparks flying from the blades. He roared and punched the soldier in the face with his left hand and then brought his pommel crashing down on him. As the man collapsed he brought the sword around in an arc and struck him a second, finishing blow.

'Sir John!' Jack Perry was sprawled at Hawker's feet. He'd been knocked down and was scrambling to get hold of his spent crossbow. The enemy were nearly upon them again. The other crossbowmen had dashed back to what was left of the square and Hawker hauled up Jack and propelled him up the slope. Hawker saw Jack drop his bow and try and draw out his arming sword.

'Keep moving!' Hawker cried out, breathless. Blowing hard, he trudged upwards after Jack.

'The captain is dead!' yelled Jack, finally drawing out his blade. 'I saw him fall!'

They had outdistanced the enemy and the dying phalanx had now become two huge hedgehogs of pikes, tightly clustering together. Hawker stopped, chest heaving, and looked back again. The Lancastrians seemed to be pulling all their battle lines forward, enveloping the remaining Germans on three sides.

Hawker grabbed Jack by the shoulders and shook him. 'Boy! The day is lost! You must get away!'

Jack threw himself into Hawker, hugging him, their breast-plates clanking. 'Forgive me!' He was sobbing where he stood, clinging to the old knight.

Hawker pushed him away. 'Come!' They moved closer to the remnants of the square. Hawker heard a horse neigh and turned to see that Jacob had followed him down into the *melee*. Hawker violently shook Jack's shoulder with his left hand.

'Get out of here now, my lad! While there's still time. Take my horse!'

Before Jack could protest, a storm of arrows cut across them. Hawker pushed Jack to the ground even as he heard the horses scream. Jacob cried out and his horse went down, struck, throwing him. Jacob picked himself up and Hawker saw a shaft protruding from his leg armour. The Fleming broke off the arrow, picked up his spear again, and then retrieved the reins to Hawker's mount. Jacob's horse lay in agony, head thrashing and forelegs kicking. It had been struck in the belly.

'Sir John! *Gottverdammt*! Fly! Now!'

'I fight with you!' cried Jack, enraged. 'I'm not running!'

Half crouching as a few more arrows swished past, Hawker seized Jack's arm again. 'Get out! If you survive this they'll hang you afterwards for a traitor! You know where to go. Do it! Do it for my sake if you still hold any love for me!' Hawker reached down to his sword belt and yanked out his *cinquedea* dagger – his constant companion of many years. He shoved it into Jack's belt and wedged it as securely as he could, hooking a curved quillon over the leather.

Jack's mouth gaped. His eyes searched Hawker's but he couldn't speak.

'Go now!' ordered Hawker, his voice quieter, pushing Jack towards the last remaining mount. Jack nodded, seized the reins from Jacob, placed an unsteady foot in the stirrup, and hauled himself up. Hawker stood alongside and pulled off the long war hammer which was still lashed to the saddle. Jack looked down at his knight as he tightened rein.

'God save you, Sir John!'

Hawker laid his gauntleted hand on Jack's knee. 'Get out of here, lad. Be well.'

Jack nodded and then he spurred the horse forward up the slope.

Jacob limped closer to Hawker using the spear as a support. 'So… Here then?'

Hawker gave him a knowing look and nodded slowly. 'Aye, Jacob. There be no better place.'

Jacob grinned, his scar rising high up his cheek. 'Well chosen.' The Fleming raised up the spear, butt end pointed to the ground, and drove it down into the soft, churned soil. The knight's pennon atop fluttered lazily. He slowly drew his arming sword from his scabbard. Hawker planted his feet firmly, left foot forward towards the advancing enemy. He rested his long war hammer against his shoulder. Jacob moved alongside him, his foot touching Hawker's. They stood as one.

'*Komm! Jetzt!*' cried out one of the Germans, desperately urging both men to join their ranks for protection. Others joined in, exhorting Hawker to withdraw into the slowly disintegrating formation. Hawker could already see some men dropping their weapons and running up the hill.

'We don't give one inch!' cried Hawker, looking over towards the Lancastrians.

Jacob turned and shouted to the Germans that they were holding firm where they stood. Moments later, a dozen pikemen silently moved forward to either side of Hawker and the Fleming. A veteran halberdier who was probably as old as Hawker stepped into place between two pikemen and winked at the knight. Bravado in the face of death. Their colourful hose and doublets were dirty and torn after ten days of marching south, but they were still standing. The *landsknechts* raised their pikes to their shoulders, spear heads pointed to the approaching wall of steel, now just a few yards ahead. Hawker grunted to himself. He had done what needed to be done. Saved who needed to be saved. And, at long last, he had unburdened his soul.

He pulled down his visor into place again. Encased in his helm, Hawker listened to the muffled sound of his own measured breaths and stared out through the eye-slit at the faceless enemy ahead. A sense of calm descended upon him.

And they came on.

The knight recognised the tabards of the men. Red with a white star upon them. The Earl of Oxford's men. The same nemesis as at Bosworth Field. Hawker's lips broke into a smile at the irony of it, but no one could see it. The enemy rushed upon them like angry foaming surf breaking upon a quay. Jacob was at his side, sword gripped with both hands, the Fleming leaning in and preparing for the first onslaught. The Germans thrust with their long pikes, holding off the attack for a few brief minutes, but once a few of the pike heads had been deflected downwards, the Lancastrian soldiers poured forward and inside what remained of the makeshift *landsknecht* square.

Jacob aimed a high, two-handed thrust towards the face of his first opponent, jabbing. The man fell back but Jacob's momentum carried him forward on his bad leg and the Fleming stumbled and fell. Hawker gave a yell and moved to fill the gap. He brought his hammer head down hard upon the shoulder of the Lancastrian, dropping him. Jacob hauled himself up but another soldier was upon him immediately. Hawker swivelled his stance and jabbed with the spike of his weapon, forcing the man backwards.

'Jacob! To me!'

Jacob managed to gain his feet but he was swaying from his arrow wound. He let out a roar of defiance but Hawker knew full well the Fleming's strength was leaking away, second by second.

'I am with you!' the Fleming cried out. And then, Hawker was fighting for his own life against a rush of flailing pole weapons. He moved as he had a hundred times before in a hundred fights – each thrust, parry and blow swiftly transitioning to another – blocking and striking as if a single motion. It was unthinking, an instinct honed by many battles, and men fell at his feet screaming and groaning. From the edge of his limited view, he saw Jacob kill a man in close but then swiftly receive a blow to the head and a thrust to his side simultaneously. And he was down again.

A pile of Lancastrians lay around Hawker, some writhing still. The Germans had back-pedalled in the face of the assault and any remaining protective thicket of pikes was now gone. This unknown knight in black armour – his pennon still flapping aloft upon a spear – had taken a deadly toll and drawn the attention of a few Lancastrian nobles who now sought to engage him. The enemy redoubled their efforts and Hawker found himself fending off opponents on three sides at once. He took aim at the throat of a Lancastrian knight, timed his lunge, and stepped forward. The spike of his war hammer slid up the man's shining bevor and pushed up the visor of his sallet helm and as Hawker leaned in, the spike penetrated the knight's face. Hawker pulled back to release it, but his pole-axe caught and the Lancastrian jerked forward, screaming.

A blow landed on his breastplate, staggering him. And even as he freed his pole-axe, a glaive strike caught his helm, sending his head spinning. He felt his legs give way and Hawker found himself upon his back, a sky of azure blue filling his view. Then, a sudden burst of agony as a blade found its way into the gap between the top of his thigh and his tasset plate. He never felt the death blow delivered by an unseen hand, only dimly aware of the fumbling at his visor and chin strap.

Then the taste of cool, salty wetness in his mouth.

Chiara. Live… and be well.

Over his head, the swirl of coloured tabards, the cries of men, the blue sky. All faded to darkness and then reformed as a firmament of white satin. For a fleeting moment he thought he saw the laughing face of a small boy. His Nicholas. But this too melted into the whiteness which seemed to envelop him in its strange warmth.

Remember me… and forgive.

40

The little broad-beamed carvel listed as it came away from the wharf and Sir Giles Ellingham braced his feet with the sudden movement. He let out a long breath and took in another, slowly. They had made it on ship. The journey down river from Boston would take a while and they were still not out of danger.

He worried the pommel of the sword at his side and clutched at his woollen cloak, pulling it closer about him even though it was full summer. He was exhausted. A gnawing sense of chill went deep to his bones and he shivered again. Their armour had been discarded outside the town and only their weapons remained upon them. He still wore his sweat-soaked padded gambeson under the cloak – an obvious tell-tale of what he was and where he had been.

Though many hours had passed, he still could not make sense of what had befallen them. The sally they had made on the left flank at Stoke Field had been absorbed by the Lancastrian enemy and Henry's bowmen had made easy work of them. He'd watched his cousin Lincoln fall, violently unhorsed by arrow shot and then swarmed over by a dozen men-at-arms. Lord Lovell had somehow managed to stay in the saddle and fought his way back out. Ellingham had followed the path Lovell had made, trampling the dead and the dying.

On the main deck the man next to him said nothing as they made their way out with the ebb tide. His face was puffy and blotched, streaks of sweat and tears dried upon his cheeks. He leaned against the railing and warily watched the sailors as they readied the ship for open sea. It was not until they could see the gaping mouth of the Haven that Ellingham's companion deigned to speak.

'The Scots will give us sanctuary. I've shown you the letters. We can fight on. With new support.'

Ellingham half turned to look again at Lord Lovell. 'Scotland. To what end? If we could not win these past days – convince all to rise up – how will the future be any different?'

'The burr under the saddle will fester as time goes on. The country will see Henry Tudor for the usurper he is. There *will* be a new rebellion. I swear it.'

Lovell's vehemence sounded more like he was trying to convince himself. Ellingham didn't bother to argue. Lovell had abandoned his young changeling king to his fate on the battlefield so he'd be needing a new one, it seemed. A blast of cool, salt-tinged air hit Ellingham's face, the river opening wide and the flat, calm sea spreading out ahead of them.

He felt that he was leaving not just England behind him. He was leaving his illusions there too. He was not the son of a dead king. He was Giles Ellingham and no one else. And that would have to do. An exile, again, he would cast his fortunes to the wind. He remembered Sir John. He hoped – he prayed – that he might have survived and made his escape. Why not? The wily knight had done so many times before. A man of such deep loyalty is rare indeed. But if he had met his end, then his penance had now been paid, and Ellingham believed – for he had to believe – that Sir John Hawker had found redemption waiting for him.

–

Many miles away, Jack Perry approached the courtyard of a manor house. He was cold, hungry, and had not slept in nearly two days. He slid off the back of Hawker's horse, rested his head a minute on its flank, and then made his way, shaking, up to the great studded oak door. He was past caring what reception he would receive. Good or bad it would be God's will for he had reached his end. With a clenched fist he pounded three times upon the door.

It opened wide. A middle-aged woman, grey eyes lined with crow's feet, stood at the threshold and beheld him. After an instant of disbelief he saw her face then soften into wondrous recognition. And all that he had held locked inside of him for days, now came pouring out in a breathless, wordless cry of exhaustion and surrender. Lady Catherine opened her arms and enveloped him in an embrace he had not felt for many, many years. And Jack Perry, suddenly at peace, let himself sink deeply into it.

Epilogue

Chiara heard the excited cries of the local boys before she even approached the window. Once there, she saw through the wavy, distorting panes the approach of a noble retinue along the cobbles: halberd-wielding soldiers in livery escorting a gentleman clothed in a fine doublet of russet brocade. His sable-trimmed black gown and chain of office shone in the morning sun. As she watched, it became quite clear that they were coming to her door.

At once, her whole body was seized with a deep and piercing grief. The overwhelming rush of emotion forced a single, gasping sob to burst forth from her, followed by a sharp intake of breath which she could barely manage. Her hand quickly covered her mouth as if to stop her soul from flying out of it and ascending to another place. Finally, the dreaded moment had come, as she had long known it would.

The maidservant answered the knocks which followed. Chiara slowly moved to the stone hearth, her gaze resting on Nicholas who lay nearby in his cot. She turned to face the doorway and stood rigid, her arms at her side.

'It is the châtelain of the palace, my lady!' said the maid, rushing in to the little *salle*.

Chiara nodded.

Sir Olivier de la Marche entered and swept off his black velvet bonnet. His very round, pale face, topped by his short-cropped, thin grey hair, gave him the look of the man in the moon.

He looked at her with almost overly large eyes and then lowered his chin and gaze. 'Donna Chiara, I do beg your pardon for disturbing your peace.'

She did not reply but instead waited for the *châtelain* to speak again, his words – already anticipated – were ringing inside her head before he even uttered them.

'It grieves me to deliver this news, my lady. Your husband has fallen. In battle.' He raised his eyes to hers again. 'He joins the Earl of Lincoln in death – and many other men of worth who were slain. The herald reports Sir John fought honourably and mightily until he was overwhelmed by the enemy.'

The words now landed dully upon her ears and she thought it strange that tears had yet to come forth from her. 'And what of Sir Giles, his companion?'

Sir Olivier's bulging eyes winced a little and he lowered his head again. 'He is not accounted for, my lady. Nor is Viscount Lovell. We do not yet know if they managed to flee the field alive.'

Nicholas began to cry, hesitantly, as if he had understood the message just delivered. The maid moved swiftly to lift him up from his cot and place him over her shoulder. She gently bounced him in her arms, soothing his cries, and then made to exit the room. But Chiara raised her hand to stay her departure and the maid curtsied, clutching Nicholas to her.

Sir Olivier's face took on an awkward cast, one of embarrassment. He flushed a little, and Chiara took some small pleasure in this as the anger welled up inside her belly. Did it show upon her? She hoped it was so. The Burgundian lifted his chin and regarded her as if she did not comprehend him. 'My dear lady, our great enterprise is at an end. Henry yet holds the English crown. The duchess is bereft.'

'But not bereft over my husband. Is she?'

She saw his eyes dart to Nicholas. They were filled with guilt.

'Donna Chiara, Sir John has provided for you. I have given my word to him as a knight of my order to look after you and your child so long as it is in my power to do so. You will not want.' He un-looped a small leather purse from his belt and extended it towards her. 'We had an arrangement… which I honour.'

She made no move to retrieve it. 'So then… blood money.'

'It is recompense. One he negotiated. How else will you survive here? Or hope to prosper?'

She was silent a long moment, then, without averting her gaze from him, she plucked the sack of coins from his hand. 'As a widow twice over, I thank you, Sir Olivier. I will accept it. But I also demand an exemption. An imperial indulgence. I desire to import silks from my contacts in Genoa and Florence. To conduct trade. But I am not allowed to petition the Mercers' Guild here. Not as a woman. Not even as a widow. For they saw fit not to let my husband join their number. *You*, however, can ask the duchess to make them grant me the widow's privilege.'

She could see his chest visibly swelling with the soft intake of breath. His lips pressed tightly together, the colour fading from them. He seemed to be at a loss for words to address her insolence. But she was not yet finished.

'Allore, sir! Can you not give answer to a woman who was wife to a knight? A knight who fought and fell in your cause. A knight whose young son is here in your presence. You think I do not know that it was you who told the guildsmen not to let him in? I am not a witless Flemish housewife, sir. I am a lady of the Venetian Republic. And in Venice, one grows wise quickly. A *true* man of honour would have only one answer to my demand.'

Olivier de la Marche took a breath and looked over to the window facing the street. Chiara could see one of his gaudy German guards looking back at them. The *châtelain* slowly turned to face her again. He frowned. 'My lady, I am no monster. Indeed, I have raised a daughter who is very likely the same age as you.'

'And has she borne a son? A grandson for you?'

366

Sir Olivier nodded slowly.

'Then, good sir, what do you think she would tell you to do?'

She heard his sigh from across the chamber, his short, round-shouldered form sinking a little. 'Donna Chiara – *Lady Hawker* – I give you my word I will deliver your request to Her Grace. And I likewise promise that I will present it with the seriousness that it merits.' He paused a moment. 'That you and your son merit.'

'Dio vi benedica,' she replied, bowing her head. 'With your aid, I pray that she will grant it.'

The man in the moon smiled faintly. 'I still have a *little* influence at the palace, despite my years.'

When the old knight had departed, she plucked Nicholas from the arms of the maid and held him close to her breast. She leaned in, kissed the wispy dark hair on his head, and then spoke softly into his ear. The Venetian trilled gently from her tongue.

'One day… Nicholas Hawker… one day, when you are grown… you will make your father very proud.'

Only then did the tears which had somehow eluded her finally come to her eyes. And Chiara wept as she had never wept before.

Afterword

From the outset, I had conceived these adventures of the fictitious Sir John Hawker to form a trilogy, one which tells the story of an ageing, jaded knight and another who is newly christened and cocksure, both thrown together in the most challenging of times. Their relationship, at first one of fealty sworn, changes to one of master and student, and then to an almost uncertain friendship of sorts despite the vast chasm between their ages and experience. The long and dangerous path they cover together across fifteenth-century Europe changes both of them forever. Ultimately, Sir John and young Sir Giles must part ways: the older knight senses that his life's adventures are coming to an end while the other is still on a journey to find his life's meaning and his own destiny. It was also my intention to portray their world in all its wonder and brutality, following as closely as possible the true timeline of history but still leaving room for the historical unknowns and tantalising 'what-ifs' that we may never know for certain. I hope I have succeeded in these things and that you, the reader, have enjoyed the journey. Finally, I'd like to thank all those at Canelo for making these books possible and, in particular, to my talented, stalwart editor, Craig Lye, for all his support.

Ethan Bale
Battle, East Sussex

Historical Note

The Battle of Stoke Field, 16 June, 1487

Of all the battles of the Wars of the Roses, we probably know the least about what is considered to be the last: Stoke Field.

The battle resulted in another victory for young Henry VII, coming two years after Bosworth Field, and crushed the Plantagenet rebellion, which had been brewing since King Richard's fall. It is often said that history is written by the victors but in this case, rather strangely, the victors have left a rather paltry record of the event. One can speculate as to why this was. Perhaps Henry was eager to quash any remaining embers of Yorkist revolt by quickly sweeping away memory of the event, and showing mercy to many of the high-ranking vanquished who survived the field. This was what he had done after Bosworth too, with mixed results. His was always an uneasy crown with threats and rebellion dogging him his entire reign. Was it his strategy that it was better to win over an enemy rather than make more? In any event, the accounts that do exist of the Battle of Stoke Field were written many years after the fact and by people who were never there. These vary wildly.

In this novel, I have attempted to portray the events leading to Stoke Field as those living then might have perceived them: full of contradictions and rumour, false hopes and false intelligence. Through 1486 and into 1487, Henry Tudor's spies and informants had done their best to stay abreast of Yorkist developments in the Low Countries as well as in the north of England. In April of 1486, a rebellion led by Yorkist stalwart

Sir Francis Lovell fizzled to nothing and he fled abroad to the court of Margaret of York, Duchess Dowager of Burgundy and sister to the slain Richard III. With funding from Margaret and her son-in-law, Maximilian, the King of the Romans, Yorkist loyalists began to plot a new uprising to overthrow the Tudor regime. This effort was led by Lord Lovell and John de la Pole, the Earl of Lincoln – King Richard's nephew and chosen successor.

Hopes eventually settled on crowning a new Plantagenet king in exile. Ostensibly, this was to be the twelve-year-old son of Edward IV's treasonous and executed brother, George, Duke of Clarence. The young Edward Plantagenet, however, was in the hands of Henry and lodged in the Tower. This led to an imposter being procured, the so-called 'Lambert Simnel', and eventually crowned in Dublin (still a bulwark of Yorkist support) in May 1487. To quell doubts, the rebels maintained that the boy held in London was the actual imposter. Whoever the imposter was, low-born joiner's son or even the real Earl of Warwick, it is likely that de la Pole intended to take the throne once the rebellion succeeded.

For her part, Margaret of Burgundy had managed to procure the services of the infamous German mercenary Martin Schwarz who commanded between fifteen hundred and two thousand well-trained *landsknecht* soldiers: pikemen, halberdiers, crossbowmen and gunners. These men were a mix of Germans, Austrians and Swiss, along with a few Scots. It was a small but impressively equipped force of professionals, schooled in the latest tactics of pike warfare. Combined with the personal retinues of Lovell and Lincoln, this force set sail in early May for Dublin where the plan was to raise several thousand Irish soldiers under the Earl of Kildare. But much also depended upon a general uprising happening in the north of England once the invasion force landed there. It was hoped that disaffected noblemen, both Yorkist and even lukewarm Lancastrians, would rise up and supply retinues of foot soldiers and mounted knights to swell the ranks.

In Ireland for but a few weeks, local lords assembled a force of lightly armed foot soldiers, called *kerns*, enthusiastic and brave but largely without armour and equipped mainly with short throwing spears, long daggers and a few longswords. In addition, some number of better-equipped Anglo–Irish retainers were gathered, traditional bill-men and elite galloglasses, these would have had armour and better weaponry. It is estimated by some historians that the total Irish contingent may have numbered up to four thousand men, but there are no records to prove it. Once the young pretender had been crowned as 'Edward VI', the entire army, both Anglo–Irish Yorkists and German mercenaries, embarked on several ships (paid for by Burgundy) and crossed the Irish Sea bound for England's western shore.

The fleet made an unopposed landing near Furness, ready to begin what would be an arduous trek across Cumbrian hills and into the Yorkshire fells and dales, their initial destination most probably being York. When they set out from Furness on 4 June, the outlook remained promising. In Cumbria, the invasion force had been bolstered by the arrival of Sir Thomas Broughton, his retinue, and others in the region who responded to the Yorkist banner. The force passed through the old Neville and Yorkist stronghold of Middleham before reaching Masham on 8 June. Sending heralds to York, they were told by the city fathers that their army would be denied entry and indeed that the city would resist them. It was the first indication that the hoped-for uprising was in trouble. Many of the northern gentry ignored the call to arms, equivocated, or openly rejected the Yorkist rebels. Whether it was a case of 'the devil you know' or weariness of the battles of the previous few years, it must have become obvious to Lincoln and Lovell that they would have to make do with the men they had. Numbering some eight thousand soldiers, it was not an inconsiderable force, although nowhere near the size of earlier armies fielded during the Wars of the Roses. The question remained though, how many men would Henry Tudor be able to field against them as they moved further south? According to accounts penned a few years later, Martin Schwarz is said to have berated Lincoln and Lovell over the failure of the uprising, accusing them of deceiving him. But he pledged to remain faithful to his oath to the duchess dowager Margaret of York. He would see the invasion through, come what may.

Henry Tudor was not oblivious to the challenge to his throne. His informants and spies had kept him abreast of the arrival of the rebels in Dublin, the coronation and the departure. No doubt he was told of the landing in the north within a few days of it happening. He had already taken up station at Kenilworth Castle in the Midlands to better respond to the threat and indeed had issued the call to arms across England. His army would be led by his uncle, Jasper Tudor (the Earl of Bedford), and by the Earl of Oxford, the man who had secured victory for him at Bosworth Field. Contingents from the earls of Devon and Shrewsbury, the Viscount Lisle, and five barons rounded out the force. Historians estimate the total number of fighting men available to Henry was around fifteen thousand, giving him the numerical advantage. But numbers did not always tell the whole story: his mainly mercenary army had defeated the larger force of Richard III just two years earlier. Nothing could be certain once battle was joined.

And first victory went to the Yorkists. South-west of York, near Tadcaster, a force of some four to five hundred led by Lord Clifford was routed by the rebels and sent fleeing back to the safety of York's walls. Lincoln and Lovell continued their march south. They were covering roughly seventeen miles per day, an impressive feat for a medieval army encumbered by a baggage train. A Lancastrian force led by Sir Edward Woodville was also driven back around Sherwood Forest as the Yorkists proceeded southwards. Alarming reports began to arrive to King Henry who had now begun his own march northwards from Leicester. The rebels were in striking distance and final battle would be joined somewhere in Nottinghamshire. Henry must have been concerned. Some nobles were yet to commit their forces to him upon being summoned, and the ghosts of Bosworth must have surely been foremost in his mind. Last-minute changes of allegiance had helped win him the day in August 1485. Would he fall a victim to an earl switching sides?

There were reports of Lancastrian contingents fleeing encampment on 13 June and others may have also fled towards London. As rumours swirled, Yorkist supporters in London staged an abortive uprising, thinking Henry had already been defeated. In the royal camp itself, outside Ruddington, some soldiers ran away in the night, further weakening morale. On 15 June, the royal army proceeded to Radcliffe, scouts riding ahead to find the Yorkist host.

The rebels had forded the Trent, probably near Fiskerton, on the evening of Friday, 15 June, their own outriders soon thereafter detecting the advance guard of the Lancastrians. Lincoln, Lovell and Schwarz then chose the ground upon which to make their stand. It lay a stone's throw from the town of East Stoke. There is disagreement as to how the Yorkists deployed and the fields and meadows today are somewhat different than they were five hundred years ago. That said, it is likely the Yorkists used a bend in the river (and the steep incline leading down to it) to anchor their right flank, the hedgerows and fences of Stoke village to anchor their left, and deployed their line along the crest of a gentle rise looking southwards. Although consensus is lacking, the centre was probably formed by the *landsknecht* 'square' with the Anglo–Irish contingents on both wings and whatever mounted troops and guns were available flanking these.

Marching northwards early on the morning of 16 June, the Tudor host saw the deployed line of their enemy on the ridge of a gently rising meadow. But whether by accident or design, Henry's force had been divided on the march and it was only Oxford's vanguard of around six thousand that had arrived.

Henry and the remainder of the army still lay a few miles to the south. Based on numbers alone, if the armies engaged now, the odds were nearly even. Oxford immediately deployed his line opposite at the foot of the rise and brought up his mounted knights, men-at-arms, and archers to secure his right flank, the steep slope down to the Trent helping to secure his left from any envelopment.

No doubt the situation was not lost on the Yorkist commanders. They could wait for the enemy to advance, knowing they themselves held the commanding high ground, but this might give time for the remainder of the Lancastrian army to join the battle. Or, they could advance downhill and attempt to defeat the vanguard, hoping an immediate victory would cause the rout of the remainder of Henry's forces arriving late to the game. It was this course they decided upon.

Sometime after nine in the morning, the Yorkists began their advance forward. The chaos and confusion of a medieval battle cannot be overstated. Once joined in combat, command and control was difficult to maintain and victory would depend on breaking and rolling up a flank to 'turn' the enemy onto itself or punching through the vanguard and dividing it that way. When within two hundred yards or so, they would have been met with a rain of arrows from Oxford's longbowmen. Sources say that the unarmoured Irish were killed in great numbers. Those in armour would have been in less danger, but this would increase as the distance narrowed. Several volleys would have been possible before the lines engaged in hand-to-hand combat. We know that the mercenaries had some number of crossbowmen but these would have had a slower rate of fire.

At first, the sheer momentum of the Yorkists and their phalanx of German pikes had some success, hard pressing the Lancastrians. For more than an hour, the two lines of pikes and pole weapons struggled to break the other. But as the battle went on, losses on the Yorkist side took their toll. We can still only speculate on how the battle played out. Did the un-armoured and ill-trained Irish give way to the onslaught of pole weapons and arrow fire? These troops accounted for nearly half the entire army. Was the German square then exposed on its flanks? Did the arrival of additional Lancastrian troops turn the tide? What kind of leadership was demonstrated by both Lincoln and Lovell, recognising that neither (unlike the Earl of Oxford) had probably ever faced large-scale battle before? Within not much more than two hours, the Yorkist line began to disintegrate with some men fleeing back towards the slope and the River Trent.

The counter-attack of Oxford threw the Yorkists into disarray and one source claims this was when the principal commanders all fell. The Earl of Lincoln, Martin Schwarz and Sir Thomas Geraldine were slain, possibly by the withering volleys of arrows. High-value figures would not normally have been killed outright without the chance to offer surrender. The manner of their deaths was not recorded. Herald tallies for the carnage counted some four thousand rebels killed. Some number of mercenaries survived the battle, were given quarter upon surrendering, and allowed safe passage out of England. As for those rebels who were English or Irish, many were cut down in flight or executed on the field for their treason.

Of the rebel leaders, only Lord Lovell appeared to have escaped the field, but whatever his fate, he was never heard of again. A letter of safe conduct from the Scottish King James IV has been unearthed naming Lord Lovell and other English gentlemen, dated *after* the battle of Stoke Field. Did he manage to survive? It is this tantalising theory that I've made use of at the conclusion of *The Knight's Redemption*.

Henry Tudor himself did not arrive until the battle was over. He was never one to jeopardise his personal safety or that of his dynasty by directly engaging in combat as had Richard III. As for the 'boy king' – Edward VI or Lambert Simnel – he was captured on the field, apparently abandoned by his keepers. Famously, he was pardoned by King Henry and put to work in the palace kitchens as a spit-turner. He was later appointed a royal falconer and lived to at least middle age. King Henry would face another threat to his throne in the 1490s: the pretender Perkin Warbeck or, as some historians have claimed, the real Richard of Shrewsbury – the younger of the princes in the Tower. However, it is widely accepted that the Battle of Stoke Field was the high watermark of Yorkist hopes in which – in just a few violent hours – the fate of the kingdom was decided.

The most definitive historical assessments in print are *Lambert Simnel and the Battle of Stoke* by Michael Bennett (1987) and *Stoke Field* by David Baldwin (2006). More recent developments can be found online at English Heritage and at: https://meanderingthroughtime.weebly.com/wars-of-the-roses-blog/battle-of-stoke-the-battlefield-site.